AF269193

Byegones

by Stephanie Osborn

Chromosphere Press

Huntsville, AL

Chromosphere Press
P.O. Box 252
56 Hughes Road
Madison, AL 35758
www.chromospherepress.com

Table of Contents

Chapter 1 1

Chapter 2 34

Chapter 3 61

Chapter 4 79

Chapter 5 102

Chapter 6 130

Chapter 7 157

Chapter 8 188

Chapter 9 218

Chapter 10 249

Chapter 11 283

Chapter 12 307

Chapter 13 330

Chapter 14 360

Author Notes 372

About the Author 373

Chapter 1

"No, girl, I don't know what to tell you," Zebra said as Omega got dressed from her latest session in the medlab. "Not yet, at least. I swear to you, we've put the whole team on it—me, Zarnix, Dihl, we even called in Doron as an active consultant—but we don't have it figured out quite yet."

"Do you have any ideas at all?" Omega wondered. "I mean, I just…worry. Especially now Echo an' I are married. I'd feel a lot better knowing that everything would be normal if we had a wupsie."

"You know that there's not really much in the way of wupsies possible, not with galactic medicine, right? I mean, it's probably not COMPLETELY impossible, but I've never heard of it happening. Not with humans."

"I know, but…"

"It still makes you anxious."

"Yeah. I'm trying to overcome it, and Zz'r'p is counseling me—he added that to our sessions—but, well…" Omega looked at the physician. "Have you got ANY ideas?"

"The best we've been able to come up with is to remove your reproductive system—or, well, your ovaries at the very least; we think that'd be sufficient, though to be safe, we'd probably take the uterus and fallopian tubes, too—and toss 'em in a small tank with a special regeneration fluid," Zebra, the assistant chief of staff of the Medical department in Division One's headquarters, told Division One's top female Agent…who was now happily married to Division One's top male Agent: her partner, Echo.

"Well, that'd do, I think," Omega said, pondering the suggestion. "Because Doron knew how to get ME back to 'normal human' status, so you should just be able to do the same thing to my ovaries."

"It's not quite that simple, according to Doron," Zebra said, wincing. "First off, we need to determine what parts of the genome should go in the egg; it's not as basic as just grabbing your entire genetic sequence and running with it. Plus we'd need to figure out…well, look. You're an exceptional human being, Meg, and you would have been, even if Slug hadn't kidnapped you and mucked with things."

"Eh," Omega grunted; she hated being reminded of the atrocity that had been performed on her pre-pubescent body, all with no anesthesia whatsoever. It had amounted almost to a vivisection, never mind the genetic restructuring, and when the memories had surfaced about a year and a half earlier, they had been hard to handle. Knowing that it had all been intended as a multiple-layer revenge plot against Echo—one that almost succeeded, several times over—didn't help. The fact that, in the process, Slug had set her up to be unable to forget the memories once remembered, even with technological means, even with telepathic assistance, only made it that much worse. Still, Zebra was doing her dead-level best to be delicate about the reference, and Omega appreciated the fact. "I guess. It's hard, not knowing what's me and what's Slug's tinkering."

"Well, exactly. So we have to sit down and try to figure all that out," Zebra noted. "Is this here due to a slight mutation, or Slug? Is that normal to Meg, or not? All of that. It's doable, it's just gonna take some serious effort."

"Okay, I hear what you're saying. It's gonna take a while to work it out. But I think that's the best bet," Omega decreed. "The last thing I want is for our kids to turn into next-generation Echo assassins."

"Which is what Slug intended. Right," Zebra said. "But it's even more complicated than that."

"How?"

"Um, it's Doron. Well, it's not HIM, per se; it's the way he says we'd have to do it, to make sure it worked properly. He seems to think that, in order to ensure that everything ties back in once we replace the ovaries, and your body doesn't reject 'em—because the ovaries we take out of you won't be the ovaries we put back into you, when you get right down to it—we might have to…" Zebra broke off, pulling a face.

"Damn, honey, I don't even wanna tell you this…"

"Just tell me," Omega said, matter-of-fact.

"We'll certainly have to ensure the attachments remain what he calls 'viable,'" Zebra explained. "And maybe even leave the cavity open while it's in work."

Omega stared at her, face paling, expression blank, as the ramifications of what Zebra was saying hit home. Finally she spoke.

"You're saying you'd have to open me up and leave the scalpel cuts raw," she said in a low voice. "Keep my abdominal cavity sliced open for the duration. Like what Slug did. Only longer, because it'll take more than a few hours to do this."

"Only we'd certainly put you under to do it, honey," an anxious Zebra said, extremely apologetic. "But yeah, now you see why we're looking for some OTHER way to do this. ALL of us. Not one of us wanted to subject you to THAT." She shook her head. "It's just…not even on the table, right now."

"Uhm." A badly shaken Omega cleared her throat. "I… damn."

"Yeah."

They were silent for long moments. Finally Zebra drew a deep breath.

"Anyway, that's where we are right now," she said. "We're working on it hard, I swear to you. But no, right now, we are flatly not willing to use the regen process on your ovaries under those conditions — it's unanimous across the whole team: NO — only we don't have anything else that we're as certain of working. Not yet."

"But," Dihl, the chief medtech in the department, commented, as she walked in and overheard the last, "we need to figure out something. Because not only does Omega want them, tough guy image notwithstanding, Echo wants children, too."

"He's told you so?" Omega wondered.

"No, my shich'ee'ké, my daughter by marriage, he has said nothing about it to me, not directly, at least," the Apache woman said with a slight smile. "But I'm his mother; I see it in him. I hear the offhand remarks he makes. He is in love, and at last he feels the desire, the need, to establish his own heritage. He deeply wants a family. He wants children. Children that will carry on the Bryant lineage…and the McAllister line, as well."

Omega slumped, discouraged.

"And I can't give him one," she murmured.

"Yet," Dihl said. She moved to Omega and eased an arm around her, gesturing at Zebra behind Omega's back; the other woman came to her other side, and together they hugged the younger woman. "Be patient, dear one. We are far from done yet."

"Right," Zebra added. "We're only just getting started. So don't fret your head over it, sweetie."

"Well, if it comes to it, we dunk my ovaries," Omega determined, steeling herself. "I love him that much. I'll give him kids, one way or another, dammit."

"Hush that," Zebra said, stern but gentle. "Give us time, honey. You haven't been married six months yet!"

"Exactly!" Dihl agreed. "New York is still recovering from the exoheteroc attack, and you have not been off your cane but a couple of weeks, after your foot was broken and the tendons torn. You have plenty of time, my dear, dear girl."

"Besides," Zebra tag-teamed, "it would take Alpha One out of the field, having a family, and I don't think either of you is really ready for that yet, are you? After all the shit that's landed on the two of you in recent months?"

"No, that's true," Omega agreed. "But I'm not in my twenties, and there IS such a thing as a biological clock…"

"Pssht," Zebra waved a dismissive hand. "Look at Fox. He lived through the Nazi occupation, and he only looks like he's early fifties, max. And once he retires from Division One and goes back to work for Pulgey Entiyti, he'll get another regeneration dunk, and look like he's barely thirty, if that. Which," she added, thoughtful, "means I better dunk, too, or

I'll look like I've robbed the cradle!"

They all laughed.

"Look at ME," Dihl said. "I'm Echo's MOTHER, nearly thirty years old when he was born, and I don't look more than ten years older than my son, if that. Galactic medicine is nigh unto miraculous, my dear child. You have plenty of time to work out the family conundrum."

"Well, you both have a point," Omega decided, considering the information that had been presented. "I'm used to viewing the regen process as a means to heal a bad injury, or to regrow stuff. I'm not really used to thinking about it as a means to stay YOUNG and healthy. But it can do that just as easily. Maybe we have more time than I'd realized."

"Let's just all relax about it—especially you, Meg—and understand that as we work, we're going to uncover more potential techniques, and develop more medical procedures, honey," Zebra said. "We'll get this figured, yet. And then you and Echo can leave the field work, he can step up to full Assistant Director, then Director, and you'll step up to department head of Alpha Line, and Fox and I will retire from the Agency and go gallivanting around the galaxy with the Coalition President." She grinned. "And then you can start a family, and I expect Alpha Two will start a family at some point, and Fox and I will start a family…"

"This sounds wonderful," Dihl decided. "The whole adoptive family Omega has constructed around all of us only gets bigger, with more love."

"Exactly," Zebra agreed. "Because we WILL come back to visit, as often as we can. With the kids." She chuckled, then added, "And I'll be surprised if Pul doesn't come along for that visit, while he's about it!"

"Who knows?" Dihl said with a smile. "From what I hear, he and the captain of his flagship are getting along quite well; there may be a wedding and children there, before too long, also."

"Ooo!" Zebra exclaimed, excited. "I didn't think about

that!"

"And that's all something to look forward to, I guess," Omega concluded. "Every bit of it."

"It really is," Zebra said.

* * *

"Hey, baby," Echo said, as Omega entered the Alpha Line Room a little while later. "How'd it go?"

"Same ol', same ol', I guess," Omega said with a sigh.

She headed up the central aisle between rows of college-style desks, to the dual U-shaped workstations at the front of the room, one of which Echo occupied. On the back wall, overlooking the big organizational room, were two large logos—one, the black and white circle with inscribed horizontal line and conjoined Greek alpha/lambda that formed the Alpha Line logo; the other, the equal-armed black cross inscribed in a circle, overlaid with a big red 1, that denoted Division One. Below that was a credenza full of documentation, as well as a coffee station, a high-tech safe, and an extensive first-aid kit. On the side walls were more than half a dozen large flat screens, currently dark, where the Alpha Line branches scattered at Division One offices around the planet reported to their leaders.

"Still no fun, huh?" Echo wondered.

"Nope."

"Still reminds you of what Slug did?"

"Always."

"Have they figured out how to return your reproductive system to human norms?"

"Not yet," she said, hedging a little. "They have a few ideas, but nothing that they're comfortable attempting yet."

You're hiding something, sweetheart, he said through the mental bond—called an nd't'lq—that their telepathic Deltiri ambassador had helped them set up during their wedding ceremony; the fact that Omega was a low-level telepath after the extensive modifications that Echo's old enemy had done to her had made it possible. *What's going on?*

Oh, it's no big deal, she said. *There's a way that might work…maybe…but it would require some pretty icky things to happen.*

Like what?

No big deal, like I said. Let it go, hon.

Like WHAT? C'mon, Meg, you know me better than that. Don't allude to something and not tell me. Besides, we promised each other we wouldn't hide shit from each other.

Omega sighed.

Like maybe leaving me laid open while they modify the ovaries. In the regen pod. For days. Given the whole Slug vivisection thing, they don't want to do it.

Oh SHIT! Well, no wonder they don't wanna do it, then! I'm glad to see they have some sense. And sympathy.

I've told 'em it's a definite backup, though.

Uhn-uh. No way in hell. I am NOT letting them — or anybody else — fillet you like a hunk of meat, no matter what. So you KNOW I'm gonna try to talk you out of THAT, baby. If not outrightly put my foot down and pull rank on you.

You'd make it an order?

Hell yes.

Had you rather not have any children at all, Ace?

Children, versus additional torture to the love of my life? I'll pass on the kids, if that's the only way to get 'em. I will NOT put you through more shit, sweetheart. Especially not just to grant me offspring. You've had more than enough shit in your life already. I'm here to take care of you, not put you through agony.

Seriously?

Dead serious. He met her sapphire eyes, his golden-brown gaze solemn. *I mean, I know you want kids too, but damn, baby. Not just no, but HELL no. I love you way too much to put you through that.*

Aww. Omega threw him a wobbly smile. *Okay, well, we got plenty of time to figure something out, like Zee and your mom pointed out to me.*

What do you mean?

Well, I brought up the whole 'biological clock' thing, and they reminded me that if it takes longer than my body clock has, they just dunk all of me and reset the clock, essentially.

True. That'd work. And if it looks like my systems are getting too much wear and tear, we do the same to me. Maybe we just dunk both of us at the same time, so we're still 'young' at least physically, by the time the kids come along.

Yeah! Otherwise we'd never be able to keep up with 'em, Ace! I mean, really—kids by the two of US? Mr. an' Mrs. Action Agents? They're gonna be all over the place. Bouncing off the walls, most likely. Especially in the Agency, given some of our tech!

Ain't that the truth, baby! Heh. Oh, I can SO see that! Hahaha!

Heehee! I can, too! Oh, geez, I gotta stop giggling over here. We got a job to do, and here we sit giggling together, and nobody else knows what the HELL it's about!

I know, I know! Okay, sobering up time. You ready to get back to work?

Yup. Heh. Pass me the latest stack of department applications and I'll weed through 'em.

Done. He handed her the stack, though his lips were still twitching; she moved to her desk and sat down, stifling a giggle, and he turned back to his computer at the desk opposite.

* * *

The pair were still hard at work a couple of hours later, when Fox wandered down from the Director's office.

"There you both are," he said cheerfully, coming into the Alpha Line Room. "How goes it, Omega? Is that foot all better?"

"According to the medlab it is, Fox," she said with a smile, looking up from her work. "But you'd do better to ask your missus. Zebra can tell you all about it."

"Oh, Zebra has been keeping me apprised about its healing," Fox admitted. "I think I ask her each evening over dinner how you are both doing—as well as verifying that Romeo's dislocated shoulder is doing well—and she tells me. And the word I've been hearing, on all three of you, is very good. I mostly wanted to know if it feels any better, tekhter."

"Aha. Well, in that case, yeah, Abba Fox, it does," Omega said, smile growing wider, and Fox grinned. "It feels great to be able to use it again, and really open up more in my workouts with Echo."

"I'm making sure she stretches and warms it up really good first, though," Echo averred. "And I massage that foot and leg after, just to keep everything flexible."

"The stretching, especially, feels great," Omega added. "And I'll never complain about getting a massage from Echo. He is really SO damn good at loosening me up, it's amazing sometimes."

"Good, good. And how are you, zun?" Fox wondered then. "Is your counseling going well? Are the limbs and eye behaving properly?"

"It is, and they are," Echo said, nodding. "And Meg returns the massage favor when she thinks it might be good for me, which makes the medlab AND me happy. Zz'r'p is really pleased at how well I'm coming along now, too. I mean, there are certain things that are always gonna affect me now, I know. I think getting your leg and hand chopped off, never mind an eye gouged out—and being helpless to stop any of it, or even fight back, really—then having it all regrown…well, it does things to your head." He tapped his temple.

"I'm sure."

"But he says I'm handling it pretty damn well, all things considered," Echo continued. "And Meg helps in all kinds of ways, including just being there as a wife and companion—somebody to bounce things off of, somebody to care, somebody to watch out for things I hadn't thought about…all that. And of course, being active again helps a whole damn lot."

"Zz'r'p told me about the fragmentary mind, from when you almost died during the space plane rescue, being the cause of a lot of the self-doubt," Fox noted. "And Zebra and I discussed it a good bit, not that there was much we could do to help. She said that made a damn lot of sense. But just so you know, we…sympathized."

"Yeah. And I appreciate that, no end, Fox. But at a certain point, once I started having to just GO, just DO, during that little extended debacle with the exoheteroc, I think that that part of my psyche finally realized I wasn't lying to it and we—as in, agents in general, not the 'imperial we' or the busted-psyche we—really COULD do everything we claimed." Echo looked thoughtful. "At any rate, once that happened, things settled down and I stopped doubting and started getting back to normal."

"And he IS," Omega vouched. "I can tell that through the nd't'lq. He doesn't even hesitate any more before doing something; he just does it, same as he would have before the Cortians captured and tortured him."

Echo shrugged.

"I don't think about it," he said, "and I don't OVER-think it. Or at least, I try not to. I make my plan, then I let instinct and muscle memory take over."

"And that's good," Fox decreed.

"Yeah, it is," Echo agreed. Then he pulled a face. "Because, frankly, if I start thinking about it too much, too hard, I WILL tend to go off the rails into the whole torture scenario and 'Is it gonna work this time? What if it didn't grow back quite right, and this time it gives out?' an' shit like that. Then I get wrapped around the axle and don't act at all…"

"Which tends to result in simulated deaths for Alpha One," Omega finished for him.

"In the sim training room?" Fox asked.

"Yeah," Echo sighed. "So I'm still working on THAT aspect of things. But like I said, the trick seems to be not over-thinking it."

"And he's doing really well at it," Omega averred. "When he first started getting back into the simulator training, he had a couple bobbles like that, and rather than letting him beat himself up over it, I insisted we went back home, and we talked through it in detail. See, I was in his head with the nd't'lq and saw what happened to him mentally, and I could show him what happened."

"He couldn't tell for himself?"

"I didn't have a feel for the timeframe," Echo admitted. "You know how you can lose yourself in your thoughts and not know how much time has gone by. Maybe it's fast, and maybe you've been sitting there for an hour…"

"Ah. Right."

"And once we got that all figured out, he knew what he needed to do," Omega continued. "So now he just goes and does it."

"When is the last time he had an episode of wrapping his mind around the axle, then?" Fox wondered, curious.

"Not since the first week he got back in Alpha Line's sim training room," Omega determined, pleased, her pride obvious. "And it's been way over two months now, probably close to three. Of daily workouts."

"Good, good. That's an excellent sign, I'd say."

"And while we're talking about such things, how is the Kydeen scientist who lost his hand to the exoheteroc?" Echo wondered.

"He's doing quite well," Fox said. "Zebra told me he was decanted from the regen pod on a proper time schedule—they learned a lot from you on that—and he's been in rehab ever since. The hand is flexible and dexterous, Zebra said, and he's likely to have full functionality by the time they're done."

"Was it his dominant hand, or…?"

"Non-dominant, so we're good there," Fox answered. "She said they've been lucky with him and with you, in that regard. The dominant hand is always going to be harder to re-train, apparently — all the fine motor skills and whatnot. At any rate, he'll be going home to Kydeen soon with his friend, who has stayed staunch at his side, and even assisted in the physical therapy. I'm only waiting on Zebra and Zarnix to give me the high sign before arranging their travel, as we promised."

"Good," Echo decided. "That all sounds great. So. What's up?"

"Hm? You mean with me?"

"Yeah."

"Oh, nothing really."

"Then why'd you come down here from your office? You usually do that when something's up that you need us for."

"Heh," Fox chuckled. "Not this time, kinder. To be honest, I've been cooped up in there SO LONG doing after-action paperwork to help get things back to a semblance of normal after the mega moth took out a significant chunk of Manhattan, I just needed to get away from it for a little bit and stretch my legs. Never mind my brain."

"Ohh, so this is a social visit," Omega said with a grin. Fox returned it.

"Yes, tekhter, this is a social visit," he chuckled. "I thought I might come down here, grab a cup of coffee, and the three of us sit and unwind for a bit. Assuming I'm not interrupting YOUR work."

"Nope, I was just coming to a stopping place, and thinking about coffee and snackies myself," Omega confirmed.

"And that works, and it's good timing for me, too," Echo said, opening a cabinet and fishing out the spare mug that was reserved expressly for the Director's occasional visits—the fact that his office was almost directly across the Core from the Alpha Line Room, never mind he was the 'patriarch' of the cobbled-together 'family' Omega had assembled from within the organization, meant it happened every now and again, in despite of Echo's concern. "Here we go."

"I've got it, zun; don't trouble yourself," Fox said, catching the mug from the younger man and moving to the pod brewer on the end of the credenza between Echo's and Omega's desks at the front of the large room. He selected his preferred brew from the carousel of prepared pods next to the brewer, then popped it in, stuck the mug under the nozzle, and initiated the brewing process.

"Oh, that makes me think," Omega said, opening a desk drawer and digging in it. "I brought in a tin of shortbread and another tin of Echo's homemade beef jerky this morning, before I headed off to the medlab. We can snack with our coffee."

"Ooo, nice, tekhter," Fox said, popping out the used pod and dropping it in the nearby waste can before fetching his steaming mug. "That sounds delicious."

"I second that," Echo said, prepping his own fresh mug of coffee, and reaching for Omega's empty cup. While Echo brewed their coffee, Omega located and pulled out the two tins, and sat them on the end of her desk, along with a stack of paper napkins to catch crumbs. "So, Fox, how IS the city rebuild going, after that whole mega moth rampage?"

"Reasonably well," Fox decided, pulling a small desk to the opening between his two leads' desks, then grabbing a couple pieces of shortbread and a napkin before sitting in the desk and sipping his coffee; the shortbread contained dairy and was therefore not kosher to eat with the jerky, although Omega and Echo, not being Jewish, would both partake of each. "The civilians all think it was a terror attack using a fleet of drones, just like the story we put out, and other than the one building that collapsed, most of the rest of the damage was relatively non-structural. Rip out and replace some burned walls and false flooring, replace some dropped-ceiling tiles, pop in new windows, bring in new furniture, and they're ready to go. That's a considerable oversimplification, of course, but you two understand what I mean, I'm sure."

"Yeah, Fox, we got it," Echo said, handing Omega her mug of coffee with cream already added as she preferred, then grabbing a napkin, a couple of shortbread cookies, and a large hunk of jerky to go with his own coffee, placing the food on the napkin, and the napkin on his desk. "How are the missing persons cases coming? I mean, WE know the mega moth ate well while it was on Earth, but…"

"We actually managed to come up with enough evidence to declare them all dead in the 'terror attack' except Kanapkey—remember, the zoo keeper? And our Forensics people think they might even have some evidence on him, now."

"That's good," Omega declared. "That means maybe we can give all the families closure."

"That's what I'm hoping for, Omega, yes. And we've pushed hard for it. Kanapkey is the only one still hanging out to dry, and we're pushing even harder on that." He paused, then admitted, "I still don't know, though. From what the Forensics people believe, he got pretty much completely consumed, soft tissue, bones, and all, and while they found a goodly-sized patch of dried fluids in the landscaping near the petting zoo, they're not yet sure if it was him, or if they can get enough DNA from the residue to confirm it one way or the other. We're hoping, though."

"What about that collapsed building?" she asked. "What's gonna happen there?"

"There's some discussion," Fox admitted. "Some want to do a memorial to it, same as for a certain real terror attack a good few years back, and others want to rebuild. Given nobody actually died in it this time, there's a fair bit of pressure to just rebuild. Frankly, that's what I expect to happen. But I'm keeping my oar out of it; while it wasn't an actual terror attack, people still died in the greater scheme, and if the city decides to raise a memorial there, I certainly can't take issue with the notion."

"That works, I guess," Echo said around a mouthful of shortbread. "Fortunately, we didn't lose one of our own in that, either."

"Thanks to you, Ace," Omega pointed out.

"Yes, and that's another nice little notation that's gone into your personnel record at the Galactic level, Echo," Fox said. "You're already Lord Commodore Echo of the Emdalian Fleet, after that whole thing Pulgey did last autumn for the two of you. But there's noises in the Council At Large that it's high time the Pan-Galactic Coalition had some proper over-arching designations, titles, and awards for those who go above and beyond. And between us, I fully expect that the first recipients will be you two."

"You know we don't expect anything," Echo said, earnest. "Nor particularly want it."

"Alla that," Omega agreed, firm.

"I know. But that doesn't argue it shouldn't be done, just the same," Fox pointed out, polishing off his second shortbread cookie and reaching for a third. "Damn, tekhter, I forget just how good your shortbread is, every time."

"Thanks, Fox," Omega said with a pleased, dimpling smile. "I'm glad you enjoy it."

"I never met a sentient yet that didn't," Fox said with a grin. "And that includes Pul, Suud, his wife, his son, Zz'r'p, Zarnix…! Never mind Echo, who practically inhales it." He paused and grinned at the younger man, who froze with his mouth full of shortbread, and the half-eaten cookie—his fourth—still on his lips; Echo flushed, looking sheepish. "Only now I'm going to have to work out extra, to make sure my Suits still fit!"

"I always do," Echo managed to get out around the shortbread. "I swear I work out at least half again longer than I used to, before Meg became my partner. She is a helluva damn good cook. And NOT just the shortbread, either."

"Ha! Well…" Omega began, then broke off, growing thoughtful. Both men sat up straight, on the alert for whatever had diverted her attention.

"What, baby?" Echo wondered.

"I was just thinking…"

"About…shortbread?"

"No, not exactly." She grinned ruefully. "That went off on a different train of thought. We do have that private little 'blowing off steam' room down in the gym, now," she pointed out. "I think all three of us have used it at various times…but never TOGETHER. It might be worth the three of us doing a few joint workouts to come up with some three-fers tactics."

"Yes, I remember we talked about that, back when Echo was still in the regeneration pod," Fox recalled. "And then we all got busy with the mega moth, and the lot of it went on the back burner, and I'd forgotten about it until just now. Hm. You're right, though. It's still a good idea, especially with Echo doing more as the Assistant Director now." He glanced at their desks, then waved a hand at them. "How far are the two of you from a good stopping place? Not just a pause, but the task completed? If we're going to do this, I want to spend some serious time on it and do it right. So figure you'll be out of the office for a couple-three hours, kinder."

Echo blinked, then considered. "Mm…maybe half an hour, thirty-five minutes?"

"Same," Omega confirmed.

"Good," Fox said. "I'll go finish what I was doing, then meet the two of you in the 'blowing-off-steam' room in forty-five to start warming up?"

"Done," Echo agreed.

* * *

An hour later, all three Agents stood in the special room, clad in their workout gear and properly warmed-up.

"Okay, tekhter," Fox said. "You're the training guru here, and I've cleared a couple of hours of my schedule so we can work with this. What do you want to do?"

"I think first I want to hear about a few more of the specific situations you've been in, Fox, maybe back when Echo and X-ray were providing escort, even before you became Director," Omega pointed out. "I need to get a feel for situations, and then we can start developing some techniques. Or modifying some of Alpha One's techniques to include you."

"I like that idea even better, Meg," Echo said. "Fox and I can set up the scenario using the kickboxing bags or whatever to stand in for the perps, and show you what we're talking about. Then we can show him what sorts of sequences you and I have already worked out for given situations, and let him tell us how he wants to work into the sequence. If we start getting really involved, we can move into the Alpha Line training room and set up some simulations to try, and actually bring our weapons into it."

"Heh," Omega chuckled. "In here, for now, just point a finger and say 'pew-pew' and we'll know you fired a weapon."

"Ha! Right," Echo agreed, grinning.

"This all sounds excellent, kinder," Fox said, his lips twitching as he stifled a laugh at Omega's sound effects. "I think this will work. It may take a few sessions to develop a process and a repertoire, but it'll be damn near perfect by the time we're ready to go live with it."

"Great," Omega declared, pleased. "Can you think of a good starting situation?"

"All right, I think so, yes; I remember a situation early on, when there was some resistance to Earth joining the Coalition, and a couple of factions tried to cause some trouble…"

* * *

Two hours later, all three humans were sweaty and tired, but also extremely satisfied.

"Next time, I think we need to try this in the sim training room," Echo said. "I want to see what we can do in real-time against the simulated perps."

"This looks like being very, very good," Fox decided. "I think we three can, as you like to say, 'mop up' if it should become necessary."

"I agree," Echo said, "and lemme tell ya, if we call Alpha Two in on a bodyguarding session, we can tear up jacks."

"What he said," Omega agreed. "Because if I wound up escorting the Director AND the Assistant Director, there's no way I'm doing it all my own self."

"No, and you shouldn't," Fox said, serious. "I understand about that. And nominally I'd have Echo and myself on separate vehicles, even, if it could be arranged. But kaka happens, as we all know."

"Maybe we want to come up with a twin to the *Genesis*?"

Echo wondered. "Or, well, just another battleship; I don't need one that big or powerful, I don't think. Not as 'just' the assistant director. If you're not going, I can take the *Genesis* anyway…"

"It's something to think about, and truthfully, I've already put in a requisition to upgrade one of the other battleships, with the *Genesis'* chief engineer overseeing the upgrade," Fox confirmed. "I already considered the matter and ran it by Pul and Suud—AND Lydhuu, for tactical considerations—and we all decided it needed doing. Pul also said that any ship you commanded could be considered a flagship of the Grand Emdalian Fleet, as well. Either of you, for that matter, since you're joint commodores. I'm most likely," he added, "to see about making Omega the executive officer of whatever battleship I assign as your personal flagship, Echo. I assume that's acceptable."

"More than," Echo agreed. "It makes a lot of sense, actually. Especially if she's heading up my bodyguard unit."

"Okay, this is all starting to come together," Omega said, thoughtful. "In that case, maybe what I want to do is to put together a special training procedure for director bodyguards, and get volunteers for who would like to be put into a bodyguard rotation…?"

"I am definitely liking how you think, tekhter," Fox said, approving. "I'm available to help you develop the criteria, if you like, since I do have a bit of experience there, doing it for Pul all those years. You might open that up to the standard Field agent department, too; I'm sure Crutch would appreciate it, and some of those folks are quite capable of handling it. The Security department as well, for that matter. Bodyguarding is, after all, a form of security."

"Good plan," Omega said, still thinking hard. "Maybe we need to create some special testing for that, too. As in, you don't get to be a bodyguard unless you can do these things, and have this mindset. That latter also eliminates anybody who might have any resentments, or might be an implanted agent like we had back at my first Christmas with the Agency…"

"All good," Echo decided. "I think we have something going here."

"I agree," Fox said. "We used to have a bodyguard corps back when Oboe was the Director, but she just picked her people and had them trained by me, since I'd been Pulgey's chief bodyguard…"

"So we never had a standardized method of staffing a bodyguard unit," Echo confirmed.

"Exactly. And maybe now, we need one. Because we have a Director AND an Assistant Director," Fox added. "And frankly, we probably needed one before now. Omega, I hereby give you the official order to go forth and put this together."

"Okay," Omega said, nodding firmly. "I think I have this in hand."

"I have no doubt," Fox said. "Let's go get cleaned up."

* * *

Fox worked closely with Alpha One over the next week or so, developing techniques in the 'blowing-off-steam' room and in the simulation training room, as well as working on criteria required for bodyguards. Fox and Echo both jointly considered that Omega was currently the logical person to head up the bodyguard unit, as she had an obvious vested interest in keeping her husband safe, as well as counting Fox a father figure; as the assistant chief of Alpha Line, the logical future chief of same, and the training coordinator for that department, it only made sense.

When the trio had figured out a system for smoothly and seamlessly fitting Fox into their established fighting routines, they brought Alpha Two into the mix, in the simulation training. That proved an excellent combo, and easy to modify, since Alpha One and Alpha Two trained and worked together so much anyway. When Alpha Four found out what was going on, they asked to join, as well, and demonstrated themselves to be almost as flexible as Alpha Two.

"And we know this whole lot has proved themselves to us already, Fox," Echo noted, after a successful bout that involved

Fox, Alpha One, Alpha Two, and Alpha Four against fully fifty simulations of the enforcers from Adita's Coup. Fox and Echo were encapsulated by the other Alpha Line Agents, while still using their own weapons through rolling 'slots' predetermined in the fight routines, even as the five remaining Agents kicked simulated ass.

"Yeah," Omega agreed. "I think we have the core of a bodyguard unit right here."

"But we need more," Fox pressed. "What you have is the full leadership of Alpha Line, and if Alpha Line is already in the midst of a brouhaha, you will not have all of these."

"No, that's true," Omega confirmed. "But it gives me a model to go on, now. See, with this to go by, I know I can put together a team from Alpha Line, the Field department, and Security lickety-split, just based on what we've already done."

"Good. Do it," Fox ordered.

* * *

It was the beginning of summer—early June—when the bodyguard unit was full up and nearly ready to go online. By that time it consisted of a rotating roster of Alpha Line, Field, and Security agents—a little over twenty in all.

"We want to keep it somewhat small," Fox told Omega and Echo, "because that will make it seem like a privilege and an honor to be part of an elite team that protects the Director and Assistant Director."

"I get it," Echo said. "I think we're gonna be okay with that. Meg, who's in the unit?"

"Right now, we have five Alpha Line teams—not counting me—plus four Field teams, and six Security agents, twenty-five agents in all, counting me," Omega said, looking at the roster on her tablet. "We have Alpha Two, Alpha Four, Alpha Seven, Alpha Eight, and Alpha Sixteen—that last team is Dog and Quebec, so adding me and Romeo into the mix, we have several hotshot pilots in the unit. Never mind you two."

"That's also all the leadership of Alpha Line," Fox said. "Do you have provision for...?"

"Yes sir," Omega acknowledged. "At no time will we ever have BOTH Alpha Two AND Alpha Four on bodyguard assignment; at least one has to remain in Headquarters to run the department. I mean, that can be overcome in a major emergency, but the general protocol is gonna be one or the other. Now, if the Praetorians are working in concert with Alpha Line, we could conceivably have both teams…"

"Good. That works."

"…Then from Field," she continued, "we have Beta Twenty-Eight, which is Echo's old buddy Queen and his partner Como; Beta Fifty-Two, which is MY old friend Chi and his partner Genova—and they're gonna be applying for Alpha Line when Chi has reached the right level of experience; Delta Twenty-Three, which is Berta and Carmen; and Delta Twenty-Nine, which is York and Quintal."

"So far, so good," Echo decided. "And from Security?"

"Well, those are individual agents, since Security doesn't use a partner system," Omega said, "and those are Oscar, her significant other Eagle, Topsail, Horse, Oyster, and Page."

"With additional backup available from all three departments?" Fox asked.

"With additional backup available from all three departments," Omega confirmed, nodding.

"Wait," Echo said. "I thought Oscar's significant other was Easy."

"He was," Fox said. "That was a glitch in code name assignments. He and Alpha Four's Easy joined our ranks at about the same time, and we didn't realize they'd gotten duplicate names. Since Alpha Line outranks Security in normal situations, he offered to change his code name, and suggested Eagle. He liked it, I liked it, Oscar liked it, and Omega liked it — plus, Alpha Four's Easy was relieved — so we went with it."

"I suppose stuff like that happens once in a while, as big as the Agency is," Omega said with a shrug.

"It does," Fox affirmed. "We try not to, but when they

come in at the same time like that, the computers don't always flag it."

"Right. What's the reporting scheme?" Echo wondered. "I mean, normally Alpha Line teams take the lead…"

"We discussed that," Omega said, "among all the new unit members. It was decided that, under nominal circumstances, there will be no more than two Alpha Line teams in rotation at any given time, and the other bodyguards will report to them, and them to me."

"So the hierarchy is maintained, it isn't a steep hierarchy, and we have good reporting," Fox said, satisfied.

"Exactly, sir. It's all matrixed, but it's a fairly flat structure. In an emergency situation, however, we call in all hands, plus whoever else we can get out of Alpha Line, Field, and Security. All of the latter of whom would report to the bodyguard members, preferably the Alpha Line bodyguards."

"Understood. And training is underway?"

"It is, Fox," Omega vouched. "I've given them all the tactics we three worked out, along with the explanation that they're intended to be modular; they can put them together in whatever ways they decide, that are appropriate according to the situation. And they've been training hard in teams of at least six in the sim room, with simulated versions of the two of you as well as simulated perps, and it seems to be working very well. I make sure that there's a rotation through the personnel, so each time they run it, they don't know who else they'll be working with. I figured that's the way to show up if there are any…" Omega paused, thinking of the right word, then tried, "um, incompatibilities…among the personnel. It also familiarizes them with the way each guard works; just because we're all using the same tactic doesn't mean we all move the same exact way."

"Good," Echo said. "Meg, baby, this is great. It sounds like you've thought of 'most everything."

"Well, I've been talking to Fox a lot," Omega admitted with a slight grin and blush. "And I also called and talked to

Uncle Suud several times, too."

"Excellent," Fox decreed. "You picked our brains?"

"Bingo."

"What about Lydhuu?"

"I did, once," Omega said; Lydhuu Rait was an Ergisol, looking like nothing so much as a six-foot-tall semi-bipedal June bug, complete with a lovely iridescent carapace. But she had followed in Fox's footsteps, being Suud's protégé as Suud had been Fox's, and had turned out to be brilliant at the job. She was currently considered one of the galaxy's best tacticians, a subject she now taught at the university on the Coalition capital planet of Aleancë. "She's got a heavy load this semester, teaching, and she's hard to catch. But we kind of condensed it, and I learned a lot."

"Even better," Echo decided.

"In fact," Omega said, a bit hesitant, "I was wondering if, at some point, I could take some of her courses? I think I could use the strategy stuff. I mean, I understand a lot of it already, but…at that level? I was an astronaut, not a tactician," she pointed out. "I'm learning tons working with y'all, but I still have a long way to go. And I'd rather not learn it on the job, and maybe put others at risk from basic mistakes."

"No, I agree, and I think that's a very good idea," Fox said, as Echo nodded. "If you look like being the Alpha Line Chief someday—and you do—then the more you know, the better off everyone is. Going to Aleancë to take the courses is problematic, without doubt, but I'm thinking some virtual learning coursework would do the job quite nicely. I'll talk to Lydhuu and see what we can figure out for you."

"That sounds great, Fox. Thanks." Omega smiled.

"Tekhter, you have a very good head on your shoulders, and it is capable of a great deal," Fox said, very serious. "I cannot think but that it is a good thing to keep providing input to the brain inside that head. It helps all of us, in the short AND the long run."

"Amen to that," Echo agreed. "When do you think we can

call the bodyguard unit operational?"

"Give it about another week, I think, and we can do this," Omega said. "I do have a couple of questions."

"Shoot," Fox said.

"Is this only for trips, is it for forty-eight/seven, is it for…?" Omega tried.

"Ah," Fox said then. "Yes, I understand. Because if it were continuous, you would need to remove the agents in rotation from the active rosters of their principal departments."

"Right," Omega said. "Crutch, Nab, and Uncle are waiting to hear back from me on that."

"I don't see it needful around the clock, not with us in Headquarters," Fox decided, after a moment to think. "Do you, Echo?"

"No, Fox, I don't," Echo agreed. "Not unless we had, say, a Level 3 Facility Alert called on Headquarters, or any of the higher alerts, depending on the exact nature of the alert. All things considered, though, it may mean that Alpha One needs to start taking along an extra team or two whenever we hit the field, and maybe Alpha One doesn't need to be doing quite so many routine patrols, not any more, I guess. But I'm thinking we'll use 'em mostly for trips offworld, or any situation that may arise on-planet. Like, if you or I had been on-planet during Adita's Coup."

"Right," Omega said. "And we're working with Facilities, too, to gin up a few safe spaces for the two of you, both here and in some of the larger Offices. Places we guard-types can shuffle you off to, if something starts going down."

"This works," Fox decided. "I likely should have been a little less independent during my tenure as Director, I suppose, but that's my nature. At least, after Majdanek got done with me."

"And that's understandable," Omega murmured; thanks to galactic medicine, Fox was much older than he looked, and as a young teen, had been imprisoned in the Nazi concentration camp, where he had seen the rest of his family exterminated.

He himself had survived, and lived to meet Pulgey Entiyti during that being's first term as Galactic President; after a brief retirement, Entiyti was once again overseeing the Pan-Galactic Coalition.

The trio was silent for a long moment, in respect of Fox's memories. Then the older man cleared his throat.

"Well, that is neither here nor there, I suppose," he noted, trying not to sigh. "It is what it is, and we are doing it now. Any other questions, Omega?"

"Do either of you have a preference as to what guards are assigned to you?" Omega wondered.

"Not especially," Fox said, after a moment to ponder. "I think those are all excellent people, and I should have no problems working with them. Though I suppose that Echo and I would do well to replace those simulacra of ourselves at least a few times, to ensure we can fit in well."

"True. I'll try to squeeze in a few sessions there, 'cause you're correct, Fox. Meg, if you're running it, I don't guess that means I can specify you, because you'll have to float between us," Echo mused.

"Right, but I'll still try to make sure my shift aligns with yours, if at all possible," Omega said. "In fact, the others pretty much TOLD me I was gonna do that. They don't want us separated on account of me running the bodyguard contingent."

"And that's considerate of them," Fox averred. "I note you say, 'If possible.' So you're prepared to change that?"

"If it means keeping you two safe, hell yes, Fox," Omega determined. "I'll work whatever hours are required to ensure that, with whichever of you I need to."

"Then we are good, tekhter, we are good. Anything else?"

"No, that's pretty much it."

"Let us know when you are ready to go online."

"Wilco, Fox."

* * *

The very next day, Echo joined the training sessions for the bodyguard unit, working with different combinations of the guards to give them a better feel for how Echo operated during a fight.

"But I have a question," Oscar, the security agent, wondered, after one of the sessions in the sim room.

"Shoot," Echo said, replenishing some of his gear in various warp pockets, in preparation for the next training session.

"Why are you even fighting with us? We're protecting you. Shouldn't you be moving more to the rear and letting us guard your escape? I mean, you are, to a point, but…"

"Because it's not who I am," Echo noted, "and it's not who Fox is, either. Both of us came up through active agency sorts of positions. I didn't get to be head of Alpha Line by taking a back seat when shit hit the fan, and Fox didn't get to be Director that way, either. Yes, he's mostly known for founding the Diplomacy department, but you, of all people, should recall that he also founded the Security department, too. He was, after all, Pulgey Entiyti's chief bodyguard for many years. And his experience goes back a long ways beyond that."

"Whoa," Eagle, another security guard and Oscar's significant other, murmured. "Good point. That's some serious prowess, there, in you both."

"Exactly," Echo said, "and we both want to lend those skills to the efforts to protect us."

"In other words," Monkey noted, "you're both used to protecting yourselves and others, and want to continue doing that."

"Bingo," Echo confirmed. "We're part of this unit. Just because this unit is set up to protect us doesn't mean we're not an active part of the process."

"Let's go, then!" Carmen, half of the Delta 23 field team, declared, enthusiastic.

* * *

Fox came by the next day, and while he couldn't stay more than part of the day, he came back the day after that, as well. He also confirmed Echo's explanation of why they were participating in defense and evacuation, rather than simply moving straight to the rear.

"I'm used to roughing my way through matters," Fox said. "I've been doing that for decades, and I don't think I can change now. I had independence drilled into me at a very young age, and it was done extremely thoroughly. I'm not foolhardy; I know what you lot are trying to do, and I'll let you do it…but I plan to help in my own defense, thank you very much."

"Makes sense," Golf noted, giving Fox a knowing look; unlike the standard Agents' Handbook that the others had read, Alpha Line got a non-redacted handbook that contained personal information about some of the Originals, including Echo and Fox. So he fully understood that Fox obliquely referenced his time in a Nazi concentration camp as a juvenile. Fox raised an eyebrow at Golf's comment, pursed his lips slightly to hide the appreciative smile that threatened, let his eyes twinkle at the Alpha Line Agent, and checked his blaster before the next training session.

* * *

A couple of days after that, Fox and Echo cleared their schedules for the whole day, and met the entire bodyguard team, including Omega, at the simulation training room.

"All right, let's see what this elite bunch can do, when we pull out the stops," Fox decreed.

"We're ready when you are, Fox, Echo," Omega said. "I've got a series of simulations already programmed in. This simulator room is amazing; I've got the bulk of Headquarters — INCLUDING the warp tunnels — programmed into it. We won't be able to tell that we're not in the real thing."

"Let's roll, then," Echo said.

* * *

They started out with the full unit—all twenty-five agents, plus Echo and Fox. The scenario Omega programmed was an attempted coup by the Andromedan rogue faction, similar to the one that had briefly taken over Headquarters the previous autumn. It therefore constituted every single level of emergency alert that the Coalition possessed: a Maximum General

Emergency, a Level 3 Facility Alert, a Level 2 Planetary Alert, a Level 1 Division Alert, and a Level 1A Galactic Alert.

To that end, there were more Andromedans than there had been in the real-world scenario—seventy-five Scuttles, as the Agents called the rogue Persans, just to storm the Core, compared to the original fifty-some-odd—against the twenty-seven elite agents…and several other simulated Alpha Line partnerships. The Core, the Alpha Line Room, the Director's office, and all adjacent structures and facilities were also simulated. Omega had, as she had said, programmed in virtually the entire Headquarters facility, to allow for off-book, spur of the moment tactics.

The simulated Scuttles—comprising a mix of the several species that made up the Andromedan galactic empire known as the Persis Federation, including the Ka'agand and the Uzshei, as well as four more that Omega had seen on the Persan flagship—came at the group from the up-escalators from Grand Central Station to the Core. Fox was in his office, and Omega and Echo were in the Alpha Line Room, along with the Alpha Line members of the bodyguard unit and several simulated Alpha Line partnerships. When the notification came in, Omega promptly hit the emergency button on her cell phone and flagged the bodyguard unit.

"Echo! Fox! We have a coup attempt! It's the renegade Persans, trying again! Fox, please send out the alerts at once!"

"On it, Omega," Fox declared. "Opaquing my windows. Sending the Boys into hiding, as well."

Within seconds a klaxon began to sound, and the ATLASS system annunciated, "Level 3 Facility Alert. This facility has been invaded by hostiles. Level 2 Planetary Alert. This planet has been invaded by hostiles. Level 1 Division Alert. This division has been invaded by hostiles. Level 1A Galactic Alert. The Pan-Galactic Coalition has been invaded by hostiles. All personnel, secure work stations and take evasive response. Notification to other Offices, other planets, and the Ennead under way. Evacuation of this facility recommended."

"Alpha Two, Alpha Four! Get Echo into the warp tunnel!" Omega ordered, shouting to be heard over the ATLASS alert system. "Alpha Seven, Eight, and Sixteen! Go to the Director's office and take Fox into the warp tunnel there! All other Praetorians, you are activated! We'll all meet up at the saferoom nexus! All other Alpha Line units, you are assigned to slow down the invasion force! Divert them if you can! Taking 'em out is even better! GO!"

India activated the door in the wall between the big logos on the front wall of the room, then shoved the credenza aside, which effectively opened the door. Romeo pulled his primary blaster and ran through, verified the tunnel was clear, then came back, holding out a hand to Echo and ushering him through the door. Golf and Easy followed, and Omega brought up the rear, closing the door behind them, even as Yankee, Tare, Monkey, Kako, Dog, and Quebec ran across the Core and up the ramp to Fox's office, leapfrogging and laying down cover fire as they went. The other simulated Alpha Line teams split into two groups; the larger group headed for the escalators to block the invasion force, the other headed for the bank of elevators to stop any Scuttles that might be attempting a flanking maneuver.

Moments later, Alpha Seven, Eight, and Sixteen had hurried Fox into the warp tunnels via the secret down room he had hidden behind his office.

* * *

This exercise was designed for conditions to deteriorate as soon as the Praetorians had the upper hand. So, to that end, as soon as the Praetorians had Echo and Fox in the warp tunnels, the simulated Scuttles gradually took out the simulated Alpha Line teams as those teams ran interference for the Praetorians.

Meanwhile, Echo and Fox rendezvoused in the safe room within the warp tunnels that had been created for this purpose—except it wasn't the real thing, of course. It was another simulation, to avoid a war game running throughout Headquarters and getting in the way of regular business...never mind frightening the visiting aliens.

"All right, Echo," Fox said. "Are we good with the standard evacuation plan? Offworld via the *Genesis* and the *Revelation*?"

"I think so, Fox," Echo agreed. He turned to Omega. "Have we verified the Lunar Farside Drydocks is intact and secure?"

"Affirm," Omega said, double-checking a readout on her cell phone display. "Yeah, still clear, thanks to all the stealth equipment on that facility."

"What about the new L5 Docks?" Fox wondered.

"Also clear," Omega confirmed. "The *Genesis* and the *Revelation* are both safe and legitimate destinations."

"Good," Fox decreed. "Omega, please execute Plan EA-1A."

"On it, Fox, Echo," Omega ordered. "Fox Team, Grand Central Station Emergency Concourse X, Gate D1A. Destination, Penn Station Gate D1AA *Genesis*. Sound off."

"Romeo copies. X, D1A."

"India copies. X, D1A."

"Dog copies. X, D1A."

"Quebec copies. X, D1A."

"Queen copies. X, D1A."

"Como copies. X, D1A."

"Berta copies. X, D1A."

"Carmen copies. X, D1A."

"Oscar copies. X, D1A."

"Eagle copies. X, D1A."

"Horse copies. X, D1A."

"Oyster copies. X, D1A."

"Page copies. X, D1A."

"Good," Omega said. "Team Fox—GO."

They headed out at speed, Fox in the center of the group, all weapons drawn.

"Okay," Omega said. "Team Echo, we're headed to the North Emergency Departure Concourse XX, Gate D1B. Destination, Big Indian/Willowemoc Local Station, Gate D1BB *Revelation*. Sound off."

"Golf copies. XX, D1B."

"Easy copies. XX, D1B."
"Tare copies. XX, D1B."
"Yankee copies. XX, D1B."
"Monkey copies. XX, D1B."
"Kako copies. XX, D1B."
"Chi copies. XX, D1B."
"Genova copies. XX, D1B."
"York copies. XX, D1B."
"Quintal copies. XX, D1B."
"Topsail copies. XX, D1B."

"Good copy," Omega decreed. "Echo, with me. Everybody fall in; let's go."

Seconds later, the safe room was empty.

* * *

But as soon as the Fox Team came out of the warp tunnels at the emergency concourse, the simulated Scuttles were waiting. Within moments, and by sheer overwhelming numbers, five of the team went down in the simulated attack, the simulator computer deeming them incapacitated-injured or outrightly dead: Queen, Berta, Carmen, Horse, and Page.

The exit they'd chosen was right across from the D1A gate designated for Fox's emergency evac offworld, however, and the remaining eight agents, plus Fox, fought their way across the concourse. But while they took out more than half the Scuttles, the Praetorians lost Quebec, Como, Oyster, and Eagle in order to reach the gate. Romeo positioned himself and India between Fox, Dog, and Oscar.

"Go! GO!" Romeo ordered. "Get through the hatch and go! We got this covered!"

Dog grabbed Fox and Oscar and hustled them through the hatch of the heavily armored maglev train, as India and Romeo opened up with all four blasters, scything through the ranks of the Andromedans. Romeo took a hit just as the hatch closed and the maglev detached, and India instinctively crouched over him...and went down under the remaining Scuttles, who dogpiled the Alpha Two team.

It was the last thing Fox saw before the maglev shot away.

* * *

Team Echo exited the warp tunnels in the same emergency departure concourse that had seen Omega's very first maglev train ride, en route to the T-bird and nabbing a gang of saucer jackers. But here, too, the Scuttles were waiting, and by the time they had Echo out of the passage, Topsail, York, Quintal, Chi, Genova, and Easy were down and out of the fight — fully half of their contingent. The simulation was sufficiently real that, when the simulation computer considered Easy 'dead,' his real body disappeared thanks to a projected sensor scrambler field, and a solid hologram of a 'dead Easy' appeared on the floor in his stead; this did his partner, Golf, no favors mentally or emotionally.

Like Team Fox, the exit from the warp tunnels was very near the emergency maglev train. Team Echo simply had to reach it…across a concourse swarming with armed Scuttles. An angry Golf—it was often the case that the agents forgot they were in a simulation, especially as the equipment used in the training rooms became more and more sophisticated— took the point, taking out as many Scuttles as he could. Behind him, Tare, Yankee, Monkey, and Kako surrounded Echo, with Omega bringing up the rear.

Within moments, Golf went down, followed by Tare.

"GO! GO! GO!" Omega ordered, hitting a remote button with one hand while still firing with the other.

The armored maglev hatch opened, and a distraught Yankee, along with Monkey and Kako, hustled Echo through it…

…Just as Omega took a shot to the leg.

It happened to be a real shot of sorts, a practice projectile round soft enough to prevent any real injury more than some ordinary bruising, but with enough momentum to take her leg from beneath her. She fell to the floor, still firing at Scuttles. Echo, already in the maglev car and about to seat himself and strap in, spun.

"Meg!" he shouted. "Baby! NO! *NO!*"

"GO, Ace!" Omega cried, and hit the button on the remote.

The hatch closed before Echo could reach it; the maglev hummed loudly, and shot away from the gate...

...Just as a Scuttle stood over Omega, firing point-blank at her head, while Echo stared out the hatch window. The last thing he saw was her simulated headless body slumping to the floor.

"DIRECTOR AND ASSISTANT DIRECTOR HAVE ACHIEVED ESCAPE FROM HEADQUARTERS FACILITY," the simulator's stentorian voice declared then. "ENDING SIMULATION NOW."

And suddenly everyone—all of the Praetorians, as well as Fox and Echo—were standing or lying at various points across a huge, gray, featureless room.

"Damn," a shaken Echo breathed, and sat down hard on the floor.

Chapter 2

The debrief was a quiet affair. Most of the team, as well as Echo, were shaken by what they'd seen, what they'd had to do, in order to accomplish their chosen mission. It had even hit Fox in the midst of the firefight that, had the simulation been real, he would be leaving Zebra behind, with no idea of when he would see her again, if he ever did. And the probability that his 'son and daughter,' Romeo and India, would have died protecting him was high, as well.

"That said," he remarked, "we were successful on our very first run, against overwhelming odds. That speaks to skill, and it speaks to dedication. And I am very proud of all of you." But his voice shook slightly at the end.

"Alla that," Echo agreed, though he was a bit hoarse.

"I'm thinkin' maybe we need to add Meg in there with Echo, though," Yankee noted. "Echo knee-jerked bad, and almost undid all our work, when she went down."

"I did," Echo sighed. "And I know it, and I'm sorry. I...it was the first time I've really ever seen Meg go down in front of me and get mock-killed since we've been married. An' we haven't been married that long. I...didn't handle it well at all."

"Good thought, Yankee, and something we'll consider going forward," Fox agreed, holding up a hand as Omega made to protest. "No, tekhter, it won't do. Never mind I'm now considering how to evacuate Zebra, as my wife and a potential target of blackmail against me, we need to look at your safety as well. You ARE the head of the Praetorians, after all, and you're most likely the third in the Division succession—I've already gone forward to the Ennead about that, and Pulgey says they're discussing it, but like the idea, given your reputation and how you held up during Echo's Ennead trial—and so while you can command, it's probably a very good idea to do as Yankee suggests. Does anyone in the Guard have an issue with that?"

All heads shook in the negative.

"But then do we need ta split 'em up?" Romeo wondered. "We might need a bigger guard unit, if we do that..."

"Nah," Monkey said. "You didn't see those two in our end of the firefight. Hell, put them together in the middle of Team Echo, let 'em go back to back, an' shit, dude. You almost don't need the rest of us!"

"Let's put together some more fighting moves like that, and see where it takes us," Fox decided. "I think that's an excellent idea, based on what I've seen of those two in action."

"Consider it done, then," Omega said.

* * *

That night, the joint quarters of Alpha One were very quiet. Echo tended to stay close to Omega, even cooking dinner for her but insisting she sit in the kitchen on one of the bar stools while he did, then cuddling close on the couch after dinner.

But once they climbed into bed, he couldn't get close enough.

* * *

It took a while for him to settle, and when he did, he still held her tight against his body.

"I never wanna see what I saw today, ever again," he murmured. "I'll go out with you, but I won't watch you be taken out."

"Shh," she shushed him. "We're gonna fix that. But we might need to think about getting out of field work sooner, if it affected you that bad."

"I'm seriously considering it, now," he averred.

* * *

A week later, and after several more intense practice sessions incorporating Fox, Echo, and both at once, as well as the new concept of Echo and Omega working together as the core of Team Echo, Omega called Fox and Echo together in Fox's office.

"We're ready," she declared. "When the two of you went down and spent an entire day in the sim room working with 'em two days ago, that was the last thing we needed to confirm it."

"You're calling live on the guard unit?" Echo verified.

"Affirmative," a formal Omega stated crisply, nodding. "The Division One Praetorians are officially online and active, Director, Assistant Director. You may call on us as needed, sirs."

And that means you're my Batava, Echo told her silently, hiding the smile that she still sensed through the mental link.

That'll work, she told him in response. *Your special bodyguard of sorts. 'Cause I can be there at night.*

And you ARE special. In lotsa ways, but especially to me.

"Excellent," Fox decreed. "Our lead Praetorian is dismissed."

* * *

After that, things settled down as far as work was concerned…but ramped up even further in the Medical department. Fox had told Zebra about the work on the bodyguard corps, and requested that the medlab back off on working directly with Omega as regarded her reproductive system until she had completed assembling the corps. Zebra found herself somewhat relieved at the thought that her husband the Director would soon have an entire team of bodyguards to protect him, and agreed at once to his request.

Now, however, with the Praetorians officially online, the intense effort required to put it together was at an end, and the medlab called her in for more analysis.

Consequently, Omega spent parts of every other day in the medlab, as the 'Omega team' tried to determine what they could do to ensure that any offspring she produced would be normal humans. Slug had, unfortunately for Omega, rather thoroughly tampered with the genetics of her eggs to ensure that, had she mated with the other 'enhanced' human Slug had created as the gastropoid had intended, their children would have been genetically-programmed Echo hunters. The programming wasn't really programming in the standard sense of the word, but it was an extremely sophisticated bit of biochemistry…as well as possibly a few other technologies, up to and including quantum entanglement.

It was uncertain if that genetic 'program' still held, however, if the father of Omega's children was another, unaugmented human. But Omega flatly was not going to risk putting Echo in danger from his own children. And the medlab staff was in full agreement.

"So we're going to biopsy some of the tissues in your uterus, your Fallopian tubes, and your ovaries, in turn, and analyze them in depth," Zebra told her. "Once we have a feel for that, we'll nab a few of your eggs and check them out."

"This is not gonna be pleasant, is it?" Omega wondered, wincing.

"Well, no," Zebra said with a sigh. "Biopsies aren't fun. But we're gonna keep you knocked out for most of it—which normally isn't done, but you're a special case, and we're not gonna make this any harder on you than we can help—and hit everything with some Rejuvic after the biopsies but before you wake up. I'll want you to come in every other day until I say otherwise, while we run these analyses."

Omega sighed.

* * *

Joe Bob Cardiff was a member in good standing of the Facilities department at Headquarters. But few people knew him. Still fewer liked him. He handled all of the trash disposal that the Sluuites didn't get, usually gathering it up from around Headquarters — bags of garbage from the various trash cans and bathrooms, even the food court in Grand Central Station, sweeping up the Sluuite inedibles, cleaning restrooms and wiping up spills — and taking it all down to the third level sub-basement, where he loaded it into the special incinerator in the corner, the one that ensured nothing coming out was identifiable, so they could compost or recycle it for other, Earth-bound, uses. So despite his Agency-issued coveralls, Joe Bob tended to be dirty all the time. His personal hygeine wasn't the best anyway, and between that and the garbage he handled, he usually smelled bad.

But that was all right, because he rarely saw any of the high mucky-mucks anyway. Or anyone else, really.

Which suited him just fine.

So no one noticed when Joe Bob was replaced one night.

Nor did they hear the screams that came, all too briefly, from the incinerator.

* * *

There was an extra five pounds of ash in the incinerator the day after Joe Bob disappeared. But given the variations in waste from day to day, depending on what alien species was passing through, no one really noticed.

Joe Bob's replacement looked almost exactly like Joe Bob. He acted just like Joe Bob. He smelled worse than Joe Bob. He answered to the name Joe Bob, on those rare occasions when he was addressed at all.

And he made the rounds of Headquarters...

...just like Joe Bob.

* * *

Several evenings—nearly a Division week—after the Praetorians went on-line, Omega sat at the dinner table, staring at her dinner...but not eating. She had taken perhaps two bites, then laid her flatware down, sighed, and simply stared at the plate.

"What's wrong, baby?" Echo wondered. "Don't you like it?"

"Oh, no, it isn't that, Echo," Omega said, offering him a weary smile. "It's delicious, and I'm hungry. I'm just...too tired to eat."

"What? What's wrong?"

"It's all this medical testing," she sighed. "Poking here, biopsy there, let's get a blood sample, wupsie, let's knock you out before we do this part...it's past old. And it doesn't matter how careful they are, I'm just...TIRED."

"Are they hitting the biopsy sites with Rejuvic, or giving you some Regenic after?"

"Yes to both, but it still takes energy to HEAL," Omega

said. "And the site is usually sore for a day or two. And by the time that place isn't sore, they've done made a NEW place."

"Ooo," Echo said with a wince, pulling his cell phone and swiping his fingertip across the screen several times, then tapping twice. "Well, lemme ping Fox and Zebra and tell 'em you need a break. Then I'll sit down beside you and shovel food for you."

"You know what? That all sounds…good. Really, really, damn good."

"You ARE tired, if you'll let me feed you."

"Yeah. Pretty bad. I nearly nodded off in front of my computer today in the Alpha Line Room. And that was with all that coffee I drank, too. I didn't mean to; I mean, that's WHY I was drinkin' all the coffee."

"Ugh. I think it's good after all that Alpha One has been proscribed from doing routine patrols."

"Yeah, I thought about that, too. And it helps me now, 'cause I really don't think I could do that, too. I just don't have enough energy for it. Though it's supposed to be for you, as the Assistant Director."

"Well, I guess it's about time you and I started commanding, rather than leading, so much," Echo said, finishing the text message and sending it. Seconds later, his phone dinged and he read the response.

"Zebra says, 'Oh shit, she shoulda told me, I'll tell the others she gets a break from all the testing,'" Echo noted, "and Fox says, 'Hell yes, tell her to sleep in tomorrow.' So it's official. You get a little time off for a change, baby. In fact, if you want to take all of tomorrow off, I'd say go for it. I can handle things with Romeo's help."

"No, we were gonna review the newest batch of applications, remember?"

"That can wait; there's no urgency on it. YOU, however, need to unwind and let your body recover." His phone dinged again and he checked it, "Aha. And no gym for a couple days. That's per Zebra. As well as an apology; she had no idea it was doing that to you, 'cause apparently you didn't let on."

Omega sighed.

"All right," she capitulated. "I don't think I'mma fuss. Don't think I got the energy to fuss if I wanted to, anyhow. And I was just sort of…dealing, so no, I didn't let on. I guess I should've, but I didn't think. I was too damn tired to think, to tell the truth." She paused, considering. "Let's just take it nice and easy tonight—nothing energetic, nothing that requires a lotta thinking, just a real quiet evening, just us two—then I'll sleep in tomorrow as late as I feel like I need to, and take it from there. If I don't feel good when I get up, I'll ping you and tell you I'm taking a sick day. If I feel better—I mean, you know how fast I heal up, so I MIGHT feel better—then I'll come on in for part of a day. Just the notion that I have time off from all the pokin' an' proddin' perks me up mentally, to be honest."

"That all works for me. Given that our days run forty-eight hours, it's perfectly reasonable. But we don't need you getting sick, let alone injured again, just because you're run down from all the medical testing and shit."

"Point."

Echo did indeed sit down and feed her—a nice sirloin, cooked exactly as she liked it, with salad, baked potato, and steamed asparagus drizzled with balsamic vinegar, and one of Zebra's homemade cheesecakes — just a small one — to share for dessert. Echo simply moved his plate close to hers, used one fork, and patiently fed them both, alternating between bites. With him at the wheel — or fork, as it were — Omega ate, and ate well, tucking away her share of everything.

When they were done, he picked her up and carried her into the den, putting her on the sofa and wrapping her in the Orion Nebula sublimation-print throw.

"Now you sit there and just unwind and relax," he told her, "while I go put the dishes in the washer, then I'll come back out here and we'll 'make like Brussels sprouts' for a while, as you like to put it, then we'll go to bed early. Are you going to want your evening whisky?"

"Not tonight, I don't think," Omega said, her voice low. "I might go to sleep before you could get back from loading the dishwasher, if I did. Maybe a glass of wine. Maybe. No, scratch that; I'll still go to sleep if I do."

"That bad, huh?"

"Pretty bad, yup. Maybe a soda, or some lemonade. Iced tea. Whatever's handy."

"Do you want to just go on to bed?"

"Not yet. Not really. My body's tired, but my brain's not ready for bed yet."

"Okay, stay put and I'll be back in five."

It took six, but Omega didn't mind. Echo brought two cans of Diet Coke, eased under the throw beside her, pulled her into his side, and they snuggled together, chit-chatting of nothing in particular; just two lovers talking and occasionally planning their future together.

They never even bothered to turn on the television.

* * *

After a couple of hours of this — interspersed with a few kissing sessions — as Omega flagged more and more, Echo slipped out from under the throw.

"I'm gonna turn down the bed, then come back and get you," he told her.

"Nah, I'll come with," she protested, pushing aside the throw and standing. "I'm not that far gone, and sitting there quietly, snuggling and talking, helped a lot. Plus the soda."

"Good. Let's go on to bed, then. Even if I'm not ready to go to sleep, I'll cuddle you."

"That sounds good. I…I hate to say it, hon, but I just don't think I'm up to more than cuddles tonight."

"That's okay. I already figured. I can feel just how tired you are through the nd't'lq, even after the caffeine from that soda. You're wiped. You need to just lay down and zonk for a change, honey. I bet you barely move all night."

"I wouldn't take that bet right now."

41

Fifteen minutes later, they were snuggled together in the middle of the big bed, Echo spooning Omega, protectively enveloping her smaller, exhausted body with his tall, powerful one. She sighed, profoundly weary, and he hugged her.

"Sleep, baby," he breathed in her ear. "I'm here, and I'll take care of things. You're safe, you're protected, and you're loved."

Not more than sixty seconds after that, she was soundly, deeply asleep. Snippets of her dreams—happy, sunshiny dreams full of family, her husband, and children yet to be—floated to Echo through the nd't'lq.

Echo smiled and gently held his exhausted wife as she slept.

* * *

A lone Echo was heading to the Alpha Line Room the next morning, walking across the Core, deep in thought about the agenda order for the morning departmental meeting, when he heard a vaguely-familiar voice squeal his name.

"ECHO!"

And suddenly a female figure slammed into him and wrapped around his body, even as a fervent kiss was pressed to his lips.

Meg? he thought in startlement, but got no response save a few flitting images of dreams; he had left his wife and partner sleeping in, after the latest round of testing to determine how to repair her reproductive system and return it to human norms had left her more debilitated than he had seen her since their final confrontation with Slug. And this behavior didn't fit her, anyway.

When the being whose arms and legs were wrapped firmly around his torso finally pulled its head back, he stared into familiar purple eyes in a heart-shaped, pale, slightly blue-tinged face, a curtain of pure white hair framing all. It still took him several moments to pull the memory to the fore…though a sudden whiff of scent helped.

"REE?!" he exclaimed, surprised.

"YES!" the alien woman exclaimed. "I KNEW you would recall me! Oh, Echo, it is so good to see you again! It has been much too long!"

And she kissed him another time.

But this time it wasn't remotely platonic; to his increased startlement, her tongue entered his mouth and explored, even as her scent became deliciously heady.

With an effort — she was hugging him tightly with arms AND legs, and it didn't give him much leverage — Echo pushed back, then gently pried her off his body. Other agents and aliens stared at the pair as they passed through the Core—given that Echo had stopped dead in the middle of the huge room, it wasn't hard, because they were in plain view from all angles.

"Ree, it's good to see you, too," he murmured. "But you can't do that any more."

"Why not? You kiss as good as ever!"

"Because I'm attached now. I'm with someone else."

"Aw! That is cute. But you and I both know I am your first love, Echo dear."

"That was a long time ago, Ree." He turned for the Alpha Line Room.

"Where are you going?" she wondered, mildly shocked.

"I have a department meeting in a few minutes, and I have to go deal with that. You're welcome to come by later and we can chat and get caught up, if you like."

"Oh no! I am not letting you get away this time."

"'Get away'? You're the one who ended our relationship, Ree," Echo said, cool.

"And that was a mistake," the petite, shapely alien woman decreed.

She hooked her arm through his and shadowed him across the huge room to the joint departmental office and meeting room of the most badass group of law enforcement agents in the entire Milky Way Galaxy: Alpha Line, Division One's special forces unit.

* * *

"Ree, you can't stay here," Echo said firmly as she followed him into the room. "This is business."

"I accompanied you on business back when we were seeing each other," she pointed out. "I do not see a difference."

"The difference is, this is a special forces team, and some of the information may be classified due to division security," Echo pointed out.

"Pissh," she said, dismissing the matter with a nonchalant wave of her hand. "Oh, by the by, where is X-ray? I wanted to tell him hello…"

Echo winced.

"X-ray is dead, Ree," he said, and she turned to stare at him, shocked. "It's…a long story. I'll tell you later; I don't have time right now."

"All right. Well, you just sit right down here in one of these chairs, and I shall sit beside you and be very quiet, and you can find out all of your mission details."

"I'm not attending the meeting, Ree," Echo tried to explain, feeling more than a bit put out. He was trying hard to be nice to an old flame, but that old flame was being rather petulant and decidedly demanding, and he was becoming more than a little annoyed. "I'm running it. I'm the department chief."

"Ooo!" the alien woman squealed. "I am the girlfriend of the department chief!"

Several Alpha Line Agents, including Alpha Two, who had arrived early for the meeting, raised eyebrows at that. Echo raked a hand across his face and up into his hair.

"Y'all, meet an old girlfriend of mine. This is Nreefluvan Daagnadan of Kochav. She and I used to…see each other, years ago."

"And we have not seen each other in so long! I am so happy to be back on Earth with my Echo!" Daagnadan exclaimed. Echo sighed.

"Ree, I've already told you. I'm with someone else. I'm espoused to another Agent."

"No, of course not, Echo," Daagnadan said with a smile. "I am certain I would have heard about it if that had happened. You are simply trying to…how did X-ray term it? Oh! You are 'playing hard to get.'"

"No, he's serious," India, the female member of the Alpha Two life partnership, declared as she stepped into the breach, to Echo's relief. "And his wife—his mate—is the assistant department chief, Agent Omega. His partner."

"You are so confused, dear female," Daagnadan said with a laugh. "A partner is not the same as a mate."

"It is in this instance," Romeo averred. "We got life partners an' marriage, now."

"What is marriage?" Daagnadan wondered. India and Romeo exchanged glances, then Romeo started to speak, but an exasperated Echo cut him off with a wave of his hand.

"Leave it be, Romeo," Echo sighed. "I'll try to get this mess straightened out after the meeting. Ree, you need to go. Now."

"No, boopy," she told him, still smiling. "I will stay right here with you."

"Boopy?" Romeo repeated, trying not to look cross-eyed at his superior and adoptive brother of sorts. "Dude, don't tell me you EVER let her call you THAT when you 'uz datin'. I don't care HOW young you were!"

"No, I didn't," Echo declared. "It's Kochavi for…well, it's the equivalent of honey or sugar, I guess. But no, Ree. You still don't get to call me that."

"Aw." She grinned. "But I think you make such a cute boopy."

"Come with me, Ms. Daagnadan," India volunteered. "I'll take you on a tour of Headquarters. I'm sure it's changed since you were here last, and that'll be more interesting for you than this boring old meeting. And Romeo can fill me in later."

"But Echo…"

"You can come back after the meeting, and we'll sit and catch up until Meg gets here," Echo said. "Um, Omega, my wife. Then I'll introduce the two of you, and we can all go out to first lunch."

"Oh, that sounds nice," Daagnadan said. "But I had much rather you leave your partner behind and go to lunch with only me."

"I think you'll like Meg," Echo insisted. "All three of us will go to lunch."

Daagnadan pouted, but India all but dragged her out of the room.

Echo drew in a long, deep breath, then let it out in a very tired sigh. He briefly noted that he could still smell Daagnadan's perfume, because the clinch in which she had held him—she had barreled into him so hard it had nearly knocked him down, then fairly enveloped his torso with arms and legs; fortunately she was wearing a pantsuit, or it might have become even more familiar—had gotten the fragrance all over his Suit. *Oh great,* he thought, becoming annoyed. *And Meg will smell it and know somebody's been hugging on me. I'll have to make sure to explain fast, or I'll have a jealous wife to deal with. And,* he recalled the way Daagnadan had held him, trying to put away a certain stirring it engendered, *not without reason, I guess.*

"No shit, bro," Romeo agreed with the unspoken message contained in the sigh. "She a thang on wheels, that one."

"She wasn't like…THAT…back when we were a thing," Echo said, shaking his head. "Damn. Talk about clingy. And insistent. Never mind wanting things the way she wants 'em and ignoring all statements to the contrary. Well, a little bit of that last, I guess. But not nearly like this."

"Alla that," Romeo confirmed. "Meg still sleepin'?"

"Yeah. Between having just got off her cane after the busted foot healing up, then putting together the whole Praetorian thing, and THEN all the tests the medlab has been putting her through—since way BEFORE she got off her cane—well, she was pretty damn tired last night. To give you an idea, you know how hungry she gets?"

"Yeah?"

"She was starved, but too tired to eat. I had to help her eat.

Like, shovel it in her face. She just kinda sat there and chewed and swallowed, then periodically opened her mouth like a baby bird, so I knew when to shovel more in."

"Damn, dude. I'll let India know they needa ease up."

"I pinged Zebra and Fox last night and told 'em that already, but you two are welcome to emphasize it," Echo said. "Anyhow, I told her to just sleep in until she felt like getting up today, and if she didn't feel like coming in, don't — and Fox AND Zee agreed, and approved it. Some of that shit they've been doing in the medlab—biopsies an' stuff—they're not fun at all. Even if they do have galactic pharmaceuticals to help it not hurt, and heal up fast, an' shit. It's still getting cut on, after a fashion, and that takes energy to deal with the healing." Echo shrugged. "Damn, sometimes I think it takes MORE energy to heal up as fast as we do, all things considered. And they did several biopsies yesterday, for various reasons. At one point last night over dinner, she told me she felt like a Thanksgiving turkey, all carved up."

"I know whatcha mean, an' I agree. India an' I been talkin' 'bout it a little. Nothin' real medical, an' no private shit, jus' kinda cussdissin', ya know? Concerned f'r our friends, is all. She got an idea what's goin' on, bein' a doctor herself an' all— never mind occasionally consultin' on it—an' damn, Echo. Me 'n India, we jus' trying not to have kids 'til we're ready an' all. We feel bad for you two, havin' to go through all that crap just to see if you CAN have kids."

"It's okay, Junior," Echo told the younger man with a slight smile. "I appreciate it, and I know Meg does too. But either it'll happen — or it won't. We both kinda really hope it will, but hey. You don't always get what you want. Shit happens."

"I never thought I'd see you wantin' kids, man."

"I never did…until Meg came along. Now I want the whole 'happy ever after' scenario with her. And that includes kids." Echo turned to the room, which was filling up; screens on the wall bleeped softly, and he reached for the remote control to activate them, revealing departmental Agents from Offices around the world. "Okay, guys, let's get started, here…"

* * *

Joe Bob's replacement was gathering up the bags of garbage from the trash cans around the Core when newly-arrived Nreefluvan Daagnadan fairly tackled Agent Echo, planting several deep kisses on him and wrapping her legs around his waist in a very erotic position. He paused and watched, as did most of the other passersby, and saw him help her back down to the floor. Then she took his arm and walked with him to the Alpha Line Room.

'Joe Bob' pursed his lips, considering, then nodded to himself and went about his business.

* * *

Echo hurried through the more classified security aspects of the daily briefing, worried that Nreefluvan would drag India back too soon. As it turned out, she did, but the more sensitive matters had been handled already, and India insisted the pair sit quietly in the back of the room—only after Romeo gave her the high sign that it was clear. And then she shushed Daagnadan every time the alien woman made to speak up. Echo shot India a subtle *thank you* code—which sailed right by Daagnadan, of course—and India nodded slightly in response.

The meeting finally came to an end, and the Alpha Line Agents filed out as Echo shut off the wall monitors. After the crowd cleared a bit, India and Daagnadan rose and worked their way toward the front of the room.

"Hey, Ree," Echo said, as the pair moved to the desks where Romeo and Echo coordinated departmental matters; with Omega effectively taking a bit of leave that day, the third in command—Romeo—filled in for her.

"Hello, Echo," Daagnadan sang. "You are a wonderful leader."

Echo flushed despite himself. "Thank you."

"We agree, he is," Romeo averred. "So's his wife, Omega. She's number two in th' department."

"Then why are you the one working with him?" Daagnadan

wondered.

"She been havin' the medlab workin' on her," Romeo said, acknowledging the subtle code Echo sent him—*The real reason is none of her business.* So he hedged a good bit. "We had a…whadda them things called…oh! We had an exoheteroc—somethin' between a giant moth an' a giant hummingbird, but with kinda an acid sorta chemistry, so if it spit at ya and hit ya, you died—get loose in th' city couple months back, an' she got injured. She's sleepin' in a bit, today. The medlab worked 'er over pretty good yesterday. So as number three in th' department, I 'uz fillin' in for 'er today."

"Oh, I see," Daagnadan said, wincing. "Yes, that is a very good reason." She turned back to Echo. "But it gives us a good chance to catch up!"

"It does," Echo agreed, sitting down in his desk chair and waving to a visitor chair nearby. "Have a seat, Ree. You were asking about X-ray earlier, so let me tell you about what happened, there…"

"C'mon, baby," Romeo told India, keeping his voice low, as Echo began to tell Daagnadan about X-ray's death. "Let's go over inna corner, an' I'll fill you in on what you missed in th' meeting."

"Shouldn't we step out?" India wondered.

"No, I kinda think Echo wants us here, to ride herd…"

* * *

Just under an hour later, Echo had finished telling Daagnadan about how X-ray died, as well as how he'd partnered with first Romeo, then Omega, and was well into telling her about his adventures with Omega and how they fell in love. About that time, and as Alpha Two was headed out for their daily patrol, Omega entered the Alpha Line Room.

"Hey, Ace," she greeted her spouse cheerfully. "I'm up and alive, finally. And feeling a lot better for the sleep in! How'd the morning briefing go? Anything I should know about?"

"No, Meg," Echo answered, standing and leaning past Daagnadan to give her a kiss…missing the scowl that briefly appeared on the alien woman's face. "Nothing we haven't already discussed between us, at least. Um, listen, there's somebody here I want you to meet. You remember me telling you about my first girlfriend, after I joined the Agency?"

"Yeah? You called her 'Ree' or something like that, didn't you?"

"Yes. Well, meet Nreefluvan Daagnadan, of Kochav. She's evidently on Earth for a visit. Ree, this is my wife and current partner, Omega."

"Hello, Omega," Daagnadan said, reserved.

"Hi there!" Omega said, offering the other female a smile… that only Echo could tell was slightly hesitant. "Welcome back to Earth! Was your trip good?"

"It was fine, yes," Daagnadan said, rather primly, Echo thought, rather to his surprise. "I reserved a flight on a very reputable carrier, and it was quite comfortable."

"Great! I hope all your business on Earth goes well," Omega said. "So you're catching up with an old friend, huh?"

"Yes, I am," Daagnadan responded, still prim.

* * *

Echo noted Omega did not use the term boyfriend, and sent to her, *It's cool, baby. Ree has been really familiar since I ran into her—pretty much literally; she nearly knocked me down—but she doesn't seem to understand yet that I'm happily married now. Evidently she didn't hear about our wedding or something. I never thought to ask if Fox damped down the publicity, given how large the wedding was and all, but he might've. Intel and security and whatnot.*

No problem, Ace, Omega responded in kind. *I'm just kinda…unsure how to behave. And I think she feels the same.*

I'm sorry about that. I wasn't expecting her visit at all. And I'm serious; she fairly barreled into me in the Core, hugging all over me. So don't get upset if you smell her perfume on me.

No, it's good. But it does explain the perfume on you.

Sorry.

Not your fault.

The mental conversation took place in only a couple of seconds; Daagnadan never knew it occurred.

* * *

"Well, now," Echo said then. "Meg, have you got anything you need to do at your desk right off, baby?"

"No, I was just gonna check my email, and then get a debriefing of the morning meeting from you," she told him cheerfully, as Nreefluvan watched their interaction in silence.

"Okay," Echo decided, "then why don't you boot your computer and check your email real quick, and then the three of us will go to first lunch? I was just filling in Ree on everything that's happened since she was on Earth last—you know, losing X-ray, and bringing in Romeo, and the invasion, and Romeo and India hitting it off, and bringing you in, and forming Alpha Line. All that stuff. I can finish that while you check your email and answer anything urgent, then we'll head out."

"That works for me, Ace," Omega said with another smile, turning to her desk and hitting the wake-up button on her desktop screen.

"Why do you call him 'Ace,' Omega?" Daagnadan asked then.

"Oh, that's a nickname I gave him, early on in our partnership," Omega said with a laugh. "Way before we ever even started dating. Before we ever realized we were interested in each other, even. Hell, I was still in training! Hey," she turned to Echo, "she knows I was an astronaut when y'all brought me into the Agency, right?"

"Yeah, I already told her," Echo said with a nod.

"Okay, so you know I know from pilots. And he seriously impressed me with his flying skills, and there's a term for a skilled fighter pilot on Earth called an ace—so I started calling him that. I'm not sure he liked it at first, so I teased him with it a little. And then he started calling me 'baby,' like 'baby agent,' and teasing me with that, and that stuck, so he hadda just deal with being called Ace after that!"

"And after a bit, I realized I didn't really mind at all,"

51

Echo said, "I just hadn't had anyone nickname me in a long, long time, and wasn't used to it." He shrugged. "Hell, at this point, Meg could call me 'Hey, You!' and I'd answer to it, and cheerfully, I think."

"Not that I'd ever disrespect you that way, hon," Omega protested.

"I know. I'm just sayin'. I know you well enough now that you COULD, and I'd know what you meant, or that something was going on where you didn't wanna call my name out loud and risk identifying me."

"Well, that's good, I guess," Omega decided. "An' yeah, that makes sense."

"Yeah. And that's why, when you tried to shoot me under the programming, I knew things weren't right."

Daagnadan leaped from her chair, jumping in front of Echo.

"She tried to SHOOT YOU?! Echo! Why are you continuing to work with her?? That is foolhardy!"

"NO!" Omega cried, suddenly upset, throwing out a hand. "I didn't! I mean, well, my body did, but I couldn't stop it, couldn't control it!" She took a step forward.

"Get away from him, you filthy drekul!" Daagnadan snarled, raising her hands and curling them into claws; given her long fingernails, painted blood-red, it was not an idle threat.

"STOP IT!" Echo ordered from behind her, his voice brooking no denial. "Ree! Stand down!" Startled, Daagnadan looked back over her shoulder.

"But…but Echo…she…"

"Was being controlled by an old enemy," Echo said, letting his voice drop to a quieter level. "Do you remember my bringing Slug into custody?"

"Oh ragnadang," Nreefluvan whispered. "He returned to attack you…through her?"

"Yes," Omega said, bowing her head. "It's…a long story."

"One I was debating about telling Ree," Echo said. "Are you okay with that, Meg?"

"Y-yeah," Omega said, then telepathically added, *Just the*

basic story, though, please. Not the...the details. Of what he did to me, I mean. You know...the genetics...

No way, baby, Echo confirmed. *That's private anyway. I'll let her know that you were tortured, and restructured an' enhanced, and then telepathically programmed, but not anything more than that. I'll just explain Slug's plot from there.*

"Okay, yeah, but YOU tell her," Omega repeated aloud. "I'll, um, I'll try to go through email while you do that, then we'll see about lunch."

* * *

By the time Echo had finished a very basic explanation of how Omega had been used—and abused—in Slug's revenge plans, and how the pair had finally managed to kill him with Alpha Two's help, along with the failsafe programming that nearly forced his own partner to shoot him, Omega had finished running through her email. Echo had been well aware she was trying hard NOT to listen, and had kept the explanation as quiet and as simplistic as he could.

"So," Echo said, when Nreefluvan nodded her understanding, and Omega turned from her desk, "how 'bout lunch, ladies?"

"I would love to have lunch with you, Echo," Daagnadan practically purred, throwing her patented sultry smile into the mix.

"I...dunno," Omega said, pulling a face. "You know how much the whole Slug shit upsets me, Ace..."

"I know, baby, but I also know you gotta eat," Echo encouraged, coming to her side and laying a gentle hand on her back. "You can't afford to let that boosted metabolism get ahead of you."

"I know, but damn, hon," she sighed. "All right. I'll just have to be careful what I choose off the menu. Where you wanna go?"

"I've been thinking about that," Echo said, silently adding, *I don't want to make a big deal out of this, with Ree-ree here. She seems to think you're JUST a partner, and that doesn't lead in a good direction. I don't want her thinking of this as a date with a chaperone or something.* Then he said aloud, "I thought maybe Ree might enjoy visiting the deli; she and X-ray and I ate there a lot, back in the day."

"I thought we might try something a little nicer," Daagnadan interjected. "Perhaps that very nice place over in Manhattan? The steakhouse…?"

"Ooo, that's a bit much for me right now," Omega commented quickly, deliberately not looking at Echo. "You wouldn't know, Ms. Daagnadan, but—"

"Call her Ree, like I do, Meg," Echo said, not seeming to notice when Daagnadan scowled for a fraction of a second. Omega saw, and raised an eyebrow, then went on with it. She was uncomfortable with the nickname, hence slightly hesitant, but only Echo recognized the fact.

"…Okay. Ree, see, when I get really upset—and getting dissected with no anesthetic is a good way for ANYBODY to get upset, and I remember it all now—I have a tendency to, um, barf."

Daagnadan stared at her blankly.

"Barf?"

"Regurgitate," Echo tried. "Vomit."

"It's a bad way to waste a really expensive, really lovely steak," Omega added, as Daagnadan pulled a disgusted face.

"I am surprised you are an agent of any sort, if that is your reaction to growing emotionally perturbed," she said, somewhat condescending. "Let alone one of the elite agents."

"Assistant chief of the elite agents," Echo corrected, deliberately stern verging on hard; it was a point about which he wanted no misunderstandings. "And she doesn't get upset in the field. Only about personal stuff, almost always to do with what Slug did to her. And I've telepathically seen the memories of that, and believe me, Ree, she has reason to be upset. And the term 'dissection' isn't an exaggeration at all." When Daagnadan looked skeptical, he tried again. "Okay, Ree, let's put it like this: how would you like to be on an operating table,

WATCHING while your abdomen was sliced open, and your liver, spleen, stomach, intestines and more were all removed and laid on the table around you, to be cut apart, modified, and reassembled? While feeling every single scalpel cut?"

The Kochavi woman's slightly bluish-tinted skin paled, turning almost gray, as her jaw went slack and her mouth popped open. Purple eyes dilated in horror. Instinctively, she placed a hand to her abdomen.

"That is what…?" she began, turning to Omega. "He did THAT to you? Truly?"

"That, and a lot more," Omega confirmed, solemn, almost grim. "Brain, eyes, nose, tongue, ears, throat, chest, abdomen. Every single organ. What he couldn't cut apart and put back together, like the rest of my nervous system, he dinked with biochemically. And that hurt, too. Like fire burning through me."

"Drekulik," Nreefluvan said blankly. "Ik grak abul dos ardrekag."

Omega, who didn't speak Kochavi, glanced at Echo.

"She said, 'Son of a bitch. It must have been hell,'" he translated.

"Oh. Yes, forgive me," Daagnadan said then, wincing and flushing slightly bluer than normal. "I never learned to curse properly in English."

"Not for lack of X-ray tryin' to teach you," Echo said in amusement. Omega snorted, and they all laughed, breaking the tension.

"I can imagine, if this guy here is anything to go by," Omega said then. "But to reply to your statement, yes, it was, Ree. And I was a child at the time. I try not to think about it, for obvious reasons."

"I see," Daagnadan said with a nod. "It…makes sense to me now. In that case, can you find something to eat at the deli that will not exacerbate your upset?"

"Probably," Omega decided. "Like Echo said, I'll need to eat a good bit—Slug boosted my metabolism by a substantial amount to be able to do what he wanted me to do, so if I don't eat well and often, I can drop weight kinda fast—but I'm thinking maybe some matzoh ball soup, some basic stuffed knishes for the main course, and either a blintz or a piece of kugel for dessert, depending on what the deli has today. Mild and easy to digest. It's kinda heavy on the carbs, but I can make up for it at a later meal once I've had a chance to settle more, and it should sit on an upset tum okay."

"Good," Daagnadan said then. "As I recall, the deli is just down the street…?"

"Right," Echo agreed. "A nice little stroll to stretch our legs. Shall we go, ladies?"

"Let's head out," Omega agreed.

Echo offered his right arm to Omega, and his left to Nreefluvan, and they headed for the exit.

He would regret that chivalrous familiarity later.

* * *

Omega managed to tuck away a decent first lunch, and Nreefluvan behaved herself…though neither member of Alpha One was especially happy about the lingering touches to Echo's arm and hand that she kept applying. No one at the deli had been there long enough to remember Daagnadan—the current owner was the son of the previous—and Echo explained her away as an old friend from college days come to visit unexpectedly; it worked well enough, under the circumstances.

The friendly deli owner knew exactly what sort of friend was being referenced, however, and he gave Omega a querying glance, eyebrow raised. Omega responded by quirking her mouth and cocking her head, in a plain, *What can you do?* expression, and Echo shrugged and rolled his eyes, as if to say, *This wasn't my idea, and I'm not any happier about it.* The deli owner's eyebrows both shot up in understanding, and instead of giving them the private little corner booth they usually got, he gave them a table out front, in plain sight from all directions. Echo subtly murmured his thanks.

They finished their meal at last and headed back toward

Headquarters, Daagnadan trying hard to hold onto Echo's arm again so she could snuggle in close to him, and Omega finding ways to prevent it…much to Echo's gratitude.

* * *

Nreefluvan spent a significant portion of the rest of the day in the Alpha Line Room, one way and another, only occasionally being diverted by this or that activity, and determined to 'chat' with Echo. After a couple of hours of repeatedly-interrupted attempts to go over the proposed budget for the department, Echo finally told her that he had work to do, and any further catching up would have to wait until Alpha One's shift ended. Daagnadan accepted this, and continued to sit in the room and mostly watch Echo in silence, as he and Omega worked on various administrative things. Alpha One thought it odd, but at least she wasn't interfering with their work any further — for a wonder — so they let it go.

After several hours of this, however, she seemed to grow bored, and asked if it would be all right if she tried to find other agents she used to know, to say hello. Echo gladly gave permission, but told her not to simply wander about. He gave a heads-up to several department leads, notably Crutch, who was still in rehab from her mega moth injuries and therefore on light duty, while her assistant, Nab, actually ran the department. Crutch remembered the alien woman, and agreed to come fetch her from the Alpha Line Room and take her around her own department to greet old friends.

Once the two were out the door and out of earshot, Echo slumped in his desk chair with a sigh.

"No shit," Omega noted, responding to both the sound and the relief that flowed through the nd't'lq. "Kinda nerve-wracking to have somebody continually watching you while you're trying to work. Never mind interrupting all the time to make herself the center of attention."

"You got that one right, baby," Echo confirmed. "In spades. I'm not even sure why she's here. SHE broke up with ME, back in the day, and made it plain that she'd decided I was too young for her, and she wanted somebody more mature for a permanent mate. This, when I'd been thinking about asking her to make it permanent. 'Course, X-ray was against that idea; he said I was way too young to settle down, and that her…I can't remember the term he used, but when you introduced me to the concept of pheromones, I remembered that, and knew it was what he meant…anyway, he said her pheromones were affecting me. See, she's an historian, and there was this old Kochavi legend she was fascinated with, of an adept who'd learned to control his pheromones to such an extent that he could essentially influence the people around him to do as he wished, and she was constantly trying to figure out where that concept had even come from."

"Ooo. That IS an interesting concept. Can it really be done?"

"Yeah, no. It can't. Anyway, I guess X-ray figured she'd been practicing on me or something…not that she was ever able to do that. It was just a myth, she said, and never really happened. At least, not like the legends said. She said it was impossible, but it fascinated her anyway. She was constantly trying to figure out what it was supposed to symbolize, and just how much WAS possible. She even wrote some research papers on it. Anyway, X-ray said she was right about one thing—I needed to let her go. It wasn't like I had much choice, really," Echo said, a certain pain entering his eyes as he remembered, "because she was determined to go, but in the end, X-ray was right. And then I finally found you, and you pretty much eclipsed everybody that ever came before. And then you and I got married. And I'm forty-nine an' a half kinds of happy about THAT fact. All of it."

"Me, too," Omega agreed with a shy smile. "There's one thing I noticed, though."

"What's that?"

"She's not very observant. She never seemed to realize that we were communicating even when we weren't SAYING anything—out loud, anyway. So she has no clue we have a mental bond."

"No, you have a point there," Echo decided, thoughtful. "She never was particularly observant. X-ray and I used to sometimes use her as a distraction for the perps when we were on missions, if she insisted on coming along. Most of the time, she didn't, though—we didn't let her. It was just one more distraction for US, having to keep up with her and keep her out of trouble." He shrugged. "I guess she hasn't gotten any better at that in the meanwhile."

"Well, let's see how much we can get done before she comes back. Crutch is good, and knowing her, I'm betting she understood even what you didn't say, so she'll keep her busy as long as she can. And since Nab is doing most of the departmental work right now while she recupes, she has the time, and she can — and almost certainly WILL — do that for us."

"True, and yeah, you're right. Let's get going. And I'm voting for ordering delivery something for second lunch. Pizza, Chinese, deli delivery…something. Anything. That way we can bypass any more going out to eat and use the time to get some extra work done."

"Absolutely. We are WAY the hell behind today."

"No shit, baby. Let's go."

* * *

Late in the shift, one of the Sluuites that worked in the Facilities department, helping to keep Headquarters clean, went missing.

Given they were such small creatures, and easily injured should a larger being stumble and fall upon them — or lost in a tiny nook, should they become ill — the Agency had made the decision to require them to wear specialized locator beacons, implanted just under the skin near the spine in the back of the neck. So as soon as Timerrn Dhin failed to check in with her supervisor, Facilities alerted on a missing Sluuite and pulled up the locator beacon coded to Dhin's body.

Only to discover that the beacon no longer functioned.

Facilities issued a missing-persons alert, and several Security agents and Field teams swept the building.

But they never found Dhin.

* * *

Crutch managed to keep Nreefluvan Daagnadan away from the Alpha Line Room for most of the rest of that shift, though she did swing by with the Kochavi woman to see if Alpha One wanted to go out to second lunch with them. Upon discovering that they were behind in their work and had ordered delivery from their favorite Chinese place—whose owner, along with most of the employees, 'wasn't from around here'—she hauled Daagnadan away again, giving her a tour of the outlying facilities and downtown Manhattan in the course of getting lunch, so the alien woman could see the damage from the mega moth.

Alpha One didn't see Daagnadan again until almost the end of their shift.

They got a lot of work done as a result.

Chapter 3

In the end, however, she came home with them for dinner. Omega, realizing that the pair—Echo and Ree—had some issues between them, decided to let things play out and see if Echo couldn't find some closure with his old flame, given she had come to realize over the Christmas holidays that Echo's past experiences with women had left him somewhat—and uncharacteristically—uncertain in the romance department, thanks partly to his job repeatedly interfering with certain aspects of his personal life. He was a handsome man, strong and well-built, and confident in almost all other matters, and she knew he was finally confident in her affections for him… and she was finally confident of his, for her. But she decided she wanted to allow him the chance to resolve some lingering resentments.

So she offered to prepare a nice dinner for three, choosing to make a large salad, a delicious, creamy pasta alfredo with an excellent smoked salmon liberally flaked into it, and serve shortbread and ice cream for dessert. Echo assured her that Nreefluvan had no especial problems with Earth food, though he still wasn't sure he wanted his old lover to come home for dinner with them.

Because I'm not at all comfortable about it, he said. *I just flatly don't want her in our home, yours and mine. That's our refuge, baby. Our private domain. And she plain doesn't belong there. Especially as… 'friendly'…as she's been being. I don't wanna give her any more ideas than I can help.*

I know. But this isn't about her, as such — YOU need the closure, hon, Omega told him as they carried on the silent conversation; Daagnadan was already in the Alpha Line Room, waiting for them to finish work and end the shift, but all she knew was that they were still working. She had no idea of the discussion that was actually occurring in parallel with that work. *Besides, the two of you can get better caught up on what's been going on since you saw each other last. That might help with that closure, showing her that you've both moved on. Especially you. And I'm gonna be there, so it's not like anything can happen. We might even play up our newlywed status a little, you know, kiss an' flirt an' stuff, to make sure the idea gets across — You Are Not Available.*

True. And that's a good idea. Well...okay, Echo relented. "You about done, baby?" he wondered aloud.

"Yeah, gimme about two sec…there," Omega said, as she hit a key on her computer. By this time, the virtual keyboard technology that Fox had been using for the last couple of years had filtered down as far as the Alpha Line and Field leads, so it meant all she needed to do was to switch off the screen and deactivate the keyboard, and her workstation was safed. "Now I'm ready."

The trio headed for the agents' quarters.

* * *

Echo and Nreefluvan set up shop at the dining table just off the kitchen while Omega prepared the meal, so that the female Agent could hear and participate as the pair caught up. This pacified Echo a bit, as did setting the table for three while Omega cooked, and helping her fetch the items from the refrigerator, pantry, and cabinets—it kept him close to his wife and generally moving too much for Ree to get touchy-feely, which he was concerned about happening. Eventually, however, once Omega began cooking, Echo joined Ree at the table, sitting opposite her, with Omega planned to sit at the end of the oblong table—it currently had no leaves in it, but even so, it would easily seat six, so they were using only half the table for dinner.

The pair reminisced a bit while Omega cooked, and Omega occasionally asked questions about this or that event. Several stories Daagnadan told on Echo made her laugh, and Echo flushed but grinned.

"Yeah, I was a wet-behind-the-ears greenhorn sometimes," he admitted. "I was learning fast, though. X-ray and Fox saw to that."

"I wish I could have met X-ray," Omega said, wistful.

"No, you should not wish it. X-ray may have been a good agent, but he was not a nice man," Daagnadan declared then, and Echo scowled, as Omega stared at her, startled. "He did not like me, and he did not approve of my relationship with Echo. And he told me so. Many times."

"He did not, Ree," Echo chastised. "Stop that."

"He did," Daagnadan insisted. "He never said anything while you were around; he knew you would defend me. But he did not want me about. You were of age, or he would have prevented it—he said so to me, directly."

"Well, if I'd been under age, it would have been illegal anyway," Echo pointed out.

Daagnadan huffed in irritation, then silenced. Omega blinked, then hurriedly added a couple of last touches to the alfredo as she began plating the food.

"Dinner's ready," she called. "Echo, hon, would you come help me bring everything to the table, please? I'll wait to scoop the ice cream once we're done with the main course, else it might melt before we're ready for it, even with the kitchen stasis field, I'm afraid."

Echo rose and helped Omega bring the trays of plated food from the kitchen to the dining room.

* * *

Daagnadan consumed the meal with alacrity, thanking Omega for providing it and noting that the human woman was an excellent cook.

"And I love this crisp, or biscuit, or cookie, or whatever it is called," she noted, reaching for another piece of shortbread as she finished her ice cream.

"So do I," Echo agreed, having already eaten four pieces himself. "It's the best I've ever had, and I've eaten it in Great Britain. Meg says it's an old family recipe; her family was originally from Scotland, some few generations back, and brought it to America when they emigrated."

"Really? No wonder it is so good," Nreefluvan decided. "It has had many generations of her family to perfect it."

"Exactly," Omega said with a smile. "And Mom started teaching me to make it when I was only about eight years old. Um, a small youngling, only eight annums of age."

"Ah. And you are a highly trained adult. Then by now you are an expert in its preparation."

"Some say so, yes." Omega rose and took away the last of the plates. "I'm glad I'd just made a big, fresh batch! We can take the platter of shortbread into the den with us, and sit on the sofa and chat. Echo, would you please grab the platter and take it in the den while I stick this stuff in the dishwasher, then I'll be right out."

"Okay, baby. You want your usual whisky?"

"Yes, please."

"Ree, do you still drink the top-shelf bourbon that Fox introduced to you?"

"Ooo! That would be a lovely treat! I have not had any in a very long time—I fear Kochav does not import many Earth liquors, perhaps a couple brands each of whiskies, rums, gins, and vodkas, though not bourbon—but I would like some if you have it, Echo. Fox always had excellent taste in such matters, and I liked it very much."

"All right. I can do that. Rocks, or neat?"

"Rocks, please. Ice."

"Got it."

"Why not bourbon?" Omega wondered from the kitchen. "I mean, if they imported the other, why didn't they import bourbon?"

"Oh, they do not understand the fine points of whisky, Scotch, bourbon, rye, and the like," Daagnadan explained. "They assume they are all essentially the same, and that of those, whisky must be the best and the others merely subsets — though I have no idea why they concluded that. So the importers pick only the top brands of whisky and ignore the others."

"That's a shame," Omega remarked, coming into the den. "They lose a lot of the flavor variations of the different beverages."

"Yes, it is, and they do," Daagnadan agreed.

Five minutes later, Echo was in one of the swivel recliners and Omega in the other, which in the course of their home decorating they'd ended up placing opposite the sofa, with a low occasional table between for drinks and snacks and books, and a small end table for each. They could turn them to face the sofa in a conversation circle as they had them positioned currently, or turn them to watch the television on the front wall of the den. In the event that they were having a TV watching party of some sort, the chairs could be shoved apart, forming a semicircle with the couch.

Daagnadan sat tucked into one end of the sofa, facing them, her bourbon on the end table. It was obvious to both members of Alpha One that she had expected Echo to sit beside her, but he had very deliberately taken his recliner—which was his usual seat, in any event, unless he and Omega were cuddling on the couch.

"This is a very nice, and very big, quarters, Echo," she said, looking around, as she sipped from the old-fashioned glass. "Is this because you are that department chief?"

"Partly," Echo noted. "I used to have the same quarters you remember, up until this past autumn. But when Meg and I got married, um, espoused, they merged our quarters. And since I'm the Alpha Line Chief, Meg is the Alpha Line Assistant Chief, and I'm the Assistant Director for Division One, we—"

"Ooo!" Daagnadan squealed. "Assistant Director! So it IS true! I had heard, but it was only rumors on Kochav! My boopy has made good, as you used to say!"

"Ree, I'm not your boopy," Echo said, shooting an annoyed, worried glance at Omega. "I've told you that several times today. And the word has a different connotation on Earth—an infantile one—and wouldn't do my reputation any favors."

"Oh! I am sorry, Echo, but I thought of you as my boopy

from our first date," Daagnadan admitted, looking sheepish. "Sometimes it slips out."

"What does 'boopy' mean?" Omega wondered.

"It's like honey or dear, only in Kochavi," Echo explained.

"Ah. Then no, I'd say you're MY boopy," Omega said with a huge, teasing grin. Nreefluvan frowned.

"Oh, good grief," Echo said, raking a hand over his face. "Don't you dare, baby."

"Nah, you're good," Omega said, still grinning. "I won't do it to you…until the next 'family' dinner."

"Shit," Echo grumbled…but the corners of his mouth were twitching. "You will, too."

"You betcha." Her grin grew wider. Finally Echo snorted in amusement and allowed himself a grin of his own.

"What is 'the family' of which you speak?" Daagnadan wondered.

"Oh, it's a little gathering of close friends, really," Echo explained. "Meg lost her family to Slug—he evidently wanted her to be a free agent, so he took 'em out, some years ago—and once she landed here, she started gathering close friends around her, to ease the loneliness a little, I think." He shrugged. "Somewhere along the way, we all started thinking of ourselves as a surrogate family."

"Oh," Daagnadan murmured, casting a sympathetic glance at Omega. "And so who is in this surrogate family?"

"Us two," Omega said, "Fox and his wife Zebra—Fox is the Director now; you knew that, right? Okay," she said, as Daagnadan nodded. "Zebra is the Assistant Chief of Staff of Medical. They're kind of the mom and dad of the family. Well, Zee says she's the stepmom, sorta, 'cause she's so much younger than Fox."

"But you can't tell it," Echo noted. "Not with Fox."

"No, you can't. And then Zarnix Chifejuz, the Chief of Staff of Medical, is an uncle, as is His Excellency Ambassador Zz'r'p ob Tii'rkin of Deltir. Then there's Alpha Two, Romeo and India; they're kinda like Echo's and my brother and sister. They're married, too," Omega added. "The head of the medtechs in Medical, Dihl, is another elder—if Fox is the patriarch, I guess Dihl is the matriarch." Omega carefully avoided telling Daagnadan that Dihl was Echo's birth mother. "Fox's assistants, Lima and Bravo, have kinda become Fox's 'grandkids' of a sort, though I dunno whose kids they're supposed to be!" Omega laughed. "And an old friend of mine that I recruited to the Agency, Chi, is sort of a brother, I guess, and his partner Genova…"

"Yeah," Echo chuckled. "Alla those. Then there's 'Uncle' Pulgey Entiyti—"

"The galactic president?!" Daagnadan exclaimed in surprise.

"The same," Echo averred. "And Lord Admiral Suud Guurn is another uncle…"

"Not to mention his wife, 'Aunt' Eetii," Omega interjected, "and all their kids are cousins, including Uncle Pul's current head bodyguard, Duuniiss."

"Yep, and Lady Admiral Lydhuu Raiit is another cousin," Echo finished. "I think that's about got it."

"Dear Maker," Daagnadan whispered. "How ever did you manage such illustrious people?"

"Looooong story," Echo said with a chuckle.

"I think I should like to hear it," Daagnadan decided.

Omega and Echo exchanged a grin.

* * *

Alpha One alternated between bantering good-naturedly— occasionally, and deliberately, becoming blatantly risqué— with each other while a silent Daagnadan took in the fact, and conversing with her. They told her all about how they had come to know such illustrious people, then Echo finished catching up his old girlfriend on how he'd gotten from last seeing her to the present. In turn, Daagnadan told him a few things about her life—she was a schoolteacher in the equivalent of a Kochavi high school, teaching Kochavi history, but they were on 'summer break' equivalent currently—while occasionally querying Omega for more about her background, as well.

As the evening wore on, and Daagnadan had a second glass of the bourbon, she grew tired and mildly inebriated, being unused to the Earth intoxicant after so many years without. Within another half-hour, she had leaned her head back on the sofa and closed her eyes. Thirty seconds after that, her jaw went slack and her body limp; she was asleep.

Whu-oh, Echo thought to his wife. *I didn't expect that.*

Me too neither, although I guess we shoulda thought. If she hasn't had any bourbon in some years, she's not gonna be used to it these days. Not like she would have been in your younger days anyhow.

Yeah, I didn't think of that either.

Was she prone to overdoing the alcohol when you were seeing her?

No, but she had a similar reaction on the rare occasions when she did. I'd forgotten until just now.

Mm. We got us a sitch, here, Ace.

I know, baby. Lemme run into our home office and call Housing. They'll probably know where she's staying; if it's a hotel, we can call a cab. Romeo and India can probably help us get her down to the main entrance with some sense of decorum—for poor Ree AND us.

Okay. It's almost time to crash anyhow. I'm good with that.

All right. Stand by.

Echo rose and headed down the hall.

* * *

He came back about ten minutes later.

Well, this ain't good, he told Omega.

What's up?

Housing can't find that she has ANY place to stay. No request for temporary quarters here, no hotel reservations in the City as a whole, nothing. I hate to say it, but given that when she showed up, she had no idea I was married and pretty much glompled me, she mighta figured on staying with me.

You think she expected to pick up where you two left off?

Maybe. I'm kinda puzzled by the whole thing. I can't tell that she has any business here on Earth at all, other than visiting me.

Well, she ain't gettin' you, Omega determined. *You're mine, and that's that.*

And happy to be, baby. Still, we got a problem, here. He waved a hand at the sleeping Kochavi.

Yeah. She's zonked. She's barely moved since you left to call Housing. She even let out the Kochavi equivalent of a snore, a couple times. I think it's the way her head is tilted way back like that. It can't be comfortable, and she'll have twelve kinds of kinks in her neck in the morning. But she's out like the proverbial light.

Yup. She ain't wakin' up 'til tomorrow. Look, I sicced Housing onto finding a place for her to stay, but they aren't gonna have anything lined up until in the morning…the agents are really the only part of this place that works around the clock, and most of the embassies are closed for the 'night' and…

Eh. We gotta do what we gotta do, Ace. You go get a spare pillow and blanket from the linen closet, and I'll get her turned around on the couch, here, so she doesn't kink her neck all up, and slip her shoes off. I'll tuck the pillow under her head, you spread the blanket, and she can just crash here for tonight. We'll close and lock the bedroom door to ensure she stays out if she wakes up, there's a couple nightlights around so she can see if she DOES wake up, and everything will be fine.

Done, Echo said, headed for the bedroom.

* * *

Five minutes later, Nreefluvan was put to rights, and settled into the sofa to sleep even deeper. There was a soft knock on the door, and a barely-above-a-whisper voice annunciated over the household system, "Housing, with Ms. Daagnadan's bag from Baggage Claim."

Echo went to the door to fetch it, while Omega sat Daagnadan's shoes down at one end of the sofa. Echo returned with the bag, setting it beside the shoes.

Then Omega and Echo tiptoed out of the den into the bedroom, turning off lights as they went.

There, they prepared for bed themselves.

* * *

"It feels funny—like, weird-funny—me being in here with you while your old lover is out there on the couch," Omega murmured, as she and Echo crawled into their big bed together. "I'm not really keen on it, to be honest. I mean, it is what it is, but…"

"Yeah. Neither am I, but I'm not sure what else we could have done," Echo said. "Judging by the fact that Housing couldn't even find a hotel room in the whole greater City in her name—I'm talking ANYWHERE in the Five Boroughs— she apparently thought she was gonna make up with me, then move in with me, or something. Never mind the fact that I'd have been—and am—pissed at her for breaking up with me in the first place, even if you and I hadn't made a go of our relationship. It has nothing to do with remotely considering getting back together with her. She flatly just didn't handle it well—she was really blunt, and kinda callous, like 'I'm done with you now'—and it hurt." He sighed. "If I'd known then what I know now, my love life history would look a lot different. I'd 'a probably done more like you did. And then we wouldn't be in this mess."

"Yeah, I get it, sweetheart. It's okay. At least Housing fetched her bag from the Baggage Claim for us."

"Well, I told Housing in no uncertain terms to come up with a place for her to stay as of tomorrow morning, no excuses," Echo determined. "Preferably NOT in Headquarters, but I guess if they stick her in the Kochav Embassy area, it'd do. We're unlikely to go anywhere near it, you an' me."

"You really are unhappy about this, aren't you?"

"Yeah, I'm not thrilled at all, Meg," Echo said, settling into the bed. "We haven't even been married quite six months yet! I don't want somebody coming in, making a play for me, trying to make you feel insecure! Especially when Zz'r'p is finally starting to get you past all the shit that's come before."

"Well, you could look at it as a backhanded compliment, I guess," Omega said, scooting over to snuggle against his warm, nude body.

"How so?" He gathered her close, enjoying the feel of skin on skin.

"Because if she doesn't back way the hell off real soon, you're gonna have two women cat-fightin' over ya."

Echo stifled a guffaw.

"You'd really do that?"

"Oh hell yeah. She was entirely too touchy-feely today. If that keeps up, I'mma stop being so polite. Closure is one thing. Trying to come between us is another. She needs to keep her damn hands off my husband."

"C'mere then, and lemme show ya how much your husband appreciates that."

"Okay," Omega agreed, "provided you do one thing."

"What's that?"

"Forget the whole 'old girlfriend' problem for a while, in favor of your 'new wife.' I want your undivided attention."

"I can do that. Gladly."

And he kissed her with his characteristic thoroughness.

* * *

The next morning, a mildly chilled Echo—he'd kicked off the covers in his sleep during the wee small hours—rose and grabbed his robe, throwing it on loosely over his nude body, not bothering to tie it closed. Their normal morning routine, when it included a robe at all, left said robe open and loose, each member of Alpha One having early on in their marriage expressed pleasure in watching the other in the nude; they were, after all, in the privacy of their own home. Omega headed for the kitchen without even bothering to grab hers.

"I'll get something going," she told her partner, "if you'll set the table."

"Done," Echo said. "Lemme get our phones off the chargers

and I'll be right there."

"Hokay."

Echo grabbed his cell phone from its charging pad on his nightstand, then headed around the bed to fetch Omega's, slipping them into opposite pockets in his robe to avoid mix-ups. Then he headed for the dining room, and the little breakfast nook in its corner.

Just as he reached the open archway into the dining room, he heard the voice.

From BEHIND.

"Oh my. You really have filled out and matured very nicely, Echo. You were always handsome, but now you are gorgeous."

Echo's feet left the floor, he startled so badly.

"SHIT!" he exclaimed, grabbing the sides of his robe and closing it over his naked body. "Dammit, Ree, you could have said something sooner! You KNEW we forgot you were sleeping on the couch!"

* * *

Alarmed by the commotion, Omega came to the door of the dining room to see Ree looking over the back of the couch, a wide smile on her sultry face as she ogled Echo. Meanwhile, Echo was cinching his robe tightly closed around his waist, ensuring no more skin than he could help showed through.

It hit Omega just then that she didn't even have a robe on—she stood before her would-be rival for her husband's affections, stark naked.

"EEP!" she exclaimed, covering breasts and crotch with her arms and hands as she spun to put her back to the other woman, shuffling over to hide behind the edge of the wall.

"I'll go get your robe, baby," Echo said, intensely annoyed.

"Please!" Omega pleaded.

"I do not know what YOU are worried about," Daagnadan grumbled. "I am not interested in looking at YOU."

"You shouldn't be looking at my husband, either!" Omega fired back.

"It is not my fault," Daagnadan protested. "If I judge by the pillow and blanket, you both put me to bed here. I cannot help it if you forgot you did so and paraded your nudeness in front of me." She shrugged. "Besides, the view was nice." Then she smirked. "I look forward to joining you both in bed tonight."

"Oh, no, you don't," Echo said, coming back in with Omega's robe—the heavyweight terrycloth bath robe, not the black lace and satin peignoir—and a pair of lounge pants covering his lower half, in addition to his own robe. "You're gonna have a place to stay of your own, tonight; Housing is taking care of that." He helped Omega shrug into her bathrobe and tie it firmly closed; Nreefluvan eyed it with distaste.

"Do you not have something more attractive?" she wondered in disdain.

"She most definitely does," Echo shot back, "quite a few, actually, but that's not for YOU to look at. Meg, what were you fixing for breakfast?"

"Um, I'd just put a breakfast casserole in the oven to heat. I…we'll have to do something else; it's only big enough to serve two."

"Okay. Here's what's going to happen, then," Echo decreed. "Since she's here, Ree will be joining us for breakfast. I'll set the table for three, then come in the kitchen and help you fry some bacon and eggs, maybe grate some cheese, and we'll top the casserole with all that. It's layered as it is; we'll just add more layers. That should eke it out to be enough for three people. While we're doing that, Ree can go freshen up in the powder room," he pointed down the hall toward the front door, where that facility lay, "and then we'll eat. Then SHE is going to report to Housing, to find out where they're putting her up, while WE get ready for our shift."

"That works," Omega decided, heading back for the kitchen.

An annoyed Echo put his hands on his hips and glared at Daagnadan, who silently stood, picked up her bag, and carried it down the hall to the powder room to freshen up as best she could.

* * *

Omega put a frying pan on the stove to heat, while Echo fetched the eggs and bacon and a chunk of Omega's favorite Cheshire cheese from the refrigerator. He put the eggs and bacon beside the stove, along with a medium-sized mixing bowl and whisk, then got out the grater, and commenced grating a good-sized pile of the cheese. Meanwhile, Omega laid several thick strips of the hickory-smoked bacon in the pan, then cracked four eggs into the bowl, added salt and pepper, and whisked them thoroughly. When the bacon was crisp, she removed it from the pan and laid it on a stack of paper towels to drain, then poured the beaten eggs into the pan and began scrambling them in the fat from the bacon.

When Echo had a considerable quantity of grated cheese on another paper towel—they were trying to minimize the additional cleanup—he opened the dishwasher and emptied it from the night before, putting the various pots, pans, plates, glasses, and utensils into their respective cabinets and drawers. Then he grabbed the grater, mixing bowl, and whisk and put them into the now-empty dishwasher.

When he finished that, he washed his hands and set the dining table for three. Nreefluvan was now in the dining room, sitting at the end position—the one where Omega had sat, the night before, effectively maintaining distance between Echo and Ree. So Echo put one place setting in front of her, and the other two down the side of the table. She scowled, and moved to the corner side seat. Echo grabbed the plate past her, and set it on the table across from her. When she made to switch chairs again, he balked.

"STOP," he ordered. "SIT. Right there. You do not get to usurp Meg's place at my side. Not after the way you ended things with me years ago, and not after all Meg has done for me. Even if I wasn't married to her, that would all still be true. But I AM married to her, she's my wife and I love her, and I don't care what you may want, I'm not letting you come between us."

Just then, the savory scents of cooking breakfast deepened, becoming somehow sweeter.

"All right, Echo," Daagnadan said quietly, remaining where she was. A loud bleat came from the oven, and a mollified Echo headed for the kitchen to help his mate.

* * *

After topping the breakfast casserole with the bacon and scrambled eggs, then spreading the shredded cheese over the top of everything, they ran it back into the oven long enough to melt and lightly toast the cheese, then Echo put a hot pad on the table and Omega brought in the casserole dish while wearing oven mitts, and Echo doubled back for a serving spoon. While Omega had been waiting for the casserole, she had gotten a container of mixed fresh fruit from the fridge, spooning small servings into little bowls, as a healthy side. The coffee pot, with just-brewed chicory coffee, went on another hot pad, alongside cream and sugar containers.

Omega took the end position again, and Echo sat next to her, across from Ree. The atmosphere was strained, but relaxed a bit after Nreefluvan tasted the casserole and complimented Omega on it.

"It is very much like one Echo and X-ray used to make," she mused. "Did you get the recipe from them?"

"I did," Omega admitted. "I got it from Echo; X-ray was already…gone…before I came into the Agency. And yes, this is one of mine. Echo and I share the cooking duties most of the time, though. In this particular instance, I think we had a dual assembly line going on our day off—he made several of his version, and I made several of my version, and then we froze 'em all, so we just have to heat 'em up while we get ready, then eat, throw the dishes in the washer, and head out."

"Very intelligent," Daagnadan decided. "You spend only a couple of hours preparing them, when you have TIME to do so, and it saves you time cooking when you do NOT have time."

"Bingo," Echo affirmed. "Meg and I've been working together for a few years now, and we've got certain systems down that work for us, like that."

"You are very harmonious," Daagnadan agreed.

"Thank you," Omega replied. "We try hard. I think after some recent events, we're even more harmonious than we were."

"And we always got along pretty damn well," Echo noted. "From the very first. Oh, everybody has their fusses and misunderstandings now and then, and we've had a few ourselves, though not really that many. But Meg and I always work together on everything. We only get crossways when something or someone interferes with our understanding."

"I can see that," Daagnadan decided. "And certainly, as attractive as you are, Echo, I am sure Omega likes to make you happy and agree with you. I meant what I said earlier—you have matured well. You are a strong, healthy, adult human male, with an excellent physique. You were never small, but your build now better matches your frame. The muscle has filled out quite well."

Echo flushed, picking up hints of annoyance from his partner through the mental bond. Abruptly he thought of a counter.

"Well, thank you, Ree-ree, but you know what? I think much the same thing about Meg. She's got a great body—strong and muscular, but curvy. I enjoy watching her just as much."

"Eh," Nreefluvan sniffed. "Not so much, I think. Especially given the horrible scarring on her back."

Omega paled. She dropped her fork, along with the food on it, splattering it across the table.

Echo saw red.

"How. Dare. You," he snarled, as Daagnadan's purple eyes went wide in shock at the furious expression on his face. He shoved back from the table and came around it, grabbing the alien female by the collar, lifting her out of the chair. "First of all, that supposed 'horrible scar' is a patch smaller than my hand—MAYBE the size of my palm, if that. Second off, it was obtained when she nearly died protecting ME from the damn Cortian slavers' ion drive during their first attempt to kidnap me! It burned away whole chunks of her body that had to be grown back! That one little bitty scar is the only real external mark left of that incident! It's her TROPHY from where she protected ME from being enslaved! From being KILLED! Look here!" He dropped Daagnadan back into her chair with a thud and shoved up the sleeve of his robe. "Do you see this scar here?" He yanked up a lounge-pant leg. "How about this one, down here below my knee? Do you know what the hell those are? Did you even notice those earlier, when you were eyeballing me without my awareness?"

"N-no," Nreefluvan whispered. "No, I…I did not."

"These are the scars where the Cortians, when they finally DID capture me last autumn, whacked off my hand and my leg!" Echo almost shouted. "They also gouged out my eye! I was a mangled WRECK, Nreefluvan! Do you get that? And do you see that woman there?" He pointed at Omega. "THAT brave, loving woman INFILTRATED the Cortian ship, ALONE, and with only the telepathic help of a handful of Deltiri aboard a cloaked Division One vessel nearby, crept through that enemy ship, found me, freed me, and SNUCK ME BACK OUT OF THEIR SHIP! She even brought back the remains of my hand and my leg, so when the medics dunked me in their regeneration pod, it all grew back the way it was supposed to!" He jerked open the top of his robe and pointed to a slight pockmark just below his rib cage. "Do you see THIS?! That's where I got SHOT, in a plot to take down the leadership of the whole damn Division! I was bleeding out! That woman right there," again he pointed at Omega, "actually managed somehow to PICK ME UP and HAUL my ass back to Headquarters, so the medics could patch me up! And gave me from her own blood to do it! More than she was supposed to safely give! THEN offered MORE! Is it any wonder I love her with everything I've got?! What did YOU do? YOU dumped me for trash, once you'd decided I wasn't the MAN you wanted me to be! You're right,

I wasn't—I was still a boy! But I was TRYING to be, not that you cared! And you DARE to comment on HER scars! Meg is orders of magnitude more beautiful to me than you'll ever be!"

"Echo," Omega murmured from behind him, as a very pale Daagnadan whimpered softly in her chair, cringing and trying to hold back tears. His partner put a gentle hand on his back, and he calmed slightly. "Echo, ease up, sweetheart. She was only making observations. Yeah, it hurt, but she didn't know."

"I…I am sorry," a deeply perturbed Daagnadan whispered. "She is right. I did not know. I…I am sorry."

"Yeah, well…think before making crass observations next time." Echo stalked back around to his chair and dropped into it. "The Housing people fetched your bag from the baggage claim last night. When you finish eating, take it and go to them. They'll have a place for you to stay."

"V-very well…"

There wasn't a whole lot left to breakfast after that.

Chapter 4

In the end, Housing assigned Nreefluvan Daagnadan temporary quarters in the Kochavi Embassy floor. This sort of thing was not uncommon, and since there was space on the floor, and several empty temporary quarters appended to the embassy, it was the easiest and quickest thing. She moved in within an hour of leaving Alpha One's quarters, and settled in for an indefinite stay. As she unpacked and put away her things, she pondered matters.

That did not work at all as I had expected, she thought. *I had no idea X-ray had died—damn the male for coming between me and Echo!—or that Echo had taken a female partner, let alone married her! This complicates things.*

She placed her hygiene kit in the bathroom facility, extracting its contents and placing them in her preferred locations. Then she paused and studied her heart-shaped face in the mirror.

He said he found her much more attractive than me. That... hurt. I wonder if he truly no longer finds me attractive. I AM older than I was then, though I have tried hard to keep it from showing on my face and in my mannerisms.

She sighed, then went back into the bedroom and unpacked her clothing, hanging most of it in the closet.

They are obviously very much in love, if I read things correctly. And certainly their pheromones indicate it. The woman has been through much, as well; I hate to do this to her. The simplest and least painful thing for her would have been if I could have convinced them of allowing me to participate in a three-way relationship. I could even teach her new ways to please him! But I knew that had scant chance of working with Echo, and it stands to reason he would espouse someone of like mind on the matter.

She tucked away a considerable quantity of lacy underthings in a drawer of the dresser.

Hopefully this will get used, she thought, looking at one of the negligées. *I am sorry for Omega's sake, but I MUST have Echo back! It is simply not a negotiable thing. But now I have angered them both. I could smell the bitter, almost sour, biting pheromones from both of them. That will not do. I must find a way to apologize sufficient to allow me back in their company and their good graces, or it is all for naught. And that cannot be allowed.*

Finished unpacking, she tucked her case into a corner of the closet, went into the tiny den of her temporary dwelling, and sat down to think.

* * *

For a wonder, it was quiet in the Alpha Line Room that day, and Echo and Omega got a lot more work done as a result. They did not bother taking time off to wander back down to the deli for first lunch, but ordered a kitchen-sink pizza from Trifles' Pizzeria, and had it delivered. By midafternoon—or at least, what passed for it in the Agency—they had not only caught up from the day before, they were ahead of schedule.

"Today sure seems a hell of a lot easier than yesterday did," Echo decided.

"Yeah, I noticed that, too," Omega agreed. "We need to send Crutch a thank-you something in appreciation of keeping our visitor busy, or we'd still be diggin' out from under."

"Good point. Got any ideas?"

"One or two, yeah."

"Okay. Can I leave you to take care of it?"

"Sure thing, hon. I'll do that first thing in the morning. Different subject: What did you think about that latest batch of Alpha Line applications?"

"Hold 'em with the others, until we get enough to run 'em through testing," Echo decided. "I didn't see anybody who was disqualified, offhand. Did you?"

"Nope, not in this batch. Okeydoke, I'll file 'em with the others until we get a big enough stack." She laughed.

"Yeah, really," Echo agreed, grinning. "I'm beginning to

think we need to just hire some folks to run the testing for us. This is a BIG department. And it'll get even bigger when we go Division-wide with it."

"It's an idea," Omega said. "And yeah, it is, and it sure will. I'm just not sure where to get testing coordinators."

"Yeah, me neither." Echo shrugged. "We need somebody who will go with what WE want, and abide by our rules. Well, just ponder over it in your spare time. I think we have better uses of our time than running fifty candidates through at a go, but I still want to maybe watch video on any that get flagged, and I still want to do the final culling, just us."

"Absolutely. That way, we can ensure everything's consistent."

"Bingo. Hey, wanna go out to dinner tonight, maybe see a movie?"

"I could probably be talked into it, sure."

* * *

It was getting late in their shift when Daagnadan somewhat hesitantly entered the Alpha Line Room, choosing one of the desks partway back, along the center aisle, and sitting silently, patiently waiting. A whiff of perfume-like fragrance was the first indication the hard-working couple had that they were no longer alone.

Oh shit, Echo sent to his partner. *Guess who?*

Not again, Omega replied. *What do we do?*

She looks pretty chastened, Echo decided. *I dunno. What do you think? Should we hear her out, or throw her out? That stunt she pulled this morning was way the hell beyond the pale.*

Eh. Maybe hear her out. She might be gonna apologize.

Fair enough. I'm willing to give her that chance, I guess.

"Hey, Ree," Echo said, glancing directly at the Kochavi woman. "We'll be done here in about…what, Meg? Thirty, forty-five minutes?"

"Better make it forty-five, Echo. I just got started on this requisition, and it looks like it's gonna be more involved than I thought."

"Aw shit. Okay. We can talk in about forty-five minutes, Ree. Is that okay?"

"Yes, Echo," she said, quiet and reserved. "I can wait. I will be quiet and will not disturb you in the meanwhile."

"'Preciate that. Do you want a cup of coffee while you wait? I have some disposable cups over here…" Echo pulled out the pack of disposable cups and laid them beside the pod brewer.

"That would be nice, thank you." Daagnadan rose and moved to the brewer, then watched closely as Echo stepped her through its operation. She selected a pod, placed it into the brewer, and initiated the brew. Echo gave her a friendly smile, then turned back to his computer screen and resumed perusing the latest intel reports from offworld; he had the screen optics set so that its contents would only be visible from his eye angle, so security was maintained, even though Daagnadan was behind him.

When she had prepared her coffee—most non-humans preferred black coffee for some reason, but she loaded hers with both cream and sugar—she moved back to one of the desks, but chose one a little closer to the front than before.

* * *

"There," Omega said, hitting a couple more keystrokes nearly an hour later. "I'm finally done with that!"

"Good timing, baby," Echo said. "I just finished the latest offworld intel reports."

"Anything we need to worry about?"

"I didn't see anything, no. The Cortians are still out there— well, a few are—but they're over on the other side of Aleancë right now, and mostly getting mopped up."

"Good," Omega declared darkly.

"Heh. Yeah. No shit. So, Ree, what's up?" Echo wondered, as he and Omega commenced shutting down their virtual workstations.

"I…wished to apologize," Daagnadan said then, keeping her voice low in volume and pitch; she looked rather ashamed.

"I meant no harm this morning, but I can see where it was…unpleasant, even insulting…and I wanted to tell you both how sorry I am."

"Well, provided you don't do any of that again, I'm willing to accept an apology," Echo offered. "How 'bout you, Meg?"

Briefly, Omega thought she smelled something extremely sweet, like the sweetest flower she had ever smelled, but it was gone almost as soon as it registered on her semi-conscious mind.

"Sure, Ace, I'm good with that," she said.

"Oh, excellent," Daagnadan said in relief. "Would you allow me to make up for…let us call it, a lack of understanding of human mores in espousal…by taking you both out to dinner tonight? I had thought we might go to that lovely steakhouse in Manhattan that I recall from my first time on Earth…I think I mentioned it yesterday…"

Omega and Echo exchanged another glance.

"That's awfully expensive, Ree," Echo noted. "Are you sure you can afford it? We don't need any place nearly so fancy, and we don't wanna put you out financially."

"My teaching position is quite good, my old friend," Daagnadan said, and smiled. "My school is a private one, a preparatory school I think humans call it, and my salary is a very nice one, as X-ray would have said. Plus, I perform subsidized historical research at the university. I am not rich, but I can certainly do well by my friends when I have done them a wrong."

"Meg, how's the tum?"

"Doing okay today, Ace."

"Feel like the best steak in the Big Apple?"

"I could do that, yeah."

"Then we accept, Ree," Echo said with a smile. "Give us about half an hour to run home and freshen up, and then we'll meet you in the Core, grab the 'Vette, and head out. Will that work?"

"I think that will do very well, Echo," Daagnadan said,

matching his smile.

* * *

Daagnadan had already made reservations for three, and they were seated at a private window table in a corner almost as soon as they arrived. This was one of the poshest restaurants in all of New York City, situated in the penthouse of a Manhattan high-rise—fortunately well out of the region of the mega moth's rampage, so it was undamaged—and the views of nighttime New York were amazing.

"This is lovely," Omega noted, looking around.

"I take it, you have never been here before?" Nreefluvan wondered.

"No, I haven't," Omega said with a smile. "We don't often get to go out, at least like this; we tend to stay really busy."

"Meg is being a little modest," Echo said then. "In addition to being the chief and assistant chief of Alpha Line, with me as the Assistant Director into the bargain, we've been considered the premier team in Division One. Fox calls on us a lot when there's something bad in the wind. Plus she's the training coordinator for the entire department. Yeah, we stay really busy — and that's an understatement of some considerable quantity."

"Oh, I see," Daagnadan said, raising an eyebrow. "No wonder you know all the restaurants CLOSE to Headquarters."

"Exactly," Omega said with a chuckle. "If we do get to head out, we tend to stay close, just in case."

"If you'll remember, Ree," Echo added, "when you and I came here, we were in company with X-ray and Fox, who were in a 'we need MEAT' mode."

"Ha! Yes, I had forgotten that detail, but you are right!" Daagnadan said with a laugh. "I remembered that they were with us, but not that they were craving meat. X-ray was definitely a carnivore, was he not?"

"He was," Echo chuckled. "He said, as hard as we worked, we needed the protein. And based on my experiences, I think he was probably right. I know THIS lady," he patted Omega's hand, "has to be kept topped up on her protein reserves, for sure."

"I can imagine. I hope you are feeling better tonight, Omega," Nreefluvan said sincerely.

"I am," Omega said with a smile. "I think I'm looking forward to this meal!"

"Good. I also hope you are enough like Echo—as you seem—to like the same things…"

"She is, and she does," Echo said, confident.

"Good. I decided to choose the full-menu option for our meal tonight, so there is no need to order," Daagnadan explained. "I selected the meal plan that looked the most like something I thought Echo would enjoy, and trusted to your affinity for the rest."

"Ree," Echo chastised gently, "that's the most expensive option on the menu."

"This is an apology, Echo," Daagnadan replied, equally gently. "It is my way of saying I am sorry, and I should like to remain friends. I think there is no expense too great for that, do you not agree?"

Echo glanced at Omega, who shrugged, then nodded.

"Thank you, Nreefluvan," a very sincere Omega said then. "I think I speak for both of us in that we appreciate that, on many levels."

"What she said," Echo agreed.

"Good." Nreefluvan smiled, and suddenly the very air around them seemed sweeter and more relaxing. "I have signaled the waiter, and they will be bringing the first of five courses soon."

* * *

The five-course meal was delicious, and consisted of a wild mushroom bisque for the first course, with a wild-greens salad with candied walnuts and an orange-pineapple vinaigrette for the second. The third was broiled oysters Rockefeller. The entrée was, of course, filet mignon with a Bordeaux sauce and lobster tails, with steamed asparagus drizzled with Hollandaise and pan-fried herbed potatoes. Dessert was a chocolate-cinnamon pecan torte drizzled with cinnamon sauce and garnished with whipped cream and crushed pecans.

And it was accompanied by a different, and very excellent, wine with each course.

"Oh my goodness," Omega murmured, as she took one final bite of the torte. "That was fantastic."

"It really was," Echo agreed, shoveling away the last of his slice of torte. "Thank you very much, Ree-ree."

"I am so glad you both liked it," Daagnadan said with a smile. She had given up on her slice of torte a few minutes earlier, unable to finish it after such a huge meal. "I, too, thought it was excellent."

The waiter popped by just then. He took one look at their plates, then addressed Nreefluvan.

"Would madame like to add the rest of her torte to her tidbit bag?" he wondered.

"Yes, please," she said with a smile. "Those two have very active, very physical jobs, but I have not so much, so I cannot eat all of it!"

"Very good," the waiter said, responding to her smile. "I think madame likely has another very nice meal in her tidbit bag. I will ensure the chef adds instructions for the best way to reheat each item, so you enjoy it, as well."

"Thank you," the alien woman replied. "And the cheque should be already handled, is it not?"

"Yes, madame," the waiter replied. "I can bring coffee, if you like, and you may sit and catch up with each other; I understand you have not seen each other in some time, prior to your visit to our fair city. Or you may leave whenever you like."

"I think some coffee would be nice," Daagnadan decided. "Perhaps with a shot of whisky."

"An Irish coffee. Excellent. Would Madame's guests care for coffee, fortified or otherwise?"

"Coffee's always good," Omega said. "No whisky in mine,

thanks."

"I'm driving, and I've already had plenty of wine," Echo said. "Fortunately with lots of food." *And a DeTox tab,* he added mentally to his partner. 'But yes, some coffee would be good."

"Very good, then. I'll bring that out shortly."

The waiter collected the plates, then departed, and the trio were left to chat quietly.

* * *

"Echo, Omega, I have a favor to ask of the two of you," Daagnadan said, when the conversation finally lagged a bit. Echo and Omega sat back, exchanged a glance, then nodded as one.

"Shoot," Echo said, turning back to Daagnadan.

Omega promptly replied, "Bang!" and the pair snickered. A tolerant Daagnadan rolled her eyes.

"If I did not know you better by now, I should think you had both had too much to drink," she teased. "But no. This is, I hope, a simple request, borne mostly of curiosity. Could I, perhaps, be allowed to watch the two of you train, at some point? Given your affinity, and your reputations — about which I have done a bit of research, and am already duly impressed — I think it would be fascinating to watch you train together. And Echo, I should love to see how far you have come, from when I knew you last..."

Echo sat back again, somewhat surprised at the request, and shot another glance at his partner. Omega raised her eyebrows.

"I don't see why not, Ace," Omega pointed out. "It isn't like we don't do training sessions that way for other agents, after all. Even record it for later viewing, sometimes."

"Yeah, it isn't gonna be classified, I don't guess," Echo agreed. "Sure, Ree, we can do that. In fact, our regular session is coming up in the rotation tomorrow morning. Show up at the Alpha Line Room first thing, and we'll take you to the observation room, then do our training."

"Wonderful," Daagnadan said with a smile. "I look forward

to it."

* * *

When they finally arrived back at Headquarters, Omega and Echo glanced at each other.

You know what we need to do, to be polite, he told her. *Damn, she dropped some bucks on that dinner. It's only fair.*

Yeah, I know. Omega sighed inwardly. *Okay. It's been a good evening, and she behaved herself. Go ahead and do it.*

"Um, Ree, would you, uh, like to come back to our place for drinks?" a somewhat hesitant Echo asked then.

Daagnadan gave them both a slight smile.

"Thank you for the invitation, but no, not tonight. I do not believe that would be wise, after last night's…unpleasant aftermath. Your wines I can handle, and whisky, for they are imported from Earth, and so I have had them whenever I wished over the years, but the bourbon…! Let us allow some time to pass before we try such a thing again. And I promise I will be better behaved, and will drink less of the bourbon. Good night to you both; sleep well."

"You too, Ree," Omega said, as the alien woman lightly touched their hands, then turned and headed for the elevator that would take her up to the embassy levels.

Once she was well out of earshot, Echo let out a long sigh of relief.

"Whew. That's over with."

"Yeah," Omega agreed. "And it wasn't too bad, after all."

But she wondered why she picked up a faint hint of disappointment through the nd't'lq.

* * *

Back in her quarters, Daagnadan sat in the armchair and pondered for a time.

It works while I am with him, she thought, *but not when I am away. And there is a substantial period of time when the two of them are in their quarters, alone together, and I am not anywhere near. And now, thanks to my tongue's carelessness, I dare not go there for a time. I must find another way to handle matters.*

She thought for a long time, tossing around ideas in her mind.

"Oh!" she finally exclaimed, sitting upright. "Yes, that will work, I think. It will not be as good as if I were there, and it will not diffuse so far, or adjust to situations and moods. But if I am wily, and position it close by, it should do." She paused, considering. "It may take me a few days to manage this, but I think it will work."

Then she stood and went to her luggage, digging in the hygiene kit for long moments before producing a small, empty glass vial.

She stripped down to the waist, then gently massaged the inner sides of both breasts, along the cleavage, until tiny ducts revealed themselves.

Then she delicately 'milked' the clear, slightly oily liquid they produced into the vial.

"There," she said, when she capped off the full vial. "That should do nicely."

* * *

The next morning, Daagnadan was waiting for Alpha One in the Alpha Line Room. She sat near the front, a cup of coffee in hand.

"There we are!" Echo said with a smile. "Good morning, Ree."

"Hello, Echo, Omega," the Kochavi woman said, responding to his smile. "I hope you are both feeling well."

"Pretty damn good," Omega decreed with a smile of her own. "I feel great today!"

"Shall we go, then?" Echo asked, grinning. "I believe we have a training session to do."

"We shall go," Daagnadan said.

The three turned and left the Room…

…But behind them, there was a small square of cloth, saturated in a clear, slightly oily substance, tucked under the pod brewer…

…Which sat on the end of the credenza nearest Echo's desk.

* * *

Alpha One led Daagnadan to the observation room.

"Here," Echo said, indicating the seating. "Grab a chair and get comfortable, Ree. Meg and I will be onscreen there, and you can watch our training."

"All right. Thank you," Daagnadan said, moving to a chair and sitting. "I look forward to it."

Echo and Omega left, and Daagnadan settled in.

Moments later, Crutch arrived.

"Well, hey there, Ree," the older agent greeted the Kochavi woman. "I hope you don't mind a little company."

"Not at all, Crutch," Daagnadan said with a welcoming smile. "I enjoyed our time together the other day, and you are very welcome to keep me company!"

"What are you doing here?" Crutch said, gimping a bit as she made her way with a cane to a seat beside Daagnadan.

"Oh, I asked to watch Alpha One train, out of curiosity, and they agreed," Daagnadan explained. "Why are you here?"

"Ah," Crutch said, settling in and discarding the cane in the adjacent empty chair. "I'm here because, at Omega's request, I had a little input into the training scenario today, and I wanted to see how it went."

"Oh! This should be VERY interesting, then," Daagnadan decided.

"I sure hope so," Crutch said, and they leaned back to watch.

* * *

Echo and Omega entered the sim training room and Omega moved to the control panel beside the door, while Echo double-checked his equipment.

"So what's the scenario today, baby?" Echo wondered.

"Dunno, Ace," Omega said, checking over the controls before setting the simulation to initiate on a thirty-second countdown.

"What do you mean, you don't know? You're the training supervisor for the whole damn department," Echo pointed out.

"I don't know because I didn't set up the scenario," Omega explained. "I decided we needed to occasionally be surprised, you and me, by what we went up against. So, given she's back on light duty and still on a cane, I thought it could be good all the way around, if I asked Crutch to program in what she thought might be a good scenario. It gives her a task to work on, and it gives us something unexpected in our training."

"Ohhhh, shit," Echo groaned. "THIS is gonna be interesting."

"Along the lines of the ancient Oriental curse?" Omega asked with a grin.

"Hell yeah." Echo shook his head. "Do we at least have a starting point to go from?"

"Yeah. We have an illegal alien — one Dar Gerhin, of Valestia — on the run from Division Eight for a series of robberies, currently loose in a section of Mumbai called Dharavi," Omega said. "We have to track it down and bring it into custody."

"Lovely," Echo sighed…

…And suddenly they were in one of the most crowded slums to be found on planet Earth.

* * *

Echo and Omega reconnoitered their immediate area, and Echo discovered that his phone now had an image of their perp. So while Omega broke out a spectral imaging scanner and set it for their perp, then scanned the area, Echo approached some locals with the image, asking in English and reasonably fluent Hindi if anyone had seen the being. Omega got no immediate hits, but Echo did, so they followed the trail laid out by the eyewitnesses.

Two streets down, and per the directions of the locals, they turned left, then right.

Then came to a complete halt.

"Well, that didn't work," Echo noted, staring at the

91

ramshackle wall ahead. "We're in a dead-end alley."

Omega turned.

"That isn't all we're in," she said. Echo spun, to find the way blocked by a military contingent of a race that both members of Alpha One recognized.

And despised.

"At last," the leader of the Cortian crew said, as the rest of his people came out of hiding and surrounded Alpha One, "we have both of you. Thank you, Dar Gerhin, for bringing them right to us. Their offspring should make wonderful slaves."

And their smirking perpetrator stepped from hiding, a blaster in hand, to join the ranks of the Cortians enclosing Alpha One.

The Cortians pulled their weapons.

"Oh HELL no! I don't think so," Omega snarled. "Y'ALL don't even get the 'Halt, you're under arrest' treatment."

"Terminate?" Echo growled.

"With extreme prejudice, Ace."

"I'm all over that."

The pair went back to back. Abruptly blasters appeared in all four human hands.

Alpha One opened up with all four…

…Simultaneously.

* * *

Their instinct was to scythe the blaster beams through the pirate slaver crew plus one, but given the dilapidated buildings behind them, and the pedestrians and peddlers on the street beyond, the likelihood of injuring or even killing an innocent bystander was high.

So instead Alpha One chose to apply as much gun-fu as their highly-trained bodies could manage…which was considerable, taken all in all.

Target, aim, fire; target, aim, fire — with both weapons — was the sequence of the hour. Alpha One's precise aim was swift and deadly. Cortian after Cortian took gut and head shots, falling before they could fire their own weapons — which were intended to stun, in any case, in order to take their prey captive without harm. There were fifteen Cortians, one Valestian, and only two Alpha Line Agents…

…But within seconds, and in just four rounds of fire, the only ones standing were the two Agents.

* * *

"Oh, great Maker!" Daagnadan exclaimed in astonishment, mere moments later. "What just happened?!"

"Those simulations were a bunch of the same beings that kidnapped and tortured Echo, wanted to rape him to 'harvest his genetics,' and were going to sell him off to the highest bidder to be killed," Crutch said softly. "Never mind torching Omega under their ion drive on our FIRST go-round with the bastards. I thought the sight of that many Cortians might give 'em pause, but it looks like I was wrong. It only made 'em mad." She shrugged, a wry grin on her face. "I'll have to come up with something better next time."

"They…they…" Daagnadan tried, shocked.

"They wiped 'em out," Crutch supplied. "In seconds. I knew Omega was pissed at 'em generally, but I wasn't sure how Echo was gonna react. Looks like he's past any inhibiting responses and into, 'kill 'em all' mode. Especially given how I had the commander lead off in that little excuse for a negotiation."

"That was…impressive," Daagnadan murmured, dumbfounded, and struggling to process what she had just seen. "Certainly Echo was, of course, very good when I knew him, but he is so very much better now…I, I have no words. And Omega is right beside him, and equal to him."

"She is," Crutch agreed. "And frankly, I think she has the capacity for being the fiercer of the two. Oh, she can be very gentle, especially when children are involved, but she is ferociously protective of the people she loves. And Echo is her heart and soul." Crutch let out a bark of laughter. "I've heard some of the Alpha Line teams call her 'our mama bear.' Are you familiar with what happens when you get between a mama bear and her cubs?"

"Yes, I recall that, and…I…can see why," Daagnadan said, still overwhelmed.

* * *

This may be more difficult than I had realized, a worried Daagnadan thought, as a grinning Crutch slipped out of the observation room. *They are thoroughly bonded, and he means the world to her. She is unlikely to give him up without a fight… and I have not nearly the skill to take HER on.*

She shook her head. *I will have to maximize my innate ability…and try to wield it against HER, forcing her away, while trying to draw him in deeper. This will be difficult. Fortunately they are different sexes, and I can see about using that to my advantage.*

She was still in a certain amount of awe when Alpha One entered the observing room…

…But not so much that she failed to begin using her body's biochemistry — a very unusual innate ability — to its best advantage.

* * *

"So, Ree, what did you think?" Echo wondered, as he and Omega entered the observation room.

"I have not the words, Echo," Daagnadan admitted, shaking her head. "That was incredibly impressive. I always knew you were good, when you and I were seeing each other. But you have increased orders of magnitude in your skills since then. And Omega, you stood beside him as his equal. You are both…" She paused, searching for words. "Imposing. Remarkable. Extraordinary. Almost frighteningly so. I had no idea."

Both Agents flushed, then smiled, finding the atmosphere especially congenial.

"Let's go grab first lunch," Echo suggested, and the trio headed out to eat.

* * *

It was a good two Division days after Timerrn Dhin

vanished when Narrbeg Kath went missing.

Like Dhin, Kath's locator beacon also failed in the middle of his shift. Facilities called out the search teams from Security and Field departments once more, hoping to locate the little Sluuite despite the difficulties. This time, they broke out the imaging spectral scanners, hoping to find traces that would lead them to the tiny being.

A faint trace was located on the fifth floor, between two of the embassies.

But Kath was never found.

* * *

Joe Bob had tended to be in and out of the Core all day, every day. He had been hired shortly after Slug's body had been eliminated, a couple of years prior, and he rarely took a day off. He had no family of which anyone was aware, but he was human, and he was reasonably adroit mentally, and he was willing to do the job AND keep his mouth shut about it. The pay was not the equivalent of a field agent's salary, but he was all right with that. Being a distinct introvert, he had requested a small apartment in a corner of Sub-basement Three when he was hired, in lieu of actual quarters. So Facilities had provided him with a bed, a wardrobe, a tiny kitchenette, and a small bathroom in a corner of Sub-basement Three, not that far from the incinerator he tended. It was walled off on three sides, but the front opened onto the incinerator area...which also served as a den of sorts for him. He had no television, no stereo, nor much of anything else, though he did have a substantial bookcase, filled top to bottom, in his bedroom across from the bed. Most of his pay went toward food and books. On the rare instance when anyone asked about it, he replied that it was food for the body and food for the mind.

Omega had met him once, not long after he had been hired, and he had been able to hold his own in conversation with her, which Echo found interesting. The female Agent had been interested in trying to befriend the janitor, but Joe Bob had let her know — rather more gently than his usual method —

that he preferred to be alone, most of the time. Thus she had acceded to his wishes and left him be.

So Joe Bob meandered on a semi-regular schedule throughout every floor of Headquarters, cleaning and gathering trash, keeping his equipment on a janitorial cart, on which he hung the full bags of trash until it was too unwieldy to maneuver through the corridors. Then he trundled it down to Sub-basement Three to unload the lot into the incinerator, and headed out again. It made for a long day, but Joe Bob hadn't minded.

That was all okay with 'Joe Bob' as well. It meant he could be where he wanted to be whenever he wanted to be there. The addition of a discreet and very specialized shotgun mic to his janitorial equipment also meant that he could hear what he wanted to hear, wherever it was occurring around the Core. And the isolation of his personal quarters also meant that the addition of a few offworld bits of comm equipment would never be noticed.

So he knew whenever Daagnadan was in the Alpha Line Room. Which, he discovered, was at least once a day. Given that it had transpired that Agent Echo was now married to his partner, 'Joe Bob' could see why that sort of frequent visitation might be a necessity, and certain matters be taking longer to accomplish than Daagnadan had anticipated.

Still, he decided, she was diligent, and sooner or later the matter would be taken care of.

One way or another.

He would see to that.

* * *

Daagnadan did not spend a great deal of time in the Alpha Line Room once she walked Alpha One back to it after first lunch. Instead, she retreated to her quarters, and Alpha One settled down to their usual work.

As the day progressed, Echo became mellower, more relaxed.

But Omega became more irritable, headachy and tired.

That night, they sat in their loungers, Echo reading while a worn-out Omega absently channel-surfed.

They went to bed early.

* * *

In her quarters, Daagnadan sat on the sofa, deep in thought, all evening. She rose from the sofa and prepared meals in her stocked kitchenette when they were required, but she did so without spending a great deal of thought on it.

Finally, shortly before she retired for the evening, she nodded to herself.

"Yes, that should work," she murmured to herself. "It will take a bit of doing to convince him, but it should work nicely. If not right away, then…soon."

Daagnadan attired herself in a filmy négligée, then went to bed.

Alone.

She slept surprisingly well.

* * *

Omega woke the next day feeling lethargic and mildly nauseated. It was her turn to fix breakfast, so she managed to scramble a couple of eggs and fry some bacon without getting sick, heating up some canned biscuits in the oven in the meanwhile. She dished all of the eggs onto Echo's plate, along with all but a couple of pieces of the bacon and two biscuits. Then, from the rest, she made a couple of bacon biscuits, putting those on her plate.

"What's up, baby?" Echo wondered, when she brought their plates to the breakfast nook. "You normally eat a lot more than that."

"Still not feeling great," she admitted.

"Still?"

"Yeah, it comes and goes," she told him. "Between all of the medical testing, the push to get a bodyguard corps prepped, staffed, and trained, and your old girlfriend showing up and bugging the hell out of us, I'm just feeling kinda stressed lately, I think. I've had worse; I expect it's the medical testing and some of the meds they've given me for those that's made me feel so…blarg. I expect I just need time to get past it, while they've backed off on the tests."

"Well, try to take it easy, as much as you can," Echo said, as he tied into his breakfast. "We got this. Oh, we have another batch of Alpha Line applications in; can you have a look at those today and sort 'em into the usual groupings?"

"Sure, Ace," Omega murmured, stifling a sigh as she nibbled on one of the biscuits.

* * *

Omega had just finished going over all of the newest applications to join Alpha Line in detail, and was about to begin sorting them while Echo prepared the departmental shift report for Fox, when Daagnadan walked into the Alpha Line Room.

"Hello, Omega, Echo," she said in a cheerful tone.

"Well, hey, Ree," Echo said, looking up with a smile, and completely missing the brief scowl that appeared on his partner's face, given their desks faced away from each other. "What up, buttercup?"

Now who's glommin' Romeo's sayings? Omega thought with a desperately stifled snort, and Echo grinned, having picked up the remark through the nd't'lq.

"I was wondering if I might have your opinion, perhaps advice, on a business matter, Echo," Daagnadan wondered then.

"Sure thing, Ree. What's the problem?"

"I am considering emigrating to Earth," she noted, and an annoyed Omega bit her lip to control her expression, "likely with some family members this time, and wondered what region of the planet you thought would be most comfortable for the Kochavi people, as well as perhaps—"

"Hey, dude and dudette!" an exuberant Agent Love of Alpha Five exclaimed, as she practically waltzed into the Alpha Line Room with her partner Uniform. "What's up, guys? Guess what! We FINALLY got that Dabanoran chop shop broken and the perps taken into custody! Yay us!"

"Yeah, sorry we missed this morning's department meeting, but we figured taking 'em down was more important," Uniform said. "Once we got 'em booked and their asses in Confinement, we thought we'd swing by and see what we missed."

"Oh, right," Echo said, glancing past Daagnadan at the pair. "Great job, y'all. That's some really damn good news! That chop shop has been a pain in the ASS in the last couple of months, and slipperier than owl snot. Ree, excuse me for a few minutes; I need to debrief these two, fill them in on what's going on, and get 'em out on their next assignment. It won't take long. Then I'll see if I can advise you."

"Uh, of course," Daagnadan murmured, as the Alpha Five partnership, high on adrenaline after a complicated mission, swept by her on their way to the pod coffee brewer.

* * *

Half an hour later, as Alpha Five headed out once more, Daagnadan pulled up a chair to Echo's desk and tried again.

"I was hoping you could make some suggestions as to—"

Echo's workstation bleated with the URGENT INCOMING EMAIL alert, and he held up a hand.

"Hang on, Ree, that's probably Fox, and he never puts that level on it unless it's important and time-critical," he said. "I gotta have a look at this."

Daagnadan sighed.

Omega bit her lip again…this time, to hide the grin.

* * *

After three more interruptions, during which Daagnadan became more and more frustrated, and Omega continued biting her lip to stifle perverse laughter, the alien woman huffed as soon as Echo got off his cell phone.

"May we PLEASE go somewhere else to discuss this?" Nreefluvan finally demanded. "Somewhere you will not be interrupted every five seconds?"

"Aw. I'm sorry. Perils of being a department lead AND the assistant director, I guess. Sure thing, Ree," Echo said, apologetic. "We can go around to Fox's little conference room. Meg, can you hold down the fort?"

"Sure, Ace," Omega agreed. "How long will you be gone, just in case Fox calls?"

"I don't think it'll be too long," Echo decided, glancing at Daagnadan for confirmation. "Maybe an hour?"

Daagnadan nodded, and they headed out.

* * *

Well, at least she's finally out of earshot, Omega thought. *That, and...would it be 'smellshot'? Damn, I can't stand whatever perfume it is that she wears. Granted, she doesn't wear much, but it does my head NO favors.* She rubbed her temple as a headache threatened, and it eased slightly.

Okay, now maybe I can concentrate on these applications an' get 'em sorted, she decided, flipping through the stack once more, and beginning to sort them into the pre-established categories she and Echo had set, and determined by their qualifications.

* * *

Echo led the way across the Core toward the small conference room that Fox often used. As he passed the Director's office and saw Fox glance up, he waved, then shot a couple of obvious hand signals at Fox that said, *Can I use your conference room?*

Fox read the signals immediately and nodded, giving Echo a thumbs-up.

"Okay, good," Echo told Daagnadan. "Fox doesn't need the conference room; we can go in there and talk and be undisturbed."

"Oh, can we not find someplace more...comfortable, more...convivial?" the Kochavi woman wondered, slightly petulant by this time. "A conference room is so cold and, and anonymous..."

Echo raised an eyebrow.

"What did you have in mind?" he asked.

"Well, now that you mention it..." she began.

100

* * *

"No, I don't think so," Echo said, leading her across the huge room. "We can always sit over here, in a corner of the Core, and chat…"

"MUCH too busy," Daagnadan countered. "And visible from your departmental room. Anyone who wanted you there would simply detour, and keep interrupting us."

Echo sighed.

* * *

"No, this is even worse," she said, as Echo aimed for the small food court in Grand Central Station. "There are so many people coming and going I can hardly hear myself think."

"Ree, we don't have a lot of options, here," Echo pointed out.

"We do," Daagnadan replied. "You simply do not wish to consider them."

"Well, your quarters are right out," Echo said. "That's just not good, I don't care what."

"There is still another option, Echo, and you should be comfortable with it…"

"Not especially, no."

"But it would be comfortable…"

"Ree, I think it's a bad idea."

"I don't think so. I think it would not be minded at all."

"What in the name of common sense makes you think THAT…?"

Chapter 5

"Are you sure about this, Ree?" Echo wondered, as they finally headed for the agent's quarters; Echo had tried several other venues, but Daagnadan turned them all down flat for one reason or another. "I really just do NOT think this is a good idea at ALL..."

Just then, and without his conscious awareness, his nostrils flared in a subconscious response to...something.

"Oh, I think it is a very good idea, boopy," Daagnadan said with a brilliant smile. "And what Omega does not know will not hurt her. We will have a nice long chat, perhaps over drinks, in your apartment, and it will go well, and it will be fine."

"All right, if you say so," Echo said, pausing in front of the door that said, *Alpha One—Echo and Omega.* "Come on in."

He never seemed to notice the affectionate endearment that Daagnadan kept insisting on using.

* * *

'Joe Bob' was in the corridor, gathering the full bags from the wastecans beside the elevator banks, when Agent Echo arrived with Ms. Daagnadan. He pretended to ignore the conversation between the pair as Echo headed down the hall and opened the door to Alpha One's quarters, then ushered Daagnadan inside.

Interesting, he considered. Perhaps matters were progressing faster than he had expected. This looked promising. Very promising indeed.

* * *

"Okay, have a seat," Echo said, "while I get us something to drink. Coffee, water...?"

"I think we should have whisky," Nreefluvan decreed. Echo raised an eyebrow.

"All right," he said, raising the lid on the coffee table to reveal the hidden warp-pocket wet bar. "I'll need to take a DeTox tab, 'cause I have to go back to the office when we're done, but that'll work. Do you want a DeTox?"

"No, I do not have to work," Nreefluvan pointed out. "But I promise I will be careful. I will not drink too much."

"That's…a good plan," Echo agreed. "Now lemme see here…" He poked around in the wet bar, pulling out two old-fashioned glasses and the decanter of his favorite whisky, then hunting for the bottle of DeTox. He came up with the small pharmaceutical bottle, but it was empty. "Oh shit. We forgot to replace this the last time we used it. I know we have more, I just have to find it."

"Where would it be?"

"I think Meg put it in one of the bathroom cabinets," Echo said, rising and heading for the master suite. "Let me go find where it is, and I'll be right back."

"That is fine," Nreefluvan said, standing, moving to the thermostat on the wall, and adjusting it. "Take your time." She moved to the end table beside Echo's recliner, producing a small piece of cloth and a tiny vial of clear, slightly oily liquid; she saturated the cloth with the liquid, then tucked it under the lip of the end table. There was sufficient oil, and it was viscous enough, that the cloth adhered there on its own.

"Dammit," came grumbling from somewhere within the master suite, along with the sounds of rummaging. "Where the HELL did that bottle of DeTox go?"

Nreefluvan wandered into the bedroom on silent feet; Echo was not visible through the bathroom door, and she took advantage of the fact. Another swatch of cloth, saturated from the vial, went into the corner of the drawer in Echo's nightstand — it was obvious which was which, because Omega's had a block of pink resin containing a rose and a worn book covered in some sort of black animal hide, and Echo's had a small dish with various man-type trinkets such as spare change, an extra pocket knife, and a disposable lighter. Then she slipped over to the dual closets, peeking into each until she determined which was Echo's; another saturated square of cloth was secreted on the top storage shelf. *There,* she thought. *That should take care of matters when I am not around. Not as well as I should like, but it will be close enough for him to feel the effects. And for the moment, I AM around, so let me see what I can do.* She headed for the bathroom door.

Just as she reached the open doorway, however, Echo appeared on the other side, a bottle in hand.

"Finally!" he said with a wry grin. "It got knocked down behind some other stuff, and I thought I'd never find it."

"Good," Nreefluvan said with a smile. "I was coming to help you look, but it seems I was not needed after all. Let us go sit down and discuss what the process is to move me and my family to Earth. Permanently."

* * *

On the same floor where Alpha One's quarters were found, another Sluuite member of the Facilities staff vanished. As per the previous disappearances, the locator beacon for Nirrded Vult simply ceased function.

The locate-and-rescue team comprised of Security and Field agents was sent out once again. Again they took along spectral imaging scanners, set to identify Sluuite presence; again they found an odd site that indicated considerable contact with a Sluuite — down the corridor and around the corner from Alpha One's quarters — but nothing definitive.

Again, Vult was never found.

* * *

"…And so I had hoped to apply for permanent residency," Daagnadan told her old lover. "I find I miss Earth, miss my old friends…miss you, Echo. I made a mistake in leaving Earth. I want to return."

"Are you sure that's wise, Ree?" Echo wondered. "You've already seen that I'm not available, and if your intent to return is predicated on getting back together with me, you may be sadly disappointed."

"I do not think so," Daagnadan replied, sanguine. "There are more reasons than that. I like it here. Yes, I have a good job on Kochav, but there is more to life than a job, as you must know, else you would not have espoused. I fit in better on Earth than, I think, I ever have on Kochav."

"Well, I can understand that," Echo considered. "Still, I'm not sure…"

"Echo, may I ask a personal question?"

"I suppose. I may not answer, depending on what it is."

"Do you have fond memories of our time together?"

"Yeah, I do, Ree. It was fun."

"Good. So do I. And…" Daagnadan broke off, then tried, "The more I get to know your spouse Omega, the more I like her. She is…attractive, and intelligent, and quick-witted, and…"

"You sure didn't like her at first. And you didn't think she was attractive," Echo pointed out, sharp. "That crack about the scar on her back demonstrated that."

Daagnadan flushed a rather deep blue.

"I…was jealous," she confessed, and Echo's eyebrows shot up as he realized Nreefluvan was telling the truth. "It IS only a small scar, though I can tell by it that what happened to her was…bad. But yes, I have grown to like her. If…I do not know how either of you would feel about it, but my comment about sharing the bed with you both, that first morning, was sincere. And I find the idea even more appealing now I have come to know her better."

Echo gaped for a moment, managing somehow not to drop his jaw, though the muscles in it went slack. After what seemed to him an eternity, but evidently to Daagnadan was a span of only a second or so, he found his voice. It was hoarse, and he had to rather force out the words, but he managed reasonably coherent speech.

"Uh, no, Ree, I uh, I appreciate the compliment, and so would Meg, I'm sure, but…but we don't, um, that's not the way we, uh, operate," Echo tried. "Meg and I are, ah, kinda private that way."

"I see," Daagnadan said, seeming disappointed. "Well, my old love, the offer is there, should the two of you wish to take it. I promise you, I could teach her things that would take your love to new levels."

"Maybe so," Echo said, glad to find his voice was finally starting to return to normal. "But we—"

He was interrupted by a knock on the door, as the intercom annunciated.

"Agent Echo? Agent Omega? Are either of you there? This is Musket, with the Security department…we'd like to speak with you for a moment…"

"Oh, great Maker," Daagnadan fussed. "Someone found us HERE, to interrupt us?"

"Shit," Echo said in surprise. "I need to go answer this, Ree. Stay here, stay out of sight, and be quiet. I doubt it'll take more than a minute."

Daagnadan nodded agreement, and Echo rose and headed for the front door.

* * *

Agent Musket, in standard Security body armor but carrying a spectral imaging scanner, was just about to turn away from the door when it opened. Agent Echo stood framed in it.

"What's up, Agent Musket?" he wondered.

"We have a small situation, sir," Musket responded. "We've had a disturbing trend develop among the Sluuites in the Facilities department."

"Tell me."

"Well, in the last week, ish, we've had something like three or four Sluuites go missing, sir," Musket explained. "Always while on duty. They just suddenly stop reporting in."

"What do their locator beacons say?"

"That's part of the problem, sir. In every case, the beacon ceases function about the same time they stop reporting in, give or take a few minutes."

"Hm. That's interesting. When you find them, are they badly injured?"

"That's just it. We haven't found them. Not one. It's like they vanish into thin air. Sometimes we get a little bit of a spectral signature," Musket waved the scanner, "but what with the automated cleaning systems AND the janitorial services, what little we get has always been cleaned over already."

"Okay, that's interesting, but not necessarily unexpected."

"No."

"So what do you need me to do? Are you asking for Alpha Line involvement? Did Meg send you to find me and get my approval?"

"No sir, it's a bit more direct than that. The latest disappearance occurred within the hour, on this floor. Nirrded Vult went missing. And we found a reasonably fresh, if already cleaned-over, spectral signature for Sluuite down the hall and around the corner from your quarters, here. We're going around to all the quarters in this wing and canvassing for any eyewitnesses."

"Oh, I see," Echo said then, nodding. "Unfortunately, I'm afraid I don't have anything for you, Musket. I've had a… personnel…issue to deal with, and I came back here to find some peace and quiet to think it over…"

"Ah," Musket said, grinning. "Yes sir, I bet you get a whole lot of interruptions, don't you? And here I went and created another."

"No, no, this was important, and I understand that," Echo said, holding up a hand. "I just wish I had something to offer you."

"That's fine," Musket said. "If I might ask, how long have you been in your quarters? Or more to the point, when did you come back to them?"

"Mm," Echo glanced at his wrist chronometer, considering. "Maybe half an hour? Give or take maybe five minutes."

"That would likely be before Vult went missing, though not by much," Musket decided. "Which means whatever happened likely did NOT happen in this wing of the floor."

"That makes sense," Echo agreed. "My wife and partner, Omega, has several friends among the Sluuites, so I'd have probably said hello if I'd seen one around."

"Understood. Okay, thank you, sir. I'll let you get back to your problem, and see about canvassing the rest of the floor."

"Thanks," Echo said, slipping back through the front door as Musket headed down the hall.

* * *

"Okay," Echo said, resuming his seat on the couch, "that should take care of that."

"What was it about?" Daagnadan wondered.

"Oh, a couple of the Sluuites have gone missing," Echo said. "I probably need to get with Fox and see what's up. We don't need an entire group of offworlders going missing like this. But that's for later. Let's finish deciding what to do about your situation…"

* * *

Echo had been gone over an hour, pushing an hour and a half. When Omega began to get too tired and headachy to concentrate on the department applications, she sighed and rubbed her eyes.

"Whassup, pretty lady?" Romeo wondered, as Alpha Two came into the Alpha Line Room. "You look grumpy. An' you ain't usually grumpy. 'Specially since you an' Echo done got married."

"And she looks a little pale, too," India added.

"Oh, I'm just tired, guys," Omega murmured. "All the medical testing an' whatnot has picked back up, you know. Between the biopsies, and the blood draws, and the scans, and the dyes for the scans, and the special shit I gotta eat or drink or swallow — or NOT eat or drink or swallow, as the case may be — before some of the tests…" She sighed. "It throws off my system, sometimes kinda bad, and I just don't feel that great."

"Mm. Yeah, you make some damn good points, girlfriend. You ought to go on home, Meg," India said, scrunching her face in concern. "The medlab HAS been doing a lot of testing on you. Again. If you need me to, I can talk to the team and tell 'em to back off a little more and give you another break. In fact, maybe we oughta just pause the stuff for a little while. You're trying to do that plus half a dozen other things, including Alpha Line and the bodyguard corps, and even enhanced metabolisms run outta steam sooner or later. Especially when the testing dinks with your biochem like that — and I'll be the first to admit, some of 'em do. I mean, some of it, we gotta, just to see what's going on. But there ARE limits! You must be blitzed, girl."

"I am. Alla that, and then some. Stress is the operative word, for sure. And given everything that's been going on with Echo's old girlfriend adding TO that stress, yeah, I think that's a damn good idea, India, and I think I'd appreciate that a lot," Omega admitted, as India got out her medscanner and ran it over the Alpha Line assistant chief. "That woman has been a pest. I mean, she CAN be nice…usually ONLY after she's gone completely over the top, and is apologizing! It's starting to verge on ridiculous, as far as I'm concerned. I have no idea why Echo ever even put up with that shit, back in the day."

"I kinda gathered she wadn't like that, back when they 'uz seein' each other," Romeo offered. "Leastways back when he an' I were partners, that 'uz the impression I got, from what he told me 'bout 'er. Not that he told me a whole lot — you know how he is — but hey." He shrugged. "Some folks change as they age, y' know. Maybe she got more bitchy. Bitchier? More bitchier," he decided, raising a mischievous eyebrow while India stifled a snort, as he tried to coax Omega to smile. He wasn't successful.

"Could be, I guess," Omega sighed. "She's a pain in the ass now, though. And at least initially, she just didn't seem to understand boundaries. At. All. And she still isn't great at 'em. At least where Echo is concerned."

"Whu-oh," Romeo muttered, sobering at the information. "That ain't good."

"Nope, trust me, it wasn't, and isn't," Omega grumbled, expression darkening. "You do NOT want to know what happened that first morning. Seriously. But I think Echo was ready to throw her out on her ear. He picked her up by the collar out of her chair as it was. He was furious. And I wasn't far behind."

"Whoa," Romeo groaned. "F'r Echo t' do THAT, he musta been 'bout ready t' hit somethin'. Or somebody."

"Oh, he was, believe me," Omega responded, wry. "An' for a second there, I was afraid he might. Fortunately, he's a lot more level-headed than that. But I think it might be the angriest I've ever seen him."

"Damn. Well, I think I'll ping Zee and Zar and let 'em know to keep holding up on more testing until further notice, while you two get that resolved," India said, deliberately cutting off Romeo, who had opened his mouth to ask further about the referenced behavior. "That'll give you a nice extended break from medical shit, so you can focus on the problem at hand, rather than split your attention between the old girlfriend and the medical testing, PLUS Alpha Line, PLUS the bodyguard shit. Thank the good Lord you don't actually have a mission about to start! I think — I mean, I'm pretty sure that we have enough test results now so we can work for a while on analyzing what we have, anyway."

"THAT...would be much appreciated, gal. And yeah...alla that."

"Good. Consider it done, honey. Meantime, I am seriously telling you, as the department physician, go home, 'sis,'" India said, studying her medscanner. "Like, now. This thing says you need down time, in a big way."

"Sick leave?"

"At least for the rest of the day, yeah. Maybe tomorrow, if you still don't feel good in the morning. Eat well, stay hydrated. All the usual."

"Am I coming down with something?"

"Not that I can see. No, I think you're just run down and stressed out. You need down time, rest, and good nutrition, to pull out of the funk, here." India waved at the door again. "So go home, already."

"Okay," Omega sighed. "Dammit. I do NOT need to take

any more time off, with as much as there is to do. But I wasn't expecting everything to whip my ass like this." She shook her head. "I feel like the universe is dog-piling me, somehow."

"It's awright, pretty lady," Romeo said. "We'll get Echo t' come handle it."

"No, he's off trying to do SOMEthing about Daagnadan," Omega said. "WITH Daagnadan, no less."

"Do what? What's the problem now?" India asked.

"Believe it or not, she wants to move back to Earth," Omega noted, rolling her eyes. "With her whole damn family, apparently."

"Oh great," Romeo grumbled. "Jus' what you an' Echo do NOT need."

"Exactly," Omega sighed. "Listen. Can you an' India handle things here in the office for a while? Echo will show up once he's got things straight there, an' then you can do your patrols. Oh, and make sure you tell him where I am, when you DO see him. If I'm honest with myself an' y'all, I really would like to go home, take something for this sick stress headache, an' maybe put my feet up for a little bit an' close my eyes. A cold compress on my eyes and forehead would feel awfully damn good about now, too, I b'lieve. Maybe even take a nap. And I just don't think I'm up to waiting until Echo gets back; I need to go lie down now, or I'm liable to barf."

"Ooo. That bad?" India wondered.

"Not good," Omega replied, shaking her head.

"Sure thing, Meg; I got this," Romeo said. "Department Rank Number Three, here, will be happy to take th' chair f'r a while if you'll lissen to India an' go home an' just unlax."

"Oh, I will, I swear I will," Omega said, popping a message to Fox before logging sick leave for the rest of the day, then standing. "There. I let Fox know what was up, too, just in case."

"Can't you tell where Echo is through the nd't'lq-thing and tell him?" India wondered.

"Mm, not at the moment," Omega said, checking the mental link. "He's gotten really good at erecting telepathic blocks in the last few months, see — I think Zz'r'p has been showing him how, in their counseling sessions, plus he's learned mine. Anyway, he knows it bothers me, him having to interact with her, an' he's evidently got a bit of a block up, so I can focus on my work 'stead of piggybacking on his putting her straight. Hopefully that'll include telling her to stay on Kochav, but first he'll have to beat it through her head, I expect. So maybe not this go, but soon, I hope."

"Ah," India said. "Well, we'll tell him when we see him, then. Off with you."

Omega headed for the office door.

* * *

But when she entered the joint quarters she shared with Echo, she heard voices. Heading down the hall at speed, she emerged in the den, to find Echo and Nreefluvan sitting on the sofa together—fairly close together—talking. Two partly-empty old-fashioned glasses sat on the coffee table, with a bottle of Echo's favorite whisky and a small, brand-new bottle of DeTox tabs nearby.

Just then, Nreefluvan leaned toward Echo with a sultry smile, well inside his personal space, apparently aiming for his mouth. Much to Omega's surprise, Echo did not pull back.

"Excuse me?!" she said in a loud voice.

Both parties on the couch sat up straight and spun in surprise.

"Oh, hi, Meg," Echo said then. "What are you doing here?"

"I can—and will—ask the same question," a deeply irritated Omega said, staring at Daagnadan. "What the hell are the two of you doing?"

"We are just talking, my dear," Daagnadan said with a smirk. "What did you think we were doing?"

"Well, the conversation has ended, effective immediately," Omega determined, waving a dismissive hand. "Please leave, Ms. Daagnadan."

"I thought you were calling her Ree these days," Echo pointed out.

"When I find another woman alone in my home with my husband, trying her damnedest to kiss him, I don't call her by a damn nickname," an irate Omega riposted. "I call her OUT. Or I THROW her out. Please leave, Ms. Daagnadan. Right. Now."

"I don't think we're done—" Echo began.

"Oh, you're done, all right," Omega said, rubbing her temple, as the headache ramped up, beginning to throb. "I feel crummy and I took sick leave at India's medical orders, and she and Romeo are waiting in the Alpha Line Room for YOU, Echo. So they can find out how you want them to handle some stuff that I wasn't able to finish doing. So YOU need to be headed there, and Daagnadan, here, needs to get the hell out before I start throwing something heavy at her head, and generally pitching a hissy fit." She paused, waiting, then glared at the pair on the couch. "NOW."

Echo, catching her ire through the nd't'lq, sprang up immediately, though he didn't make for the door right away. Nreefluvan lingered, taking her time and moving in a very languid, almost indolent, fashion.

"I will walk Echo down to the Alpha Line Room," she declared.

Omega stepped between the pair.

"No. You won't," Omega decreed. "Because you are going to leave now, and Echo is going to leave in five minutes, after he and I have had a private little chat."

"Then I shall wait."

"Then I shall call Security," Omega noted, firm, and mocking Daagnadan's tone. "Or handle it myself. The hard way...for you."

"Meg," Echo began.

"Can it, Ace. I am NOT in the mood," Omega tossed over her shoulder without looking. "I'm handling this, since you won't. Right now, you just need to be quiet."

"I think he—" Daagnadan started.

"And you need to get out, or I will take you out," Omega told the Kochavi woman. "Right. Now."

"And if I say no?"

"That doesn't matter. You're going, one way or another," Omega stated, calm. She rolled her shoulders, flexing and warming muscles, just in case. "You have three choices. One—you go under your own power..."

"I do not think so."

"Two—I physically pick you up and throw you out. And thr—"

"You cannot pick me up and throw me out! You are not strong enough!"

"Want to watch me?" Omega challenged, taking a step forward and seeming to become bigger as she flexed more muscles; Daagnadan instinctively backed up a step, even as Echo's eyes widened in alarm. "I can deadlift and carry Echo, and you're a whole helluva lot smaller and lighter. And won't fight back if I've already decked you."

"How dare you!"

"Oh, I think that's my line, sister. And option three, I call Security and have you removed and placed in Confinement."

"On what grounds?!"

"Trespass, and refusal to obey a direct order from an Alpha Line Agent."

"I was invited!"

"I doubt that."

"Go, Ree," Echo sighed. "She's serious, she means business, and she can do what she says. I'll talk to her and see if we can't straighten this out. If she's not feeling good, you're only gonna make things worse, going on like this."

"Oh, very well," a deeply annoyed Daagnadan said, spinning on her heel and heading for the front door. "I will be protesting my treatment with the Kochavi Embassy, however."

"You do that," Omega said, raising a blonde eyebrow. "Be sure to tell them the situation when I found you with my husband, alone, on the sofa of our apartment, trying to force a kiss on him."

Daagnadan slammed the front door on her way out.

A glaring Omega spun.

"Oh shit," a dismayed Echo murmured, seeing her face… and realizing the nd't'lq reflected that expression.

* * *

Well, thought a very self-satisfied Daagnadan as she made her way toward her assigned quarters in the Kochavi embassy. *That should help my progress considerably. And not only did Echo invite me in, when I started to kiss him, he did not pull back. That…is an EXCELLENT sign. I am progressing well, I believe. And Ms. Alpha Line Heroine does not seem to have so firm a hold on her mate as she thinks, perhaps. Which means I should be able to wrest him from her. Especially with my advantages and experience.*

The only thing I need to consider now, she thought, *is whether or not to actually file a complaint against Omega with the ambassador.*

She sauntered on.

* * *

"Meg," Echo went on the offensive, hoping to cut off what he sensed was coming, "that was just plain rude, baby."

"Oh really?" Omega queried, tone disbelieving. "So her coming into my home and trying to monopolize AND kiss my husband was NOT rude?"

"She wasn't trying to kiss me."

"Damn sure looked like it from my perspective. She was MAYBE three inches from your face, if that, and her lips were puckered and parted. And YOU were not moving back."

"Well…"

"What were YOU thinking, Echo?" Omega demanded to know. "Why did you even consider bringing her in here, after all the…shit…she's already pulled on us?"

"She wanted to discuss some things about maybe moving back to Earth, like she said in the Alpha Line Room in your hearing, and she felt maybe it would be best done in private," Echo started. "So I suggested Fox's conference room, but she said that was too impersonal, and—"

"Did it ever occur to you what it would look like? What she would have access to?"

"No." Echo shrugged. "But I'm really not worried about it."

"You SHOULD be!" Omega cried, flailing one hand in the air in frustration. "YOU'RE the guy whose reputation we had to fix, after we got caught in a no-win scenario just a few months back! Had you thought about what it would look like if she'd actually managed to plant one on you, then somebody saw you both coming out of OUR quarters, with HER lipstick on you? Even if you didn't kiss back, even if it was all one-sided," Omega pointed out. "The rumor mills would fly, Ace! Think about what happened to me, my first Christmas with the Agency! People would think you were cheating on me, whether you were or not! They'd be absolutely convinced that you were lying to me!"

"I'm not worried about gossip, baby. Seriously."

"You didn't have to worry about gossip when you were a regular field agent, Echo! But you're NOT, now! You're the head of Alpha Line, you're the Assistant Director, and one day you'll BE the Director! How the hell many people do you suppose would want to follow a leader they believed lied and cheated? On his partner and spouse, no less! How many agents do you think would be loyal to a man they thought did that? How do you figure to lead Division One if nobody trusts you?!"

"I—oh," Echo said, as the AC came on and air blew through the room. "That's weird."

"What is?"

"I THOUGHT it was getting stuffy and hot in here," Echo noted. "I don't think the air came on the whole time I was talking with Ree."

"How the hell long were you IN here?!"

"Um..." He glanced at the grandfather clock in the corner. "Maybe forty-five, fifty minutes? We meandered around for a good long while — prob'ly half the time I was gone, at least — 'cause I was trying to find a place she'd be willing to sit and talk. Finally she just said we should come sit down here and talk things over. By that point, I...” He wandered over to the thermostat and checked it. “Well, no wonder. How the hell did the temp get set that high?”

“Maybe one of us sleepwalks,” Omega suggested. “Seriously, Echo, you gotta not do that again, honey. I trust you implicitly, but after everything she’s done, I don’t trust her any farther than I can throw her. No, that’s not right; I can probably chunk her a good piece, ‘cause she ain’t that big,” Omega changed her mind. “I don’t trust her any farther than I could throw YOU.”

Echo turned to face her, feeling the emotions that played across her face through the nd’t’lq—anger, largely directed at Ree, as well as a certain jealousy; irritation at him for not considering the repercussions of gossip; protectiveness of her mate; deep trust, and an equally-deep love.

But he also sensed the headache, and the general malaise she was experiencing. And which seemed to be getting worse by the moment.

“Are you okay, bab—” he began.

“Uck!” Omega suddenly choked, and she spun and sprinted for the master bath.

Startled, Echo stared after her for a moment, then ran after her.

* * *

He found her in the water closet in the master bath, throwing up in the toilet.

Not a lot came up except a little bit of bile and stomach acid. As she responded in panting gasps to his soft questions in between retching, it transpired that she hadn’t eaten since breakfast, and he vaguely recollected that she hadn’t eaten a lot then.

He laid a light, gentle hand on her back, then pulled her silver-blonde braid out of the way of her dry heaves, just in case something did manage to come up.

“Ugh,” she grunted in disgust, as the retching finally

receded. "Sorry. I already had a sick headache. Now it's pounding. And I think that little emotional upset didn't help the tum."

"Looks like it," Echo decided. "Listen, honey, I'm sorry. You have a point. I tried to come up with some better places to meet, but Ree wasn't having much of it. She wanted someplace private and comfortable, and declared you wouldn't mind. I kinda thought differently, but the only other alternative she was offering — HER quarters — was just not an option; I knew better than THAT! So I figured maybe if we could get it done and over with fast, it'd be okay. I mean, this is Alpha One's quarters, yours and mine, so I sorta thought it would be safe. I know it bothers you, her being around me, but I really need you to kind of ease back and try not to be so jealous…"

"I will, if she'll quit hitting on you."

"Well, I'm working on that. I thought about your wanting us to have closure over the breakup, and decided you were right. See, I'm trying hard to repair that relationship and make it a friendship now."

"Why?"

"Huh?"

"Why do you want to be friends with her at all? She dumped you, and from what you've shown me in your memories, she was pretty callous about it. There's closure, and then there's stomping in where angels fear to tread." Omega stepped out of the water closet into the bathroom proper, and reached for the glass by 'her' sink, running water into it before rinsing her mouth and spitting into the sink…several times. Then she sipped the water slowly.

"I dunno," Echo sighed. "I thought maybe it'd be better if Ree and I were friends, rather than at loggerheads or something."

"Were you really gonna let her kiss you?"

"She was gonna kiss me?" Echo said, startled. "I mean, really for true? You were serious about that?"

Omega just stopped and stared at him.

"You gotta be kidding, right?" she wanted to know. "If a woman comes at you like this..." She let her lips part, curving them slightly into an open-mouthed, smiling pucker, and leaning up until she was only a couple of inches from his face. Echo could feel her breath on his skin, and instinctively he let his own lips part, bending his head toward his wife's face. Suddenly she jerked back.

"Yeah, you obviously know what it means," she noted, raising an eyebrow in mild irritation. "Why'd you let HER do it?"

"I swear, baby, I didn't realize she did that," Echo said, holding out his hands, palms up. "I never saw it."

"How could you miss it?!"

"Is that when you interrupted?" he wondered. "Like, when you said, 'Excuse me'?"

"Yeah..."

"Oh. Well, that's why, then. I'd just spotted you over Ree's shoulder, and while it may have looked like I saw her, I was looking at you, not her."

"Hm. That makes sense, I guess," Omega decided, leaning back against the vanity with a sigh. "But seriously, I think I need to go lie down now, hon. And you do need to go to the Alpha Line Room; I was only just getting started good on sorting the latest batch of applications, and I think Romeo needs to know where you want to go with this batch. He and India aren't as familiar with that last tweak we made to the sorting groups, and they need a little help."

"Okay. But lemme get you in bed first, baby," Echo said, slipping an arm around his partner and mate and helping her cross to the bed; she was still a little wobbly after the retching incident. He saw her seated on the bedside, then crouched before her. "You wanna strip down, or just kick off shoes, tie, and jacket?"

"I'm seriously not feeling that great," Omega admitted. "I think I wanna...I think I wanna actually put on some pajamas and go to bed."

"Whoa. You really aren't feeling good," Echo realized, putting a hand to her forehead. "Huh. You don't feel feverish at all; if anything, you feel a little on the cool side. Okay, baby, lemme help you strip down, then I'll dig out whatever you tell me to look for in the p-j drawer, and help you get situated. I'll bring in a carafe of water and a glass, too, so you can stay hydrated. You want me to bring in a trash can and put it by the bed in case you barf again?"

"It...might be a good idea," she confessed. "My gut is not doin' happy things right now."

"Consider it done. I'll make sure it's got a double bag in it, so if you do barf, all I gotta do is pull 'em out, tie 'em closed, and dump 'em down the trash chute to get incinerated, then rebag the can."

"Okay, that'll work." She caught his arm as he turned away to fetch a waste can. "Echo?"

"Yeah?"

"Please don't risk bringing her here again. Not without me here. And don't go to her quarters, either. Not alone. I'll gladly go WITH you, but whatever you do, please don't do it alone."

"Okay, baby."

"Promise me, Ace. PROMISE me."

"Pinky promise?" He grinned. Omega snorted.

"Sure, why not?" she chuckled.

They hooked their little fingers together.

"Pinky promise," Echo said, meeting her eyes.

"Pinky promise," Omega replied, and smiled in relief.

Then she sighed and leaned back against the pillows.

* * *

Echo finally showed up in the Alpha Line Room about half an hour later.

"Hey, bro," Romeo said. "There ya are. You seen Meg?"

"Yeah," Echo replied, being careful not to say where, or how. "I hustled her off to bed...after she tried really damn hard to barf. Only reason she didn't was 'cause she didn't have much in her TO barf. Turns out she hasn't eaten since breakfast, and I

120

remember, she didn't eat much then."

"Uh-oh," India said, concerned. "She really isn't feeling well, then. We might want to see about getting a look at her in the medlab. If she's picked up a gut bug from one of the offworlders, it'll be unpleasant for sure."

"You an' your ol' girlfriend get things squared, finally?" Romeo wondered.

"We, uh," Echo began; by the time Echo had gotten Omega settled in bed with anything he thought she might need, and they had finished discussing the matter from the bedside, he understood the need—and Omega's desire—to keep the matter under wraps, in order to protect his reputation and safeguard their relationship against gossip. So he had left their quarters to return to his office only a few minutes before, prepared to divert the topic as per Omega's wishes, should the matter arise.

He never had the chance.

The newly-assigned Kochavi ambassador, Her Excellency Rnaalti Isahuutob, stormed into the room, a smug Nreefluvan Daagnadan at her side, a perturbed Director Fox trailing.

"Agent Echo! Where is that ragnadang drekul you call a partner? How dare she treat one of our people so rudely as to throw her out of your quarters, after you invited her there! I want your partner in Confinement!" the furious ambassador demanded.

* * *

An hour or so after he had spotted Echo escorting Daagnadan into his quarters, 'Joe Bob' was collecting the trash bags from the cans in the Core, when he saw Her Excellency, Kochavi Ambassador Rnaalti Isahuutob stalking regally from the Director's Office toward the Alpha Line Room, a smug Daagnadan and a concerned Director Fox in her wake. It was patently obvious that the ambassador was in what some would have called 'high dudgeon,' and she addressed Agent Echo in a loud, demanding, imperious tone before even crossing the threshold of Alpha Line's realm.

'Joe Bob' nodded to himself, hiding a smirk, then hurried

to complete his task; there were far too many important people assembled in the area, and he did not want to do something that might inadvertently draw their attention. That would, he considered, be very bad for his real task.

Within a couple of minutes, and before anyone had left the Alpha Line Room, 'Joe Bob' vanished from the Core.

* * *

Echo raised an eyebrow, folded his arms, and stared at the Kochavi ambassador, sparing one long, VERY irritated glance for Daagnadan, who shrugged it off. Shocked, Romeo and India stood by, trying not to gape. Fox simply watched the interaction in silence, wearing his best Great Stone Face. After several moments of the big Agent silently staring her down, the ambassador backed off slightly, her body language relaxing just enough to indicate the fact.

"Your Excellency," Echo said then, "on what grounds, and what are the accusations against my WIFE?"

"Wife? I thought she was your partner," Isahuutob wondered, now puzzled.

"She is both," Fox explained. "Echo and Omega worked together for several years before deciding that they wanted to be espoused. They are legal, bonded mates. And very much in love."

Isahuutob rounded on Daagnadan, who flinched.

"You did not tell me that!" the ambassador declared. "That puts a completely different light on the matter."

"No, it does not," Daagnadan protested. "I was carrying on a very private...discussion...with Echo, when Omega interrupted and very rudely ordered me out of their quarters."

India and Romeo both dropped their jaws. Fox pressed his lips together, carefully hiding his displeasure.

"Dude!" Romeo hissed to Echo. "You had her in y'all's quarters? Jus' th' two of you? 'Thout Meg there? That's ASKIN' f'r trouble."

"No shit," India muttered.

"It is a very different situation," Isahuutob insisted to

Daagnadan. "You have, yourself, just referenced it as THEIR quarters! As his wife, and given they share their quarters as spouses, it was as much her home as his. She therefore had every right to be there, and to require you to leave. Especially if you were having such a 'very private discussion' with her mate, and she did not know about it in advance, nor approve it."

"She did not, and she did not," Echo confirmed, maintaining a formal diction in his replies. "In fact, it was not my idea, but Ms. Daagnadan's, that we meet there…after I spent nearly a full hour trying to find a venue acceptable to her to discuss BUSINESS. But Omega is ill, and she took sick leave to come home and rest. Once the—private, but innocuous—interaction with Ms. Daagnadan was over, my wife ended up vomiting— which she only does when she is either very ill, or extremely upset about…personal matters."

India scowled. Romeo frowned.

"Where is she now, Echo?" Fox asked, eyebrow raised in concern at that news.

"At home in bed, where I helped put her, with a barf bucket next to the bed, and a carafe of water and glass to sip from, to stay hydrated, on the nightstand," Echo replied, his tone slightly more casual with his superior, who would understand Omega's condition. "I've already let India know, as our department medic, that she tried to throw up, and she or one of the other physicians is going to follow up and check Meg for an intestinal virus or infection if she gets worse, or isn't better in the morning."

"Good," Fox noted. "Your Excellency, is there still a problem, in your estimation?"

"No," Ambassador Isahuutob replied. "I think not. Evidently there may be somewhat of a personal issue between my citizen and yours as yet, but no, there is no longer a diplomatic problem, and apparently never was. I was…misled." She glared at Daagnadan, who flinched again, and looked anywhere in the room but at the ambassador, Echo, or the glaring Alpha Two team.

"Then let us go back to my office and discuss a few matters, Your Excellency," Fox offered smoothly. "And...let me strongly recommend that your citizen go back to her quarters for now."

"Yes, and stay there..." Isahuutob glared at Daagnadan again, "but I shall want to discuss this with her later," the Kochavi ambassador added, by now practically staring holes through a flushing Daagnadan. "This little misunderstanding could have caused a diplomatic incident between our peoples — all because two females are vying for one male, when the male is already happily espoused to one of them. It will not do. This was entirely uncalled-for."

"Most certainly, but now is, perhaps, not the time," Fox said.

"Indeed. Ras Daagnadan, please return to your quarters at once, stay there, and await my summons," the ambassador ordered. "Director, attend me, please."

"Of course," Fox said, shooting a concerned glance at Echo as he followed the two Kochavi women out of the Alpha Line Room.

* * *

As soon as the trio left the room, Romeo went to the door and closed it, then joined a scowling India as she spun on the department chief...who also happened to be, along with his wife, one of her best friends, as well as 'siblings' in the adoptive family they had constructed.

"What the HELL is going on here?" she demanded. "You're telling me that you were ALONE in your quarters— the quarters you SHARE with MEG—with HER?" She jabbed a finger in the direction of the departing Kochavi women for antecedent. "And that Meg walked in on the two of you, and got so upset at what she saw that she threw up? What the HELL were you doing with that Kochavi bitch?"

"I was trying to advise her on the possibility of immigrating to Earth," Echo responded, curt. "Nothing more."

"That don't sound like somethin' that'd upset Meg,"

Romeo pointed out.

"Meg claims Ree was trying to kiss me, or some such shit," Echo replied with a shrug. "I think I'd have noticed if she had."

"You're kidding. You're calling your own wife a liar?" an incensed India demanded to know.

"No, not at all. I think she honestly thought she saw that," Echo said. "I just don't think she was at an angle to actually tell, and she was upset and not feeling good, so she read more into things than were really there."

"It still ain't smart, man," Romeo noted. "Ev'rybody knows the Kochavi bitch 'uz tryin' ta get her claws inta you when she first got back here—hell, tons o' people saw her glomp you in the Core! Frankly, dude, th' way she 'uz wrapped around you then 'uz almost obscene! At this point, even if nuthin' happened, if somebody sees you two comin' outta your quarters together, just you two, they gonna wonder what th' hell is goin' on."

"He's right, Echo," India agreed. "And Meg's not the type to go imagining things. If she thinks Daagnadan was trying to kiss you, chances are, she might have seen something you missed. Maybe you were looking the wrong direction, and Daagnadan tried to use that as an opportunity to plant one on you."

"That's what Meg said," Echo admitted reluctantly.

"Uh-huh," Romeo said knowingly. "Bitch still tryin' ta get 'er hooks inta ya, don't make no never-mind what Meg wants."

"What about what I want?" Echo grumbled.

Furious, India started to say something, but Romeo waved her off.

"You better be wantin' Meg," he retorted, annoyed. "You're married ta HER, not ta Miss Hoochy-Coochy."

An irritated Echo stalked off.

* * *

As a deeply annoyed Echo strode across the Core, with no particular destination in mind, Fox spotted him from the door of his office as the Director escorted the Kochavi ambassador out of it.

"Echo," he called. "A word, please."

Echo nodded, murmured a greeting in Kochavi to Ambassador Isahuutob in passing, and headed up the ramp to the Director's office.

"Thank you," Fox said. "Come on in and have a seat."

Silently Echo followed the order...which had been subtly couched as a request. Fox closed the door and moved to his desk chair. They sat and looked at each other for long moments.

"All right," Fox said with a sigh. "Let's start off with me in the role of Abba Fox."

Echo shrugged. "Okay."

"Is everything going well between you and Omega, or are the two of you having...problems?" Fox wondered. "And understand that I am not being nosy, but trying to help if help is needed."

"Not particularly, not that I know of," Echo noted. "Meg's jealous of my old girlfriend, because I'm trying to be friends with Ree, but other than that, I don't think we have an issue."

"Has it occurred to you, zun, that you'd be better off to maintain some distance with Nreefluvan, in order to make for an improved relationship with your wife? Turn the situation around and consider it that way: if she had an old lover show up unexpectedly, and was being very friendly with him despite your wishes — letting him interrupt your plans as a couple, trying to come between you — would you like it?"

"Uh," Echo grunted. "No, I wouldn't. I hadn't really thought about it like that."

"You might want to start," Fox suggested. "You'll be living with Omega the rest of your life, hopefully; Nreefluvan will be going home to Kochav when her D1-2 visa is up."

"Well, that's just it, Fox—the business Ree was wanting to talk to me about was about her immigrating to Earth, maybe with family. Moving here permanently."

"Uhn," it was Fox's turn to grunt. "I don't think that is at all wise. Not for Alpha One, at least. Perhaps if they move to another continent—maybe Europe, or Australia, or the like."

"No, she wants to live in the Big Apple."

"I'm likely to disapprove of that application."

"Why?"

"Like I said, Echo, for the sake of Alpha One," Fox explained. "If you want to have a good relationship with Omega going forward, I highly recommend putting—and keeping—some distance between yourself and your old girlfriends. This one, in particular. As a Kochavi, Nreefluvan has a very different view of relationships and...well, let us say, personal space and privacy...than most humans, and especially your very reserved wife. And, I thought, yourself, as well."

"Mm," Echo said, considering the matter. "I suppose you have a point. Better to keep Meg happy and not worry so much about repairing or restructuring the relationship with Ree."

"Exactly. And to that end, did anything happen this afternoon with Nreefluvan?"

"Not particularly, not that I noticed," Echo said with another shrug. "I took her to Alpha One's apartment, got a couple of drinks per her request—whisky; we found out the hard way that first night she was here, she doesn't handle bourbon well anymore, and she knows it, and didn't ask for it—I popped a DeTox tab, and we sat on the sofa and discussed the requirements for immigrating to Earth."

"I thought you were taking her to my little conference room."

"I thought I was, too," Echo said, exasperated. "But she wanted someplace less...how did she put it? Less cold and more comfortable, or something like that."

"Mm," Fox hummed. "That's...odd. Did you suggest your quarters?"

"No, she did. After first suggesting HER quarters. I nipped that one in the bud right off." He shrugged. "I figured the quarters I shared with Meg would be...safer."

"Mm. Even more suspicious. I think she is maneuvering you, alter khaver."

"How so?"

"I strongly suspect that she wants you back, and may be hoping to cut Omega out of your life to do it."

"Huh? Seriously?"

"Seriously, zun. You said you didn't notice anything. Did Omega?"

"Yeah," Echo sighed, beginning to grow concerned. "She thinks Ree was trying to kiss me as she came in. I didn't see it, 'cause I'd just spotted Meg outta the corner of my eye, and while my face was still turned to Ree, I was actually LOOKING at Meg." He shrugged. "I wouldn't have put up with it, if she really had tried, but I guess Ree doesn't know that."

"Damnation, argdug, and ragderfram," Fox cursed. "That is NOT good, zun. Not at all. Is Omega angry with you?"

"No, she trusts me—and told me so afterward. She wasn't remotely happy with Ree, though, and basically ordered her out of our quarters. And was prepared to physically throw her out, if necessary."

"And I don't blame her. And thence Nreefluvan went straight to her ambassador and filed a formal complaint by way of making as big a stink as she could, and attempting to get Omega into plenty of hot water."

"Apparently, yeah. But didn't tell the ambassador all the pertinent facts in the complaining."

"No. She weighted it toward her viewpoint, so the ambassador had a biased picture of matters. Isahuutob and I discussed that afterward, and she plans to watch that one pretty closely, I believe. She's up to something, zun, and I do seriously think it's what I said a minute ago—she wants you back, Omega be damned."

"Good luck with that," Echo said, raising an eyebrow. "I got a gal I'm happy with."

"Good. I'm glad to hear that," Fox said, "because now I have to put on my Director's hat."

"Um, okay."

"Zun, maybe you haven't considered the potential ramifications of what you did today..."

"Well, I didn't initially, 'cause that's just something I never had to bother about before, but I have now," Echo said, even more exasperated than before. "Between Meg almost reaming me a new one for not considering the ramifications, and 'siblings' India and Romeo hitting the roof just now, I know I screwed up and left myself open to gossip about Ree an' me gettin' it on or something. Even though it was nothing of the sort."

"Exactly, and good; I'm glad you're now aware of that," Fox said, relieved. "Because you cannot let gossip reflect poorly on you, if you hope to sit in this chair one day, zun. It's one thing to look for and finally find your life partner, your spouse, the love of your life — as you and I both have done, over the years — and another entirely to philander on that spouse. Or even APPEAR to do so. Especially when that spouse is your partner in the field. The former speaks to a heart; the latter, to a lack of judgement, honor, and honesty." He cocked his head. "You're a good mensch, zun. One that has already had his character unjustly besmirched in the last year. People—of any species—will gossip, as you've already seen; don't let them, or even give them an opportunity, if it's something you can avoid. You will find that sitting in this chair will go much, much better, if you follow my advice on this. The last thing you need is to discover a lack of trust — of YOU — among those who report to you." He shook his head. "It is next to impossible to lead under those circumstances. And believe me, I know — I've seen it in action. On other planets, granted, but still."

"All right, Fox," Echo sighed. "I already promised Meg. I'll promise you, too."

"Good. That way, I don't have to make it so much of an order: Stay away from Ms. Daagnadan, Echo."

"Oh," Echo said, blank.

Chapter 6

Leaving Fox's office with a good deal to think about, Echo headed back for the Alpha Line Room, to find Romeo working with India on the departmental applications. They both glanced up when he entered the room, then tucked their heads, avoiding his gaze. After pausing for a moment, gathering his thoughts, Echo headed straight for them.

"Hey guys," he said in a quiet voice. "Listen, uh, I'm really sorry I got annoyed. It's...well, it's like this: I'd only just gotten a reaming-out from Meg on the same thing, that ended not five minutes before I got to the Alpha Line Room. And then I caught it from Fox after I left y'all. I feel like a little kid that's been disciplined by the teacher, his mom, his dad…! Nothing happened, I swear, guys. I love Meg, and would never cheat on her. I guess I just wasn't thinkin', is all. I pulled a stupid, and I know it." He shrugged, then sighed. "Dammit."

"We apologize too, Echo," India said softly. "It's not our business, and we should have kept our mouths shut."

"Alla that," Romeo said, slightly shamefaced. "We jus' care a lot 'bout you two, thass all. But we shouldn't 'a said anything. It wadn't our place."

"No, it's okay," Echo sighed again. "That's what family is about. Besides, Romeo, you're number three in the department, right behind me an' Meg, and India, you're the department medic. If you see me going off in the weeds, either of you, you NEED to speak up. And I screwed up," he admitted. "I dunno what I was thinking, except I just sorta wanted to get whatever Ree wanted over and done with and get back to work."

"That makes a certain amount of sense, actually," India said, sighing herself. "Was she being...difficult?"

"I guess it depends on your definition of difficult," Echo decided, thoughtful. "She wasn't being easygoing, that's for sure. I tried, like, three other places before she told me to just go back to my quarters and us talk over drinks. An' I told her I didn't think it was a good idea, but she was kinda insistent." He paused, then added, "It was still a better option than going to HER quarters, which she suggested first."

"Ooo," Romeo said, eyebrows shooting upward. "So she IS tryin' ta get her hooks in ya."

"I dunno," Echo said, shrugging. "Yeah, I guess she is, sorta, now that I think over everything."

"I don't think there's any 'sorta' about it," India decided. "She IS trying. No ifs, ands, or buts."

"Damn, no wonder it bothers Meg." Echo shook his head.

"It would bother me, if she was doing shit like that to Romeo," India pointed out. "So I don't think Meg is being unreasonable at all. And I'd lay odds, if the situation was reversed, it'd bug the hell out of you, too, Echo."

"Okay, fair enough," Echo said, nodding. "I'll try to be more careful about this stuff. Evidently I've gotten used to Meg's politer, more respectful way of handling things, and I'm not always seein' Ree's shit. Never mind that I don't remember her being like this, back when, so I'm not expecting it. Y'all help me watch out for her crap, okay?"

"Deal," Romeo said, as India nodded with a smile.

"We'd be glad to help, however we can," India agreed. "Including diversions, if that becomes necessary. I just want us all to get along and not let some old girlfriend come between us. And that," she added, giving Romeo the stink-eye, "goes for all of us."

"Hey, girl, you got old boyfriends, too," Romeo retorted.

"Easy, y'all," Echo said with a laugh. "We all got skeletons in the closet of our past, I guess, one way or another. Hell, even Meg had an old boyfriend turn up—and now he's in the Agency, and looking to join Alpha Line!"

"And respects the hell outta you both," India added.

"Yeah, an' appears t' be gettin' along jus' fine with 'is own partner," Romeo observed. "I heard they went out on several dates already. So I don't think you got nuthin' t' worry about outta that, bro."

"No, I think you're probably right about that, junior," Echo said, considering. "Given that when I was 'mostly dead,' he was there, and he told me he offered to stay beside Meg, 'cause she was in a bad way, but she turned him down to flee...no, I think that's not any sorta factor in our marriage." He paused, then admitted, "But you're both right. And Fox is right, and Meg is right. Ree IS a factor. She's a problem. A big one, and getting bigger, I think. I'm just not sure how to handle it. I don't want to be rude, because of the diplomacy factor. I mean, look what she just did with the ambassador, for cryin' out loud! Plus, I was sort of hoping to shift the relationship into a friendship, but it doesn't seem to be going that way. Mostly, I guess, because SHE doesn't want it to go that way."

"Naw, man, that one? She flat dunno how t' take no f'r an answer. She done got dangerous to your an' Meg's marriage, I think," Romeo offered.

"Fox agrees with you."

"He does?"

"Yeah. He gave me some advice just now, and...I think it makes sense," Echo admitted. "I'm gonna try to go with it, anyhow. And yes, help would be very much appreciated. And India, I think 'diversions' might be really good, starting as soon as we can arrange 'em." He shrugged. "But for now, I guess we need to all get back to work, here. I know Ree's already taken up way the hell too much of MY time today...yet again."

"Good," India decreed. "Alpha Two is on the job, hon, and we have your back! But for now, we need to know, Echo—how do you want these applications divvied up? Romeo and I have been going over 'em, except we're not sure, based on where Meg was when I shipped her off home, exactly what it was she was doing with 'em..."

"Oh, right," Echo said, leaning over the stack of applications. "We adjusted the criteria for the individual categories, Meg an' me, a couple weeks back. Lessee here..." He flipped through the top half-dozen. "Oh, I see where she was going. Lemme

explain our current system, then I can show you..."
* * *

"Oh, hey, while you're here, I wanted to ask y'all if either of you has heard about the thing with the Sluuites," Echo said, once they'd settled into their respective activities.

"Uh, I guess not," Romeo said, "given I ain't got a clue what you're talkin' about."

"That makes two of us," India agreed. "What's up? What 'thing with the Sluuites'?"

"Oh, while I was talking with Ree, a Security agent came to the door and—"

"Oh shit," India murmured. "Did he see your old girlfriend? Do we already have rumors to deal with?"

"Uh, no," Echo said, feeling sheepish. "I stepped outside and she stayed inside, out of sight."

"Thass good," Romeo averred.

"Yeah. I had enough sense there, I guess," Echo sighed. "Anyway, it seems there's been a spate of vanishing Sluuites in the last week or two. Nobody's sure what's happening; they'll be on shift, working away, and then just stop checking in."

"What's th' locator beacons sayin'?" Romeo asked.

"That's just it — the beacons quit working about the same time the given Sluuite goes missing. Nobody can find them."

"That isn't good," India said. "Want us to look into it?"

"If you have time, maybe," Echo said. "Don't go full investigation on it; Security and, I gather the Field agents, are on it, and we don't want to usurp their place. Maybe ping 'em and suggest a few things, like asking the Deltiri Embassy to help out in tracking 'em, or find out how many are missing, if the Sluuite community is frightened, things like that."

"Sure thing, dude," Romeo said. "We'll tag up with some folks, see what we c'n find out. You got a point; we don't need th' offworld communities gettin' upset if it's got a simple explanation."

"Exactly," Echo agreed.
* * *

133

Within an hour or so, Romeo and India had finished sorting all of the departmental applications, and left on their routine patrol. Echo kept going on his own work, which involved some Division-wide items passed to him by Fox, and which they had already discussed. It was simply a matter of Echo going through and appropriately dispositioning each item, and sending it out for follow-through. Then he looked through the requisitions for departmental equipment, studying them and approving most of them.

After he had finished his shift, Echo headed home, anxious to see how Omega was doing.

He found her still sound asleep in bed, the carafe of water more than half-empty, the glass that formed the cap sitting beside it on the nightstand, a few milliliters of water inside.

I wonder if she really IS sick, he wondered, worried. *The good Lord only knows, she's had enough stress for four dozen people the last couple years—especially the last six months or so. Enhanced immune system or not, that's gotta tell on her, sooner or later.*

He put a light hand to her forehead, checking to see if she was feverish. But her skin felt comfortably cool, and at his touch, she stirred, then opened clear, sapphire-blue eyes. Echo nearly lost himself in them for a brief moment, before recovering his power of speech.

"Hi there," he murmured.

"Hi," she replied, groggy, voice little more than a whisper.

"How are you feeling, baby? Any better?"

"Yeah, I think so. Gettin' some sleep helped."

"Did you get sick again?"

"No. Felt like it for a little while after you left, but my tum finally settled, and I went to sleep."

"Good. Have you been asleep the whole time I was gone?"

"Pretty much, yeah. Woke up a time or two. Sipped some water. Rolled over and zonked back out."

"Hm. That means you haven't had anything to eat since breakfast, right?"

"Yeah."

"Want anything?"

"Dunno. Depends what, I guess."

"What about an omelet?"

"Whatcha gonna put in it?"

"What do you want me to put in it?"

"Jus' some cheese, I think. Mild cheese, at that."

"Swiss, maybe?"

"That..." she pushed up, seeming to consider the reaction of her belly, "sounds like it oughta work." She reached for the covers.

"What are you doing?" he wondered.

"Gonna come in there an' help fix dinner."

"Nope. My sick wife is gonna stay right here and rest. It won't take long to whip up an omelet with some cheese in it, and then I'll bring it in here for you, and we'll share it. I don't wanna risk you taking a turn for the worse, if you've picked up a nasty little buggum."

"Oh," Omega said, blonde eyebrows shooting up. "Which brings up another thought. If I'm comin' down with some sorta buggum, then you don't need to be sharing the omelet with me. I don't want you comin' down with this shit, too, all on 'counta we shared a meal. Alpha One has been out of th' office plenty enough in recent months; we don't need to both be in the bathroom barfin' our guts up, while Romeo an' the others have to cover for us AGAIN. Never mind I don't think the water closet is big enough for two people projectile-vomiting…let alone if it starts comin' out the other end, too!"

"Mmph. You have a point. Several, I guess. Well, I'll just make it like we were gonna share, then I'll cut it in two and put each half on different plates, 'stead of all on one plate, eatin' off opposite ends," Echo decided. "I can still eat with you if I bring a tray in here. We just won't eat off the same plate with the same flatware."

"Okay. 'At'll work."

"Now lay back down there and rest, while I ditch my jacket,

tie, and holsters, then I'll go whip up an omelet and maybe some toast an' stuff. Whatcha want to drink?"

"Jus' water, I guess. Maybe some 'a that electrolyte mix the Agency has, to go in it. Seems like it would taste good, which means I probably need it, you know?"

"Yup. That's doable. Mind if I have coffee? Or maybe a beer? I mean, the smell won't bother you or anything, will it?"

"No, I don't think so. Either one; whichever you want, I'm good."

"Okay." Echo rose from the bedside, moved to the armchair in the corner, and commenced divesting himself of the aforementioned items. "Aw, hell," he decided, "I think I'll just strip down and put on some lounging pants and a tee, then go cook."

"Works for me," came the voice from the bed. "Can I watch?"

Echo snorted a laugh.

"Sure, I suppose so," he agreed. "If you wanna."

"I wanna."

"And I like that you wanna."

"Good. Works well that way."

"It does."

* * *

Echo changed clothes with an intrigued wife-slash-partner spectating, then headed for the kitchen. In about twenty minutes he had returned with a tray containing two plates with part of a Swiss cheese omelet on each — not quite evenly divided — plus several slices of toast, a little tub of applesauce, and a tiny bowl of grape jelly. There was also a cup of coffee for him, and a glass of water with a packet of the Agency's special electrolyte drink powder for Omega alongside it. She pushed up, and Echo sat the tray down across her lap, then eased into a seated position on the bedside next to her.

"Try the toast first," Echo recommended. "That's on the B.R.A.T. diet, so it should sit okay on your tum, baby. And sip on the water."

"Okay," Omega said. "I guess, if some basic toast goes okay, I can try the jelly and the applesauce?"

"Right. Then, if all that does fine, nibble on the omelet. You'll notice I didn't give you quite half; more like about a third. You're welcome to have more if you can eat it—I'll just give you part of my piece—but I didn't want to stuff you, 'cause you might get nauseated again if I did. Anything you can't eat right now, I'll put in a stasis field and you can work on it again later."

"No, I get it, Ace, and thanks," Omega said, picking up a piece of the toast and nibbling.

"Go slow, now."

"Oh yeah."

* * *

Omega did take her time, but she polished off all the toast, the applesauce, and her share of the omelet, along with the jelly in there someplace, though Echo never knew when she ate it, as he was busy with his own dinner. It seemed to sit well on her digestive tract, and after a bit, she got up, wrapped herself in her robe, and wandered into the den to join him on the sofa.

"Wanna watch something on the TV?" he asked.

"Nah, I'm not in the mood," she sighed. "I think I just wanna sit here with you and...I dunno. Maybe read a book."

"I can go for that," Echo decided. "You want me to go get your current read off the nightstand?"

"Yeah, please do," Omega grumbled. "I didn't even think to grab it as I went by."

"Well, mine's on my nightstand, so I'd have to go in there anyway. It's no problem to grab yours, too."

"Okay. Thanks."

Moments later, he was back with both books.

"Here," he said, handing the book to her before sitting in the corner of the sofa and holding out an arm. "Stretch out on the couch, put your feet up, and lean back against me, baby. Just relax, snuggle in, and read your book. We're gonna have a nice quiet evening together, just us two, for a change. No fuss, no drama, just peace an' quiet."

"That sounds awful nice, Ace," Omega said, sighing once again, as she positioned herself against his torso and relaxed. Echo slipped an arm around her waist, helping to hold her still-tired body in position, then opened his own book and began to read, as Omega did the same.

They stayed there, quiet and content, until bedtime.

* * *

"You're kidding," Pudding, the Facilities department chief, said, staring at the agent across her desk. "ANOTHER one? We just had one disappear this morning!"

"I know, ma'am," the Facilities agent told her. "I'm just reporting what the shift ops personnel told me."

"Who is it this time?"

"Bobbeg Nelt. She was only about an hour from going off shift, too. Same scenario — she didn't check in on time, and when they checked her locator, it was offline and unresponsive."

"Shit." Pudding sighed. "What the hell is going on? How can these little guys get into so much trouble? Call out the search team…again."

"Yes, ma'am."

* * *

But Nelt was never found.

One slightly greasy spot in a corner of the Core seemed to have a Sluuite signature on it, but since it had already been partially cleaned, there was little that could be determined from it.

* * *

Once Echo and Omega went to bed—after another small plate of toast with applesauce for each of them—Echo gathered his wife close to his body and held her.

"There we go. Relax and just crash, baby. You've earned it."

"We're not gonna do anything else?"

"I don't wanna risk making you barf again, sweetheart. I think you need to just unwind, snuggle in, and zonk out."

"Aw."

Shush that, he told her through their bond, grinning. *I appreciate that your other appetites are still going strong, and I also appreciate that you want me for dessert, as it were. But you need to rest, baby. I felt bad enough this afternoon that you got upset and it made YOU feel bad enough to throw up. I don't want to have our lovemaking cause you to throw up. That's just not a good association. For either of us.*

Oh, Omega responded, seeming surprised. *Okay, yeah, I see what you mean. And yeah, I just had the toast an' applesauce, so there really IS something there to come up if I did get nauseated.*

Exactly. But given how long our nights are with a forty-eight-hour day, bedtime snacks are almost mandated. Not to mention midnight snacks, about half the time.

Yup, to alla that. Okay, I'll behave. Sorta. She reached over and patted a certain portion of his anatomy with affection, adding a slight tickling motion with her fingertips for good measure. *Okay, now I'll behave.*

A mildly-shocked Echo unexpectedly giggle-snorted at the tickling sensation in such a private area, then clapped his hand over his mouth to stifle the sound. Omega let out a howl of laughter and all but doubled up in mirth.

Echo grinned.

* * *

The next morning, when Omega woke, she felt considerably better.

Being snuggled close to Echo's body helped. Having his body spooned with hers, wrapped protectively around her, helped even more.

Breakfast was another cheese omelet with toast and jelly, and this time she tucked away fully half of the big egg dish, along with half the toast.

A quick shower, followed by dressing in a clean Suit, and Omega was at Echo's side when he headed for the Alpha Line Room.

* * *

The next day, 'Joe Bob' noticed that Agent Omega was back in the Alpha Line Room alongside Echo, and Daagnadan was once again reduced to showing up at least once a day to try to get Echo's attention.

Hm, he thought. *Something did not go right with the ambassador, I assume. That bodes ill, at least in my mind. Well, we shall see, I suppose. 'Gary' is not overmuch concerned about the situation, as he seems to have faith that the woman can do as she says, and this will end as desired. I will report to him tonight as per usual, and see what he says.*

* * *

Romeo and India had organized the applications the day before, sorting them into the various groups, so all Omega had to do that day was to run through them and determine which groups would go through qualification testing and which had not made the first cut. Then she had to pull emails and send form notifications to the two groups—one set received gently-worded but encouraging rejection notices, and the other set was given notice of when they were expected to present themselves for qual testing.

She had just sent out the rejection notifications when a bit of a scuffle made itself known at the door. Omega looked up, to see Romeo and India blocking Daagnadan's entry into the Alpha Line Room, even as Echo tucked his head and tried to look very busy.

"Hey, Nreefluvan," India said cheerily. "Listen, I was wanting to introduce you to my husband, here—my partner, Romeo. Romeo, this is Nreefluvan Daagnadan."

"Pleased t' meetcha," Romeo said, smiling, as he offered his hand.

"Likewise," Daagnadan said politely, taking his hand and shaking, as she tried to peer over his shoulder at Echo.

"Listen, Nreefluvan," India said, "I was wondering if you might want to go out to first lunch with us today; we'd like to get to know you a little better. Girlfriends are always good to have, you know?"

"Oh, um, well, that would depend," Daagnadan tried. "I... need to speak with Echo and Omega. Things...were not good yesterday."

"No, they weren't," Omega said, just loud enough to be heard across the big room, but sounding like an offhand, under-her-breath comment. Daagnadan flushed a slightly blue tinge.

"I wished to apologize," she said then.

"Been an awful lot of those lately, but shit still keeps happening," Omega retorted in the same just-loud-enough tone. Echo managed to damp down the eyeroll that threatened, and stifled a snort with an effort, managing to make it sound like he was clearing his throat.

"I'm pretty busy right now, Ree," Echo said then. "I appreciate the attempt at an apology, but it can wait. At the moment, I need to concentrate. Why don't you run on to lunch with Alpha Two, and Meg and I can discuss how to handle things with you later?"

"It...is not time for lunch yet," Daagnadan said, somewhat blank.

"True," Echo admitted.

"Maybe we can just sit here in the corner for a bit and talk, you and me," India suggested. "I know Romeo needed to run see about arranging some routine maintenance on a couple of our vehicles, so he can do that, and I'll keep you company, and we can get to know each other a little better, you and me. Then when Romeo gets back, we'll head off to lunch."

"Might Alpha One come, too?" Daagnadan wondered.

Echo shot a quick, querying thought at Omega, who responded with a decided, *NO.*

"No, Ree," Echo said, "I think we need to stay here and maybe order something in, today. Meg was out sick most of yesterday, so we're, uh, playing a certain amount of catch-up from yesterday in addition to the stuff that's going on today." Omega watched as Echo sent a quick, subtle series of signals to Alpha Two, indicating his appreciation for the work the other partnership had done, and noting that he was only offering an excuse to Daagnadan. India and Romeo both nodded ever so slightly, acknowledging the message.

"Oh," Daagnadan said, missing the coded communiqué, as they'd expected. "Um, I suppose that would be acceptable, then. Perhaps I can help?"

"No, it's pretty much classified information," Omega replied, somewhat curt.

"I see," Daagnadan said with a sigh. "Yes, India, thank you. I will accept your kind invitation. Let us sit here in the corner, while your mate does what is needed, and we can chat. And if Echo or Omega find the conversation...agreeable...they are more than welcome to join it. If they are not too busy."

"Of course," India said smoothly.

"Okay, baby, I'll be back soon," Romeo said, leaning over and kissing his wife before heading out to handle vehicle maintenance.

India and Nreefluvan settled down in chairs in the far corner of the Alpha Line Room as they began to chat quietly, finding out more about each other's backgrounds and interests.

* * *

Omega sighed to herself. *She just can't let us be,* she thought, trying to tune out the chatter in the far corner of the big room — which, at that moment, was not nearly big enough to suit her. *Just can't let ECHO be—because that's who she's after. I'm in the way, and she knows it, and I know it, and she knows that I know it...and doesn't care.*

Having finished the rejection notifications, she concentrated on scheduling the testing. By the time she had a decent schedule built, however, she felt the twinges of yet another headache coming on, even as a whiff of something bittersweet reached her conscious awareness.

Ugh, it's that perfume Nreefluvan wears, Omega thought, rubbing her temple. *I really wish she'd find something else to wear. I think I must be allergic to it or something. I was doing fine until she came in, and now all I can smell is that stuff,* *and...*She paused, rubbing her temples. *And being irritated at her single-minded fixation on Echo doesn't help. At. All.*

Oh well, she decided. *India, bless her, will have the bitch gone for a while soon, and maybe then I can get rid of this headache and get some actual work done.*

Just then, Romeo returned, and the two women stood.

"Echo, are you sure you—and Omega, of course—will not join us for first lunch?" Daagnadan asked.

"No, Ree, y'all go on," Echo said, casting a swift, considering glance at Omega, and she wondered if he had caught the fact that Omega's invitation was an after-the-fact addendum. "We have too much to do to go out right now."

"Very well."

And the trio were gone.

"Thank the good Lord," Omega sighed, once they were out of earshot. "I think I figured out what the problem has been with my gut, at least yesterday."

"Oh? What?"

"I think I'm allergic to her perfume," Omega explained. "I was doing fine until she came in, and then, when her fragrance got to me, I got another sick headache."

"Ooo. That's not good. Can you take something for it?"

"I'm gonna try," Omega said, digging in the specialized first-aid kit kept in the Alpha Line Room, looking for a dolocet and some sort of antihistamine. "We'll see if it helps. Doesn't it bother you?"

"I guess I don't notice it, no," Echo said. "Maybe it's your hyped-up senses, baby."

"I suppose it is," Omega said, downing the medications with a swallow of cold coffee. "Ugh. I need some fresh coffee."

"Dump it and make some more. How are the applications coming?"

Omega stood and moved to the pod brewer; a departmental request had recently ensured a tiny wet-bar sink had appeared beside the credenza where the brewer lived, courtesy of Facilities, and she dumped the cold, stale coffee into the drain, rinsed the cup, and popped in a fresh pod of coffee, hitting the <brew> button.

"There," she said. "Um, applications. It's coming along. I got the rejection emails out. I always hate to do that..."

"Yeah, I know what you mean."

"And I just did finish the testing schedule, 'bout five minutes ago," Omega continued. "Now I can run the spreadsheet through the automated email system and send out the testing times for the applicants we're considering. I'm sure glad we finally got THAT system worked out. It speeds things up amazingly."

"Yeah, it was starting to be a pain in the ass, doing it manually."

"Yup. So I'll start doing that as soon as I get some more coffee in me. Speaking of getting stuff in me, it IS time for first lunch. What do you want to do?"

"Uh, maybe we can get an order from the deli again? Will that work with your gut and the sick headache?"

"Probably, yeah. Maybe a cheese plate or a fruit salad. Or both. Something mild, but with some protein. I'm hungry despite the sick headache."

"Okay, let's do that. 'Cause I just got in a buncha stuff from Fox that he needs done, in my capacity as Assistant Director, and I'm trying to sort through it. An' there's a damn lot of it."

"Anything I can help with?"

"I dunno yet. But I think I'm gonna see about getting your security upgraded to something approximating Directorial levels, Meg. You're my exec, as it were, and Fox has Lima and Bravo, and they have near-Director security levels, so it only makes sense. And it means there IS something at that level, too! So I'd like you to be at least at their level, so you can help me the way they help him."

"Okay, I'm game. I wanna help, if I can."

"I'll talk to Fox about it and see what we can work out with Security."

"Yell if I need to do something in all that."

"Right. You probably will, but I dunno what, yet. I'll find

out and let you know."

"Okay."

Omega got her steaming mug from the brewer and moved back to her desk, while Echo placed an order for delivery with the deli down the street, then pinged Fox about her clearance level.

* * *

That night, in his little corner of the sub-basement, 'Joe Bob' got out a special device, hidden under the bed.

It was not of human make, this device, nor yet that of any race in the Pan-Galactic Coalition.

That said, there were many worlds in the Milky Way Galaxy that were not part of the Coalition, and who had very sophisticated technology. It was arguable, however, whether it belonged to any of them.

He activated the device and spoke into it.

He did not speak English. Or any other Earth language.

('Gary', this is Arg. Do you read?)

(Arg, 'Gary' here. What is your report?) came the reply.

(Echo took the female into his quarters yesterday, as I mentioned. They were there for some time, for they were still inside when I perforce had to leave that floor to continue my cover task. Later, the female brought her ambassador to Echo's office, along with the Director. I thought this boded well, as the ambassador was demanding imprisonment for Omega. However, today Omega was back at her desk near Echo, the two of them working as usual, and the female is once again visiting their shared office daily. I think perhaps the ambassador's visit did not go as anticipated, and our agent has had to regroup.)

(That sounds probable. She is resourceful, however. Give her time. I have little doubt but that she can do as she says.)

(And if not?)

(If not, then you may kill her and dispose of the body as you deem appropriate; you are well positioned there to do so, in any event, and the incinerator may prove useful once more. I will handle matters here.)

* * *

The next morning after Alpha Line's departmental meeting, Omega went down to the medlab to see about getting some antihistamines, thinking that maybe that would help her reaction to Daagnadan's choice of personal fragrance. The generic antihistamine — it was an Earth over-the-counter brand, so it wasn't at galactic pharmaceutical levels — hadn't done a lot of good, but had at least abated the worst of the nausea.

"Ooo. I getcha. Yeah, that sure coulda done it, all right," Zebra said, writing out a prescription for a specific medication on her tablet, then popping it over to Agent Prep in the pharmacy, once Omega had finished explaining matters. "Some offworld perfumers use some junk in their formulations that we'd think was downright damn weird. I guess Earth perfumers do, too, when you get down to it — I mean, let's face it, verdigris is a component of whale poop. Then there's the other stuff. Anal secretions? POOP extract?! But at least that shit — literally! — is compatible with our biochemistry, even if it seems disgusting; some of the offworld stuff — which, for some reason, follows the same pattern of disgusting shit — is definitely NOT compatible! And as a consequence, not all of it is good for a human system. Yours in particular, I expect, due to…the way you are."

"Yeah, that's kinda what I suspected," Omega agreed, accepting the addendum without rancor. Zebra was, after all, one of her dearest friends, a member of the 'family,' and had made it obvious she was tiptoeing around the subject of Omega's 'enhancements' so as not to hurt her. "So you think a good galactic antihistamine will help the situation?"

"It should," Zebra averred. "It might take a while — anywhere from a couple days to a couple weeks — to kick in to the degree you need it by now, though, 'cause you've been exposed to it for several days already, here. So try to be patient, and realize you'll still have symptoms until it does, so you'll have to grit your teeth and wait it out. But it should help. Meanwhile, if you're willing, I can shoot you up with something that oughta do the trick right off, until the new med kicks in. It's a fairly new medication that we don't have in pill form yet, so it HAS to be injected."

"Good," Omega said, offering a smile to her personal physician and sometime-stepmom. "That'll work. And thanks. I flatly did NOT feel at ALL well, the other day."

"Uh-huh, an' if this is what caused it, I'm not surprised in the least," Zebra said, getting out an osmosive hypo syringe and a little bottle of a specific drug. "Between that, and Echo's old girlfriend behaving a little TOO friendly, and all the other shit India told me about, hey. I'd be feeling pretty damn rough, too, honey. You have my sympathy, and Fox's, too, for that matter. So I'm sure you'll be glad to know that Zarnix and I discussed some stuff in detail, he feels the same, and we've decided we are holding off on doing ANY more testing of any sort on you until you get back on an even keel. However long that takes. I mean, if you get well and truly sick, all bets are off; we gotta get you well, after all. But we're putting a temporary moratorium on further baby-making tests. And it has an indefinite time limit. We're going to have to all get back together and determine to start it up, before it starts up — and that 'all' means you, too. You'll have to specifically tell us you're ready to resume."

"Oh BOY does that help," Omega confirmed, as she removed her Suit jacket and rolled up her sleeve to allow Zebra to inject the medication. "If Echo an' I can manage to get 'Ree-ree' off the planet, I can unwind a bit, maybe take an extra day off to relax, snooze, soak in the hot tub with a book an' a glass of wine, generally kick back some. And that should get me back to something approximating normal, I think. Then we can start the testing back."

"That'll work," Zebra agreed, as she injected the medication. "Meanwhile, we have plenty of data to analyze, so it isn't like it puts a hold on the work, after all. So listen up, honey, on this," she tapped the now-empty syringe, just before she dropped it in the medical waste receptacle, "I'll want you to come back each morning for the next, oh, week. I suspect it's gonna take that long, at least, for the antihistamine to really grab hold and start working, at least based on your personal biochemistry, and you'll want this to help you fight off the effects of the shit in the Kochavi gal's perfume. Which means we'll have to maintain a consistent blood level of the medication in your system, while the OTHER medication's blood levels get up to snuff. So if you can, just pop in here before you go to your office, and we'll take care of matters. I'll run the medscanner over you to help me determine dosage, then pop a shot into your other shoulder, and alternate shoulders each day until the pills kick in properly. We're talking five minutes; maybe up that to fifteen if I have to tweak a dosage. It'll take longer for you to walk down here than it'll take me to do what needs doing, so it isn't gonna be a big hit to your day."

"Okay, yeah, I can do that," Omega said. "I'll just let Echo know, and we'll work things around it. It'll be way the hell better than me having to go home sick every other day."

"Good. And yeah, it will. See you tomorrow, then. Go get the pill script from Prep, and go ahead and take one."

"Once daily, or twice?"

"Today, twice — morning and evening. So, right now, and again before bed tonight. After that, just once a day, at whatever time works best for you."

"Got it."

"Get outta here, then, kiddo."

"Gone!"

And Omega headed for the in-house pharmacy.

* * *

In the Alpha Line Room, Echo worked alone on the various tasks a leader of Alpha Line had to do: he had several requisitions of equipment to review and approve, then route to the appropriate channels to see it ordered, a couple more department applications to add to the current batch, a departmental report to compile and fire at Fox, and a couple of items Fox had bumped down to him as the Assistant Director. He was hard at work on the departmental report, having handled the equipment requisitions and the applications, when a soft fragrance dimly caught his conscious awareness. He looked up.

"Hello, Echo," Nreefluvan said with a soft smile, as she approached his desk. "I hope I am not disturbing you. This will only take a moment."

"I really wish you wouldn't do this, Ree."

"Do what?"

"You created enough of a ruckus for twelve people, bringing in the ambassador like that, the other day. Fox was NOT happy, and he doesn't want me having anything to do with you now. And I'm sure you know that, after he and the ambassador were done! Yet you keep coming by to see me."

"Oh, surely not," Daagnadan protested, seeming taken aback. "We are old friends, you and I. What can Fox possibly have against my visiting with you?"

"You've caused some major problems, Ree, like it or not," Echo pointed out. "What do you want now?"

"We never finished discussing my emigrating to Earth," she noted. "I was hoping to finish that, so I can get the paperwork under way…hopefully, with your help in doing the paperwork."

"No. Way," Echo said flatly. "I'll send you to Sugar, but I can't afford to be seen working that closely with you right now. Fox would have my hide, even if Omega didn't. And both of 'em would be fully justified in doing so."

"Well…" Nreefluvan paused to think. "Perhaps we can meet away from the Headquarters building? It should not be too hard, nor take too long."

"I really don't think I should."

Dimly, Echo became vaguely aware of a sweet, almost heady, fragrance wafting about his old girlfriend, drifting around him. *That must be the perfume Meg's talking about, that she's so allergic to,* he thought. *Hm. She can't stand it, but it smells really nice to me. I like it a lot. Maybe not quite as good as Meg's, of course. Then again, it isn't giving ME sick headaches, either…which seems…kinda weird, to me. Oh well. Must be Meg's odd biochem, maybe. Which could also explain why it smells different to her.*

"Please?" Nreefluvan pleaded. "I need your help to know how best to handle matters, Echo."

"Oh, all right," he said in exasperation. "It's against my better judgement, though."

"Oh good! Maybe we could meet in the deli and have something to nibble while we talk?"

"No, that's too close to Headquarters and frequented by too many agents," Echo demurred. "Word would get back to Fox and I'd be in hot water before you could sneeze. Let me think…oh! I know where we can go. There's a relatively new coffeeshop over on Bedford, between 8th and 9th Streets. It's several blocks away, kind of 'behind' Headquarters and not on any of the main drags, so it's not usually used by Agency personnel, but it's easy to find — go up Division Avenue to Bedford, turn left, and it's a block and a half down, on the right."

"Bedford is the intersection before you reach the deli, correct?"

"Yeah. Across from the traffic triangle, as it were."

"Oh, yes, I know now. All right. What time?"

"Let me get back to you on that. I need to see what Meg's schedule looks like before I can set a time."

"I…do not think she should be there," Nreefluvan said, hesitant. "I do not think she likes me."

"I don't think you're giving her any kind of a real chance to even try," Echo pointed out. "We're protective of each other, Meg and me, and a little possessive of one another, and she's not happy about some of your culture's…habits."

"She thinks I am too close to you."

"She does, yes. Given that I'm not married to you, but to her, she definitely thinks that. And, by human lights, she has every right to think that."

"Well, for now, then, let us do this very quietly, just the two of us," Nreefluvan suggested. "I think we can have matters worked out in a few days, if we meet each day for a few minutes. I do not wish to upset her any more than she already is."

"…Okay," Echo agreed, trying not to sound exasperated. "But I'm only doing this because of old times' sake, Ree. And I'm not entirely thrilled about going behind Fox's and Meg's backs to do it. You're asking an awful lot of me, and you need to realize that."

"I understand. I will keep things brief."

"I still need to figure out Meg's schedule," Echo pointed out. "If I'm to meet you without her knowing, I can't just get up and walk away from my desk."

"Oh. Yes, I see," Nreefluvan said, thinking. "Well, contact me when you can. You have my personal communications device contact now, after we met yesterday — I did give it to you, did I not?"

"Yeah, I have it in my phone now."

"Good. If you can meet me today, all well and good. If not, perhaps tomorrow?"

"I'll see what I can do, but I can't promise," Echo said, then waved her toward the door. "Get outta here, before somebody sees you. And try to look put out, like I fussed and told you to let me alone."

"All right."

* * *

Omega swung by the medlab pharmacy to pick up her antihistamines, feeling a little better about her ability to handle matters as long as she could end the malaise produced by Daagnadan's perfume. "Hey, Prep," she said as she approached the dispensary window.

"Hey, Omega," Prep greeted her with a smile. "Yeah, hang on; I saw your allergy 'script come through and filled it myself, just a little while ago. Lemme go grab it."

"Okay, thanks," she replied, smiling back. Prep disappeared into the back of the pharmacy, then came out with a vial of pills.

"Here you go. This oughta make you feel better, based on the info Zee put on the script. Some of those offworld fragrances can just play hell with human biology."

"Yeah, and it has been," Omega decreed, accepting the vial he proffered. "I'm glad to have this. I've felt kinda under the weather in recent days."

"Well, I can't say as I blame you," Prep said, then leaned forward and murmured conspiratorily, "especially if the gossip I've heard is any indication. Echo didn't really take his old girlfriend back to your joint quarters for a 'visit,' did he? Tell me it's just baseless rumor, please."

Omega felt the blood drain from her face.

* * *

Echo was once more working busily on the last of the departmental report when Omega arrived in the Alpha Line Room.

"Hey, baby," he greeted her, glancing up from his computer display. "Was Zebra able to help?"

"Yeah, I think it's gonna help," Omega informed him. "Turns out this sorta thing isn't that unusual; some of the offworld perfumers use chemicals that don't work well with human biology. I got a prescription for a special antihistamine, an' that's already filled and in my pocket, with the first dose down the hatch. She said it'd take up to a couple weeks for it to really kick in and get rolling, though, so in the meantime, she's giving me daily shots of a special, fast-working antihistamine-thingie to try to cut through my body's reactions until I have enough of the pills in my system to start doing the job. Something about 'sufficient blood levels' to take care of things."

"Oh?" Echo said, turning to follow her as she moved past him and sat down at her desk. "How often do you have to have these shots?"

"Only once a day," Omega told him. "I'm supposed to go back every day for a week, 'bout eight-thirty in the 'morning' D1 time, so she can get readings on me and give me the shot. I'll probably just go straight down there when I leave our quarters in the morning, until this is over and I'm not reacting to Nreefluvan's perfume any more. Which will be a relief."

"Gotcha. Eight-thirty every morning for the next seven days. Do we need to adjust the department meeting to allow for it? Maybe shift it later?" Echo turned to log the series of appointments on his computer's calendar app.

"We've been having it at ten, right? Shifted back an hour from when we used to have it?"

"Yeah, ever since we opened the other Office branches. Helps 'em with the time zone differences an' meshes up better for most of the Offices. It's still not great for a couple of 'em, but it's better than it was, at least."

"Right. I think that'll be fine; it won't take that long to do all this. Maybe a quarter of an hour in the lab, plus down there an' back. Total of around half an hour, ish. I'll be back in the office in plenty of time for the department meeting."

"That'll work, then. Okay." He hit a few keystrokes. "There, I got it in my calendar. We're good, here, Meg."

"Well, on that," Omega said, drawing a deep breath and letting it out in a sigh. "Not so much on other things."

"What do you mean?" Echo turned back around to face her.

"I mean, the gossip problem I was afraid of seems to have surfaced," she told him.

"Huh?" Echo cocked his head in confusion.

"I mean," she tried again, "Prep down in the pharmacy had heard that you and your old girlfriend were in our place by yourselves." Omega's voice was slightly sharp. "The gossip has begun, and people apparently aren't happy about it. Especially given we're barely six months out from our wedding."

"Uh-oh," Echo murmured.

* * *

"…No, it's okay, Meg, I swear," Echo explained. "Yeah, she made a big stink with the ambassador, who then got pissed at her when she found out what really happened. I'm sure there was some gossip about it, 'cause the ambassador was in what Madrid calls 'grand high dudgeon' pretty much all the way across the Core — twice; once from the elevator to Fox's office, then from his office over here. Then, arguably, back to Fox's office again, I suppose. But Fox is gonna help scotch things, and so is Alpha Two. Just like you told Prep, Ree was being…difficult…and I was trying my damnedest to be diplomatic. Never mind getting her outta sight before she pitched some sorta snit fit. Damn, she was pissed about all the interruptions. And then she went and pitched a snit fit anyway, and got the ambassador involved in it. But yeah. Believe me, baby, it's gonna be all right."

"Okay, Ace," Omega said, offering him a slight smile. "And of course I believe you. And I'm glad we have Fox, India, and Romeo on our side of things." She paused, then her eyes widened. "Oh! That's why they intercepted her yesterday and dragged her off for a long lunch!"

"Exactly," Echo confirmed, nodding. "It'll be okay with that trio on the matter. Plus us, troubleshooting every chance we get. And if we can make it obvious in public that she IS being difficult, so much the better. It'll be fine, Meg, I swear."

"Yeah, you're right. It will." Omega nodded, obviously relieved. "Okeydoke, lemme see what we have, here, and get my butt to work." She turned back to her desk and woke her virtual keyboard.

"Right," Echo said, picking up his cell phone and sending a text message.

* * *

Ree, this is Echo.

Hello, Echo. Do you have a time worked out?

Yeah, if you can meet me at that coffeeshop around 8:30 D1 each morning, I think I can shake loose for maybe twenty minutes or so for the next week.

Yes, that sounds good. I believe I can do that. Starting tomorrow?

Yeah, starting tomorrow.
I need to work out one thing, then we're good.

> *Please work out that thing, then.*
> *I look forward to seeing you.*

Well, thanks, but it's no big deal.

> *It is, to me.*

You damn well better appreciate it, then.
And behave yourself.

> *I will.*

* * *

Golf, this is Echo. Please respond as soon
as it's convenient.

> *Go, Boss. We're just on patrol,*
> *and Easy's driving today.*

OK. Can you and Easy stay about an hour
late on your shift for the next week?

> *Sure thing, Echo. What's up?*
> *Is something wrong?*

No, Meg just has some allergy stuff going,
and Zebra is trying to treat it. That's part
of what's made her sick the last couple days.
So we wanted to kind of try to get it under
control. Zee's got some special shots for Meg.

> *Oh, right. Not a problem, Echo. You need*
> *us to handle the department meeting, or are*
> *you gonna get Romeo to do it?*

Neither. I'll be back in the office in plenty of time for the department meeting, and Meg will likely be there soon after me. We got that covered, no prob.

For how long?

About a week. Maybe more, maybe less. Depends on how Meg responds to the meds.

OK no big. Consider it done, then.

Thanks. Solves a scheduling prob for me.

That's what we're for.

* * *

Half an hour later, Echo had the departmental report finished, and sent it to Fox.

Omega took the handful of new applications for Alpha Line membership from Echo, and started folding them into the rest of that cycle's batch.

Chapter 7

The next morning, Echo and Omega got ready for work together like they always did since marrying, and headed out together. But upon reaching the Core in the elevator, they went in separate directions. Omega headed for Medical…

…And as soon as she was out of sight, Echo headed for one of the least-used rear exits, making sure to raise a rudimentary telepathic block as he went.

* * *

Aha, 'Joe Bob' thought, as he watched Echo slink out of a rear entrance to Headquarters, having already seen Daagnadan exit the same way. *Matters have accelerated, I believe. This looks like an assignation of some sort.*

'Joe Bob' resumed gathering trash. A little Sluuite scuttled by, and he tossed it a particularly good tidbit of food from the bag he was tying shut. It caught up the bit, tasted it, and called a high-pitched thanks. Then it turned to go.

But before it could get far, 'Joe Bob's' very large foot came down on it, hard. The Sluuite was dead in an instant, crushed beneath the much larger being's weight.

'Joe Bob' picked up the body and took a bite.

Mm, he decided. *Nice snack.*

Moments later, there was little left of the poor Sluuite. Even the greasy spot on the floor had been carefully cleaned away by the wipes and spray cleaner the janitor kept on his cart.

* * *

Nreefluvan was already there, waiting for Echo in the café. She was seated in a little corner booth, and had already ordered coffee and a danish for him. She was, herself, leisurely sipping a latte while nibbling on a slice of quiche Lorraine.

"All right, Ree," he said, easing into the opposite side of the booth, "let's get started. I need to get back before I'm missed, or there'll be hell to pay."

"Of course, boopy," she said with a smile.

Echo didn't even notice.

* * *

He was back in the Alpha Line Room, handing over to Golf and Easy, well before anyone else was about. They left, and Echo sat down at his desk and began going through his email, dumping some things to the printer and dispositioning others.

About fifteen minutes later, Omega came in.

"Hi, Ace," she sang cheerily.

"Hi, baby," Echo responded with a smile. "How'd it go?"

"Pretty well, I think," she decided. "Zebra said I should start feeling better soon. If I don't, then it might be something else, and after about a week of this, if it's not helping, I should come back down and let 'em scan me more thoroughly. What I definitely don't have is a bug of any sort — bacterial, viral, fungal, or other."

"Well, that sounds promising," Echo concluded, after a moment to consider. "And I'm glad it isn't an infection or something nasty like that."

"Yeah, me too."

"Okay, ready to get to it?"

"Yup!"

"All right. I popped you some requisitions that have come in that I'd like your input on, so take a look at those. Oh, and Fox likes the idea of you having the same level clearance as the Boys, but he needs to present a rationale, because it isn't OUR Security department that has to approve it, it's the Security department at the PGLEIA top level — you know, Chief Wux's people — so be thinking about that. Start setting down our rationales for doing it around your other stuff, if you can. I'll put down my thoughts on it, too, and then we can consolidate when we're done."

"Okay."

"Oh, and there have been a couple of specific requests for training on certain items; one of the team members over in Hong Kong managed to sprain an ankle pretty badly on a recent foot chase — you remember how hilly it is, once you're away from the coast — and they need some workarounds in the gym, while it heals."

"Ouch."

"Yeah. But since you're the training guru for the department, they want your feedback to go along with the physical therapist. So they're asking for the appropriate routines to keep the rest of 'em in fighting shape, while allowing the ankle to heal up properly."

"Oh geez. Okay, I can do that…"

* * *

A notification came in later that morning to Fox from Facilities that another one of the Sluuites on the staff had gone missing.

"Huh," Fox murmured, studying the report. "Gesstun Sish reported at the beginning of his shift, started work, then disappeared partway through. He never came back at the end of his shift, and his locator beacon just stopped working. That's… odd. The Sluuites, being small, well, I made sure there was an accounting procedure so nobody got lost or accidentally hurt or whatever, when I brought 'em on to help. They're so small, if one got incapacitated someplace, we'd never find 'em in time to help."

Fox nibbled at his lower lip, thinking.

"I think I'm going to talk to Crutch and see if she has anyone to recommend who can look into this in more detail. I'm thinking it doesn't bode well for Gesstun, but we need to get onto it fast, just in case. With this being the fifth Sluuite reported to me as missing, we have to do something."

He hit the intercom button.

"Lima here, Boss-Daddy."

Fox snorted despite himself.

"Hello, zun. I need for you to get me Crutch as soon as possible. We may have an injured Sluuite somewhere in Headquarters, and we'll need a team to sweep the facility, looking."

"Ooo, right. Who is it?"

"Gesstun Sish."

"Oh damn! He's a great guy!" Lima exclaimed, dismayed. "I'll get on this right away!"

"Thank you, zun."

* * *

Later that morning, a little while before first lunch, Daagnadan showed up in the Alpha Line Room again.

She moved to the front, fished one of the disposable cups from the stack that Echo silently got from the cabinet and sat beside the pod brewer, and made herself a cup of coffee, adding lots of cream and sugar as she preferred it.

Then she moved to the middle of the room, sat down, and waited.

Omega and Echo exchanged puzzled glances, but said nothing, either verbally, or through the nd't'lq.

Half an hour later, India rushed in.

"Oh damn, Ree, I'm so sorry I'm late," she exclaimed. "With it being our day off, Romeo decided he wanted to reorganize some stuff in our quarters, and it ran longer than I figured it would."

"That is quite all right, India," Daagnadan offered with a smile. "You had not contacted me to tell me you could not, so I fully expected that something had simply delayed you."

"Exactly," India said, returning the smile, before shooting a surreptitious apologetic glance at Echo and Omega. "So, are you ready for lunch and some shopping in Manhattan?"

"I think so! It sounded very fun when you proposed it!"

"Let's go, then!"

The two women headed out.

* * *

As soon as they were out of sight and earshot, Echo turned to Omega.

"How are you doing, Meg?" he wondered.

"Hm?" Omega said, looking up from where she worked on the justification for her security clearance upgrade.

"Your head and your tum," Echo elaborated. "Ree-ree was

just here for an extended time. How are you feeling?"

"Uh," she said, understanding. She paused, assessing. "Okay, I think. No headache, and no upset stomach, at least for now. Oh, I'm not happy that she showed up here, but she didn't bug you this time, and I guess it IS a reasonable location to meet an Alpha Line Agent, even if it's for a social activity." Omega shrugged. "I can't complain, I guess."

"Good," Echo said, mildly surprised, but pleased. "It looks like the new meds are working. And maybe soon things will take care of themselves."

"What do you mean?"

"Well, Fox isn't happy with Ree these days. Not with all the problems she's caused. Even if Ree submits an application to immigrate — which I know, sure for certain, she's got in work — I seriously doubt he'll approve it."

"Oh," Omega said, sitting up straight. "Really?"

"That's what he said the other day, anyhow. I doubt he's changed his mind since then."

"That's some good news, then."

"I suppose it is, yeah. So hang onto that, baby. This, too, shall pass. It may pass like a damn rock of a kidney stone, but it'll pass."

They laughed.

* * *

Late that day, Crutch hobbled into Fox's office on her cane.

"What's the word, old friend?" Fox asked, looking up from his computer work, then turning to face her.

"Not good, I'm afraid," Crutch said with a sigh. "Nab and I put three teams on the search for the missing Sluuite this time, then started adding to the search as the day went on. We didn't find Gesstun Sish anywhere. We think we found some genetic traces — I hesitate to call it DNA, because Sluuites don't have the same genetic structures as humans, but you know what I mean — in one of the back-entrance lobbies..."

"That sounds promising," Fox said. "Maybe we can at least find out what happened to him?"

"Not really," Crutch said, throwing up her hands. "Evidently Joe Bob had already been through on his cleaning rounds, and…"

"Ah," Fox sighed. "Most of whatever evidence would have been there got obliterated. Just like all the others."

"Judging by the cleaning chemical residues, yes. It seems our efficient janitor is a little TOO efficient for our purposes, here."

"Shit, farkakte, argdun, abdab, and gronk," Fox cursed.

"That's — what? — the fourth Sluuite to go missing in the last week?" Crutch wondered.

"Fifth," Fox noted. "Our Sluuite cleaning team is starting to get well past frightened. And frankly, I can't say I blame them. I'm seriously considering putting a moratorium on Sluuite cleaning until we get this little mystery figured out."

"I think that's a plan, Fox," Crutch agreed. "If I were you, I'd go forward with it, effective this next shift."

"Mm. I think I agree with you," Fox said, turning back to his virtual keyboard. "Hold on a second, while I get that under way."

"Standing by," Crutch said with a slight chuckle. Fox shot her a grin, then resumed typing. After several moments he looked back up.

"There," he said. "I just curtailed all Sluuite operations anywhere in Headquarters, and verified that there are still no disappearances at other facilities…"

"Which means something's going on here, and only here."

"Right, and I've asked them to please voluntarily confine themselves to their quarters for their safety," Fox added. Just then, a series of dings went off, and he turned back to the viewscreen to check it. "Ah. Excellent. They've all responded back in the affirmative, and there are several heartsfelt thanks, into the bargain. Poor little guys have been running scared, and I don't blame 'em a bit."

"Neither do I," Crutch agreed. "Never mind that I've devoted more and more agent-power to the investigation into what's happening."

"Should we bring in some Alpha Line people to help out? Some of those folk have some specialized skills that could help…"

"At this point, I wouldn't complain, if they're available," Crutch admitted. "Nab and I had so many teams on it this afternoon, we didn't have a full slate for our usual patrols."

"Damn. Yes, I'll call Echo and Omega and see if they can throw some people at it."

"Copy that, and thanks," Crutch said. "Anything else I can help with?"

"Not at the moment, not unless you've developed a liking for budget analysis."

"Oh HELL no," Crutch declared with a snort. "I do not envy you that task in the least."

"Are you sure, meyn khaverte? There were murmurs, when I named Echo as my successor, that I should have named you instead. We talked, you and I, and I had understood you didn't want the position, but if that was wrong, or if you've changed your mind…" Fox held out his hands in invitation. "I would certainly understand. And perhaps there might be something we can do…"

"No, we're fine, Fox," a calm Crutch stated. "I am where I want to be, and I don't want your position, and there isn't enough money in the whole damn galaxy to convince me to swap places with Echo. I like being den mother to a buncha field agents."

"Ha! And they love having you there," Fox chuckled. "You and Alpha One are, I think, the most beloved agents in the whole place."

"Add yourself in there, and I'd agree with you," Crutch said with a smile, before reaching for her cane. "All right. I'll get back to my desk and pop you the formal report on what we do have on the missing Sluuites, and you can ping Alpha One and see who they can add to the investigation."

"Right. At this point, it probably won't be until tomorrow,

but hey."

"Yup. When you have a series of cold cases, every little bit helps."

* * *

The next morning, once both members of Alpha One had arrived at their desks, they got a summons from Fox. The cracks between the floor tiles of the Core flashed a deep crimson as the pair walked across it, en route to the ramp to the Director's office.

"Here we are, Abba," Omega murmured, as she and Echo slipped through the closed door of Fox's office. "What's up?"

"We need you to assign some teams to help out Crutch's folks for a bit," Fox noted. "We have a bit of a situation, and we're not sure what to make of it."

"What's up, boss?" Echo wondered.

"Omega, you know some of the Sluuites that work in Headquarters, right?"

"Yeah, Fox, I'm friends with a couple. Why?"

"We've had some Sluuites go missing lately. Five in the last week. The latest was Gesstun Sish, who went missing yesterday morning. He'd only just come on shift about the time he went missing. No check-in. Locator beacon abruptly stopped working. No sign of him after that."

"Damn," Echo said, surprised. "And nobody can find 'em?"

"No, none of them. Not even much in the way of clues," Fox affirmed. "I gather that Delta-Forty-Eight found what might have been some genetic evidence in one of the rear entrance lobbies, at least for Sish, but unfortunately, Joe Bob had already been through the area, cleaning…"

"Shit," Echo grumbled.

"Exactly."

"Has anybody talked to Joe Bob?" Omega wondered. "Maybe he saw something."

"I gathered Delta-Forty-Eight did, but he saw nothing," Fox said with a shrug. "I mean, the biggest Sluuite we have working for us is only about a foot tall, max. And that's on his tiptoes. So…”

“If something happened, there isn’t gonna BE a lotta sign,” Omega murmured, thoughtful.

“Exactly. I was hoping you could have some of your experienced investigators have a look.”

“Right now, I think that’s gonna be us two, Fox,” Echo said, gesturing to Omega and himself. “The others are all on cases of various sorts already.”

“Ah. Well, do the two of you have time to have a look?”

Omega and Echo exchanged glances.

You’re already kinda stressed, baby, Echo noted through the nd’t’lq. *Do you wanna take this on, or pass on it?*

I think I kinda have to, Ace, Omega responded. *If my friend Nubuv is in danger, I need to help. I WANT to help. I guess I need to make sure he’s not one of the missing, first, though; I haven’t heard from him in a while. He may just be busy, or he may be among the missing.*

Good point.

“Hey Fox,” Omega said, “I think our answer is yes, we’ll help. But I was wondering if my buddy Nubuv Kiish is one of the missing…?”

“Mm, let me check…” Fox murmured, pulling up the list and scanning it quickly. “No, he’s present and accounted for; I’m sure you’re happy about that. And for what it’s worth, I’ve placed a moratorium on Sluuite work at Headquarters for the duration of the case; they’re all going to remain in their quarters for safety. If you want to run by and say hi, maybe interview the others, I’m sure that would be appreciated. As would an offer to provide supplies, so they don’t have to get out and risk the danger, whatever it is; I expect Alpha Twenty-Four can help you with that, given their part-time status.”

“That’ll work,” Echo said. “We’ll run by and interview the Sluuites. If you can pop ‘em a message that we’re coming, it’d be good.”

“On it,” Fox said, turning to his keyboard.

* * *

But while Nubuv was glad to see Omega, and the rest of the Sluuites — there were some forty-five or fifty of them on payroll working in Headquarters at any given time, taking care of the odd bit of trash in tiny, out-of-the-way corners, often eating it to supplement their diets — were relieved to see such prestigious Agents working their missing-persons case, they had little to add other than what was already in the formal reports. Over the last week or so, five of their number had gone missing, three during the course of their work shifts, and the remaining two between their quarters and their work areas. No one had seen what happened, and none of their locator beacons worked.

"All of them just…stopped," Nubuv noted to Omega. "All at once. Nobody else has been having any problems with the locators, and none of them were having problems with their locators before they disappeared."

"That definitely argues for intelligent interference," Echo decided, listening.

"Yeah, it does," Omega agreed.

"Well, I think that's about all we can do here for the time being," Echo concluded. "Y'all get together in your meeting hall and put together a list of things you're gonna need for the duration — supplies an' shit — and anything Supplies can't handle, pop it to Meg, and she and I will see you get it. Y'all know Alpha Twenty-Four, right?"

A general chorus of, "Yes," went up from the tiny creatures.

"Good, 'cause while they're still recuperating, they do a lot of this sort of thing for the Alpha Line department," Omega tag-teamed Echo. "So what I'll probably do is pass on your list to them, and they'll acquire the items and bring them to you at your embassy."

"That works for us," Nubuv said. "Thank you both for helping out. We are very small compared to most beings in the Coalition, and we are used to being forgotten. We appreciate that your Agency does not forget us."

"Just because you're little doesn't mean you're not people,

or not important," Omega pointed out. "You're friends. We have to help."

"What Meg said," Echo agreed.

And Alpha One headed out, to a chorus of thanks from tiny voices.

* * *

A quick trip to the rear entrance yielded little. Omega located the area with a spectral scanner, then took several swabs to try to get something. Just then, Echo, who had been holding the scanner while Omega swabbed, to ensure that she swabbed inside the very tiny crime scene, started.

"Hey, Meg, come here and look at this," he said then.

"What?" Omega stood, tucking away the last of the swabs into its special transport container, doffed gloves and mask, and headed for her partner-slash-husband.

"Look at these overlapping shapes in the scanner," he said, pointing. "I mean, they're sorta smeared, yeah, prob'ly by the cleaning stuff. But doesn't this sorta look like a lizard body…" his finger traced part of the image in the scanner, "and doesn't THIS look like a footprint?" He traced another part of the image.

"Shit," Omega murmured, studying the imagery. "Save the original image, here, then outline each of those, and save those down. I think we have a murder scene."

"I think you're right," Echo agreed.

But he also noted, with some private and carefully-hidden relief, that it was NOT the rear entrance he had used that morning.

* * *

They spent the rest of the day that day poking around the various sites that seemed to be associated with the other disappearances. Unfortunately, since those had been cleaned several times by that point, there was nothing to be found.

Omega discovered that the field teams assigned to investigate had also used spectral scanners to locate the last place the missing Sluuite had been, and she requested that

Crutch make the saved images available to Alpha One.

Soon she and Echo had close to two dozen images to review.

"And that tells the tale," Echo noted after only half an hour of review. "We have a serial killer of Sluuites in Headquarters."

"Yeah," Omega agreed. "A Sluuite body print, and a honkin' big biped footprint overlaid and outlined in Sluuite body fluids, in every missing-persons case."

"It's not obvious unless you're looking for it, though," Echo said.

"No shit." Just then, Omega's cell phone went off, and she answered it. "Hey there. You got anything? It did? Oh shit. Yeah, that's not good. Yeah, we do. Now we gotta figure out what to do about it." She hung up and turned to Echo, who was waiting with a curious expression. "That was Forensics. Those swabs I took?"

"Yeah?"

"No doubt. The genetic material belonged to Gesstun Sish. I'm gonna send along our reckoning of the various sites, and Forensics is gonna try to sort out the swabs that the Field agents sent along, and maybe we can verify victims."

"I think we need to notify Fox," Echo said, moving to his desk and waking the virtual keyboard and display.

"You do that, and I'll do this," Omega said.

"Done."

* * *

But thanks to the smearing of the outlines during the cleaning, and the faintness of the images to begin with, there was no real way to take the evidence any farther.

And with the Sluuites sequestered for their own safety, the serial killings stopped.

"Which means we have cold cases," Fox sighed.

"Which means we have cold cases," Echo agreed.

"Shit," Omega grumbled.

* * *

'Joe Bob' ensured he was gathering up garbage bags on the

168

rear entrances each morning for the next several mornings, and watched Echo and Daagnadan leave by the same entrance, at slightly different times, each day.

Roughly half an hour later, Echo would return via the same entrance.

Daagnadan's return was rather more varied. Sometimes she would return within a few minutes of Echo. Other days, she was gone an hour or more. Occasionally she entered through the main entrance of Headquarters.

And she still tended to find a reason to pop by the Alpha Line Room later that day.

'Joe Bob' stifled a laugh.

But he was disappointed that there were no more snacks to be had.

* * *

The next morning, Echo arrived at the café with his electronic tablet in a warp pocket. Once again, Nreefluvan had his coffee waiting, just as he liked it, but this time a fresh glazed doughnut waited beside it. She had another latte, and an egg sandwich.

But when she had finished eating, which didn't take long as she'd already started by the time he arrived, she moved around to Echo's side of the booth so she could work with him on the tablet, filling out immigration forms.

As they worked, she leaned closer and closer, though Echo didn't notice.

What he did notice was that her perfume seemed especially sweet that day.

Or maybe, he considered, *it mixes well with the scent of good, fresh coffee. 'Cause this is good shit.*

He took an appreciative sip of his coffee, which the waitress had just topped off, and resumed work on the immigration form.

* * *

This time, however, he left the coffeeshop with Nreefluvan, and they walked companionably back to Headquarters, where they slipped into the little-used back entrance before splitting up. Echo headed for the Alpha Line Room to hand over with Golf and Easy, and Nreefluvan headed for her quarters within the Kochavi Embassy.

Echo handed over with Alpha Four, then set to work.

Fifteen minutes later, Omega arrived, chipper and feeling well. They coordinated their activities, and Echo helped her work on her clearance upgrade justification.

That afternoon, just in time for second lunch, Daagnadan showed up again. She greeted Alpha One quietly but in a courteous and friendly fashion.

Again, she came to the front of the room and made herself a cup of coffee, very sweet and very creamy, in the pod brewer. Then she moved to an empty desk in the middle of the room and sat down, waiting.

This time, however, Crutch showed up to go out to lunch with the Kochavi woman.

And Omega developed a mild sick headache after they departed.

* * *

That night, Echo prepared dinner for a slightly debilitated Omega, choosing a basic sliced roasted turkey breast with gravy and mashed potatoes — a small, relatively light meal, easy on the seasonings, and with little to offend an already-offput digestive tract. He set it in front of her, then sat down beside her and helped her eat it, along with some fresh lemonade to drink in an effort to ensure her electrolytes were in balance. Omega nibbled and sipped slowly until it was all gone, and it stayed down.

"There," Echo said, taking the dirty plates and putting them in the dishwasher along with the pans used to prepare the meal, then starting the dishwasher. "Do you feel any better, baby?"

"Yeah, I do now," Omega decided, though he thought she was still a little pale. "I think I wanna try to just chug some water tonight, and see if I can flush stuff outta me. If I can hang on until I can do that, after getting exposed to Ree's perfume, it seems like it helps."

"Which is a good indication that that's what the problem is, I guess," Echo concluded.

"Yeah, that an' the fact that I always feel okay afterward… until she shows up in the room," Omega pointed out.

"Okay, lemme grab your spare water bottle outta the cabinet and fill it, and I'll bring it to you," Echo said. "Go have a seat in the den an' I'll be there in a sec."

"Awright. What do you wanna do tonight?"

"Dunno. Would a long soak in the hot tub help, do you think, or make you feel worse?"

"Mm." Omega hummed as she considered. "I think that sounds really soothing, actually. You wanna get in together and just cuddle and talk, me with my water, and you with your whisky? Or something else?"

"I think I'mma get my water bottle and chug some dihydrogen monoxide, too," Echo decided. "And yeah, we can get in and just cuddle and talk."

"Let's do it, then. And after?" Omega offered Echo a suggestive grin.

"If you feel better after, we might get, um, 'busy,' as you like to put it," Echo noted, remaining serious, "but if you still feel even a little off, we need to just crash. I do NOT want you to barf in the middle of our lovemaking, sweetheart. That just…" he shook his head as he came out of the kitchen with their water bottles. "I think I'd feel really bad if I thought I'd caused that. And then we'd both get anxious about it the next time we made love, and…" He tilted his head. "We don't need to get into a cycle that interferes with things like that."

"I get it, and I'm okay with that plan," Omega sighed. "I hope I feel a lot better after that, though."

"Let's go strip an' soak, and we'll find out."

"Right behind you."

* * *

The hot tub relaxed Omega, but she still felt rather limp when she got out — even more so, in fact, due to the loosening

171

effects of the jacuzzi on her muscles. The cold water in their bottles was good, however, and she simply sat in the vanity chair, wrapped in her terry bathrobe, and sucked down the water while her body dried, content to do so. Echo dried off, then wandered into the bedroom and turned down the bed, making it ready for them to retire for the night.

"Okay, baby, up an' at 'em," he said, coming back into the bathroom. "Bed's all ready. Let's go crash."

"All right," she sighed. "I guess we just cuddle some more, huh?"

"I think we oughta, yeah. I mean, you're some better, but now you're about like jelly."

"Dammit."

"I know. But maybe I can rub your belly a little and help. I was taught a few things like that in my massage classes to help in situations like this, I just never had much chance to use 'em before. I went back to my old textbooks and refreshed my memory earlier, so I think I can do this. We can spoon, and I'll rub your tum, and you just try to relax."

"Hokay."

* * *

Echo was as good as his word, and it wasn't long before a deeply relaxed and considerably relieved Omega was asleep in his arms.

He smiled to himself, pulled her a little closer, and let himself drift into slumber as well.

* * *

The next morning, Echo and Nreefluvan got a little farther along in filling out the extensive list of immigration forms on Echo's tablet. Echo had told her the previous day that he had just had breakfast, and while it was appreciated, she only needed to order coffee for him — and she was paying for it, by way of thanking him for helping her. So she had another slice of quiche — ham and cheese this time — and they both had coffee, but Echo didn't bother with anything more to eat.

They walked back to Headquarters together, arm in arm.

* * *

Daagnadan made a habit of using the Alpha Line Room as a meeting place at various times each day, grabbing a cup of coffee before meeting this or that person in the Agency for a social outing of one sort or another. She tried not to bother Alpha One any more than she could help during these times, and once, when another Alpha Line Agent — it was Yankee — politely but pointedly asked what she was doing there, she simply explained that it was an easy-to-find location for everyone, since it opened off the Core.

As the week wore on, Omega grew ill again whenever Daagnadan came into the room. Zebra worked with her to try to find some combination of medications that would ease her reaction to the alien woman's fragrance.

"Because I see the histamine response, right here," Zebra told her while waving her scanner, several days in. "We just need to find the right combo to knock this in the head. Are you still taking the prescription I gave you?"

"Yeah," a glum Omega remarked. "But I'm not seein' it helpin' much."

"Just give it time," Zebra soothed. "I told you it could take more than a week to get everything right."

"I know," Omega sighed, extremely discouraged. "But I barfed dinner last night, and it was a GOOD dinner! Plus, this has completely killed our love life, Zee — Echo doesn't wanna risk the physical activity of, um, of lovemaking because, well, he's afraid I'll throw up in the middle of things. Which, I have to admit, I might. And THAT…is a pretty damn big turn-off."

"Yeah, that'd be a real mood-killer," Zebra agreed. "And then the two of you get your heads wrapped around the axle NEXT time — 'will she or won't she?' and the whole intimacy thing goes right to hell in a handbasket!"

"Exactly!"

"Just hang on, girl. I'm gonna try something different today. Zar and I discussed and dissed and cussed and cussdissed the hell out of it last night — he even joined Fox an' me for dinner, just so we could discuss it some more, an' lemme tell ya, Fox is worried about ya, too — and so we're gonna try a little cocktail of antihistamines and inflammation reducers that we devised, and see what that does for you."

"Whatever works," Omega fumed. "I'm tired of this, and I can't make the woman go away, and I don't think the Kochavi Embassy would like it if I tried something more…permanent." She crossed her eyes. "But I have to admit, at this point, I've considered it."

"No! I don't think so," Zebra laughed. "I don't think Fox would like it, either. At this point, from what you've told me, Echo might not care, but I still don't think it'd be good for your career. Never mind your long-term future." She turned to the pharmaceutical cabinet. "Now, lemme put this mix together that Zar and I worked out, and see how that does for you. I might even throw in an anti-emetic to help with that nausea."

"Oh, I like THAT idea. Let's do that, for sure."

"Okay, we can do that. I can even write you a script for an oral anti-emetic…"

* * *

The next morning, while Omega went back to the medlab to report the failure of the latest medical cocktail — though the anti-emetic had helped considerably in that regard, and she hadn't thrown up — Echo headed for the seldom-used rear exit to Headquarters…

…To find Nreefluvan waiting for him in the foyer.

Echo led the way out, checking the area to ensure no one was watching. Only after he gave her the high sign did Nreefluvan join him. They walked side by side, chatting companionably about matters inconsequential, down to the coffee shop several blocks over.

"Okay, let's get started," Echo said after they'd ordered, pulling out his tablet.

"Oh, boopy, let us simply sit here and chat, for a change," Nreefluvan suggested.

Echo didn't demur.

To anything.

They walked back to Headquarters, hand in hand.

* * *

Back inside the little foyer, where they were alone and were fairly certain of remaining unseen, Nreefluvan turned to Echo with a smile, pressing close. Her arms slid around his neck, and she stretched upward, aiming for his mouth, even as a swirl of honey sweetness reached his nostrils, reminding him of an equally sweet memory, just out of reach.

"Come with me," she breathed, and he could feel her breath, sweet and warm against his face.

"Where?" he wondered, voice very low.

"Back to my quarters. It is time we had our own opportunity to be together."

Echo's breath caught, and he bent his head to hers.

But before his lips could cover hers, the memory he had been trying to recall surfaced…a memory from The Beach, the previous summer.

* * *

Echo retrieved a book from his gear, turned on a lamp in the common area as the sun went down, and sat down on the couch to read.

"Echo?" Omega's voice filtered through the vagaries of the book's plot to his conscious awareness.

"Hm?" he answered without looking up.

"If you want your partner…back, you've got it, Ace. But I thought I'd better show you what you're letting yourself in for." The couch gave slightly next to Echo as Omega sat down beside him, and automatically, he glanced up.

"Damn," he whispered involuntarily. Echo's eyes widened and darkened as the pupils dilated — he knew they did, because the dim room got a lot brighter; his nostrils flared slightly, and he caught his breath. The book slid to the floor, forgotten.

Omega sat close beside him, almost but not quite nestled into his side, wrapped only in clinging black silk and lace; bare skin was visible through the openings in the lace. She had unbraided and brushed her hair, and the shining platinum tresses cascaded down her shoulders and back. The sapphire eyes appeared lit from within.

She met his gaze steadily, withstanding his scrutiny silently. Omega maintained a demure, reserved posture, even when Echo extended his hand and lightly fingered the silver hair, letting the back of his hand gently brush her soft cheek.

Omega extended her own hand to run a featherlight fingertip fondly down the bridge of his nose to its tip, and he closed his eyes for a brief moment at the sensuality of her touch, exhaling slightly.

"You see, Echo?" Omega said. "Pheromones work both ways. But you're not even aware of 'em, only how your body responds to them. It's completely and purely involuntary. And I can't turn mine off. I can't turn ME off. When I've been keeping you at a distance, it's because I've been trying to protect you, not me. This is what you'll have to deal with, every minute of every day, if Bet, India, and the others fail. But if that's what you want...if you're okay with that...here I am."

"Meg...what do YOU want?" Echo asked in a low voice. Is she really...offering herself to me? Does she want us to become lovers? *he wondered.* Is she asking...to become MY lover?

The blue eyes met the brown ones steadily. "I would've thought that was obvious," came the reply.

Echo's breath caught again as his deepest dream faced him, offering to come true, and he raised his other hand, plunging his fingers into the silken hair to cradle her head in his hands. His head bent over hers.

* * *

And suddenly Echo's head snapped up, and he pushed away from Nreefluvan.

"No," he said. "Not now. Not this. I'm sorry, Ree. This... this isn't right. I won't do that to Meg."

"What? What are you going to do?" Nreefluvan asked, shocked and startled.

"I don't know," Echo said, confused. "Go. Just...go."

Nreefluvan left, and Echo stood there for long moments, trying to regain his composure and his sense of self.

What is WRONG with me?! he demanded to know. *What I almost did just now...that's not RIGHT. I love Meg, not Ree. I'm married to Meg! I WANT to be married to Meg! So why do I want to run after Ree, sweep her up in my arms, and carry her back to her quarters, right this very instant? This makes no sense.*

He shook himself, then stepped back outside. There, he took several deep breaths. The lumberyard nearby had just had a special-order shipment of freshly-cut cedar wood arrive, and he inhaled deep of the sharp, aromatic scent, letting it clear his mind, at least somewhat.

Then, feeling ashamed, he ducked back into Headquarters and hurried to his desk, hoping to be there before Omega arrived at hers, and thankful that, between the tutelage of his wife and Ambassador Zz'r'p, he'd learned how to raise a telepathic block sufficient to prevent leakage through the nd't'lq.

* * *

After several days of the clandestine sneaking about by Echo, and rather less sneaking by Daagnadan, 'Joe Bob' saw the pair meet up at the rear entrance and head out together.

Half an hour later, they returned, hand in hand. 'Joe Bob' had placed himself in a position where he could not be seen, but could watch, using reflections on various polished surfaces.

So he noticed when Daagnadan slid her arms around Echo's neck, and he bent his head to hers. 'Joe Bob' heard her request for him to come with her to her quarters, and he smiled to himself.

Then he made himself scarce; it would not do for them to accidentally run into anyone and spoil the mood.

* * *

Daagnadan headed straight for her quarters within the Kochavi Embassy. Her bedroom was prepared for an assignation...which was, she decided, not occurring this morning. *Though I have no idea why,* she considered, deeply puzzled. *I thought I had 'reeled him in,' as X-ray used to phrase it.*

A soft bleat on her Kochavi equivalent to a cell phone made it through her musings, and she checked the device, to find another notification of a message from Her Excellency Rnaalti Isahuutob, Ambassador from Kochav. It was the eighth one in a week, and Daagnadan essentially just ignored them.

Until she entered the door of her quarters to find a very irritated Isahuutob waiting imperiously.

"Uh-oh," she murmured.

* * *

Isahuutob sat in the armchair of the flat's den area, in formal robes, her attitude and bearing appropriate to a queen. Without a word, she pointed imperiously at the sofa, across from her. Daagnadan moved to the sofa and sat.

"I see the humans' colloquialisms have invaded your proper English," Isahuutob noted, crisp and disapproving. "'Uh-oh'? Really, Ras Daagnadan."

"I...was here many years, some two decades ago," Daagnadan pointed out. "And very close to Agent Echo at that time. His partner, Agent X-ray, took great pains to ensure that my linguistics included the local colloquialisms, because sometimes I helped them on their cases."

"I see. So this was deliberate, and you have maintained it?"

"Yes. Some of it became instinctive, I will admit. I had... hopes...of returning to that assistance with Echo."

"You did not know he was married to another?"

"No. I had not heard."

"Why is that, do you think?"

"Echo and Omega both believe that Director Fox may well have prevented the event from reaching the general news media, in order to help preserve security around the ceremony, and them."

"I see. That makes a certain sense, I suppose," Isahuutob decided. "Why have you not responded to my messages?"

"I have been...busy," Daagnadan tried.

"Too busy to respond and tell me so? To advance schedule a meeting?"

"I, uh…"

"No, do not even try to claim your communications device is malfunctioning. I heard the alert on it as you opened the door."

Daagnadan was speechless.

"You do know why I am here?" Isahuutob pressed.

"Yes. You are here to pass formal judgement upon my actions, as per Kochavi law."

"Indeed. And to that end, you will answer my questions, or be found wanting," Isahuutob decreed. "Why are you here? Was life on Kochav too boring for you?"

"I…Rasah Isahuutob, that is a very long story, and to tell it could endanger someone close to me."

"Oh! I see," Isahuutob said, startled. "Are you here for help from your old lover?"

"In a manner of speaking, yes."

"You have an odd way of asking for help, Ras Daagnadan." A skeptical Isahuutob raised a delicate white eyebrow. "You antagonize his partner and wife, you antagonize him, you cross boundaries that humans do not like to have crossed…"

"I do not have long to work, Rasah."

"And you will not tell me what is the problem?"

"It is as much as my loved one's life is worth, Rasah."

"Then you leave me no choice," Isahuutob sighed. "You are confined to quarters until I say otherwise, Ras Daagnadan. I will not have you causing a problem with the Earth humans, on whom we have for years been on such good terms. If you violate this ruling I will have you sent back to Kochav at once. Am I understood?"

Daagnadan paled.

"Yes, Rasah. You are understood."

"Good."

Isahuutob rose and swept out of the apartment.

Daagnadan flung herself across the couch and wept bitterly.

* * *

('Gary', this is Arg,) 'Joe Bob' spoke into the device in his little quarters in the sub-basement.

(Go, Arg.)

(I believe our mediary has had success at last today. I saw her and Echo kissing in a remote, unused back foyer of the Headquarters building.)

(Indeed? That shows promise, and definite forward movement in the plan, but I would not call it a success.)

(She invited him to her quarters, and I understood he agreed.)

(Ah. THAT...is very different. This sounds most excellent. Matters proceed apace.) There was a pause, then "Gary" added, (Once it appears that Echo has become our agent's mate, feel free to dispose of Omega in whatever means you consider appropriate, just as long as no one knows what happened to her. She should simply disappear, and never be heard from again. If she appears to have fled, to get away from Echo and Daagnadan, even better.)

(Understood, 'Gary'. And Fox? What of him?)

(Wait until Daagnadan and Echo are fully and firmly established, and we have ascertained her control. Then Fox should 'go away' also. Perhaps he goes looking for Omega and is unaccountably lost. You have reported to me that they are close, in a manner akin to sire and larva, so it should make sense to the humans. Yes, that is a story that should do nicely.)

(I see. That is a good idea. It will be done as you say.)

(Excellent.)

* * *

Echo was quiet the rest of the day, and for a wonder, Nreefluvan did not show up at all in the Alpha Line Room. As a consequence, Alpha One got a lot done, and Omega felt slightly better.

Echo also tried hard to be more affectionate to his wife, with some success, although he felt like he was forcing it most of the time.

And I have no idea why, he thought guiltily.

* * *

That night, after they went to bed, Omega rolled over to press against Echo. A huge, mischievous grin was on her face.

"Ree didn't come in today, and I feel lots better tonight," she told him. "So c'mere, naked cowboy."

Somewhat hesitant and uncertain, Echo pulled her close. But then Omega opened fully to their telepathic connection, and a wave of love and desire came through to him, washing through his entire being. Immediately and instinctively, he reciprocated.

Within moments, all thought of anything other than how much he loved his beautiful, intelligent wife was gone.

* * *

Confined to quarters, Daagnadan really did nothing but cry. She did change into a négligée — she had brought no pajamas, and little in the way of informal loungewear — and crawl into bed, but ate no dinner and did little else.

She got no sleep that night.

* * *

The next morning, when Omega went down to the medlab, Echo headed straight for the Alpha Line Room.

I'm done with Ree, he decided. *She pulled something — I dunno what, but something; I'd think it was pheromones, but hers were never strong enough to do THAT — plus she's been trying to seduce me from the get-go, and that flat won't wash. Not with me. Not when I'm already married to the woman of my dreams. Who really reminded me of that last night. In spades. And every other card suit. Damn. Meg is ah-maze-ing!*

"Hey, Echo," Golf said in surprise, when the department chief came through the door. "We didn't expect to see you here." He glanced past. "Where's Meg?"

"In the medlab," Echo noted. "I, uh, I had a couple things here I wanted to get done, and, well…"

"Oh, got it," Easy said, nodding. "You done with us for today, then?"

"Yeah, pal. Go head out on patrol."

"On it. Want us back tomorrow?"

"Nah. I think, uh, the medlab is starting to get things under control," Echo lied, feeling horrible for doing so; he'd never lied to his people before. *I've never lied to Meg, either,* he thought. *Not that I actually did; I just let her assume where I was going, and didn't tell her. Dammit. I'll have to figure out how to explain — to a whole damn buncha people — but I dunno how, when I don't even know WHY. What in the damn HELL was I thinking?!*

He watched as Alpha Four left the room, a cheerful camaraderie between them; then, morose, he turned to his desk.

* * *

Daagnadan did not bother changing into day clothes the next morning. She threw on the only loungewear she had brought, a true bathrobe. It was something akin to Omega's terrycloth robe, but had seen rather more annums than hers, and under no circumstances had she intended anyone to see the threadbare wrap, but it was comfortable upon exiting the shower — another thing she did not bother to do that day.

Then she wandered listlessly into the den part of her quarters, where she sat down in the armchair facing the television. She picked up the remote, but did not bother turning on the TV, either.

Instead, she began to cry again.

It never even occurred to her to eat breakfast, even to the preparing of a cup of coffee.

* * *

Omega came back from the medlab, chipper and cheery. She greeted Echo, then seated herself at her desk.

"So okay, what's up next, Ace?" she wondered.

Echo had managed to get a little work done, but not a lot; he'd been busy trying to suss out what to do about what he now saw to be a very serious problem in which Nreefluvan had enmeshed him, one which currently threatened both his job and his marriage, when he had no idea how the alien woman had managed to catch him in it in the first place.

So he turned to Omega slowly, trying to decide what to tell her, and more importantly, when and how. Omega's eyebrows shot up.

Something's wrong, she told him through the nd't'lq. *I can feel it. I know you've tried to kind of screen off your own thoughts and feelings to allow me space to deal with mine, especially since I've been sick, but I can tell — something's upset you. Talk to me, Ace. I'm here. You know that.*

If I do, you're gonna be forty-nine-an'-a-half kinds of upset and mad at me, baby, he replied in kind. *And I'm already a hundred an' twelve kinds of mad at myself. But I just don't understand it. I'm...for once, I'm not sure WHAT to do.*

Is it to do with Nreefluvan?

Yeah.

Did she con you into something?

I think so. I'm just not sure how. It's like...it's like I suddenly woke up and found myself in a mess.

Okay. Tell me, and I'll consider the source. I'll be mad at HER, not you.

Echo drew a deep breath.

She talked me into helping her apply for immigration. While you've been in the medlab, I've been at a coffeeshop a few blocks away, showing her how to fill out the forms, on my tablet. He shook his head. *I think the only reason I agreed was because I knew Fox would disapprove the form.*

Mmph, Omega grunted mentally. *Yeah, that doesn't make me happy, but I get your rationale, there. Keep her from pitchin' another snit-fit like she did to the ambassador, all while knowing the application wouldn't go through.*

Yeah. But things went...kinda hinky, as Romeo would put it. Especially yesterday, which was the last time I went...and believe me, I'm not goin' back.

What happened?

Well, I think maybe I need to dig into the details of interactions between Kochavi and humans, 'cause she managed not only to get me to hold hands with her on the way back, she tried to kiss me…though let me specifically note that she wasn't successful, though it was close…and then she tried to convince me to go to her quarters with her so she could seduce me. But I didn't do that, either. Though…it was tempting. I just don't know WHY it was tempting. Because frankly, I didn't and don't WANT to.

Omega saw red for a moment, and Echo watched it happen mentally, watched her struggle for control…and regain it.

Yeah, that's something we need to look into. Maybe there was some sort of a long-term bonding attempt she made, way back when you were together, something you didn't know about at the time, Omega brainstormed after taking a moment to settle, *and she's trying to take advantage of it now. That might explain why she's coaxing you to do shit. And ABLE to.*

Might be. Anyway, I need to tell Fox, but he's gonna be upset with me, 'cause he told me to steer clear of her, and…I didn't. So I gotta figure out how to tell him, when I don't even know WHY I didn't, and…

Shush. I understand. And he's 'Abba Fox' now, in addition to the Director.

Exactly. I am not looking forward to the look on his face.

Well, you've told ME. And I appreciate your honesty. And no, I'm just glad you didn't go with her to her quarters! I take it, you were kinda under her spell?

Sort of, yeah, but like I keep saying, I flat dunno why, Echo admitted. *And it's driving me nuts trying to figure out why, and what she did, and how I can keep it from happening again. Because I DO NOT WANT THAT.*

What broke it?

Huh? Broke what?

Her spell over you.

Oh. You.

Huh? Me? How did I break it when I wasn't even around? When I didn't even know it was happening?

I remembered you an' me down at The Beach last summer,

Echo explained. *How I was kinda almost overwhelmed by your pheromones, especially since I was already nuts over you, only you and I both knew that wasn't HOW you wanted it, and I had to pull back. I remembered I loved you enough TO pull back. So I pulled back again...because I love you.*

Aw.

Omega rolled her desk chair over to his, glanced at the door to make sure no one was about to walk in, then kissed him, very gently but passionately.

I love you, so much, she told him. *I don't think there's much I wouldn't do for you. I hope you know that.*

Yeah. An' I feel the same way, baby. An' I hope YOU know it.

Good, an' yeah, most of the time I can remember that. At least, I can these days. Look, let's think through this for a couple days, then we'll BOTH go to Fox, an' I'll try to buffer things for you. I'll also put my research-fu into action and dig into the whole Kochavi/human sexual interactions thing in the online literature to see what I can turn up.

That...would be deeply appreciated, sweetheart. Now I just need to figure out how to admit things to Alpha Four, who covered for me in the office while I was off with Ree, and MAYBE this will all settle out.

I'll take care of that. Don't worry.

Oh. You sure? How?

Yeah, I'm sure. I already see in your mind how you did it, Ace, and I can manage that without causing too many problems, I think.

All right.

Okay. Feel better?

Immensely. Thanks for understanding, honey, Echo told her, sincere. *'Cause I'm serious. I love YOU, not her, and I don't even understand why I did the things I did. But I know I want it to STOP.*

Good. Omega smiled. *Let's get back to work for now. We can talk about all this tonight once we get home, and maybe work out some plans for how to proceed.*

Sounds good.

They set to work.

* * *

'Joe Bob' noticed that Daagnadan seemed to disappear after that clinch with Echo, whereas Echo did not...nor did Omega. He had made a point of scoping out the Kochavi Embassy by way of janitorial services, however, so a quick reconnoiter of the embassy indicated that the ambassador had confined Daagnadan to her quarters for being unable to explain her actions after accusing Agent Omega of harassment.

This is not good, he thought. *This could upset everything. At least she has abided by her side of the agreement and kept her mouth shut. I suppose I should see about assisting, perhaps.*

Hm. There is really nothing keeping her in her quarters save the ambassador's word. Should she countervene the ambassador's orders, however, that could possibly result in the ambassador asking the Director to take her into custody. Or even ship her back to Kochav in irons. And either option would be a worse situation than currently.

I might, I suppose, do away with the ambassador, he considered. *But I suspect that will not help; the way such things work in most places, they will simply elevate the envoy to the position of ambassador and continue on as they were. And such an action does risk giving me away.*

Mm. I think I will tell 'Gary' tonight, and see what he recommends.

* * *

Back in harmony together, Alpha One managed to get a good bit of work done that morning. Echo felt intensely relieved, Omega was happy with his honesty and his ability to resist something that was evidently not human in origin, and their camaraderie returned.

The fact that Daagnadan hadn't been in the office in a couple of days also helped ensure Omega felt a little better physically.

So when it came time for first lunch, she made an offer.

"We are crankin' this morning, Ace," Omega said with a smile. "And you've got that whole security rationale thing to put together for Fox. So rather than break for first lunch, why don't I run down to the deli and grab take-out while you work on the rationale, and we snarf it down together, then keep crankin'?"

"I think that's a plan, Meg," Echo agreed with an answering smile. "As long as I get to eat lunch with you, I don't really much care where we eat it. But if, uh, if nobody comes back to 'visit' — you know who I mean — and you stay feeling this good, we might go out tonight. A really nice restaurant and a show, maybe. With…a private little celebration after. What do you say?"

"Ooo. That sounds great!"

"Okay, done."

"Whaddaya want for lunch?"

"I dunno. You know what I like, baby," he told her. "Surprise me."

"All right. I'm off, then," she said, kissing him and heading for the door.

Chapter 8

About five minutes after Omega left, Alpha Twenty-Four entered. Adam and Torino were much better these days than they had been after the fights of Adita's Coup, and most of their injuries from that incident were healed, but both were still on canes and limped a bit. Given Torino's back had been broken, the fact that she was walking at all was only a little shy of a miracle of galactic medicine…but it had taken months of medical treatment, physical therapy, and plain hard work to reach that point. Given several broken bones — his shin had been badly shattered — and a severely dislocated shoulder joint in Adam, he wasn't that far behind in the medical treatment, therapy, and hard work, either.

The pair of Agents was still only on part-time due to medical restrictions — a situation Echo understood all too well, and one which meant 'ABSOLUTELY NO field work' — but they liked to come by the Alpha Line Room and at least check in with Alpha One, then help where they could. Sometimes that was as simple as helping with paperwork, and sometimes it was erranding for Alpha One — Fox had approved them as 'temporary assistants' for the purpose, which of late had included specific supply requests from the Sluuites — and sometimes it was extra brainpower on a problem. But they helped, Alpha One appreciated it immensely, and that was all that mattered to Alpha Twenty-Four.

This morning, after an intense joint therapy session in the medlab, they headed straight for the pod brewer, intent on caffeine to replenish diminished energy levels. Torino leaned her cane on the credenza near the brewer, then reached for the near door of the cabinet underneath, where the team's mugs were stored.

Unfortunately, when she opened it, the cabinet door hit her cane, which slid. Torino grabbed for it and missed. Then, thrown off-center by the lunge-and-grab move, she staggered, snatched at the credenza, missed, and pitched forward with a cry…her head aimed at the corner of the very solid wood-and-metal credenza.

"Oh shit!" Echo exclaimed. He spun his chair and leaped up, as Adam also lunged for his partner, and they managed to prevent her hitting the floor…or the credenza.

Several flailing arms, however, impacted the pod brewer and overturned it. Water spilled from the top of the capacious reservoir, running all over the top of the credenza and cascading over the front to the floor in a miniature recreation of Niagara.

"Hellfire damnation!" Echo cursed. "Torino, you okay?"

"Yeah, I think so," she panted. "Sorry, boss! Oh damn! I made a MESS! I'm sorry, I'm sorry, I'm sorry!"

"No problem, Tori. Shush, it's fine. Everything's okay," Echo soothed. "Shit happens. Adam, you got her?"

"Yeah, Echo. Grab the napkins and mop up the mess fast, before any of the documentation gets wet," Adam said, nodding at the credenza's open bookcase area as he got a firm grip on his partner, who was still wobbly from the almost-tumble.

"Gonna do just that," Echo said, snatching up the entire stack of napkins that had been in the holder beside the disposable cups, and mopping the mess with it like a sponge. "Torino, park your ass in my chair and catch your breath, gal. You didn't hit the corner of the credenza, did you?"

"No, you and Adam caught me before my head smacked it," Torino said, easing over to Echo's desk chair and settling into it, while Adam steadied her. "Damn, I saw that metal corner heading for my face and thought I was a goner."

"I'm glad I'm a little farther along, owing to less damage," Adam said then. "I think Echo did most of the catching, but at least I helped direct your fall so he COULD. Thank God."

"Yeah. Me too, buddy," Torino agreed. "Rglfrz says I'm coming along fast now, and I'm glad of that, but I still tend to get wonked if I go off-center too much. And that went way the hell off-center."

"I'm just glad you're both okay," Echo said, continuing

to mop. Adam reached for the overturned brewer, but Echo waved him off, then pointed. "No, it's fine, Adam. I'll take care of it, no problem. Right now, I need you to do something else for me."

"Sure thing, Echo, whatcha need?"

"Um, go into the supplies drawer over there and get out another pack of napkins and open it, please. Maybe two. This bunch is sopping already."

"Right," Adam said, obeying the request. Echo tossed the soggy stack he held into Omega's waste-can — it was nearer than his own, at that point — and grabbed another wad of fresh napkins to keep mopping, gradually working his way back toward his end of the credenza. He dropped another wad of napkins on the floor, and used his feet to nudge them about and sop up the worst of the puddles in front of the credenza as he wiped the top of that cabinet.

"Um, if we can't help clean up our mess, maybe we should get outta the way, Adam," a sheepish Torino suggested. "We can always grab a cuppa coffee in the break room across the Core."

"Yeah, good point, Tori," her partner replied. "Where'd your cane go?"

"Huh, I saw it a second ago," Echo remarked, glancing around. He got down on his hands and knees, looking under the credenza, then fished the wayward cane out from under. "Here it is. Might wanna wipe it down with a couple more napkins, but it's only water. And you're not in the way; I just know neither of you is as flexible as you'd like to be yet, and a good half of what I'm doing is mopping the floor with napkins. And not always while standing." While he was on hands and knees, he grabbed another wad of napkins and wiped a puddle that had made its way under the credenza. "I'd hate for either of you to get down here and be unable to get back up again, or worse, strain something that doesn't need straining yet." He looked up at them, concerned. "After all, I've been where y'all are, an' I understand. So I'll take care of this, so y'all don't feel like you have to."

"Yeah, but we're still in the way of you doing that," Adam pointed out. "And we still need some caffeine, so we'll scoot and come back later, to see what we can do to actually HELP."

"Instead of making a mess," Torino added. "Yeah, it's okay, Echo."

"All right, then," Echo said, handing the cane to Torino. "Here ya go."

Torino accepted the cane with gratitude, and Adam helped her wipe it off, then the pair apologized profusely once more and hobbled out.

Echo sighed.

"Damnation. Who knew the reservoir of that thing held so damn much? It's gonna be one of THOSE days, isn't it?" he said to the air, then resumed mopping up water.

* * *

It took a full twenty minutes more before Echo managed to get all the water mopped up. He used up that entire pack of napkins by the time he was done, as well as all that had been out previously, sitting in a holder beside the brewer, and started on another pack. Once he had that done, he dusted off his trousers knees, washed his hands at the little sink, then started straightening the contents of the credenza top.

Last but most important, he set the pod brewer back upright and adjusted its position, getting it ready to make coffee again. He reached for the measuring pitcher and filled it with water at the tiny sink, then poured it into the brewer's reservoir.

I guess, he thought, *we might want to look more at automating this. If we just piped the water straight into the reservoir from the faucet supply, the piping itself would probably have held the brewer in place. It wouldn't have turned over and nothing would have spilled. And I wouldn't have taken the last half-hour or so cleaning up from the Titanic.* He flipped the lid of the reservoir closed and parked the little pitcher in its accustomed spot, then did a double-take. *What's that…?*

Echo picked up a small square of cloth with what looked

like an oily substance on it, which was peeking out from beneath the brewer. He turned it around in his fingers, feeling the texture of the cloth, slick with whatever saturated it…

…When a strong whiff of Nreefluvan's scent hit his olfactory nerves. His head suddenly spun and began to throb painfully. Nausea rose for a moment, and he considered grabbing the nearest waste-can to throw up, before he regained control.

Whoa, he thought, still a little dizzy. He grabbed the plastic wrapper that had been around the paper napkins and enfolded the scrap of cloth in it. *Somebody musta wanted to remind me she was around, even when she wasn't. And no damn wonder Meg has been sick as forty-eight an' three-quarters dogs. It took the concentrated form to hit me, but her senses are hyped. This is what she was getting all the time around Ree. Blarg.*

Echo headed for the men's room across the Core from the Alpha Line Room. There, he dumped the plastic-wrapped cloth in the trash can and thoroughly washed his hands. Then he called Facilities on his cell with a very specific request.

He got back to the Alpha Line Room just as Omega arrived from the deli, arms laden with take-out bags.

* * *

'Joe Bob' was in another part of the Headquarters building when he got a notification on his battered old cell phone, telling him that there was an urgent need for a trash pickup in the men's room off the Core.

"Huh," he muttered to himself. "It has not been THAT long since I emptied the waste receptacles there, and cleaned the toilets. I wonder what has happened. Perhaps someone got sick."

He took his janitorial cart and trundled it into the elevator, heading for the Core.

* * *

"Here we go, Ace," Omega said cheerfully, setting the bags down on the end of her desk. "I got us cream of chicken soup, meatloaf, green bean salad, and baked potatoes." She paused and looked around. "What happened here? And what's wrong? You look almost green around the gills."

"Ugh," Echo murmured. "That's one way of putting it. Alpha Twenty-Four came in, and had a little mishap — Tori nearly face-planted into the corner of the credenza, and in the course of catching her, me, Adam, and Tori managed to upset the pod brewer…"

"Ah," Omega said. "That explains the splatter over here, on my desk."

"Aw shit," Echo grumbled. "I thought I got everything."

"No, it's okay, Ace, it's not bad. It's barely anything at all," Omega protested, grabbing a napkin from the holder and wiping away what remained of the water spray. "There. So y'all had to mop up?"

"Yeah, or, well, I did, 'cause I knew they couldn't get down on the floor…"

"Ooo," Omega said in sympathy, sitting in her desk chair and focusing her attention on her partner and mate. "So you've been crawling around and mopping?"

"Yeah. Used up nearly two whole packs of napkins, 'cause I didn't have anything else to mop WITH. I was tryin' to keep the documentation dry, too."

"Shit."

"Something like, yeah. But now I think I know what you've been going through, Meg. Once I started putting the coffee station back to rights, I found a little gift Ree must have left at some point — a little swatch of cloth soaked in her perfume. As soon as I picked it up and could smell it, my head took off into orbit and started pounding, and my whole digestive tract nearly came out my mouth."

"Urg," Omega grunted. "Yeah, that's the sensation, all right. What did you do with it?"

"Wrapped it in the plastic from one of the used napkin packs, then hightailed it to the men's room, dumped it in the garbage, and washed my hands. Three times. Then I called Facilities to come empty the trash in the men's room, and use a hazmat suit. Got back here just in time to meet you."

"HAZMAT SUIT?!" Omega laughed, long and hard.

"Well, I did. Seriously." Echo grinned, slightly sheepish. Finally she sobered, as a concerning thought hit.

"Oh, drat. Are you gonna be able to eat, hon?" she wondered then. "If that made you as sick as it does me…"

"It did, 'cause I nearly tossed my cookies in the wastebasket before I could blink," he admitted. "But I think I can, if I take it slow. I hope they didn't make anything too spicy."

"Well, the chicken soup should work fine for you," Omega noted. "If you want to eat both containers of soup and the baked potatoes, I can just eat the meatloaf an' green bean salads."

"Let's…" Echo paused, thinking.

"What?" Omega wondered.

"I'm trying to work out how we can use that as a backup plan, while still letting you go ahead and eat," Echo admitted.

"Well, taste the meatloaf first, and see how that's gonna do you," Omega suggested. "Just a tiny bite. If that sits on your tum and doesn't, like, gag you, try some of the green beans. If you're good with that, then we eat like normal, only maybe way slower."

"That should work," Echo decided, digging into the take-out bags and fishing out the dishes. "And then I'mma call Facilities an' tell 'em to send the hazmat guy around to clean the top of the credenza. I'm sure some of that shit is still on the top."

"You think she was trying to make a romantic gesture?"

"I have no clue what that woman is thinking these days," Echo admitted. "I just know whatever it was, in concentrated form, made me sicker than a puppy bolting its food along with all the other puppies' food. Damn. And do I feel for you, Meg. I mean, I did before, but now I've been there."

"Yeah. Thanks, Ace," Omega murmured. "Let's see about getting things settled…maybe an indigestion chewie-thing wouldn't be amiss; they helped me a little…and then put food in you. Nice and slow."

"Okay."

* * *

When 'Joe Bob' arrived in the men's room off the Core, he found the trash bin filled to overflowing with used paper towels. An odd, strong, almost female scent came from it. He raised his eyebrows.

What has someone been doing in here, that I should smell a woman's intimate scent here? he wondered. Then he smirked. *I wonder if Daagnadan has been here with Echo. It would not surprise me.*

He pulled the bag out of the trash receptacle, tied a firm knot in the top, then hung it on the side of his cart, before heading for the elevator to resume his standard round.

In his wake, many of the agents who preferred women found themselves unaccountably aroused.

* * *

The rest of the day was relatively quiet. Echo managed to eat reasonably well, though he had moments of mild nausea off and on the rest of the day. Consequently, and because she sympathized all too well, Omega nixed their previous plans of dinner out. Instead, they went home and Omega made a fast chicken and rice casserole with a can of soup, some roast chicken from the grocery, and some quick-cooking rice — a fast text to Alpha Twenty-Four had resulted in delivery of the items not already in their pantry, notably the fresh roasted chicken.

While Omega cooked, Echo, on her orders, retired to his recliner and leaned back, putting his feet up. He'd been there about ten minutes when the AC came on, and he caught a sudden whiff of a familiar scent…one that, at this point, had decidedly unpleasant connotations.

"What the hell?" he murmured, sitting up slightly.

"What?" Omega called from the kitchen. "Did you say something, Ace?"

"Nah, nothing important," Echo replied, looking around. "At least, I don't think…"

"Yell if you need me for something."

"Okay."

After several moments he decided the slight airflow carrying the scent was coming from his left. Nothing came to his eye, although 'his' end table sat at his elbow.

Nothing on the top, he decided. *There's the lamp, and my book, and a coaster.* Remembering the pod brewer, he picked up the coaster and looked, but there was nothing under it. Then he moved the lamp, but there was nothing under it, either. The book tended to migrate around the apartment, from his end table to his nightstand or the reading nook, so it was unlikely anything was hidden under — or in — it.

Then he opened the cabinet beneath and went through it. *Nothing there, either,* he thought.

Finally he let his fingertips slide around under the lip of the tabletop. He encountered something soft, slightly rough, and oily—

—And immediately his head launched into orbit, as the nausea and throbbing head pain resumed.

"Ugh," he grunted, fighting to keep down the bile. "Meg?"

"Yeah?"

"Grab a zip-lock plastic bag, baby, and come in here. And hurry."

"What's up?"

"I found another present Ree left for me." He pulled the oil-saturated swatch of cloth away from where it had been stuck to the underside of the table lip. "Oh, and a package of cleaning wipes would be good, too."

Omega appeared in the door of the dining room moments later, a bag and a canister of wipes in her hands.

"Shit," she grumbled. "You're almost green in the face. You're definitely green around the mouth."

"Yeah, I feel ya," Echo murmured. "Hold your breath once you get close. I don't want you getting a whiff of this, or we're both gonna be in the bathroom, barfing. Assuming we make it that far."

Omega obeyed, and soon they had the bit of cloth enclosed in plastic, and Echo was carefully wiping down the area of the table where it had been. While he was doing that, Omega headed back to the kitchen and double-bagged the little cloth, then returned with a big enough bag to dispose of the contaminated wipes.

"Given she's been here a couple times now," Omega said, "I'm starting to think maybe we need to go around the place and look to see if she left any more 'presents' behind."

"I'm thinking you're right," Echo said, "but meantime, I'm gonna go wash my hands again. About twelve times. I've got whatever it is all over my hands now."

"That's fine," Omega said, headed for the kitchen to dispose of the bags at the bottom of the trash can…which was lined with a trash bag. "There's some fragrance-free hand lotion over by my sink, if your hands are too dried out when you finish."

"Thanks. Good idea."

* * *

Echo managed to get through dinner reasonably well, though he had to pause and just sip cool water a few times, while he worked on controlling intermittent bouts of nausea. Still, Omega's chicken and rice casserole was simple, inoffensive, and tasty; she had deboned and shredded the roast chicken and added it to the cream of chicken soup, then put in the rice, simmered it until the rice was cooked, dumped the lot into a casserole dish, topped it with a mild blend of shredded cheeses, and heated it through in the oven until the cheese browned lightly. Echo had never had a dish like that before, and it appealed to him.

"For something so simple, that was damned yummy, baby," he told her, as he polished off a decent-sized serving. "And it's sitting on my stomach reasonably well, for all that I keep getting nauseated."

"Good. It's something I used to make when I was in grad school — it was cheap, easy to make, quick, and filling. Never mind the 'tastes good' factor. Plus the whole thing is fairly inoffensive to the body, even to being mostly hypoallergenic. And you don't have to top it with the cheese; you can just spoon it out of a saucepan, if you want to. I thought the cheese would be good tonight, though, and add a few more calories to it for us both."

"It's great, baby. I love it. You can make this any time."

"Good. Just try to relax, for now. Are you sure you got all the residue cleaned off the end table? If so, I'll just put you in the recliner for a while after dinner. Otherwise, you're goin' on the couch while you digest."

"No, I'm pretty sure I got it cleaned off good. I scrubbed at it."

"Okay. While you rest after dinner — and keep it down — I'm gonna get some of our disposable nitrile gloves for taking forensic evidence, maybe one of the special face masks for forensics work, and some more bags and wipes, then I'm gonna see if I can't literally sniff out if there's any more 'presents' your old girlfriend left us in here."

"I can help."

"No, not right now. You've encountered the concentrated perfume twice today. If you run into it again, you might barf for reals, and keep barfing until it gets outta your system, which could take a while, if my experience is anything to judge by," Omega pointed out. "And right now you need to keep your dinner down."

"So do you. And you're more sensitive to it than I am."

"True…but that's why I'm gonna have the gloves and mask," she pointed out. "Plus, I haven't been exposed to it enough to make me really sick in a couple days. I'm betting she tried to put the shit where it would be close to YOU, not me. YOUR end of the credenza, YOUR end table in the den…"

"Eh. Good point," Echo agreed, considering her suggestion. "Yeah, you're probably dead on. All right, on one condition."

"What?"

"You come sit down and rest with me, and once our food is sure to stay put, we hunt together."

"Hm. That works, I guess," Omega decided.

* * *

After a couple of hours had gone by and they'd both had nice little half-hour after-dinner naps, Omega fetched the zip-close bags and the cleaning wipes, and Echo got out the nitrile gloves and a face mask for Omega. Then they discussed likely sites.

"There's nothing around the dining table or the breakfast nook," Omega determined, donning the mask and gloves. "I checked there when I was cleaning away after dinner. I even got down with a flashlight and looked under the tables and chairs. And I doubt she's ever been in the kitchen. Or our home office."

"Okay, that's good," Echo decided. "I'm thinking, judging by how sensitive your nose is, that if she'd put anything on YOUR end table, you'd have found it by now, anyway. Which means you're right, and they're aimed at me."

"Most likely," Omega agreed with a shrug. "It's sort of a romantic thing to do, I guess. Like spritzing a love letter with your perfume, so the intended recipient gets a whiff of it. Just a little weirder, because offworlder."

"Right. So…we check, lessee…we check 'my' side of the couch and the end table," Echo enumerated, "maybe the bedroom…"

"OH! If she managed to sneak into the bedroom while we were busy doing something else, like cooking dinner, I bet she hid one on your nightstand," Omega said. "Maybe even someplace in your closet."

"Bingo," Echo said, snapping his fingers. "Let's start there."

They headed for the bedroom right away.

* * *

Omega found nothing on the top of Echo's nightstand, but Echo opened the nightstand drawer to fetch a flashlight and spotted something.

"Here we go," he said, grabbing the tiny bit of cloth, tucked into the corner of the drawer, between his thumb and index finger.

"NO!" Omega cried. "Use the gloves, Ace!"

But it was too late. Echo's head spun, his gut lurched, his temples pounded.

He dropped the tidbit of cloth on top of the nightstand and leaped to his feet, trying to bolt for the bathroom, but staggering badly from the vertigo. By the time he got to the bathroom door, he was starting to retch, but he slammed through the half-open door to the water closet and flung the seat up just in time, as he purged what was left of the dinner still in his stomach.

Omega, already gloved and masked, followed close behind him. "Oh, honey," she murmured, as he tried to calm his retching. "Hang on a second, here."

She caught up a glass from the vanity nearby, turned on the tap, rinsed the glass, and filled it with cool water. Then she offered it to Echo.

"Here," she said, keeping her voice low. "Rinse and spit in the toilet until your mouth tastes fresher, then sip it. Slowly."

Echo obeyed, and after a few minutes, managed to stop gagging. He leaned against the wall.

"Damn," he murmured. "That was the worst one yet."

"Well, you've been exposed to the stuff several times now, directly," Omega pointed out. "I'm sure, if there's something in it that's bad for human biology, it might even absorb through the skin."

"Which was why you wanted me to use gloves to pick it up," Echo realized, smearing his — uncontaminated — hand down his face. "I am an idiot."

"No. You're just seriously affected by this shit, and not thinking, as a result," Omega pointed out. "Never mind you've eaten less than normal today, because of the nausea. Your blood sugar is low, so your brain doesn't have its usual fuel."

"Do you think you can clean up my nightstand without joining me in here?"

"I'm gonna try," Omega declared, determined. "And see

if this enhanced snoot of mine can't sniff out any other little gifties your dear 'Ree-ree' left for you."

"Please do. And she's not MY dear ANYthing, baby."

"Okay. And you're right; I'm sorry. I was only being sarcastic. Stay put here for now, but if you hear running feet, get outta the way of the toilet."

"Wilco. In fact, I think I'm gonna use your wheeled vanity chair and just park my ass for a little while," Echo decided. "That way, I can shove off and roll outta the way if you're in a hurry."

"That works. I'll be back shortly," Omega said. "Hopefully not running to vomit."

"Go git 'em, cowgirl," Echo said, waving a hand at the door as he eased into the rolling chair.

* * *

Omega returned to the nightstand and, using gloved hands, carefully picked up the swatch and deposited it in a zipper bag, closing it securely. Then she got out several wipes and proceeded to clean, first the top of the nightstand where Echo had flung the scent-soaked bit of cloth, then the corner of the drawer where it had been hidden. The wipes went into another bag, along with the gloves she carefully doffed, and that bag and the sample bag both went into a larger bag, each bag carefully sealed.

"Okay, that takes care of that," Omega murmured to herself, donning fresh gloves. "I think I might fish out the other one from the trash can, gather it all up, and run this by Item and see if she has time to run a chemical analysis on it. It would be good to know exactly what the hell it is that we're reacting to so badly." She took the bag, left the bedroom, and placed the bag in a box she'd set on the dining table, then came back to the bedroom. "I bet I'm not done in here yet," she decided, and removed her mask. "Let's see what I can smell."

* * *

It took some time. Omega wandered around the room, sniffing carefully. Echo, finally settled a little, rolled the chair to the bathroom door to watch his wife 'playing bloodhound,' as she tended to put it.

"I'm smelling something that sorta smells like it, but I'm not finding it," Omega said, frustrated, after a good ten minutes of this. "And I dunno why. I KNOW there's more here someplace, I just can't get a fix on the location. Maybe it's not in the bedroom?"

"Have you checked your nightstand?"

"Yeah. Nothing."

"What about the dresser?"

"Checked. Inside all the drawers, too. Besides," Omega said, thinking hard, "I think she'd have been more apt to fixate on YOUR stuff than mine."

"True…" Echo folded his arms and pondered for long moments, as Omega unconsciously mimicked the move while standing in front of him. "Ummm…what about the closets?"

"Huh?"

"Well, all you have to do is slide open the doors far enough to see if there's male or female off-duty wear in there," Echo pointed out. "We got his an' hers closets, after all."

"Mmph," Omega grunted, heading for Echo's closet. She pushed back the mirrored sliding door, then staggered back as her head reeled abruptly. "Urf…"

"Bingo," Echo said. "Move away from there, baby. Lemme handle this one. The right way, this time, with gloves and a mask. That's gonna make you sick, 'cause you're standing right there, and it's been mostly closed up."

"How did I not detect this when you were gettin' ready each morning?" Omega wondered, as she moved away from the closet and handed Echo a pair of gloves at his hand gesture. Then she removed her own gloves, as she hadn't really had occasion to touch anything contaminated with the mysterious substance, and rubbed her temples, where a headache was now threatening.

"Because lately you've been primping in the bathroom while I got dressed," Echo noted. "I kinda suspected maybe you were wanting to look your best, what with a 'potential rival' in the vicinity?"

Omega flushed.

"Um, yeah, kinda," she confessed in a quiet voice. "And that explains it — I wasn't in the immediate vicinity, and you aren't affected except by the actual stuff, and can't smell it unless it's concentrated. An' I still think some of that's 'cause you've touched it and absorbed some of it now."

"Could very well be," Echo said. He had donned the gloves and a mask and was now kneeling, rummaging through his closet, including looking through his shoes, holding them upside-down and shaking them out onto the floor. Gradually he moved upward…and finally found the tiny bit of oily cloth stuck to the edge of the storage shelf above the Suit jacket rack. "Jackpot," he said.

"Okay, lemme put on a mask and gloves again," Omega said, "and I'll hold the bags for you while you put it in, then I'll seal it while you clean where it was."

"All over it."

* * *

Echo's closet was cleaned rapidly, and Omega added the double-bagged materials to the stash she'd created in the dining room. They spent the rest of the evening searching their quarters, looking for more 'presents' from Nreefluvan, but found nothing else.

"But I dunno if that means there really ISN'T anything else, or if we just didn't find 'em," Omega said, as they eased tired bodies into bed.

"Yeah, I know," Echo agreed. "I guess we can set…damn, maybe Forensics? That seems like overkill for some lovesick chick's romantic gestures…"

"Maybe just Facilities," Omega suggested. "Have 'em do a special decon cleaning or something. Because allergens. I can talk to Zebra in the morning and tell her what we found. Maybe she can set that up for us, or at least prep Facilities on what to look for."

"Good plan," Echo averred, then admitted, "Meantime, I'm finding my own tum isn't in the best shape after being exposed to all of that shit…"

"Ooo," Omega murmured, sympathetic. "You sick again?"

"A little. Sorta…dizzy, I guess. My head — not to mention my belly — just wants me to lay here, really still, and not move much."

"Do you want me to sleep on the couch, so you don't get jostled by me rolling over an' stuff?"

"No, stay close. I want you close. But I'm just gonna lay here and try to go to sleep."

"Want me to get some of my anti-emetic? Zee said if you reacted to any of it at any point, I could."

"That…is not a bad idea."

Omega sat up and reached for the bottle on her nightstand, opening it and extracting a small capsule.

"Here," she said, offering it to him as he pushed up slowly. "You can swallow it dry; it won't hurt, and it slides down pretty easy. But it WILL make you sleepy awfully fast. Zee gave me two versions; one I keep here, and I conk out, and the other I keep in my Suit pocket for daytime work."

"Right," Echo said, accepting the capsule. He popped it in his mouth and swallowed, then eased back down to the pillow. "I think I'm glad I didn't try to do a bedtime snack, just at the moment. You probably need to go grab something, though. Assuming you didn't get into enough to be sick, yourself."

"Well, I'm doing surprisingly okay — once we got it all cleaned up and sealed away, that helped me a LOT — but I wasn't gonna say anything…"

"Go, baby. Get food," Echo said, waving her at the door. "Just…please eat in the kitchen?"

"I can do that."

By the time Omega came back, belly sated, Echo was sound asleep.

* * *

(…No, it did not go at all according to plan, apparently,)

'Joe Bob' told 'Gary' that night.

(I thought you said she took him to her quarters.)

(She did. However, it seems the ambassador was waiting for her within, and was displeased with her. I suspect that rather destroyed the mood, as it were.)

(I should think so! What happened then?)

(I do not know for certain, as yet; I am still trying to ascertain exactly what DID happen from that point. Evidently Echo left and returned to his office, and our mediary may have been confined to quarters by her ambassador. What I overheard sounded like it, in any event.)

(Damnation. That is unforeseen. And counter-productive for our purposes.)

(It is, on both counts. Do you wish me to dispose of the ambassador?)

(No. I think that is too much, too soon, and risks exposing us. Let us be patient and wait, and see if the woman cannot weasel her own way out of this. Do you think she has confessed to the ambassador?)

(No, this much I know — she has not. For the ambassador does not understand the rationale for our agent's behavior, and it irritates her.)

(I see. That is good, then. Our operative knows that it is worth a life if she does ought but follow the plan.)

(It seems so.)

(Good. Watch, wait, listen, and keep me posted.)

(Of course.)

* * *

Daagnadan spent the entire day in the armchair in her quarters, doing little. She had finally turned on the television, and absently channel-surfed as she sat there, crying more often than not. What she did not do was actually watch any of the programming; channel-surfing merely gave her something for her hands to do.

From time to time, when her belly felt like it would cave in, she would rummage through the kitchenette, eating whatever she could find. Discovering a bottle of wine placed there by Supplies, she fetched a handy mug from the cabinets — the wineglasses were on the top shelf, and she did not bother fetching anything to stand on, in order to reach them — and brought it and the wine bottle over to the armchair.

There, still in her négligée and bathrobe from the morning, she proceeded to drink the whole bottle while channel surfing.

She went back for another.

By bedtime, she was thoroughly drunk, and passed out on top of the bed, still in her bathrobe.

* * *

Even though he was starving — he hadn't had anything to eat since dinner the night before, and had lost some of that into the toilet when he threw up — Echo decided to play it safe for breakfast the next morning; Alpha One made a smallish cheese omelet and split it as usual, since they knew Omega had handled one well when she was so ill from the same cause. He tucked it away reasonably easily, and the pair prepared for work.

"Hey Meg?" Echo called from the bedroom, as Omega finished braiding her hair in front of the bathroom mirror.

"Yeah, Ace?"

"I'm gonna head on down to the Alpha Line Room and see about calling Facilities to get it checked out for any more little gifties."

"Sounds like a plan to me. Let 'em know they'll need to go over our apartment too, if you would."

"I was plannin' on it."

"Good. I'll run by the medlab as per usual, and I'll make sure Zee tells Facilities what they need to do to decontaminate. Do you want me to get you any meds there?"

"No, I think I'm okay now that the concentrated stuff is being taken care of. Well, maybe get some extra anti-emetics, just in case."

"Okay. See you in a bit, then."

"I'm gone," Echo said.

Moments later, Omega distantly heard the front door close.

"An' now I'mma dig out those 'gifties' and look into seeing just what the hell she did to him," she muttered to herself. "First she starts gradually messin' with his head, then we find these cloth pads hidden in his stuff with some sorta chemical on 'em, that make him even sicker than I was, when he touches 'em? No way is THAT a coincidence. An' it may not be perfume, either, or at least not ALL perfume. *I* think somebody's using some sorta offworld chemical warfare, here. Effectively, Ace got drugged. The damn conniving little bitch."

Omega paused, then considered, "The question I wanna know is, is she doin' all this just to get Echo back? Or is there something more to it all? And if so, what? And…WHY?"

* * *

Daagnadan had done little for the last couple of days save watch whatever she could find on television without really seeing it, fix tiny little meals in the small kitchen — she simply was not hungry; she was too upset — and cry. There was no more wine left in her quarters, for she had binged in an effort to ignore the pain. It had proven a useless effort.

She had, however, risen at her accustomed time, though she had neither showered, nor dressed for the day — she still wore the same négligée and bathrobe she had since that first night, and both were beginning to become somewhat grubby — when the door chime suddenly rang, and a voice annunciated, "Ras Daagnadan, are you awake and about for the day? It is Ambassador Isahuutob."

"Come in, Rasah," Daagnadan said, apathetic. There was a click, and the ambassador entered the den, where a listless Daagnadan half-reclined on the sofa, her nose and eyes blue-rimmed from crying. She managed to rise to her feet in respect for the ambassador, who then waved her back to her seat on the sofa, then moved herself to the armchair once more.

"How are you, Nreefluvan?" Isahuutob asked in a soft voice, apparently having noted the signs of tears, let alone her physical condition.

"I am...not good, Rasah," Daagnadan responded, morose. "I am despairing and afraid."

"Can you tell me any more?"

Daagnadan pondered for a moment, then tried, "I think the operative word on Earth is, 'blackmail.'"

"Great Maker," Isahuutob said blankly. "Someone in your family, you said the other day?"

Daagnadan merely nodded.

"And you are here to solicit Echo's help?"

"I was, yes."

Isahuutob sat and pondered for long moments. Finally she raised her head.

"Then I release you from your confinement...on one condition."

"What, Rasah?"

"You go straight to Echo and ASK him for his help. Stop this striking around the shrub in an effort to lure him into helping you, and simply tell him what is wrong."

Daagnadan thought for a few minutes. The room was silent as Isahuutob watched the younger woman. At last, Daagnadan nodded.

"That...yes, I think I know how to do that, now," Daagnadan said. "I will do as you say, immediately."

"Good. Then go. You are free to move about Headquarters once more. But do not let me hear of another incident, or I will have you confined and shipped back to Kochav, blackmail or no. And I have instructed Director Fox to notify me if anything else occurs, so I WILL know."

"Yes, Rasah."

And Isahuutob departed.

An energized Daagnadan rose and headed for the bedroom, to shower and dress for the effort.

* * *

"OH!" an angry Zebra exclaimed a little while later. "That can't be a coincidence! What the hell is that little bitch trying to prove?"

"That's what I'd like to know," Omega said, stern and extremely grim of visage. "Let's get Item in on this, and analyze the hell outta these little samples we have, as fast as we can."

"Oh, the head of the Sciences department?"

"Yeah. She's an analytical chemist, and a friend of mine."

"Ooo," Zebra said, then grinned. "Yeah, let's do this!"

"Yup. Then maybe you and Item can come up with a counter, so Echo regains some control, and neither of us gets sick from whatever shit it is that she's using, after this."

"It's a plan," Zebra said, reaching for her cell phone. "I'm all over it."

"Good. I'm headed for the Alpha Line Room, then."

"Go. I got this."

* * *

Several Alpha Line teams had already come into their big meeting room where Alpha One worked and kept their office; the teams were intent on cups of coffee, and were all standing or sitting around, chattering cheerfully as coworkers will do. Echo was at his desk, having taken care of urgent matters as soon as he arrived, and now he was bantering with them, good-humored as usual; the Alpha Line Agents had found him a little less reticent since marrying Omega, and the mood was chipper.

Just then, Nreefluvan came through the door and up the aisle.

"Echo, I...I must speak with you," she said, seeming almost shy. "It is very important. I need...I need your help."

But instead of gesturing her to come talk, Echo leaped to his feet, took three huge steps down the center aisle, and caught her up in his arms, kissing her deeply. Then he swept her up in his arms and carried her back to his desk chair, sitting down and placing her in his lap, where he proceeded to kiss her again. Nreefluvan, caught off guard, kissed back.

"Hey," Echo breathed into her mouth.

"Hi," came the response. "Perhaps we should go to my quarters for that talk."

"Okay."

Shocked, the other Agents moved away.

* * *

But before anyone could react further, Omega appeared in the doorway.

The smile she had worn on her face faded, to be replaced by confusion. This was succeeded by hurt, then anger progressing rapidly to fury. She scowled, her shoulders squaring even as her body seemed to expand in size, and she stalked silently down the central aisle of the big room toward her husband and the woman in his lap, who were kissing each other most intently.

"Oh shit," Yankee whispered, horrified.

"Piled higher an' deeper," Tare responded in kind.

"This ain't good, guys," Monkey breathed.

"And it is about to get vorse, wery fast," Kako observed.

* * *

Echo was completely lost in the kiss, unable to come up for air or even to think. As soon as the scent of Nreefluvan had reached him, his whole body had responded as if to the chemicals he had touched on the cloth swatches the previous day. His head swirled, and he became disoriented for a brief moment, then he suddenly had to have Nreefluvan as close as he could get her. The fact that she had just invited him to her quarters, and he had accepted, barely crossed his conscious mind...which was not really functional in those moments, anyway.

Abruptly Nreefluvan vanished, seeming to teleport from his arms. He heard her shriek in startled fear, and instinctively leaped to his feet...

...To see her doubled over, flying through the air toward the door of the Alpha Line Room butt-first, as an enraged Omega spun and followed.

Echo gave an alarmed cry, and took a step toward the door himself, just as Kako stepped forward and caught Nreefluvan, staggering backward with the momentum, before easing the Kochavi woman to the floor, on her feet.

Then Omega was there, and Nreefluvan took a hard hand-heel to the sternum, stumbling back, through the open door and into the Core. Omega stalked through after her.

"No!" Echo cried, and sprinted for the doorway.

But Omega turned to meet him just outside the door, stiff-arming his right shoulder hard in order to use his own momentum to spin him around, before delivering a strong knife-hand to his right shoulder from behind; it was carefully calculated to temporarily deaden the nerves in his arm, but do no real harm. It also made him briefly light-headed, as the blood flow in the area of the neck was disrupted. This, combined with the dizziness he had been experiencing ever since Nreefluvan got close, dropped him to his knees, panting.

* * *

An infuriated Omega turned, to see Nreefluvan, on her ass on the floor, trying to crab-walk away as fast as she could. But before Nreefluvan could get far enough away to safely scramble to her feet, Omega was there, grabbing her by the throat and lifting her up. Nreefluvan's legs dangled limply, and her hands grasped frantically at Omega's wrist, but could not pry loose the Alpha Line Agent's hold on the Kochavi.

"What the HELL do you think you're doing?! I've TOLD you before, over and over," she snarled to the gasping woman, "stay AWAY from MY husband. But do you listen? Will you do that? NO!" Omega dropped Nreefluvan so that she landed on her feet. "And I, for one, am sick and tired of it. So we'll have to do this the hard way, you and me." She raised both fists. "Let's have at it, bitch."

"Meg, LET HER ALONE!" Echo yelled from behind her, and she realized he was back on his feet and running…toward the two women.

Omega whirled and stepped to one side, extended one arm and fairly clotheslined Echo before he could react. Echo went down hard on his back, the wind knocked out of him.

Omega moved almost faster than the spectators could see — Alpha Line Agents, regular agents from several different departments, and a handful of aliens, all of whom happened to be passing through the Core. They had all stopped dead at the spectacle of Omega brawling with some alien woman while Echo tried to stop it. More, while Omega ensured Echo spent most of his time on the floor, out of the fight; no one had ever seen anyone able to do that to Echo. Of course, only Omega knew he was still reeling from the effects of the chemicals in Nreefluvan's scent.

"As for YOU," Omega snapped at her husband and partner, "you need to stay the hell out of this. You've already gotten yourself in more hot water than you'll be able to handle."

She turned back to Nreefluvan, who was cowering and backing away, whimpering, and looking at the other agents in the area...

...None of whom were coming to her aid, or even offering to help.

As Omega neared, grim-faced, Nreefluvan screamed in terror.

* * *

'Joe Bob' was making his rounds through the Core and associated rooms — the break room, the restrooms, and more — when a sudden commotion sounded from the Alpha Line Room. He rushed to the door of the break room and looked out.

A patently furious Agent Omega stalked toward a badly-frightened Daagnadan, who backed away, crying and begging bystanders for help. A broken ring of spectators formed, even as Agent Echo ran from the Alpha Line Room.

Omega literally strong-armed him, using the Agent's own momentum against him, and Echo went down. Then she spun on Daagnadan once more, grabbing the Kochavi woman by the throat and lifting her clear of the floor with one hand.

'Joe Bob's' eyebrows shot up. *The woman is extremely upset, to be able to do that,* he decided. *Human women should not be that strong, under normal circumstances. I am told by our medics, however, that this... 'adrenal hormone'...is capable of temporarily boosting strength. I had thought that a mere speculation, but now I believe it.*

212

He could not hear what Omega was snarling at the other female as he had forgotten his special microphone — he had stayed up too late the night before, attempting to work out what was happening, and had overslept that morning — but whatever was being said, it was unpleasant, to judge by the fierce, angry expression on Omega's face, and the frightened look on Daagnadan's face...even if she was turning blue; the medical problems would begin if she started turning pink, however, so 'Joe Bob' was not too worried. At least as yet. He supposed it might behoove him to attempt to assist Daagnadan should that begin to occur.

At last Omega dropped Daagnadan back on her feet and raised her fists...even as Echo clambered back to his feet.

'Joe Bob' watched as Omega spun in time to clothesline Echo with her own arm, dropping him to the floor once more.

Then 'Joe Bob' watched in fascination as Omega advanced on Daagnadan.

Daagnadan screamed.

* * *

Fox was sitting at his desk, his back to the bay windows that overlooked the Core, working on his virtual keyboard and using several screens, including two of the big wall screens, to display several spreadsheets of resources from different departments that he was trying to correlate. It was nearing the end of the galactic fiscal year, and budgets were in work, which made for a pain in the tuchus for him as he tried to juggle departmental expenditures and put together a suitable budget for the whole division.

Raised voices outside in the Core distracted him briefly, and he shook his head and tried to focus on his work. It was not uncommon, in any event, for an alien child, or a startled or frustrated alien adult, to cry out in excitement or annoyance.

But when the terrified scream rent the air, he instinctively leaped up and whirled toward the window. He stared in shock as he watched a scowling Omega advancing in a most threatening fashion toward the Daagnadan woman, while Echo picked himself up off the floor behind her. Seconds later, Echo leaped for Omega, but she swiftly sidestepped him, allowing him to hit the floor and slide away, before she resumed advancing on Daagnadan.

He scrambled for the door of his office and the balcony overlooking the Core beyond.

* * *

Omega had just reached Nreefluvan — after dodging a desperate Echo — and was raising her fist to strike when a commanding voice cut through the Core.

"STOP! OMEGA, stop at once!"

Omega froze, then looked up at the Director's balcony.

"Sir," she began.

"Don't give me any backtalk, yung froy," Fox said, firm. "I want you and Echo and Ms. Daagnadan in my office NOW. Yankee, Tare, 'escort' Ms. Daagnadan, please."

The shocked ring of spectators broke up as Echo picked himself up off the floor, Tare and Yankee fell into step on either side of a trembling Daagnadan, and an irked Omega turned toward the ramp leading to the Director's office.

* * *

In the end, Tare and Yankee told Fox what they'd seen; Fox refused to let Echo, Omega, or Daagnadan speak until Alpha Seven had given their eyewitness reports. Then he dismissed Alpha Seven and stared at the trio for long moments.

"It won't do," he declared, as Echo, Daagnadan, and Omega sat in visitor chairs in front of his desk. "It just won't. Omega, you cannot attack the citizen of another system."

"FOX! You should have SEEN her!" Omega protested, leaping up to pace Fox's office, flinging her hands in the air in anger and upset. "She was all over him! She was sitting in his LAP, playing with his hair, kissing all over his face! She has no right to do that!"

"CALM DOWN, Omega," Fox ordered his perturbed Agent, firm. "Echo is his own man. He can do whatever he likes. And let others do whatever he likes." Omega gaped at his response.

"Would you feel like that if Zebra were hanging all over another man?" Omega asked bitterly.

"That's beside the point, jung frau. It isn't going to happen. Zee is my wife an—"

"And ECHO is MY HUSBAND!" Omega cried.

"Sit down, Omega," Echo said, stern. "That's an order."

* * *

"No," Omega countered, unyielding, even as Fox suddenly shook his head in confusion. "If you would treat me like that, you don't hold my respect, and I won't be taking orders from you ever again. I'll transfer offworld first." She sneered down at Daagnadan. "Your philandering little bitch can have you."

"Fine," Daagnadan said in defiance then. "I will take hi—"

"STOP," Fox decreed, holding up both hands. "Something is very, very wrong here. We none of us are behaving normally."

"Shit," Omega said then, her eyes widening in realization. "You're right. Hold on a sec, Fox."

She moved to stand over Nreefluvan's chair, where she sat next to Echo, and breathed deep, nostrils flaring.

"Bingo," she said then, even as pain stabbed through her temple and she winced. "Damn, crap, shit, karkun, and abdab. Fox, you've got all kinds of protective shit on this office, right?"

"Of course, tekhter. It's the division director's office. It has to have all kinds of protective shit."

"Can you vent the air in the room and replace it?"

"In moments."

"What happens to the vented air?"

"It's contained and analyzed for any spurious chemicals— anything that shouldn't be there—in case there is a toxin or a drug or such like. Then any such chemicals are neutralized, precipitated out, and sent to the incinerator. The report of the chemicals in it is sent to me."

"Good. Do it. Maximum speed. Hard enough and long enough to outgas all of us. Then keep it flowing, but back it down a little."

"All right…"

"No," a suddenly-agitated Nreefluvan said, beginning to stand. "NO."

"YOU sit right down here, bitch," Omega snarled, putting both hands on Nreefluvan's shoulders and pushing her back into her seat, then holding her there. She was not particularly gentle. Nreefluvan, being considerably more petite and much less robust, was unable to escape the force of Omega's powerful grip.

"Meg, lay off," Echo growled, reaching for Omega's hands to pull them away from Nreefluvan. "Let her go. And don't you dare call her that again."

"No, Echo, stop," Fox said, as he activated his desktop's virtual keyboard and began typing in commands. "I think I know where Omega is going with this, and it needs doing."

"I don't think—" Echo began.

"I do," Fox cut him off. "And that IS an order. At Directorial level." He hit the last keystroke.

Within moments a sudden breeze stirred in the room, growing stronger and stronger, as the air was flushed out and replaced with fresh. The Agents' ties and jacket tails began to flap around wildly, and Nreefluvan's white hair-equivalent waved about energetically. Fox grabbed at the only unsecured stack of paper on his desk as it began to flutter and lift, then he moved it to another stack with a paperweight on top, and secured both with the paperweight.

"Breathe deep, guys," Omega told them, and Fox and Echo obeyed, relaxing even as they did so. "Exhale all the way. Nice, fresh air…with no Kochavi pheromones in it to manipulate us."

"Aha. I thought that was what you'd deduced…then detected," Fox said, as Echo gaped at her, bemused for long moments. Abruptly he shook his head, his gaze clearing, then he glared at Nreefluvan.

"What the hell?!" Echo exclaimed then. "Is THIS what you've been doing to me, Ree? Manipulating the hell out of me with your PHEROMONES?"

"Yes," Omega answered for the Kochavi woman.

Nreefluvan burst into tears.

"Woman," she wept, "you have just killed Echo's son."

"WHAT?!" Fox and Echo both exclaimed, even as Echo leaped to his feet and backed away.

Omega felt the blood drain from her face. The room spun, and she toppled to the floor.

* * *

'Joe Bob' slowed his work, taking his time emptying trash bins and sweeping up the Core, while several agents, including Echo and Omega, huddled in Director Fox's closed office with Daagnadan.

Either she will succeed, or she will fail, he decided. And I should very much like to see which it is. Gary was brilliant to go looking for the adept, upon hearing legends of her and her kind, in that bar on Aleancë. I wondered at it, given we were already in the heart of power, but he was right. And we are close, very close, I think.

Moments later, two of the agents emerged from the office, carefully closing the door behind themselves. Nothing could be seen through the bay windows of the office, as Fox had opaqued them.

But after about another ten minutes, Echo emerged carrying Omega, hastening toward the corridor to the medlab, while a Deltiri and several guards arrived at Fox's office.

Ahhh, 'Joe Bob' thought, pleased. *She has succeeded. Excellent. Omega is likely dead or dying. And Fox is next. Possibly within moments, at that. We are about to control Division One. Very, very good.*

Chapter 9

Omega woke up in the medlab, in a bed. Her hand was being held, and as she stirred, she heard a familiar, beloved voice with a deep, soft Texan drawl.

"There you are, baby. I was startin' to get damn worried. Are you okay?"

"Mmph," she grunted, pushing up to a semi-sitting position and rubbing her free hand across her eyes. "I…I guess so. I… passed out?"

"Yeah," Echo said, keeping his voice low…which a distinctly headachy Omega appreciated in that moment. "Zebra said that, on top of the stress that was being put on you by the pheromones and the combativeness it was creating between all of us, that last declaration of Ree's pretty much nailed your shock button." He paused, then added, "Never mind that Ree was lying through her teeth."

"Are you sure, Ace?" Omega asked, very, very subdued. "You used to be lovers, after all…"

"Yes, I'm sure, baby," Echo said, earnest. "Because before I did anything with her, especially her being my first-ever lover, I had the sense to go down to the medlab and get the birth control shot."

"Wait, wait, wait. They got 'em for GUYS, too?"

"Yup. As you and India are fond of saying, 'Ain't galactic science wonderful?'" he chuckled. "So yes. I got the shot, and I've never undone that. I've been shooting blanks ever since. There is no way in hell that there is any kid of mine out there someplace. Anywhere." He shook his head. "That just wasn't something I wanted to have happen, at least until I was ready for it. And I was never ready for it…until you came along."

"Are you sure? That it's never gone wrong, I mean."

"I'm not a doctor, Meg. I don't know the medical science, so you'd have to ask Zebra or India or maybe Zarnix. But I've never heard of it malfunctioning. And I've been around the galaxy a time or two."

Omega paused in thought for a long moment, then nodded.

"Okay," she said, accepting. "Zee and I have discussed it before, and she agreed with you. But I think I will ask Zee again, though, just to be sure, and get a little more detail. Especially in our situation. I mean, you and me, we don't need it to fail until we get this whole thing worked out with my genetics…"

"That's reasonable."

"So where IS Daagnadan?"

"Fox kept her in his office, with the airflow on, and brought in Qq'k'l ob Sii'stek from the Deltiri embassy to interrogate her and find out what's really going on, here. And called in about four Praetorians to keep an eye on things, while he was about it."

"And you don't mind?"

"No. Because that kind of coercion wasn't the Ree I knew, so there's something up, here. And we need to know what. Especially with her trying to play a trump card like that last statement of hers."

"Are you sure she didn't know how to manipulate with her pheromones back when you knew her?"

"Absolutely sure. Because there were legends of ancient Kochavi adepts who could do it and pretty much control everyone around 'em with it, but no one living who could. She was a history buff, and she was fascinated by those legends, but at the time, seemed pretty convinced that was ALL they were—legends."

"So she must have figured out how, in the meantime."

"I guess so, yeah. 'Cause she was damn sure doing it. Probably from the moment she saw me. And that makes me really damn angry. Never mind explaining several puzzling things in my behavior lately."

"Why aren't you up there helping, then?"

"Because I'm the one who carried you down here, baby, when you didn't look like waking up right away. We—okay, I—was kinda worried that, well, that maybe her pheromones had screwed up your tweaked biochem or something. And, well, frankly, Fox agreed."

"Oh. You…were worried…about ME, not her…?" Omega cocked her head to the side and looked up at him, unaware that her expression was more than a little wistful.

* * *

"YES," Echo said, as firmly as he could; the forlorn look on her face was breaking his heart and tying his gut in knots. "Listen, um, I'm sorry for, uh…" He shrugged, then sighed. "Everything. Initially I was annoyed with her, because, honey, listen, if you haven't heard already, you will…when she first saw me—I DIDN'T see HER—well, it was what Romeo calls a glomple, glomp for short, and at one point he called it plain borderline obscene. See, she didn't just hug me. She barreled into me, leaped, and wrapped arms AND legs around me! Then grabbed my face and planted several kisses on me, of increasing, uh, passion, we'll say. Think, um, well, if we'd been nude, we coulda done it, right then and there. It…was bad."

"Damn!"

"Yeah. So I told her to get down — except she didn't, so I had to practically peel her off me, and I told her to stop, because I wasn't available."

"You did? SHE did?"

"Yup, to alla that. I'm surprised nobody told you the gossip. It happened in the middle of the Core, and we were a 'right spectacle,' I think Madrid would call it. Which was also why I reeked of her perfume that day." He paused, then added, "Which is interesting, because even with all that, YOU did NOT react to all the perfume…which means it was her pheromones that were affecting you, not her perfume."

"Shit. You're right. And no, nobody said anything — not a word. Maybe they figured it wasn't their business…?"

"Dunno. Or maybe they figured I'd handle it. Which I kept trying to do. I suppose that, with increasing time in proximity with the pheromones, though — especially when I actually came into contact with the liquid form, which I'm afraid to think about where THAT came from, now — anyway, it sorta overwhelmed my usual..." Echo stopped, and screwed up his face. "What the hell word do I use? Behavior? Emotions? Brain activity? All of the above? And then some?" He shook his head. "Does it occur to you that I wasn't behaving normally, maybe for a few days now? A good week, maybe? Because I didn't even seem like me to my own self. I'd think I was behaving one way, only to dimly realize I'd just done what I was determined not to do. Shit like that. I wasn't happy about it at all, I just didn't know what to make of it. Let alone what to do about it. And then, after we found those little cloth pieces all over the place yesterday, and I touched 'em...and then, when she came in this morning, and I smelled her 'perfume'...damn. The upper brain flat-out stopped, and the lower brain took over. And I didn't even have a chance to register the fact, let alone do anything about it. And forget preventing it."

"Yeah, I know what you mean," Omega said, thoughtful. "As soon as I walked into the Alpha Line Room, something changed in the air. Then, when I saw her in your lap, and the two of you kissing, I...I was ready to beat her to a bloody pulp. I'm not usually so...belligerent."

"No, you're not," he agreed. "And the director's office is a much smaller room than the Alpha Line Room. So Fox was on the way to becoming downright autocratic just now, and that's not him at all, either. And did you notice how Fox was using a double standard, there for a bit?"

"Mmph," Omega said, thinking. "Yeah, I did. And I've never seen him do that; he's always very fair and even-handed. So her 'mones can overwhelm our innate personalities and behavioral responses."

"It looks like it, yeah. At least, when it's full bore, wide-open gas bombing us, I guess. Maybe at lesser intensities, not so much."

"That ain't good, Ace."

"No, it's not. From a lot of different perspectives, never

mind the 'where did she learn to do that, and how many others know how' aspect. But, uh, anyway, I'm sorry for the way I've behaved toward you, sweetheart. I'm crazy in love with you, baby, and even under all that shit she was pumping out an' smearing everywhere, I knew it. I just…couldn't seem to stop it. At least, not to KEEP it stopped."

"Nothing to apologize for, Ace," Omega said with a soft smile. She laid a gentle hand on his arm. "Just like you never blamed me for Slug's programming tryin' to take your head off, I can't blame you for her pheromones messing with your head. 'Cause that was a kind of programming, too."

"Yeah, I guess it was, at that. How do you feel now?"

"Physically? Okay, I guess. Sort of. I've been better, I've been worse." She shrugged. "Mentally and emotionally? Pretty churned up," she admitted.

"Hey, it didn't do me any favors, either," Echo confessed. "That was one hell of a declaration Ree-ree — no. No more intimate nicknames like 'Ree-ree,' because it sounds too much like lovers' names for one another. I'll use a nickname, because I've known her a long time, but not the most intimate one I used to use. Never again."

"I have to admit, I like the sound of that…"

"Good. So, as I was saying, that was one hell of a declaration Ree made, there at the end. Never mind the whole pheromone storm that came before. If I'm honest with you, I'm still sorting through everything. Especially what happened this morning. It's like it's all in a fog."

"No shit," Omega chuckled, but it was a wobbly sound to Echo's knowledgeable ears. She glanced down, then did a double-take. "Whoa. I musta been out for a while, if the medlab got me into a medical jumpsuit!"

"You were, girl," Zebra said, coming into the room then. "And you weren't the only one. Turns out Echo was loaded for bear with Kochavi pheromones; anyway, we had to flush those right outta him."

"No shit," Echo said, rolling his eyes. "I spent a good ten, fifteen minutes in the bathroom, peein' like a damn racehorse, while Zee was working on you. Feel better now, too. And a damn sight clearer-headed."

"Whoa," Omega murmured. "Are you better now?"

"Much," Echo declared, firm. "I feel more myself now than I've felt in days. Probably since she arrived."

"How'd she manage that on you, but not me?"

"Remember all those oily cloths we found? One in the office, several at home? We thought it was Ree's perfume, and that it was some sorta alien romantic gesture. But now I'm thinking it was concentrated pheromones, put there to be close to me and try to keep me under her chemical 'spell' or something. And that's also probably what you've been reacting to, not her perfume."

"And he's right," Zebra agreed. "And yes, Item just got back with me not five minutes ago about the samples you brought in this morning, Omega. Pheromonal components with Kochavi signatures, every one of 'em. No artificial perfume components at all. AND Fox pinged me with the news that he got virtually identical results from the chemicals in the air vented from his office!"

"Shit," Omega grumbled. "I was right. Chemical warfare via pheromones."

"That's an interesting way to put it, but I can't argue," Zebra said. "Which also explains why the antihistamines weren't helping you, Meg — yeah, you were having a mild reaction to the offworld components of her perfume 'cause you WERE having a histamine response, but that was slight, and the main reaction was to her pheromones…which was NOT an allergic response. Echo was right about another thing, too, but not about the magnitude of it — it was the Kochavi woman's pheromones that knocked you for a loop just now, at least when combined with the raised adrenaline and the sudden shock of thinking Echo had a kid without you." She shook her head. "None of that did you any favors."

"What about Fox?" Omega wondered. "He just got exposed

to a regular pheromone storm, there, too."

"Yeah, I've talked to him," Zebra said. "He's fairly clear-headed now that he has serious airflow keeping the air fresh in his office, and I'll make sure to take care of the rest of it tonight, once we're at home and can do it. Or whenever we both light in the same place for more than five minutes."

"Oh, good," Omega murmured.

"That said, he hasn't been exposed to it as much as you two, or for nearly so long a time," Zebra said. "It should be relatively easy to flush 'em out of him, and his body might have done it already by the time I can take action on it."

"Is Meg okay now?" Echo asked.

"I need to scan her pretty thoroughly, Echo, but I think so. Or she will be, by the time I'm done. All the same, I'd like to keep her here for a bit longer, if you don't mind, and just make sure. We still need to flush the pheros out of her, too, now that she's awake."

"No problem, Zee," Echo said, standing; he'd eased into a seated position on the edge of the bed when Omega showed evidence of waking. "You want me here, or you want me outta the way…?"

"Neither — it'd be your call — but Fox wants you in his office as soon as it's convenient, so you probably ought to head that way. And yes, Item and I already told him about the pheromone-soaked cloth bits that were left for you, and the way it was influencing your behavior to do what that little bitch wanted. He's not especially happy, but will probably have finished reaming Daagnadan a new one by the time you get there — WITH the Kochavi ambassador on the horn at the same time, while he's about it, so I expect she put in her two and a half cents' worth, too. YOU, he's not mad at, because I told him that's about as subtle a manipulation as you can get without a telepath involved. And he said to tell you that, and that he's already handling things for you with Alpha Line and any other eyewitnesses."

"Right. That's good to hear, all around, and thank you, Zee.

Meg?"

"I'll monitor through the nd't'lq," she said, tapping her temple. "Go find out what's happening."

"I'm gone, then, baby."

"Later, Ace."

He kissed her, then headed for the door.

"Okay, dear, let's see what's up with you," Zebra said with a smile.

* * *

"…Well, normally it's foolproof, yes," Zebra told Omega a bit later, after a fairly intense question-and-answer session that followed Zebra's scan of her patient. "No ifs, ands, or buts. These particular drugs are intended for humanoids in the Opdip morphology, and were expressly tweaked to ensure they'd work for humans, and be really effective. And tweaked again when the Agency started realizing we didn't have a marriage clause in our charter. They're as effective and foolproof as galactic medicine knows how to make 'em. Which is pretty damned effective, all in all."

"Okay," Omega said, as she got dressed with the physician's assistance, having been given a clean bill of health fairly rapidly, once the last residues of the pheromones had cleared her system with a BIG glass of water, a couple of additional meds, and a lengthy trip to the bathroom — though Zebra gave her orders to eat well, thoroughly hydrate, and get a good night's sleep, as soon as she could. "I hear a 'but' in all that."

"Yeah, sorta. When all that shit went down with you and Mark Wright late last summer, Zarnix and India and Dihl and I put our heads together. None of us have been here since the very beginning, of course, but we still had access to all the medical records. There is NO record of a galactic birth control ever failing in any human on whom it was used."

"I'm still hearing a 'but,' but you haven't said it yet."

"Here it comes. BUT, we HAVE heard of it failing in other Opdip species," Zebra noted. "The failure rates are really, really low, as in 'zero point' followed by a bunch more zeroes before you get to another number, but NOT JUST zero. Now, it may be that it wasn't modified correctly for them, or sufficiently, or something like that, and it has been, for us. OR…it could be that statistically, it happens, and we just haven't hit the number of usages in the data base that gives us a probability of 1.00 yet."

"Or we did, and didn't know it, because the mother went off the planet and is only just now telling the father about it," Omega said with a sigh.

"…And that's possible, too," Zebra admitted reluctantly. "I know it wasn't what you hoped you'd hear…"

"No shit," Omega murmured. "I adore the man, but I don't dare even try to give him a child or it could kill him, and this woman busted up with him when he was barely more than a boy, hurt him badly in the doing, and she's the one who allegedly gave birth to his only child. Maybe the only one he'll ever have, thanks to me."

"Aw, honey, come on," Zebra chastised gently. "We're still working on that. Don't give up hope."

"I'm not," Omega protested, but it was weak. "I just…"

"Don't want to think of Echo having a child with another woman."

"Damn," Omega whispered. "That, right there."

* * *

"There you are," Qq'k'l ob Sii'stek, one of the staff of the embassy of the telepathic Deltiri, located there in the Division One Headquarters, told Echo as he came through the door of Fox's office. "I felt that perhaps you should be here, Echo, as you know this female better than anyone here."

"How's Omega?" Fox asked, concerned.

"Conscious, feeling more or less decent — probably less, rather than more — but really emotionally…perturbed," Echo said. "As would be expected of my wife, given our newlywed status and the behavior and statements made by certain persons of my former acquaintance. Never mind the behavior said former acquaintance forced on ME." He shot a hard, angry, accusatory look at Daagnadan, who flinched and looked like crying again.

"If I cooperate, may I have your help?" Daagnadan asked then, in a very small voice. "Otherwise, our child may die, Echo."

"Nreefluvan, understand something right now," Echo said, firmer than granite, and just as hard. "You may have a child. But it is not MY child. Yes, we were intimate at one time, but first, I haven't seen you in YEARS, and in all that time, you have said NOTHING to me about a child. Second, at the time we were intimate, I was—and still am—on galactic-pharmaceutical birth control. There is no way any child of yours could be mine."

"Echo, things happen," Daagnadan said, as a tear trickled from one corner of her lavender eyes. "Nothing is foolproof. Believe me, I know! When we broke up—"

"When YOU broke up with ME, you mean."

"A-all right," she sighed. "I deserved that. I did not handle it well at the time, and I know it. But by the time I arrived back on Kochav, I was showing signs that I was newly expectant…"

"Were you not on birth control as well?" Fox wondered, surprised.

"I was. That is what I mean by 'things happen.' The doctors believe it was because I was in a cross-species relationship, though they never determined the failure mechanism," Daagnadan explained. "After a relatively normal gestation otherwise, I delivered a healthy youngling male…and the doctors confirmed, he was half Kochavi…and half human."

"Then it's not mine," Echo said, growing even harder, "and you cheated on me."

"I swear I did not!" Daagnadan pleaded.

"Then why didn't you contact me and tell me at the time?" Echo challenged. "Why is this only coming up now, after you tried your damnedest to manipulate the hell out of me, to make ME cheat on MEG?"

"I tried! Every way I could think of! I could not reach YOU!

The Director at the time—I do not recall her name, but it was not Fox, here—had arranged for my communiqués to route to X-ray, and he apparently never told you!" She shook her head. "Only after two full annums past the birth, I finally gave up…"

"Shit," Echo murmured, suddenly comprehending. "That's why you wondered where he was…"

"Yes. Echo," Daagnadan wept, "you do not have to acknowledge him if you do not wish it, but I love him! He is my SON! I carried him in my body as he formed, I nursed him, I have cared for him! Please help me! I do not wish him to die at the hands of that insane creature!"

"She is telling the truth, at least as best she understands it, Echo," Qq'k'l, who was a trained and certified telepathic interrogator, told the Agent, as Fox looked on. "And she is very upset and agitated, fearing for the life of her child. Which she sincerely believes is yours, also."

"What insane creature?" Fox interjected before Echo could speak. "Who has your son, and why?"

"I do not know what he is, but he is not from Kochav, or any other world I know," Daagnadan admitted. "His name, as best I can pronounce it, is Geretan Aggum. You see, I had not kept it a secret that Alexaan was Echo's son, but I had not made it public knowledge, either — because of certain…cultural taboos on Kochav. Nor had I made it widely known that I had at last learned the ancient Kochavi art of pheromone control…"

"Wait," Echo demanded. "HOW did you learn pheromone control? The last time we had discussed it, you swore up and down that it was only a myth."

"That…is a long story," Daagnadan sighed.

"Let's hear it," Fox ordered.

* * *

"After Alexaan was born, I quickly realized that the boy was patently only half-Kochavi," Daagnadan explained. "This, combined with my failure to keep from becoming pregnant, resulted in a certain degree of ostracism in Kochavi culture; the Kochavi were and are very open and enthusiastic as regards sex and sexual partners, but that comes with certain restrictions. First and foremost was not to bring children into the world until one's lifemate had been found."

"Aha," Fox said. "I see. Since Nreefluvan, here, had not married Echo—had, in fact, broken up with him, at her own instigation—she had violated that restriction."

"Yes," Daagnadan confirmed. She drew a long breath. "Sit down, please, all of you. This story spans more than five annums; it will take a while to tell."

Echo and Qq'k'l took seats, as the Kochavi woman continued her tale.

* * *

The second problem she had experienced upon her return to her homeworld, it transpired, was borne of the stricture upon genetics: Kochavi culture insisted that all efforts be made to ensure healthy offspring, and that included the child's genetics. Consequently, hybrid children—borne of two different species—were somewhat frowned upon, due to the possibility of incompatibilities in the genetics. This stricture was somewhat mitigated in her case, however, since both she and Echo had been demonstrably on pharmaceutical birth control; interspecies accidents of this sort did sometimes happen, though the medical researchers were still working on why, and how to counter them.

However it came about, and whatever the mitigating circumstances, the end result was that she had violated no less than two major taboos of her culture. and she was rather scorned as a consequence. Even her family turned their backs, disappointed in her. No amount of explaining, of pleading, or of demanding, persuaded her maman and dadan—let alone her siblings—to eschew their ostracization. She had embarrassed her family, and this was not negotiable.

Nreefluvan therefore turned her focus into raising her child and continuing her education, going back to the Kochavi equivalent of college for a PhD in history. Choosing to focus on the ancient legends of Kochavi adepts in pheromonal manipulation, she did well.

Until it was time to begin the specific research on her dissertation.

"No," her advisor told her. "I do not think that it is enough to spend all your time in ancient tomes. I think you need to try to find some of the native populations where these myths originated. Do not fear for the financial cost of the travel; you have been a good student and a diligent researcher, already producing numerous papers that have been received well by the journals, so I have little doubt that the university will assist with the finances."

So when Alexaan was weaned and old enough to spend time with those relations who would accept him without his being afraid, Nreefluvan left him with her maman, her mother—who, alone among her family, was still interested in the boy, at least—and dove into determining where she was most likely to find elders knowledgeable of the legends.

Then she set out.

* * *

Her travels took her to a very remote part of Kochav, up in the Vareelin Mountains; had Echo been there, he would have remarked how much the terrain and the culture reminded him of Tibet. She bought passage on a commercial aircraft and flew into a small city in the foothills of the Vareelins, then hired a driver to take her up into the range, to a small village. There, a local native took her in hand, and led her even deeper into the mountains, high up Mount Rneges, to a cave.

"There," she told Nreefluvan. "What you seek is in there."

"I have not the equipment for cave exploration," she answered, apprehensive. "I must leave and come back, better prepared."

"If you leave now, you will never be allowed back," the native replied. "The cave does not require extensive equipment to negotiate, and there are glowing fungi to light the way. You are here. That is all that you need. Go...or leave, and do not return."

Nreefluvan took a deep breath, hitched up the strap of her pack, and turned toward the cave entrance.

* * *

It was not quite as easy as the native had suggested, though the passage was indeed well-illuminated from the fungi growing all over the dank roof. Not ten feet in, and around a bend in the passage, was a deep pit, its bottom shrouded in darkness. From somewhere deep within, an odd, acrid smell exuded. She dropped a rock into it, then counted off the seconds it took for it to hit bottom. Eventually a faint, distant clack came to her ears.

"Almost eleven seconds," she whispered, horrified. "It is nearly an Earth mile deep! How do I get past..."

Just then, in the eerie glow of the fungi, she saw a narrow ledge to one side.

"Oh great Maker," she breathed. "I have to cross on THAT?"

She very nearly turned back at that point. But, screwing her courage to the utmost, she removed her pack, dragging it cautiously along the ledge behind her so she could press her back against the rock wall. Then she inched her way along the path, careful not to look down, into the pit.

It took more than fifteen minutes. The pit or sinkhole was not narrow, and she took her time, ensuring she would not make a mistake that could cost her life. But finally she was past, and the path widened into the full passage once more.

Nreefluvan got well away from the sinkhole, then sat down on the stone floor of the cave, allowing her body to react. She shook badly for long minutes, sucking in deep lungfuls of air, before reaching for the canteen of water in her pack and drinking until she was sated.

* * *

Eventually she regained control of her emotions. Nreefluvan rose, shrugged into her backpack, and moved forward.

But the next thing she encountered, once she got well out of sight of the sinkhole, was a swarm of crawlers. These were Kochav's equivalent of spiders, and they resembled them a goodly amount, save for the fact that they had twelve legs instead of only eight — making them that much more disturbing — and unlike most Earth spiders, they neither climbed nor spun webs, but stalked and hunted.

Kochavi were cautious around them, however, because they also tended to be considerably larger than Earth spiders— anywhere from a handspan up to over a foot, nearly two, in diameter—and like spiders, were predators, usually targeting the local rodents as their prey. These species tended to be solitary. Some species, however, swarmed, and those groups often targeted larger prey. The Kochavi in areas where swarming species lived were protective of their pets and children, for the crawler swarms had been known to target them. And once a crawler swarm was finished with its prey, there was little left but bones. A few larger swarms had even managed to kill several adult Kochavi.

This was not a small swarm.

And she could smell their venom, a pungent, sharp, acidic note in the air.

"Oh ragnadang," Nreefluvan whispered. "Drekulik, now what?"

'The cave does not require extensive equipment to negotiate,' she recalled the native guide telling her. *So that means I can get around this some other way.*

She tried to remain calm and study her surroundings, even as the swarm caught sight of her and began to stalk, gradually spreading out and attempting to flank her.

"AH!" she cried, and ran to the left wall before the crawlers could cut her off from it, grabbing several rocks as handholds and placing her foot on one of the lower stones that protruded from the wall. In seconds she was several feet off the floor of the cave, and there were sufficient protruding rocks to use as hand- and footholds that she could work her way down the corridor at a reasonable speed.

This caught the crawlers off-guard; their heads were not set on necks as such, and while they had excellent vision, including peripheral vision, it was largely planar in nature — they could not look up, and could only look down in a limited range of motion. More, fortunately or unfortunately depending upon one's viewpoint, the larger species could not climb due to their size and weight; this swarm was from a very large species, and could not follow, nor did it occur to any of them to try. So as soon as Nreefluvan was high enough to be outside their range of sight, they lost track of their prey, and wandered around in the vicinity where she was last seen.

Meanwhile, Nreefluvan had, with reasonable dexterity, flanked the swarm and moved well down the corridor. Glancing back, she found the swarm had apparently moved off; they were no longer in sight.

"Round two," she murmured to herself, as she climbed back down to the cave floor. "I wonder how much farther I have to go..."

It turned out not to be that far.

* * *

She got a good fifty feet further into the cave, where she eased around a tight dog-leg turn in the passage...

...And it opened up into a comfortable corridor, polished and smoothed, the floor and ceiling at precise right angles to the walls. Soft lighting, apparently inset into the ceiling of the passage, illuminated the floor beneath her feet.

This passage has been cut, she thought, startled and mildly shocked. *And that lighting is some sort of sophisticated technology, not the torch of a crude cave-dweller, nor yet bioluminescent fungi. What is going on here?*

"Ah, there you are," a voice echoed from somewhere down the corridor. "Come, my dear Nreefluvan. You have much to learn. And I have little time to teach it."

And a door opened at the end of the corridor, spilling light into the passage.

* * *

A cautious Nreefluvan crept down the corridor and eased through the open doorway, looking around.

Just inside the door was a comfortable little suite, not over-large, but lush, elegant, and obviously comfortable: there were overstuffed leather chairs with fur throws, tables, lamps whose light appeared similar to that in the hallway, and a large tea service sitting on a low serving table. A fireplace—Nreefluvan had no idea where it exhausted, but it obviously drew well—stood in the far wall, carved into the native rock, and a fire crackled merrily in it. Before it stood a Kochavi male.

He was very old, this male, with long locks so white they were nearly transparent, a face as wrinkled as dried fruit, almost luminous periwinkle-blue eyes, and a warm, welcoming smile.

"Come in, come in, Nreefluvan. My name is Meooln Treboojrn," the wizened old Kochavi informed her. "I am Un Groenja Arn, the Chief Adept. I have had word of you from many sources."

"I, um, I see. I...am pleased to meet you, Arn Treboojrn," she replied, uncertain, careful to use the old Kochavi term for *master*. "Adept at, um, what, exactly?"

"Why, pheromone manipulation, of course," Treboojrn answered with a chuckle. "You see, it does truly exist. The legends are not merely myth, as most of your professors believe, but true oral history." He paused, sobering, then added, "Except for your dissertation advisor. He knows of us; his great-grandfather was one of us, but none of his family since have had the interest...or the talent." Treboojrn cocked his head to one side. "When you became interested in the ancient tales, when you began to study them as your graduate speciality, he contacted us. He had, himself, been interested as a young man, but had not the raw talent. He saw in you the possibility to continue the line of adepts."

"But, but," Nreefluvan stammered, "how do you know I have any raw talent, either?"

"You have already been tested," Treboojrn remarked with another smile. "Not all of your qualifying exams were mandated by your school, my dear."

"Oh..."

"Now, do you wish to begin the training, or no?"

"May I ask some questions first?"

"Of course. But let me answer what is foremost in your mind, judging by your own pheromones," the elder remarked. "We know that you have a child, of course, for your instructor told us. And yes, we can manage to train you without your having to remain here for long periods, so you may care for him properly. You will have much to practice upon returning home, and must periodically return here for more training, but it is doable. Eventually you may even be able to bring him with you, especially if he shows promise himself, but he must be older for that. So. If we start today, you can return home on precisely the day you expected to return, a lunation hence, with no one the wiser—save your professor, who will help you with your dissertation, so as to avoid revealing too much."

"I had not heard that any Kochavi were telepaths," Nreefluvan tried, shocked, and the old one laughed heartily.

"We are not," he noted. "But you have apparently only thought of the emitting of pheromones, rather than being able to read in detail those of others. Which I can do, as well."

"O-okay," she said, and Treboojrn snorted.

"Your human lover has added to your vocabulary, I see," he said. "And so that was your first lesson: there is more to being an adept than merely controlling one's own pheromones. And here is your second. Leave your pack here, and come with me."

Nreefluvan shucked out of her backpack, depositing it on the nearby sofa, and followed the master adept back the way she had come. They exited the obviously-artificial part of the passage and entered back into the original cave system. Treboojrn strode forward swiftly and agilely for one so old, but as they approached a certain part of the passage, Nreefluvan put a restraining hand on his shoulder.

"Forgive me, Arn Treboojrn," she murmured, when he paused. "Tread carefully. There is a very big swarm of large crawlers ahead; they appear to have found their way into the cave system."

Treboojrn chuckled again.

"Did they, now?" he said. "You mean up here?" He strode forward, around a bend...

...And there was nothing. He kept going, even as a creeped-out Nreefluvan followed, watching in all directions.

Another bend, and she stopped dead, recognizing her location.

"Where is it?" she wondered. "The pit? I thought I should never get around it! It should be here..."

Treboojrn smiled.

"There never was any pit," he said. "Though I wondered what that particular pheromone would make you perceive."

"I...do not understand," Nreefluvan murmured, badly confused.

"This stretch of cavern is the final test, child," the old master said softly. "I and my fellows manipulate the atmosphere within it, filling it with this or that pheromone, which causes you to react as we wish. It is a gauntlet of sorts, and those who cannot pass through it never reach us to find out anything. There was no pit, and there were never any crawlers in the cave. We made you perceive those. You were never in any danger."

"How many people make it through?" she asked.

"You are the first since your professor, over twenty-five annums ago," Treboojrn said. "Once in a great while, one will come through the passage who can detect the pheromones and sort them out, and is thereby not affected by the pheromones and walks right through our gauntlet. But that is rare—"

"I SMELLED THEM!" Nreefluvan cried, realizing. "There was something acrid in the pit, and the crawlers' venom smelled acidic..."

Treboojrn raised a surprised eyebrow.

"Indeed. Interesting. Come," he said. "Let me see you settled in, fed, and comfortable. Then we can begin in earnest."

* * *

Nreefluvan Daagnadan was in the home of Adept Treboojrn for a solid month. And it was a month of intense training, not all of it enjoyable. In order to understand all possible emotional states, she had to undergo the conditions required to trigger those states, and analyze them in detail. This included the unpleasant states of being, in addition to the pleasant ones — annoyance, anger, fury, fear, panic, and more. The training was grueling, and she could be washed out at any time, should she fail in meeting his expectations.

But she proved an excellent student, picking up on what was being taught at a great rate, and able to analyze a situation to determine what needed doing, and what pheromones were needed.

"I simply do not know how to command my pheromones yet," she pointed out, as the month drew to a close, and her aircraft flight home neared. "We have still so much to do!"

"Not this time," Treboojrn said. "You have indeed learned much. I want you to return home and continue to analyze your environment and the people around you, as you have been doing here."

"But..."

"You will be back, and soon," a smiling Treboojrn said, soothing. "You are going to be 'doing research' with your advisor for several years yet."

"Oh..."

"Now it is time for you to pack your things," the old master said. "I will see you to the cave entrance, and your sherpa guide will be waiting to take you down the mountain and back to the village."

"The sherpa...?"

"Is one of us, as you suspect," Treboojrn nodded. "Now go, youngling."

* * *

A toddling Alexaan was very glad to see his maman when Nreefluvan returned, although her own maman was somewhat short and brusque as yet. Still, it was good to be home, and to return to the university to see her advisor.

"I gather that went well," he said with a grin, when she

arrived in his office. "Now, let us see about completing your doctorate, and assigning you to a post-doctoral research position under me..."

* * *

"It took more than four years," Nreefluvan told the Division One Agents, "before my training was complete. I was officially a groenja arn, a pheromone adept. The first thing I did upon returning home—and this was expressly planned with Arn Treboojrn—was to use it to mollify my family, so that I might have a little more interaction, for my son's sake. I did not, as X-ray would have said, 'go overboard' on it; I did not wish to control my family, only to convince them to open up a bit more. And they did," she said, "and it was not so long before they accepted, and I no longer had to use my pheromones when I was around them, to produce acceptance. But in general I am still a bit resented by my neighbors. I was not averse to coming back to Earth, let me just say."

"Did you use your abilities often?" Qq'k'l wondered.

"Not so much," Nreefluvan said with a shrug. "There were times when the Adept, the Neri Groenja Arn — 'the Guild of the Aura Adept' is the literal translation in English — were gathered together to work as one, and sometimes we would work in ones and twos. These times were usually when there was something...unpleasant...occurring, or about to occur. A war, or a riot, or an act of terror. These were the times we gathered to combat matters. We were...not secret; we did not do a great deal to hide our abilities. Which is why there are rumors and legends of the Kochavi adepts all over the galaxy, if one pays attention. Our abilities are simply not that obvious unless one IS an adept, or has the talent or potential to become one, or perhaps knows what to look for." She cast a meaningful glance at Echo. "I have never seen a non-Kochavi do what your mate did earlier."

"Well, I guess we know where that ability came from," Echo muttered. Fox drew a deep breath.

"I'll look into any Kochavi cold cases for her, zun, when

this is all over," he said.

"Right," Qq'k'l agreed, understanding the oblique communiqué. Nreefluvan raised a querying eyebrow, but no one was forthcoming with an explanation, so she continued.

"All that said, however, there were very few outside the Neri Groenja Arn who knew it existed," Nreefluvan noted. "A couple of national leaders here and there, a researcher or two such as my graduate advisor, and that was the extent of the outside knowledge. One might count them on the fingers of one hand, and still have fingers left." She paused. "But somehow this loathsome creature discovered both facts!"

"How?" Echo pressed.

"I am unsure. I think — perhaps — he may have heard the legends from some of those cultures with whom we have been in long contact," Nreefluvan decided. "And then came to Kochav expressly to look. And as I said earlier, if one already knows what to look for, it becomes easier. At any rate, he found us — he captured my advisor, I think, for Diipik — Professor Diipik Baaxegis — has disappeared, and I fear for his life, as well — and then the ragnadang drekulik took Alexaan prisoner from his school! He insisted that if I wished my son to live, I would come to Earth and resume my relationship with Agent Echo, whatever it took! And I was to manipulate matters— using my pheromone control whenever necessary—until Echo became the Director, and then I would control him and receive my orders from this being as to what Echo was to do!"

"A coup attempt," Echo noted, and the others nodded.

"But you still haven't told us who it really was," Fox pointed out.

"She gave us a name, Fox," Echo pointed out. "Geretan Aggum."

"And that sounds familiar," Fox admitted. "I just can't place it. Where is he FROM? What species?"

"She does not know how to tell us, friend Fox," Qq'k'l said. "She sees the creature in her mind, but her people have no words to describe such a being. Let me show you. I suspect you will recognize it then."

And in both humans' minds flashed an image of a strange being. It had a liver-colored, barrel-shaped body, multiple boneless limbs with suckers on specific areas of those limbs, gill slits on what little passed for a neck, and big black eyes in a bulbous head. Ear holes were arranged in an arc around the back of the head, and the lipless mouth was V-shaped. Two legs ended in foot-like protuberances covered in suckers, and four arms ended in something like hands. Each hand, as boneless as the arms, possessed six tentacle fingers, at each tip of which was a small round sucker.

"SHIT!" Fox exclaimed then, recognizing it instantly, even as Echo gasped. "It's a Ka'agand!"

"From the Andromeda Galaxy," Echo finished for him. "Looks like the Scuttles are back."

"Scuttles?" Fox wondered.

"Oh," Echo said with a wry, humorless chuckle. "Turns out, that's what the agents ended up calling the various Persan species under the fake Adita. It relates to both their general resemblance to cuttlefish, and the way they move, as well as the underhanded way they deal, and is a generic term across all the Persan races. It's not complimentary, and it's not supposed to be. I've never heard any of our people use that term against the citizens of the legitimate Persis Federation, though. Just the rogue faction."

"Good," Fox said. "They get the difference."

"Oh hell yes."

"Oh dear," Qq'k'l said, as he listened. "I think I have finally understood your conversation. With the surname of Aggum, may this being possibly be kin to the general who attempted the so-called 'Adita's Coup'?"

"That makes an awful damn lotta sense, and yeah, that's what we're speculating," Echo confirmed. "Maybe we didn't clean out all of the members of the attempted coup, after all."

* * *

"Do you have photos or images of your son, Ms.

Daagnadan?" Fox wondered. "If we are to help you with this, it would be good if our agents can recognize him."

"Yes," Daagnadan said quietly, pulling out her communications device, which like most such, also served as a tablet of sorts. She opened a folder and showed Fox the imagery of a young Kochavi boy, appearing to be around eight or nine years old by Earth standards. Fox knew the boy was older than that, but he also knew that the Kochavi did not age at the same rate as humans; the youngling likely WAS the human equivalent of eight or nine. *After all,* he considered, *if he were pure Kochavi he would look no more than six. And the gestation is nearly 2 years. Which means,* he realized, *that Ms. Daagnadan likely tried to get through to Echo, to tell him about the child, for close to FOUR years, Earth time. I suppose X-ray thought it was a scam or the like, and refused to bite, or even tell Echo. He never thought Daagnadan was right for the boy. And in the end, he was correct.*

"Mm," Fox said, after a moment to study the photos. "Yes, all right. If you can send these to me, I'll see that Division Two gets hold of them, and I'll look at maybe getting our people involved as well, since there's the paternity question. Yes, yes," Fox held up a hand as Echo started to protest, "I know, Echo, but this is Aggum's kin we're looking at, here, as the kidnapper. More than likely, from what I've heard, it's another coup attempt. And Division Two doesn't have an Alpha Line, or anything close. We do."

"Aha," Echo said, placated. "Okay, that makes sense. But I can't go in; if he's after me, then I need to stay away…and so do you."

"I know," Fox said, as a smirk formed on his face. "That's why you and I are staying in the background. I'm sending in the Praetorians."

"Oh," Echo said in surprise.

* * *

In the medlab, monitoring the interaction via the nd't'lq bond, Omega echoed her mate's reaction. Moments later, her cell phone, on the bed table, dinged with an incoming message. She picked it up and opened the message.

Omega, this is Fox.
I assume you've been monitoring this
whole meshuginah mess through Echo?

Yes, Fox, I have.
You want the Praetorians on this?
Because we can use Echo's
paternity question as an excuse?

Exactly, tekhter.
I'm going to send you the images
of the boy. That way, you'll have it
to recognize your target.

Fire when ready.

Incoming.

Moments later, she had a small folder of photographs.

Omega studied the images carefully. The boy had an odd dark-gray shade of hair—not fully black, nor was it white—and his eyes were brownish-purple. He had wide, high cheekbones and he was long and lean for his size. He was handsome by human standards, and a cute boy by any standards.

And enough resemblance to Echo to make people wonder, Omega thought. *If that's not Echo's son, then Daagnadan found his twin to mate with. And Echo doesn't even have any real close cousins, let alone a brother. Damn.*

She stifled a sigh, choking back tears, and closed the folder.

* * *

Later that day, the medlab released Omega, but sent her home to rest before resuming duty the next day. She did anything but, however, sitting in the den and studying the photos that now resided on her phone, and pondering this or that feature and mentally attempting to compare it to Echo.

She also piggybacked on the information and strategy session occurring in Fox's office.

* * *

"Where did the kidnapping take place?" Fox asked Daagnadan.

"At his school," Nreefluvan noted, as, behind her, Qq'k'l nodded confirmation. "I was a little late arriving from my school to his due to some heavy traffic, and got there just in time to see him hustled into a waiting vehicle by some men I did not recognize."

"What did you do then, Ree?" Echo asked.

"I followed their vehicle," Nreefluvan admitted. "I stayed far enough back that I hoped not to be noticed, but to keep up with them. They took him to what HAD been an old, abandoned warehouse on the outskirts of our city."

"HAD been? You mean it wasn't any more?" Fox wondered.

"Yes, that is correct," Nreefluvan said. "It had been refurbished and was now rather…I think X-ray used to term it, 'high-tech'?"

"What happened then?" Fox continued.

"They took him inside, and I started to leave and go to the police," Nreefluvan said, then bit her lip, her eyes instinctively dilating in fear. "Then one of them came to get me — they had seen me following them, after all. They said I could get my son back, but I had to talk to someone first."

"Keep going," Fox urged.

"They took me to this Aggum creature," Nreefluvan said, "and he told me that, if I wanted to see my son Alexaan again, I would have to come to Earth, use my skills with pheromones to entrap Echo, and see that he became the Director one way or another, with me as his mate. Then I would have to stay with Echo and use my abilities to control him and his decisions as Director. Only after I had proven myself might I regain Alexaan." She shuddered. "Suddenly all of the Kochavi men around me seemed to vibrate, and abruptly they were no longer Kochavi — they were creatures like this Aggum." She shook her head. "I screamed — I could not help it; I had never seen beings like them before, I was frightened, and did not know what to do."

"And?" Fox continued.

"One of them returned to Kochavi form and escorted me back to my vehicle," Nreefluvan whispered. "I did not even get to see Alexaan."

"How do you think they knew about your pheromone abilities, Ree?" Echo asked.

"I think they heard about the legends elsewhere, then came to my world, looking specifically for adepts. My supervisor at the university, the same one who ensured that I met the High Adept, went missing about a week earlier," she explained. "No one knew what had become of him. I think he must somehow have let somewhat slip about his own ancestry — like me, he was fascinated by the lore, and as a professor of historicities, made no attempt to keep the lore secret — and they first captured him to use him, then discovered he was not an adept, merely descended from one. So they likely forced him to tell them about me. I cannot say for sure, but that is what I suspect. I...I smelled traces of him, somewhere in the building."

"Mmph," Echo grunted. "This was planned. She was deliberately slowed down in traffic long enough for them to grab the boy, then take him to their headquarters."

"It looks like it," Fox agreed, having already gotten a subtle thumbs-up from Qq'k'l. "Now the question becomes, how do we make use of the information?"

* * *

They spent quite a bit of time discussing the situation, including bringing in Ciarmhac Ulseleigh, the Division Two Director, on a vidcall to try to coordinate Division One and Division Two efforts...never mind simply notifying the other division head of the situation in his own region of the galaxy. Fox also popped a notification of the coup attempt to the Ennead, along with several questions that came out in the course of the brainstorming session.

Eventually, after considerable discussion — during which, Nreefluvan Daagnadan was escorted to her quarters and confined there, with full notice as to the situation provided to Her Excellency Rnaalti Isahuutob, who was not only worried about her citizen, but concerned about the relations between Kochav and Earth…

…Echo went home.

* * *

As Omega became aware that Echo's day was winding down, she roused herself from her melancholy fascination over the child's appearance and moved into the kitchen to begin preparing dinner. She opted for Tex-Mex comfort food and decided to make carnitas — a kind of Mexican pulled-pork sandwich or tortilla — for the main course, bracketed by loaded nachos for the appetizer, and Native-style frybread dusted with cinnamon sugar for dessert.

Though I honestly don't know if I can choke any of it down, she thought. *But I guess I need to try, for Echo's sake. I'm sure he's gonna be upset, too. Which is why I cooked it, after all.*

But much to Omega's surprise, he wasn't.

"Hey, baby," he called cheerfully, as he entered their quarters. "Ooo, something smells DAMN good!"

"I thought some comfort food might be welcome tonight," Omega suggested, coming to the dining room door to meet him.

"I appreciate it, baby, more than I can say," Echo said, leaning down to kiss her. "But seriously, I'm doing fine. While you were out of it, Zee got all the residual shit outta me that Ree went to an effort to put in, so physically I feel a damn sight better. Emotionally? I am absolutely confident that there's nothing to worry about where Ree and her kid are concerned."

"You're sure?" Omega wondered, looking into his eyes. Echo gazed back, the deep brown eyes serene and calm.

"I'm sure," he said, then hugged her close. "It's gonna be

245

fine, sweetheart. And Ree knows better than to even TRY to come between us now, not when we're the impetus behind getting her son freed."

"Um, okay," she acquiesced, not sure he was right, at least about the boy. "Dinner's ready. Let's, uh, let's eat."

"Great! I'm starved!"

I'm not, she thought, stifling a dejected sigh. *Not at all. But let's see what I can do, here. I have to try, at least, for Echo's sake.*

* * *

In the end, she managed to eat by dint of avoiding most of the spicy condiments on both the loaded nachos and the carnitas, and eating a fair amount of frybread to fill the corners. Echo fairly inhaled his portion, and ate with alacrity anything that she wasn't able to consume.

"After all, baby," he pointed out, "you were in the medlab for a while today. It stands to reason your digestive tract would be a little off tonight, after all the trouble the pheromones have given you. And believe me," he added, "I know about THAT! I feel better tonight than I have in several days, thanks to getting alla that shit outta my system. But I'm not surprised in the least that you're still feeling a little off-kilter, especially as sensitive as YOUR system is. It's okay; as the saying is, this, too, shall pass."

They spent time on the sofa together watching a movie afterward, cuddled under the Orion Nebula throw and sipping wine in Omega's case — she thought it would go down easier than her usual liquor — and whisky in Echo's case.

When the film ended, they went to bed.

* * *

But even after Echo's enthusiastic, renewed attentions, Omega couldn't sleep.

Echo, on the other hand, finally at peace with what had happened, and why he had been behaving so differently from how he felt, as well as relieved at knowing that his wife and his boss-slash-father-figure did not blame him for it, relaxed and drifted into slumber right away.

Finally, rather than lie there tossing and turning, and risk waking up her husband, Omega got up, grabbed some loungewear acceptable for public viewing, and headed out.

* * *

Omega sat on the roof of the Headquarters building, staring up into the dark heavens, deep in thought. She had a tight mental block around those thoughts, because she didn't want to risk upsetting Echo, who was still quite soundly asleep in their big bed.

Now what? she wondered. *If that's not Echo's kid, his father was a cousin or something, I swear he is. But I didn't think he had any blood relatives in the Agency back then. And just Dihl now.*

So Nreefluvan gave him a child. Something it doesn't look like I can do for him. He cares about her, I can tell. And he loved her once. It hurt him when she broke off their relationship. It still hurts him, the way she behaved then. Maybe he still loves her. He's damn sure still attracted to her; I don't think she could have taken things as far as she did if he wasn't. She drew a deep breath, and let it out in a sigh. *Maybe they'd make the better family. Echo, Ree, and little Alexaan. Then maybe Baby Ree later on. As opposed to me, who maybe—MAYBE—can manage a kid...that isn't gonna try to kill him...if the medlab dinks around and cuts me open or something. And even his mom knows, he wants kids bad.*

She put her face in her hands.

I love Echo so much. But...but despite the brave face I put on for Echo an' Zee, I just don't know if I can stand to be flayed alive like that again. Even if they try to knock me out or something, I think I'd know. Especially given all the shit Slug did to 'enhance' me. Damn the monster.

Maybe...maybe if the boy turns out to be Echo's son, I should just go to Fox and...and step aside, she considered. *I can have the wedding annulled, get the life partnership dissolved, and transfer offworld. Uncle Pul would probably still like having me for his bodyguard corps, and that'd provide a human... sorta...for the corps, too, something he doesn't currently have. And then Fox and Zebra would be along one of these days, once Fox retires from the PGLEIA, so I'd still have family there, after a fashion.*

A tear welled up and trickled over.

I don't want to, she fussed at herself, arguing back and forth with the different sides of her psyche as she tried to decide what to do. *I adore Echo. He's...he's part of me. He's the love of my life. I'd never love anyone the way I love him. I'm not sure I could even try. I don't WANT to try!*

Then again, he deserves a full family, and I'm not sure I can give that to him. Not safely, anyhow. But Nreefluvan already has, it looks like. But is that what he wants?

I could ask him. But if I ask him, he'll wanna know why, and if he finds out I'm considering my options, he'll put the kibosh on it. And then that means he's stuck with me, and maybe no kids, ever. And that's not fair to him. He at least needs that option.

I dunno. I just...don't...know, she thought, and put her face in her hands, letting the tears come as they would.

She was there most of the night.

Chapter 10

Early the next 'morning'—morning being relative for a Division One Agent, for it was pitch dark out—still lost in her musings, Omega was startled into attentiveness by a mental shout.

Meg! MEG! WHERE ARE YOU?! BABY, WHERE ARE YOU? ARE YOU OKAY? MEG! ANSWER ME! WHERE ARE YOU??

"Oooh!" she exclaimed aloud, then dropped her telepathic block.

I'm sorry, Ace, she said, contrite. *I'm up on the roof, next to the observatory dome. I couldn't sleep, so I came up here to think so I wouldn't bother you. And I put up a block so you could sleep and not get bugged by me going around and around about stuff. I guess I lost track of time.*

Oh, came a slightly breathless reply; Omega always found it vaguely amusing and not a little curious that even one's mental voice tended to have aspects of vocalization in it. Then she caught a mental flash of Echo running from room to room in their quarters in an increasing panic, looking for her, and sobered instantly. *You sure you're okay, baby?*

Yeah, I'm fine, Ace.

No, you're not. You're still upset. And it's about Ree's kid.

Well…yeah.

He's not mine, Meg.

You can't say that a hundred percent for certain, Echo. You and I both know that.

She tried to control me, baby. This may just be another form of control.

Not according to the Deltiri, it isn't. She BELIEVES it, Ace. And let's face it—those photos have a certain resemblance.

So what did you conclude?

I haven't, yet, she admitted. *I dunno what to do.*

I'd come up there and hug you, but I don't think Fox would appreciate his assistant director walking stark naked through Headquarters. Even if I'm in the living quarters area.

And I can be down there by the time you're dressed. Don't bother. I'm on the way. I've just been mostly sitting here staring at the stars, anyway.

Okay. I'll be waiting. Stark naked.

Naked Cowboy? she wondered with a laugh.

If you want me to, sure. My hat's over here on the dresser.

I'll be down in three!

At a dead run, it sounds like.

Damn straight, cowboy!

* * *

Unfortunately, before she could get back to their quarters, Fox called.

"The plan is for Echo and me to disappear," he told Omega on the ciphered multiple-person call as she slowed her precipitate run through the corridors of the agent housing area. "If anyone followed Ms. Daagnadan to Earth, they may well know that that plan has now gone south. I hope not, for the boy's sake, but it's entirely possible. If that's the case, they'll be looking to enact whatever their Plan B is. And I intend to ensure that they can't."

"Disappear where?" Omega wondered.

"You know I showed you the special place, tekhter," Fox said. "Back when we were planning the whole Praetorians concept. That's phase one of my plan."

"Right. Okay," Omega murmured, finally entering Alpha One's apartment even as Echo ran around and threw on clothing as fast as he could go. "I'll see Echo gets safely there, then call in the Praetorians, like we discussed yesterday."

"Are you all right, tekhter?"

"Not really, Fox — this whole situation has me pretty damn upset — but not so much that I can't do my job, so no worries there."

"Good. I mean, bad, but…you know what I mean."

"Yeah," Omega said with a tired, wry grin.

"Okay, baby," Echo said, as he adjusted the knot in his tie. "Hand me my pieces and let's get the hell outta Dodge."

"Did you put on the body armor like I asked?" she wondered. Echo knocked on his chest.

"Neck to toe," he averred. "And I even have the special helmet, folded and in a warp pocket. I just need my weapons and I'm ready."

"Done," Omega said, reaching for the two blasters and one Winchester & Tesla on the dresser. "We'll be there to meet you in five, Fox. I won't be in my Suit, but I want the two of you hidden ASAP; I can come back and dress properly later."

"And I'll be waiting," Fox responded. "And good thought on the body armor, tekhter, zun. Fortunately, that's something I've been doing myself for some years now, so I'm good, as well. And no need to worry about your clothing for this, Omega; I understand it's very early in the morning. You'll be fine."

Moments later, Omega was escorting Echo into the warp tunnel passage in the back of her closet.

* * *

"Okay, guys, thanks for coming," Omega said, as the Praetorians met in the Alpha Line Room, later that morning. The door was closed, the windows opaqued, and Omega had set up a special acoustic-wave nullifying field around the room's periphery; no one outside that room would know what transpired there. And that was exactly how she wanted it. "We've had a situation come up, and we're needed."

"What's up?" Monkey wondered. "Did we get a threat against Fox? Echo?"

"Invasion threat?" Tare wondered.

"None of the above...exactly," Omega said, "and yet, we did...to all of that."

"Explain," Romeo demanded.

"All right," Omega said, trying hard not to flush. "By now I'm sure you've all seen the Kochavi woman, Echo's old girlfriend?"

"Yeah," went the dispassionate, almost downbeat chorus around the room. "Kinda don't like her much," someone muttered, though Omega couldn't tell who. "Big damn bitch, if ya ask me."

"Well, her son has been kidnapped by a rogue faction, and she was sent here by them to try to gain control of Echo, get rid of Fox, and thereby move Echo into the Directorship... controlled by her son's kidnappers through her, on threat of death to the boy if she didn't. That's why she's been acting like a 'big damn bitch,' not because she IS one. She's scared nearly witless for her son. We're going to go rescue the boy."

"Where is he?" India asked. "The boy, I mean."

"Kochav," Omega answered. "Capital city of Reegar, on the outskirts. In an old factory that's been modified to what sounds like a heavily-fortified headquarters for the renegade Andromedan invasion force."

"You're kidding," a disbelieving Easy expostulated. "Are you saying that the Scuttles are back?"

"Unfortunately, yes," Omega verified. "That's exactly what I'm saying."

A chorus of curses went around the room.

"Not again," Golf grumbled. "Those bastards?"

"Yup, those very bastards," Omega confirmed. "Led by another member of the Aggum clan, apparently. We're figuring brother, out to finish what his sibling started, though we don't know for sure. All we do know for certain is that he's a member of the Aggum family, aiming for the same thing as Humn Aggum, aka the fake Ordik Adita."

"Right," Easy sighed. "We might gonna have to nuke the whole damn family, at this rate."

"I hope not," Omega agreed. "But I'm ready to, if it comes down to it. I am past sick to death of this shit."

"But why can't Division Two personnel handle that?" Oscar wondered. "I mean, the woman is a Kochavi. So's her son. It's their business."

"Not...quite," Omega sighed, then screwed up her courage

and admitted the sticking point. "It's entirely possible that... that Echo is the father."

The shocked room fell silent.

"Oh shit," Yankee murmured.

"Alla that, man," Romeo agreed.

* * *

It took a while to explain all the details, but eventually Omega managed it. She struggled a bit, finding her throat kept trying to choke up, but the others were patient and sympathetic, and that helped her get through it.

"So where's Echo?" Romeo wondered, when he was done. "I'd 'a figured he'd be th' one ta tell us all that shit, not you. It's his bizniz, after all."

"Fox has him sequestered," Omega explained. "They're both kind of, of...'in hiding' isn't quite the right term, but it's the closest I can come to explaining. Out of sight, maybe, is a better way of putting it. He's worried that maybe Aggum sent somebody along after Ms. Daagnadan to spy on matters, and make sure she did what she was supposed to do."

"Or else they'd kill the kid, huh?" Dog wondered.

"To be honest, I only hope the boy is still alive," Omega admitted. "It's entirely possible, given what we know of Humn Aggum, that if that kind of ruthlessness runs in the family? Well, then the child is probably already dead, and may have been before Ms. Daagnadan ever left Kochav. No, I think Fox is trying to make sure that nobody else can get to either him OR Echo." She shrugged. "And that 'nobody' might include Ms. Daagnadan, although I think she's leveled with us and is working with us now. I hope so, anyway. The Deltiri interrogator thinks she is, at least."

The room fell silent again, this time in horror.

"We gotta go to Kochav, right?" Romeo verified.

"Yup."

"They gonna come with, or stay here? Echo an' Fox, I mean."

"I'm not sure yet," Omega confessed. "They were

discussing that when I left them to come meet with y'all and give you this pre-mission briefing. I think they're leaning toward going with us, because on the *Genesis* they might be marginally better protected — access is limited, see, and if we play it right, nobody will even know they're aboard. Plus, these bastards aren't gonna know we're coming, so it would be like both of 'em just flat disappeared, if they DO have somebody watching."

"Looks like that scenario with the Scuttles that we kept working is gonna come in handy now," Queen noted.

"Looks like it, yeah, Queen," Omega agreed. "Which is another reason why we're the ones doing it. We're gonna have Alpha Line backing for sure, but this is Praetorian driven, this go."

"How are YOU doin', Pook?" Chi wondered, then smeared his hand down his face. "Sorry, Meg. I was...worried about you, and it slipped out."

"Pook is an old nickname," Omega explained to the others. "Chi and I go way on back. Like, NASA days."

"It's kinda cute," India said with a grin. "Pointed and succinct, though. It might just work for a code name or an undercover name. Like, when we have an emergency sitch and need to contact Meg to tell her it's a Directorial security matter, we call for Pook, not Omega."

"I like it," Romeo said, raising an eyebrow. "Meg?"

"Hey, if it works for y'all, and you don't think it's too cutesy and maybe disparaging—that's what Fox was worried about, undermining my authority as an Agent lead—I'm good with using it that way," Omega said. "Guys?"

"Let's do it," Horse opined.

"Yeah! That works! Go for it!" came the response.

"Motion carries," Omega chuckled. "I'll have to make sure I let Fox an' Echo know. Especially Fox."

"Good, but nice job deflecting, Pook," Chi remonstrated. "HOW are YOU doing?"

"Yeah, nice dodge," India agreed. "And I'm waiting for the

answer, too."

Omega drew a deep breath to answer, then let it out in a sigh, not sure what to say, or where to even start.

"That says it all, right there," Romeo pointed out.

"Yeah," Yankee agreed. "Hurtin' pretty bad, huh?"

"It's not the greatest news in the world, as far as I'm concerned," Omega noted in a low voice, shoulders slumped. "I mean, what new wife wants to find out her husband has a child by a former girlfriend? Especially since HE didn't even know about it?"

"You don't know it's Echo's," Oscar offered. "Don't borrow trouble, hon. Let's just go get the boy, and then we can find out."

"I was about to say the same thing," India averred. "Let's do this. Are we gonna have backup, or is it just the Praetorians? Wait, you said Alpha Line, right?"

"Yeah, for starters; we're gonna have backup out the wazoo, I think," Omega said. "We'll have quite a few other Alpha Line Agents, plus a buncha units out of Division Two, according to Director Ulseleigh, who is supposed to meet us there personally. But the Praetorians are gonna take the point, because we've done so much wargame training against simulated Andromedans. And we have the partnership that led the resistance to Adita's Coup." She glanced at Golf and Easy, the Alpha Four partnership; they nodded. "Normally, if Alpha Two is coming along, y'all would be staying here, but since we'll have a good sized contingent of Alpha Line along — most of the Headquarters branch, including the Enigma Team — AND y'all headed up the coup resistance, Fox wants all of you along for the ride."

"Makes sense t' me," Romeo said.

"Me too," Easy agreed.

"All right," Golf said then. "The longer we wait, the more time they have to figure out that something's up. I move we mobilize."

"Seconded," Romeo said.

"Thirded," Easy averred.

"Fourth, fifth, sixth, and seventh here," Yankee declared, gesturing at the Firewall Team.

"Just say the word already, Meg," India cut to the chase.

"Consider it done," Omega ordered. "The word is said. Everybody, go gear up. I'll see that Echo and Fox get the word to prep for going offworld. Assuming they ARE going with us."

"Done," Romeo said, and the group broke up.

* * *

Over the course of the next few hours, various members of the Headquarters staff began departing Earth by ones, twos, and threes.

Zarnix, accompanied by Yorker, left first, ostensibly to 'visit his homeworld,' and take Yorker along to sightsee.

Discouraged at her failure, Nreefluvan Daagnadan requested that one of the Alpha Line teams might take her home to Kochav. Unsurprisingly, Omega approved the request without question.

Zebra decided to grab Dihl and go visit Pulgey Entiyti, to see how he was doing after all he had been through, as well as checking the replacement of his amputated wing by a cybernetic version.

Alpha Two and Alpha Four, along with Horse, Oyster, Page, and another new recruit named Tokyo, decided to take a larger saucer up to try out some maneuvers the two Alpha teams had dreamed up to use against the Cortians. Beta 28 and Delta 23 volunteered to be the 'Cortians' in the war game Alpha Two and -Four had come up with. Many of the other Alpha Teams joined the war games, as well, each partnership piloting its own craft, sufficient to flesh out two small 'fleets' in said war games.

Qq'k'l ob Sii'stek simply…vanished.

Omega offered to take Beta 52, comprising her old friend Chi and his partner Genova, as well as Alpha Seven and Eight, on a tour of the solar system.

And Delta 29 took a suborbital hop to the Sydney Office…

…But never arrived.

Nor did any of the other flights arrive at their advertised destinations.

* * *

On her way out of Headquarters with Alpha Twenty-Two, Daagnadan pulled something small out of her trousers pocket.

"Oh," she said to the two Agents, "I forgot to throw this away…"

"Waste can over there," one of the Agents told her, pointing.

Daagnadan detoured, cutting across the main concourse of Grand Central Station to the indicated trash bin, where she tossed the small object into the can.

Then she rejoined Alpha Twenty-Two and they continued down the concourse toward the gate where their small spacecraft awaited.

The small vial of liquid clattered down through the metal bin and cracked open when it hit the bottom. The oily liquid oozed out and seeped over the interior of the plastic-bag-lined container, soaking the adjacent contents and absorbing into the paper products.

* * *

A new agent, Unload, caught a ride to the Lunar Farside Drydocks facility on a small shuttlecraft piloted by Dog and his partner Quebec, and crewed by Oscar, Eagle, and Topsail. This team's advertised intent was to investigate some odd phenomena that had been occurring around Saturn's moon, Titan. A ship awaited them at the Drydocks, and they had only to take command of it before heading for Titan.

The five split up at the Drydocks, Unload and Oscar accompanying Dog, while Eagle and Topsail stayed together. The two groups surreptitiously made for a special shuttle gate designated only for…

…The *Genesis*.

* * *

Later that morning, 'Joe Bob' got a call from Facilities.

"Hey, Joe Bob, I need you to get down here to Grand Central Station in a hurry," Pudding, the head of the Facilities department, said. "Bring a damn big bucket and a couple of new mops. Oh, and bring a couple canisters of super-sopper. I got a mess for ya."

"What happened?" 'Joe Bob' wondered.

"We're not sure," Pudding admitted. "We had a new family coming in; the female is a new staffer for the Kaceerlon Embassy. She says they hit some sort of cloud of very strong scent — smelled to her like an Opdip female in heat, whatever the hell that means — and she, her mate, and their three offspring all got dizzy and sick at once, then started in with some serious projectile vomiting. The kids had some, um, explosive diarrhea, too. We have one HELL of a mess down in the main concourse of Grand Central Station. And of course it would be just off the food court for the offworlders. Hell, I don't think the food court smells very good at the best of times, given what they serve there. But now that whole area is pretty much painted in vomit and shit. Literally. If you think you need one, run by Supplies and get an oxygen mask, so you don't have to smell it any more than you can help, 'cause it's BAD."

"Well, shit," 'Joe Bob' sighed.

"Yeah, that's the problem," Pudding fired back. "Well, that and puke."

This is the disadvantage of being embedded as a janitor, an unhappy 'Joe Bob' decided. *I can go anywhere and see anything in the facility, but I also have to put up with this. Ugh. And this task sounds likely to take a while.*

He gathered his equipment — including an oxygen mask, a disposable coverall, booties, and plenty of gloves — and headed for Grand Central Station's main concourse.

* * *

Two hours after the last departure from Earth, the entire lot all found themselves aboard the now fully-staffed *Genesis*.

Nreefluvan Daagnadan was given a specially-guarded stateroom suite, with two bedrooms. She occupied one bedroom, and Qq'k'l ob Sii'stek occupied the other. He would remain aboard the *Genesis*, in order to provide for a certain level of telepathic security for various persons onboard, including Daagnadan, during its current mission.

Agents Unload and Tokyo, carefully secreted in another specially-guarded stateroom dual-bedroom suite, dropped solid hologram disguises to reveal…Agent Echo and Director Fox, respectively.

"Omega," Fox ordered, "contact the bridge and tell them to prepare for an immediate departure, under maximum security code D1-RED-0102."

Moments later, Omega looked up from her phone.

"Done, sir," she declared. "Secure *Genesis* Protocol engaged. We have priority; we will be cloaking as soon as we have cleared the docks and exited the Drydocks cloaking field."

"Good," Fox decreed. "Let's get this over and done with."

"Amen," Echo vouched.

* * *

It only took about five hours at maximum non-emergency cruising speed — at least, for the *Genesis*. It would have taken most other spacecraft nearly twice as long, but Fox and the chief engineer of the *Genesis*, Uncle, were constantly working to improve the flagship's already substantial abilities — and by now, they were very good at it. They arrived in the Kochav system, still cloaked, and sent a covert, tight-beam ciphered blip communication to Division Two Director Ciarmhac Ulseleigh.

Moments later, a highly-directional, collimated transmission pinged the *Genesis* for Fox. It was piped directly through to the special secure quarters being used by Fox and Zebra, and Echo and Omega — it was a multi-bedroom suite stateroom, so it served the purpose. It wasn't optimal, having both the Director and the Assistant Director in one suite, as Omega had pointed out, but as long as nobody knew, it would do for the moment.

"And," as Fox noted, "we stand a higher chance of being found out if we'd brought along BOTH flagships."

"True, but let's at least look at putting you two on opposite ends of the *Genesis* or something, next time," Omega said. "Or, hell, in the next couple hours, preferably."

"We'll look at doing that, right after I talk to Director Ulseleigh," Fox averred, though he smirked when he said it, so Omega figured he was not in a hurry. She sighed, just as Fox hit the remote for the wall screen.

"Mhac? That you?" Fox asked, as the screen came to life.

"Indeed, my old friend," Ulseleigh replied. The Division Two director was an Erikian, short, squat, with an egg-shaped head and distinctly greenish-tinged skin, like PGLEIA Chief Gwag Wuxullian, and the two were in fact good friends, having known each other since childhood, though Wuxullian was a few years older. "Are you and Echo safe?"

"We are, for now, at least," Fox confirmed. "Echo is here with me, along with my wife and his, and we are surrounded by our new and very skilled bodyguard contingent, many of whom are on loan from Alpha Line. And most of the rest of the Headquarters Alpha Line contingent is along for the ride, as well."

"Oh, that is very good news," the diminutive director remarked. "And speaking of news, my people on Kochav have been busy."

"Good. Let's hear it."

"All right, let me see..." Ulseleigh glanced to the side, appearing to consult notes. "Kochav; capital city, Reegar. Outskirts. Right. The building in question is a legitimate building lease, though obviously we may have some issues regarding the lessee; the lessor's paperwork is in proper order, however. The building has been renovated by the lessee at his own expense as a means of obtaining a lower rent. It appears to my people to be rather what you might term overkill, however, in that it is greatly over-secure."

"Who leased it?" Echo asked.

"A presumed Kochavi who goes by the name Gereetan Agguumbeh," Ulseleigh replied. "Based on what you told me of our perp, it seems that he chose to modify his Andromedan name in order to make it sound more Kochavi. And my operatives say that everyone there appears to BE Kochavi."

"Most likely using the same embedded tech that was used for Adita's Coup and the attack on Pulgey, Fox," Echo pointed out. "Especially given how Ree described her interactions with 'em."

"Yes, I was thinking the same thing," Fox admitted. "Keep going, Mhac."

"Very well. It has taken a bit of effort, and not a little remote sensor scanning, plus the loss of one of my people..."

"Shit," Omega murmured; she had positioned herself near the door to stand guard. "Sorry about that, Director Ulseleigh. We never meant to lose anybody if we could help it."

"Thank you, Agent Omega, but she knew the risks, going in," Ulseleigh replied. "I assume that was Omega, and not your wife, Fox? It did not sound like Zebra, but I cannot see who spoke..."

"Correct, Mhac," Fox confirmed. "Omega is the head of our bodyguard unit, the Praetorians. She's standing guard on the suite door, so is not in range of the camera."

"Excellent, excellent," Ulseleigh said. "So. Our perpetrators are guarding the building with numerous security measures. These include...let me see here...ah...video cameras, biometric readers, motion sensors and laser grids, ground sensors — presumably to listen for digging, with a 'smart' computer hooked up to learn what sounds are normal, so it can alarm on something abnormal. They also have infrared cameras whose computerized controllers are programmed to target both Kochavi AND human temperature ranges — interesting addition, I thought, especially the 'human' part — and sound an alert if detected...which supports what you told me about the Andromedans having a very different, almost amphibian, metabolic rate. They have video monitors on the roof to watch for approaching vehicles and generate an alert in the event one approaches too closely — whether by air or road. There is a force field which is up more often than not. There are, believe it or not, automated kill boxes at the nominal entrances, and booby traps along major corridors and in any potential entrances. The latter is how I lost my agent."

"That's some significant security, all right, by the sound," Zebra commented.

"No shit," Echo agreed.

"Yeah," Omega said, thoughtful, "but I can see workarounds to bypass all of 'em. We just need to know what's where, when."

Zebra's eyebrows flew up in shock, and both Fox and Echo turned knowing, pleased gazes on the female Agent.

"Attagirl," Echo murmured. "Some of that reading material Lydhuu sent you has helped you up your game."

"Yup," Omega replied with a slight grin.

"Good. Mhac," Fox said then, "by any chance were your people able to MAP any of this...?"

"I cannot be certain we got everything, Fox, but yes," Ulseleigh replied. "We anticipated the need to extract the child, as well as possibly the professor, and we have mapped the entire thing using multiple levels and frequencies of remote sensing. We have also found the location where the child is being held, as there is a small Kochavi signature in a contained room. There is also a room down the corridor from the small signature, containing what appears to be an adult body. Neither are close to the area being used by the Persans, nor are any of those signatures near the perimeter of the facility. I assume this is to keep them isolated and unable to make use of anything to call for help. But I fear it does not bode well for the professor."

"I didn't figure it would," Omega sighed. "Well, that simplifies things, I guess. Director Ulseleigh, would you mind popping that mapped data to Fox?"

"I am already doing so, Agent," Ulseleigh answered, his eyes on something offscreen as his hands moved about and they heard the soft clicking of keys. "There. You should have it momentarily, Fox, though you will need to decrypt it."

"Got it," Fox said, watching his Directorial tablet even as it dinged receipt. "I'll get on this, and get it to Omega, as soon as I can."

"Keep me in the loop," Ulseleigh warned. "I plan to have a contingent of my people there to assist, but we do not want to give ourselves away before your experienced people have a chance to effect rescues."

"Will do," Fox said. "I agree that my people should take the point anyway, as we've had the most interactions with the Persans. But we definitely welcome the backup and being-power. Anything else you have for us?"

"No, that should do it for now, I think. Do any of you have any questions?"

Fox glanced at Echo, then Omega; both shook their heads. He looked at Zebra last; she shook her head as well — one captive was dead, one alive, but it was impossible to know the condition of the live captive, so she did not bother asking.

"Not right now, Mhac," Fox said. "If anything comes up, I'll ping you on this channel."

"Understood. Ulseleigh out."

"Fox out."

* * *

While Zebra joined the rest of the medical staff in sick bay to ensure it was prepped and ready, Omega called in Romeo, Golf, and Easy, and the four joined with Echo and Fox in studying the resulting schematics and determining strategic routes through the building, avoiding most of the traps and determining workarounds and bypasses for the rest. Somehow Fox managed to access the three-dimensional holographic tank on the bridge and bring up a good-sized translucent image of the schematics in the middle of the suite's den, so they could all see and discuss it.

Meanwhile, the bridge crew brought a cloaked *Genesis* into a synchronous orbit behind Kochav's larger moon. A bleat on Fox's tablet let him know.

"Okay, that is excellent, kinder," Fox noted, after checking the message from the bridge. "We are in the L3 point relative to Kochav and its principal moon Kirdev. We're still cloaked, with sensor scrambler also engaged, just in case there are any renegade Andromedans also watching from orbit."

"This works," Omega declared. "Are the landing craft ready?"

Fox double-checked something else on his tablet.

"They are, tekhter," he confirmed. "As soon as we finish here, you can call together the rest of your people, brief them, and board. Once you've boarded, notify the bridge, and the *Genesis* will move into position to drop you."

"Roger that," Omega murmured, thoughtful.

Be careful, baby, Echo told her privately. *Don't get wrapped around the axle about this kid and end up biting it. I don't think I could deal with that.*

Aw, Omega replied, touched. *You know you'd be fine, Ace.*

I don't know any such thing. I've told you several times, Meg, one of the few things that honestly scares me is losing you. Have you stopped to think about why?

Not...really. I never have understood it, to be honest.

Okay, turn it around, then. What would you do if YOU lost ME?

Omega blinked, leaned back from the discussion over the schematics in the tank, and looked at him. *I...don't know,* she confessed, heart sinking at the very thought. *But it wouldn't be pretty. And...honestly? I might not survive the experience.*

Uh-huh. I understand THAT. So why would you think I'd be any different? he asked.

You're stronger, for one thing, Omega said. *Plus, you have a little boy depending on you.*

No, I don't, Echo pointed out. *Though I suppose he might think so, if Ree has talked to him about me.*

Look. Let's talk about all this after we get the boy out, Omega suggested. *I'll be careful. I have to be, if I'm gonna bring him back to you and Nreefluvan.*

"STOP THAT," Echo declared aloud, and the discussion

over the schematic stopped abruptly, as everyone stared at Alpha One. The very air seemed to become tense. "I've told you repeatedly, Meg, that kid isn't MY kid."

"Except you can't say that for sure, Echo," Zebra said, keeping her voice soft; she had just returned from a quick trip to sick bay to find out how preparations were progressing. "And Meg and I have discussed that, too."

"You are NOT helping, Zee," Echo snapped. "I'm getting ready to pull rank here, and insist that Meg can't go on this mission."

"On what grounds?" Fox asked, startled.

"She's so convinced this kid is mine, I'm getting worried about exactly what she's gonna do," Echo noted. "I'm afraid for her mental state, and her physical response."

"I told you, Ace," Omega replied, raising an irked blonde eyebrow. "I'm not gonna do anything stupid. We have to get that little boy out of this situation. And you know how I am about kids. And if there's even the slightest chance this is YOUR kid, then he's part of you, and I'll never let anything happen to you or yours, ever again. Ever." She scowled. "Not after what the damn Cortians did to you. Do you understand?"

The room was silent as Echo studied his angry, upset wife, pondering her comments. Finally he held up a conciliatory hand.

"Yeah, baby, I understand now," he said softly, gentling his response. "Okay. I'm all right with that. Provided you ARE careful, I'm good."

"Okay," Omega said then, and the tense atmosphere in the room ratcheted down quite a few notches. "Now let's finalize our plans and go get this little guy before something bad does happen."

* * *

Thirty minutes later, the Praetorians, plus quite a substantial contingent of Alpha Line who had not applied for Praetorian duty, met in a large conference room off the hangar bay, in the lower decks of the *Genesis*.

"...And that's the current plan," Omega finished the briefing, "plus several backups."

"Right," Romeo added, "'cause we all know th' battle plans never survive first contact with th' enemy."

"Exactly," Easy agreed.

"Question," Horse said.

"Go, Horse," Omega said, nodding at the agent.

"Can't we just bring down their computer system? Maybe a directed EMP or something?"

"No," Omega averred. "That lets them know we're coming, and they kill the boy."

"Shit."

"Yeah."

"Question," Chi piped up next.

"Go, Chi," Omega said.

"Why don't we just drop a knockout gas grenade or twelve into their airshafts and knock everybody out while we waltz in and grab the boy? 'Cause once the Scuttles are out cold, then we could bring down the computer security..."

"I got this one, Meg," India said.

"Go," Omega said, waving a hand at the Alpha Line medic.

"The various Persan — uh, Scuttle — races are not like anything we're used to, guys, except, to a limited extent, the Lambda Andromedans," India said, holding out one hand. "Not only are their bodies a lot different from most of the species in the Coalition, they have a very different sort of biochemistry. What works on us flatly does NOT work on them. And what works on them would make us really sick, if not outrightly kill us."

"But we can use breathing gear," Genova pointed out.

"Yes, we can. But the boy we're going in to rescue, Alexaan Daagnadan, doesn't have breathing gear," India noted. "While he's Kochavi, the Kochavi and humans are both Opdips, with similar biologies. AND he's a lot smaller, so he wouldn't be able to handle as much as an adult..."

"Ooo," Queen murmured. "I see, honey. It might make us

sick…but it could kill him."

"Exactly!" India said, pointing in approval at Queen. "Which is what we're here to prevent, not cause."

"Then…I guess we just haveta go in and get him out the hard way," an intense Monkey declared, determined.

"Alla that," Golf agreed. "Did I understand Meg correctly that the damn Scuttles have already killed one of our colleagues in Division Two?"

"They have," Omega confirmed. "Evidently she was sent into the facility to reconnoiter, and didn't make it back out. So we go in ready to kill. No quarter asked, no quarter given. This isn't a police action in any sense; this is a military operation against a hostile invasion force, so remember that. Moreover, the Scuttles are NOT representative of the Persis Federation or its legitimate government. And Fox and Division Two Director Ulseleigh have already approached the Ennead about the matter, and the Ennead has bought off on those terms, and approved the use of deadly force — AFTER contacting Premier Hsrs Syrsh of the Persis Federation, whose flagship is still in Coalition space, exploring our galaxy and making diplomatic niceties. I know Hsrs personally, and I can tell you for sure, 'cause I was there when we talked to him — he's not happy about this, either, and if we don't take 'em all out, he says for us to hand 'em over to him, and HE sure as hell will. Those of you who were there, remember how the renegade Persans fought during the upset of Adita's Coup, and realize that this bunch is more of the same. Do. Not. Hesitate. Because they will not hesitate to kill you if they can."

"Roger that," Yankee averred, and the others nodded. "Are they as highly trained as the ones in Adita's Coup?"

"That, we don't know," Omega admitted. "They may be the same, they may be MORE highly trained, or they may be less. This could be the backups, which argues either way. I'll admit, I'm hoping for less, as in, 'Wups, lemme scramble and get together another force after Bro's got wiped out.' But I'm not holding my breath on that, either."

"Right," Tare said. "What about if they surrender?"

"IF they surrender, I'll be surprised," Omega said, "but accept a surrender. Just don't trust the, uh, the 'surrenderee,' I guess we'll call it, any farther than you can toss 'em with a pinkie finger. Lock 'em down with force cuffs where they surrender, make sure they're weaponless, leave 'em there, and move on. We'll send somebody in for 'em when we're done."

"Gotcha," Tare said with a nod.

"Anything else?" Monkey wondered.

"Yeah," Omega said, but did not continue.

The room fell silent, waiting for her addendum, but she stared at the floor for long moments, until the forces arrayed in the room became uncomfortable with the prolonged silence. Finally she looked up.

"Okay, guys, listen up," Omega told the mingled Praetorian and Alpha Line teams in a low voice. "Something is probably gonna happen here that the rest of you have never seen before, and I need to let you know, so you don't startle from it and something gets hosed in the process."

"What's up, Meg?" Romeo wondered. The others sat up and paid attention.

"It's real simple," Omega explained. "You all already know this much: This child may be Echo's child. That alone means worlds to me — PERSONALLY. I will NOT let anything happen to Echo's son."

"Neither will the rest of us, hon," India said, as both members of Alpha Seven and Eight nodded vigorously. Omega drew a deep breath.

"I know," she said. "I didn't mean it like that. I mean that… well, we all know by now that I'm not a 'nominal human,' as the medlab has taken to expressing it, but none of the rest of you have ever seen what that really means. Even Echo only sees bits and pieces, depending on the situation, because we coordinate stuff. And there are those of you who, once upon a time, had some real issues with what I am, and what I can do…"

"I swear to you, Meg," Yankee said, earnest, "I was the last holdout on that, and I DO NOT feel like that any more. I understand a lot better how YOU feel about it, and why, but I also understand why you didn't get it undone. 'Cause we NEED it. Both Alpha Line and," he gestured around the room, "this bunch. The Praetorians. We NEED you, Omega. Just like you are. Big heart, big abilities, and all."

"I know, Yankee," Omega said with a tired smile. "You have no idea how much I appreciate the faith in me that the whole Firewall Team has now, and I try SO hard to be worthy of that faith, of the trust you all have in me — you'll never know how hard I try, 'cause there just aren't words for it, I think. Still, I've never really let loose, because there are OTHERS who don't understand, and many that don't know, and..." She sighed. "But this is a different sitch than I've ever gone into before. There's a little boy's life at stake. Even if he's not Echo's son, that little fella's life is at risk. And there's a fundamental part of the essential me that I just can't ignore: I will not let a child die if it is in me to prevent. So I can't afford NOT to pull out all the stops this time. Whether it freaks the rest of you out or not. So I'm going in prepared to max out," she said. "And what I need the rest of you to do is…keep up."

Eyebrows shot up all around.

"Whoa," Yankee breathed, eyes wide.

"Wait. You mean you can do even more than what you've done in those training videos?" Monkey wondered, mildly shocked. "Like the Nazi zombie one?"

"In terms of the way I move, the speed at which I can fight, the strength I can bring to bear in an emergency situation, yeah, I can, Monkey," Omega said, somber. "I've always tended to coordinate it with Echo, though. And I've only myself recently realized just how much, from working in that 'blowing off steam room' that Fox set up for me after we got Echo back from the Cortians."

"Which has probably also helped you hone those skills, that speed," India speculated. "And you've sequestered both

Echo and Fox for their safety during this operation…"

"Yes, it has, and yes, I did. Which means I don't have a partner to work with in this plan. So I'm not coordinating with anybody specific. It's not going to throw off anybody's timing if I go for broke. Oh, I'm not a comic book superhero or anything, but like it or not — and let me note that I don't like it, not really; I just use it, since I have it — well, I can do a bit more than a 'non-enhanced' human."

"How much more?" India wondered.

"I haven't really been able to quantify it," Omega said, "other than to do a few things like maxxing out on a treadmill, 'cause some things just don't have existing measurements for me to compare to, but by my guesstimates…I'm anywhere from, say, fifteen to twenty percent above…where I'd be if I was a 'normal' human. Very rough numbers." She waggled her hand in the air to denote the approximation.

Several whistles went around the room.

"Cool," Tare murmured, a wicked grin on his face.

"Yeah," Monkey agreed, matching the grin.

"Vhat do you need from us, Omega?" Kako wondered in his gentle way.

"I need for all of you to please try to accept it, accept me," Omega said, earnest, "not startle too much, and like I said earlier, just…keep up."

"We gotcher back, Meg, sis," Romeo averred.

"Likewise," Yankee agreed. "Like I said, I understand some things a lot better these days, and you are who you are, Omega. And I think the lot of us have yet to realize just how lucky we truly are to have you around, but some of us are trying hard."

"We might just realize it today," Monkey averred.

"Yeah. Let's do this," Tare affirmed.

"All right," Omega said with a slight smile. "Thanks, guys. I appreciate the vote of confidence. Everyone, load up with weapons and plenty of backup power packs, and ready positions for lightning strike."

* * *

"Echo," Fox said, after the Praetorians had departed the stateroom for the conference room off the hangar deck, "I know you're anxious about Omega. That little outburst of a discussion — most of which, I assume, took place telepathically..."

"Yeah," Echo all but grunted, gnawing his lower lip.

"Right. That showed me a few concerns there that you have, and, well, given Omega's history, I see why you're worried," Fox continued. "I agree, and I'd already thought about some possibilities, to be honest. So I've arranged a couple things that should help us, here."

"Oh, Fox? What have you pulled out of your sleeve this time?" Echo wondered.

"I equipped several members of the Praetorians with those miniaturized observing drones Omega developed a year or so ago," Fox said, "and instructed them to initiate those drones as soon as they got near the building. I was going to do that anyway, so we could watch and see what was happening, and send in backup or additional forces if needed, but I've just now pinged 'em all and told them to do it surreptitiously. I don't want Omega knowing they're there if it can be avoided. She doesn't need to feel like we're watching over her shoulder, but I want to be able to send in help immediately if needed. We brought Alpha Line along as swift backup, and I plan to make use of the fact, if need be. And Mhac has a large contingent close, but out of sight, that we can also draw from, if we have to."

"Oh, okay, yeah," Echo said. "Then we can also see if she tries anything...extreme, and maybe order a counter?"

"If ANYbody does," Fox agreed, "but yes. I know she's still getting counseling, and I know this whole farshtinkener meshuginah drek you two have found yourselves in when Daagnadan showed up has set things back a bit..."

"A little, yeah, I think," Echo decided. "Maybe a lot. I haven't really had a good chance to check, to be honest. Especially with me being forced into behaving like I was more in love with Ree than Meg. When I'm not in love with Ree at all."

"Good. We're on the same page," Fox noted. "So since I have the tank from the bridge mirrored in here, we can pipe in the drone footage and watch — you, me, and Zebra — and react BEFORE anything bad happens. Because I have a couple of ciphered blip relays set up to those same Agents."

"Who are they?"

"India, as the medic, and Alpha Seven and Eight. The entire Firewall Team has become absolutely the most dedicated to Alpha One you could imagine, especially after everything that's gone down. I thought they'd be good for this."

"You suspected she might go off the rail," Echo accused.

"I know my kinder," Fox sighed, "in their strengths, and their weaknesses. Especially that particular daughter. We've... talked, Omega and I. Many times, now. You know that. You've been there for some of those talks. And in some ways, I have been where she is, my own self, so I know how that line of thought can go, how it can deteriorate, sometimes faster than we realize ourselves. And having eyes on the situation in order to provide immediate backup also works in this instance. Omega is selfless — those she dearly loves are more important to her than her own life. And that is normally a wonderful and awe-inspiring thing, but in her mental state, it could play against us, and has, in the past. Let's just say I was concerned and decided to prepare for a 'just in case,' and leave it at that."

"Okay," Echo said, mimicking Fox's sigh. "Put what we do have in the secondary tank, here, and let's see what we can see. We'll pull up the drone video once we have it."

"On it," Fox said, adjusting the controls on his tablet, as Zebra sat silent and listened, biting her lip in worry.

* * *

Oh shit, Zebra thought, as she listened to her husband speak to the man he considered a son. *I understand where Fox is going with that whole thing, but this might not be a good idea to do WITH ECHO WATCHING IT. Because if something happens and they can't stop it, what's that going to do to Echo?*

272

Damn, damn, damn.

And do I say anything, or keep my mouth shut and hope for the best? If I say something, do I say it to Echo, to both of 'em, or only to Fox? What the hell do I do?

Zebra gnawed her lip almost bloody, debating with herself and worrying.

* * *

The detachment of agents moved from the conference room into the hangar deck and boarded the small saucers waiting for them in the bay. Omega donned the tiny earbud and subvocal microphone they would all use for communication, though it would NOT be routed through their cell phones; the risk of detection was too great. Instead, they would use a special quantum-entangled comm that had been developed recently in the R&D department. It did not use the standard means which came to mind at the term 'quantum-entanglement communications,' but it did provide for undetectable-signal communication, which was greatly desired at this point.

"QE comm on," she murmured into the ship-to-ship comm, and throughout the tiny fleet of spacecraft, all the agents donned their earbuds and sub-vocal mics.

"Comm on," came the reply from numerous voices, this time over the earbuds; in addition to the twenty-five members of the Praetorians, there were another eleven Alpha Line teams accompanying, as possible backup.

"All ships, cloak and scramble," Omega ordered. "*Genesis* bridge, request preparation for Praetorian debarkation."

"Zero copies, Omega; debarkation prep under way," came the response from the bridge; security chief Zero was the *Genesis'* designated captain, but he only commanded when Fox was not on the bridge. "Maneuvering to debarkation point; depressurizing hangar bay. Stand by for my command."

"Praetorians and Alpha Line, standing by," Omega murmured, as the depressurization warning klaxon sounded outside her little spacecraft. "Awaiting your command, sir."

They sat and waited for fully fifteen minutes; no one wanted to be too hasty and give away their presence at this stage of things. Finally the notification came. "*Genesis* at debarkation point. Opening hangar bay doors…now. Praetorian squadron, you may debark when you are ready."

Omega, seated in the pilot's chair of her craft, which contained five more crew — one of which was a skilled staff pilot who would remain on board — and five passengers, initiated the maneuvering engines, as the giant bay doors opened wide. "Praetorian One departing bay," she murmured.

"Godspeed, Praetorian One, and all units," Zero's voice replied. "Good luck."

"Thank you, *Genesis*. Praetorian One has cleared the bay doors."

"Praetorian Two departing bay," another voice noted, followed moments later by, "Praetorian Two has cleared bay doors."

"Praetorian Three departing bay…Praetorian Three has cleared."

"Praetorian Four departing bay…Praetorian Four has cleared."

"Praetorian Five departing bay," Romeo's voice murmured. "Aaand Praetorian Five has cleared the ship. Let's get this show on th' road."

"Praetorian fleet form up on my tag, per operational plan," Omega ordered. "Initiate flight plan."

And the five ships, effectively invisible to almost all sensors, headed for the surface of Kochav.

* * *

They formed up again in the atmosphere over the outskirts of the capital, Reegar, and went into silent hover mode. Directly below them was the former factory-slash-warehouse that was the focus of their efforts and the headquarters of Geretan Aggum's rogue Andromedan faction.

"It's show time, people. All Praetorian or Alpha Line pilots, hand over to your relief," Omega ordered through the sub-vocal mic. "Don personal cloaking and scrambler devices, as well as

274

antigrav propulsion belts — all of which should already BE on the antigrav belt, to make it quick and easy; please verify your units are so arranged and working properly — and prepare to debark at my order."

A flurry of activity occurred in each small craft as its occupants followed orders. In Praetorian One, Omega handed over to Canteen, the *Genesis* staffer who would pilot the craft, maintaining it in readiness, while the assault was made on Aggum's headquarters. Then all the rest commenced donning their equipment, which included several additional weapons in harnesses or warp pockets, depending on the preference of the agent in question. Then they moved to the hatch and formed a queue, Omega in the lead.

"Praetorian One ready," Omega said then. "Sound off readiness."

"Praetorian Two ready."

"Praetorian Three ready."

"Praetorian Four ready."

"Praetorian Five ready."

"Initiate quantum entanglement locations; don goggle-glasses and initiate smart view...Praetorian One ready for jump."

"Praetorian Two ready for jump."

"Praetorian Three ready for jump."

"Praetorian Four ready for jump."

"Praetorian Five ready for jump."

"All ships, open hatch."

The hatch for Praetorian One slid open silently.

"Praetorian One ready. Hatch open."

"Praetorian Two, hatch open."

"Praetorian Three, hatch open."

"Praetorian Four, hatch open."

"Praetorian Five, hatch open."

"Begin bailout protocol," Omega ordered.

She took a deep breath...

...Then jumped into the air.

* * *

As she hovered in mid-air, Omega's goggle-glasses depicted the view in front of her, as one would expect of basic sunglasses. However, it also amended that view with an increasing number of her colleagues, their essentially-invisible forms framed with square brackets, inside which were their codenames. She nodded to herself in satisfaction, then, when the last member of the operation's team had appeared, she sub-vocalized an order.

"Initiate silent prop, drop to designated altitude."

* * *

In the secure suite aboard the *Genesis*, Zebra, Echo, and Fox watched the deployment through the *Genesis* sensor suite, seeing a very similar depiction to the one Omega's goggle-glasses showed her, thanks to the specialized identifiers in the agents' wrist chronometers, which were linked into the quantum-entangled comm. The three watched as the assault squad eased downward until they hovered directly over the facility that Aggum's people had commandeered. A yellow-tinged dome was schematically represented over the building.

"Alpha Three: Hack alarm system," Omega's voice ordered on audio.

A few seconds went by before the response, "Alarm system hacked. All alarms should be down."

"'Should be?'" Romeo's voice replied. "Better ALL be."

"We think so, Agent Romeo," the hacker's voice —it was Alpha Line's Enigma Team member Gustav — answered. "But if there are systems we don't know about, that Director Ulseleigh's people didn't find out about, they might not be."

"Ugh. That ain't optimal, Gustav, man."

"I know, but we can only do what we know to do, Romeo. Be prepared for hostile action, just in case."

"Affirmative," Romeo replied. "We ARE ready f'r expected hostile action. More than."

"It's all right, guys, you done good," Omega's voice said. "Enigma Team: Hack force field dome."

It took a couple of minutes, but then Kilo's voice replied, "Force field open," even as a 'gate' formed in the top of the yellow dome depicted in the tank, a little detail provided to the display by the *Genesis* sensors.

They watched as the bracketed identifier icons seemed to flow through the opening.

"And we're in," Omega noted. "Guard duty, peel off and secure exterior."

"Roger," several voices answered. "Security detail chief Oscar here," the security agent responded. "Our people are on it, ma'am."

"Go," Omega ordered.

"Gone," Oscar replied. "Delta 23, Delta 29, Eagle, Topsail, Horse, Oyster, Page — move to predetermined stations as per plan Omega-Oscar A."

The three in the suite watched as ten of the bracket markers moved off, spreading around the building to secure the exterior.

"Backup Alpha Line teams, peel off and assume predetermined ready positions," Omega ordered.

"On it, Omega," Jack, of the Alpha Five team, said. "Alpha Five, Alpha Six, Alpha Fourteen, Eighteen, Nineteen, Twenty, Twenty-one, Twenty-three, Twenty-seven, Twenty-eight, Thirty-one — move to predetermined stations as per plan Omega-Alpha A."

This time, twenty-two bracketed indicators moved away, dropping to the ground in two groups of five and six partnerships, respectively.

Finally Zebra decided to speak up.

* * *

"Um, Echo?" Zebra asked softly, just as the 'door' in the force field closed again…with all the agents now inside it.

"Yeah, Zee?" Echo responded, absent, his gaze fixed on the depiction in the tank. "Keep it short, please. This is a definite situation, and I don't want to be distracted."

"Uh, I'll try. What will you do if Meg does try something, and we can't stop it, and you're watching it happen?"

Then I watch my baby, my partner, my best friend, the center of my world and the love of my life, die in front of me… with no way to stop it, was the answer that slammed into his brain. *And there is nothing I can do about it now.*

Echo froze as the import of her question — and its horrifying answer — hit him, then turned to gape at the physician in horror, even as Fox did the same.

* * *

"All right, guys," Omega murmured. "Let's head for the exhaust port. This is definitely not a moon, or even a space station, so it should be easier for us than the classic movie guys had it."

A smattering of snickers and one loud snort filled her ears through the earbuds, and she grinned.

"Bring up Infiltration Plan A in your glasses," she said, toggling her own goggle-glasses until the correct infiltration path showed in the virtual display. "Image of target on right." A small image of Nreefluvan's son, Alexaan Daagnadan, appeared in the corner of her view.

"Whoa," someone said. "No wonder we're involved."

Aaand it looks like I'm not the only one to see a resemblance, Omega considered, stifling a sigh. *Just what I need right now. Heads up, girl. You can't afford any distractions at this point.*

But in the back of her mind, the imagery still formed: *A young Echo, in bed with Nreefluvan, making love to her.* After all, Echo himself had admitted to Omega that many of his lovemaking techniques had been learned at the hands of the Kochavi woman.

No, she told herself, while Quebec, the most skilled at such work, removed the exterior plate from the exhaust vent. *I have work to do. A child's life may depend on me. ECHO'S child's life may depend on me.*

Quebec stood back, and Omega entered the exhaust vent, leading the way…

…With images of Echo and Nreefluvan still in the back of her mind.

* * *

(Milord Aggum,) one of his assistants said, entering the older Ka'agand's office. (Please forgive my intrusion…)

(What is it, Gree?) Aggum asked, sitting up and turning to look at the young Ka'agand. (Have we had word from the Kochavi adept?)

(No, milord. We have had some sort of…flag…from the security computer.)

(I heard no alert.)

(It was not an alert. It was…neither we, nor the computer, knows quite what it was. Perhaps merely an unusual vibration. We do not even know if it was inside or outside. It may only have been a poorly-maintained vehicle passing by.)

(Mmph. That is not much to go on,) Aggum decided. (Can you narrow it down any better?)

(Not very much,) the younger being admitted. (It is most likely an acoustic wave, though not of high amplitude at all.)

(Mm. It is likely nothing,) Aggum considered. (Perhaps a small ground tremor. Or that badly-maintained vehicle you suggested. Then again, that damned Division Two agent made it inside, so it may in fact BE something.) He paused to think.

(Do you wish us to take action, milord?)

(Yes, I think so,) Aggum said. (As I said, it is likely nothing of any significant import to us, but we cannot afford to become too complacent. The Division Two agent had a special personal cloak device, did she not?)

(She did, milord.)

(Have we developed a workaround yet?)

(We believe so, sir.)

(Is it ready to be implemented?)

(It is. You have but to speak the word.)

(Then the word is spoken,) Aggum ordered. (Do it. And put the guards on a higher alert level.)

(Very well, sir. It will be done at once.)

And the young Ka'agand left the office of the being he expected to soon rule two galaxies.

* * *

It was considerably easier to get out of the vent than it had been to get into it; apparently it never occurred to the Persans to secure matters in this fashion, as they hadn't anticipated anyone would try to get through the force field from above.

"Maintain maximum stealth," Omega ordered sub-vocally, as her team fanned out into the corridors, floating near the ceiling, though they could not maintain that means for long; the batteries on the antigrav belts were running down rapidly by this point. Fortunately, the cloaking and sensor scrambling units had separate power packs.

Unfortunately, and unlike the antigrav batteries, the imagery in the back of her mind seemed to be ramping up. So Omega put especial effort into trying to ignore the mental imagery…

…A young Echo and Nreefluvan enjoying a picnic together under the flowering trees on Tiniken, the Eden planet Zeta Aurigae Four.

…A young Echo and Nreefluvan making love under those same trees.

…X-ray and Echo taking Nreefluvan with them on a mission, using her to distract the perp while they set a trap for him.

…A young Echo, proud as punch, when the plan worked perfectly, and they took their perp into custody. Nreefluvan dancing happily around the pair of agents, glad to have helped.

…Nreefluvan moving into Echo's quarters, and a gentlemanly X-ray — in the quarters next door, connected by the 'back door' — teaching her to cook…

"Goggle-glasses to multi-spectral mode; watch for lasers and photoelectric beams and any other junk that could pick us up," she ordered then, disrupting the film playing in her mind. "And walk lightly once we land, like Echo showed us. You never know when they have the floor sensored for unexpected footsteps."

A soft chorus of, "Roger that," came back to her.

* * *

Behind her, as each Agent got well into the building, first Yankee and Tare, then Monkey and Kako, and finally India released their miniaturized drones, setting them to follow the team point — Omega — and watch for anything untoward, whether in her behavior, or in the environment around the infiltration team.

* * *

As each drone's cameras came online, a view popped up in the holographic tank in the secure suite aboard the *Genesis*. Gradually the big flagship's onboard computers collated these different perspectives, and finally a fully three-dimensional view of the environment around the infiltration team arose in the tank. It was largely centered on Omega, but took in essentially all of her colleagues — or, at least, their loci; the depiction still showed square brackets annotating their locations, though they were undetectable to the drone cameras. And it was capable of being manipulated — expanded, shrunk, turned around, even flipped upside-down, should the onlookers decide they needed a different perspective.

"So far, so good," Fox murmured. "Everything is going according to plan. Maybe Zebra's concern is a wild hare."

"Yeah," Echo agreed. "Let's hope so."

"Meg seems good, too," Zebra confirmed. "I mean, I can't see HER, but her icon is right where she needs to be, which argues she's alert and on top of things."

"Given the way her brain works, though, she could still have a pot of boiling shit going in the back of her mind," Echo noted. "That brain of hers can multitask like you wouldn't believe, guys."

"Can't you tell if she's simmering in the background, zun?" Fox wondered. "Through the nd't'lq?"

"No, not right now," Echo explained. "She and I discussed it in our bedroom on the way here — I made her lie down and take a nap before she had to get active, so she'd be at least a little rested when this infiltration went down, but we talked for a while before she fell asleep — and since the Persis

Federation has empaths, and we never found out for sure that they don't have telepaths, we felt like leaving the bond wide open wasn't…advisable."

"Ooo, good point," Zebra murmured. "If they do have 'em, and picked up an active telepathic conversation between you two, the gig's up."

"Exactly," Echo confirmed. "So she's not actively blocking me, as such; I'm just not going looking, because I also don't wanna distract her at a bad time. I mean, if I was THERE with her, yeah, we'd be locked together, pretty much — and then a hard block around us both. But I'm not, so we're not. In fact, it's me that's got sort of a block up; that way, SHE doesn't have to concentrate on it. It's not a HARD block; she could reach me if she needed to. But…well." He shrugged.

"Right," Fox said, nodding his approval. "We understand. That makes good strategic sense, zun. And good on making her rest for a bit, too."

"Here we go," Zebra noted. "Forward motion, here."

"Right," Echo agreed, watching as the positioning of Omega's 'brackets' shifted down the corridor and onto floor level. "Let's hope all goes accordi— oh shit!"

"Farkakte!" Fox exclaimed in dismay at the same time. "Tsu aldi rukhes, ist a kappore!"

"And what a catastrophe, hon!" Zebra added, horrified.

Chapter 11

Omega and her team had landed, switched off their antigrav belts, and made it some hundred feet down the corridor that was on Plan A, when a sudden flash of violet light washed down the corridor. Their personal cloaking units flickered and died, countered by whatever field had just been initiated, and both cloaking and sensor scrambling systems — since the latter was an offshoot of the former — failed. Abruptly their entire team was visible.

Video cameras mounted on the walls near the ceiling swiveled in their direction, and moments later, a low-pitched klaxon, almost beyond their range of hearing, sounded loudly.

Shit. Here we go, Omega had just time to think.

"ON ME!" she shouted, as a small force of some half-dozen Persans in body armor emerged from a doorway about fifty feet farther down the long hall. "KEEP UP, PEOPLE!"

And she opened up her 'enhancements' even as she broke into a hard sprint.

* * *

But in her mind's eye, in the back of her head and despite her wishes, she watched:

A young Echo, smiling widely, placed a ring on a happy Nreefluvan's finger, and filed paperwork with the Agency to list her as his mate. He handed it in to Director Oboe, who smiled back, and approved it.

Then he went home to his Kochavi wife, and they celebrated in bed together with glasses of champagne.

* * *

Doing her best to ignore the mental imagery, Omega sprinted down the corridor as fast as she could, straight at the four Ka'agands, one Uzshei, and one Trachytoid — three of the various races that inhabited the Andromeda Galaxy. The six alien soldiers drew weapons quickly, bringing them around in an attempt to target her team. But before they could train their weapons on anything — though one got off a quick shot that narrowly missed Topsail — Omega was on them. In such close quarters, their beam weapons were essentially useless against her…which had been her intention.

She delivered a swift, powerful, chambered punch to the face of one, coupled with a sweeping kick to take most of its tentacle-legs from under it, and that being found itself suddenly on its back on the floor.

Omega used its body as a springboard, leaping upward into a hard, double split-kick — each foot took a different Scuttle in the head. Both fell instantly with heads canted at an odd angle on what passed for their necks. A large indentation had also appeared in each head, apparently due to skull fractures.

She landed back on the first Scuttle, as hard as she could with both feet, and its barrel-shaped chest — largely supported by the equivalent of cuttlebone, with only a couple of 'spines' of true bone — promptly collapsed beneath the impact. It let out one slight gasp before its eyes glazed.

"Glasses: Scan remaining targets, identify kill zones," she sub-vocalized the command to her goggle-glasses, and the device promptly overlaid a heads-up display on the remaining three Scuttles. This depicted an anatomical diagram of each being based on the medical studies that had been performed on the captives from Adita's Coup — many of whom required medical attention anyway, after Alpha Line got through with them — along with an assessment of the armor and its vulnerabilities. Like most sentients, their armor was intended to protect their vital spots, but generally only from the front; the sides and back tended to be less well protected, as it was expected that the attack would come from the front.

So Omega went for something UNexpected.

* * *

"Holy shit, Fox, honey, are you SEEING this?!" Zebra cried, shocked. "I…I knew she could…I mean, she's…but not THIS!"

"Yes, I suspected as much," Fox confessed. "When we

were en route home after rescuing Echo from the Cortians, I had occasion to check on her while she was engaged in her first session of blowing off steam in the gym…" He shook his head. "She is far more formidable than she has let on, until this point."

"No shit," Echo whispered, his eyes glued to the tank, as he watched his wife pull out all the stops. "I've been working with her for a couple years now, and I've never seen her do THIS." He paused, then added, "She came close, that time she had to fight off Mark Wright up at our beach house. 'Cause that looked like a movie special effect. But this…damn."

"Why hasn't she done it before now?" Zebra wondered. "I mean, she could have saved herself AND Echo, under the Cortians' ion drive, last winter…"

"I don't think she herself has fully realized what she could do until recently," Fox considered. "I think it was her efforts at venting — after Echo's torture and rescue — that revealed to her what she was truly capable of doing."

"What do you mean, honey?"

"I think," Fox explained, "that, as Omega struggled to release her anger at the Cortians, she kept ramping up her actions, higher and higher, until she was doing things she hadn't realized she could do. And probably didn't even realize at the time that she was doing. I think it only hit her after the fact, when she was winding down and thinking about it."

"Oh," Echo said. "I get it. Then, as she kept working out and venting, she strengthened her abilities, and eventually it hit her that she'd reached a new level."

"Exactly, zun. And I'm betting that, as the two of you work together, you won't be far behind her."

"Heh," Echo chuckled, rueful. "When she was still a rookie, I was glad to have a partner who could keep up with me. Now the tables have turned, I guess. I'll have to keep up with HER!"

"But she's just now SHOWING it, revealing it," Zebra said. "Why now?"

"She believes she is helping to rescue Echo's son," Fox

said quietly. "What would she not do?"

"That's…what I'm afraid of," Echo admitted.

* * *

From somewhere, Omega produced a pair of fighting knives of considerable substance.

In the movie playing in the back of her head, matters progressed.

Some months later, Nreefluvan came to young Echo, her husband, patting her belly and smiling. A startled Echo was disbelieving at first, then became delighted, rubbing the Kochavi woman's belly in happiness and hugging her close.

Omega deliberately ignored the imagery and concentrated on the task at hand.

As her hands blurred with their speed, the two nearest Scuttles found themselves suddenly each with a large and very painful hole in the side of the torso, punched straight through their military-style armor and deep into their vitals. A quick wrist-flick twisted each knife and ensured the outcome. They gasped in shock as blue-green blood spurted, then they fell, even as Omega flipped the blades and drove both of them, one on each side, into the lone remaining Scuttle standing before her.

He fell too, as the first of the Praetorians reached her position.

The entire fight had lasted less than ten seconds.

* * *

"Holy shit, Meg," India panted, looking around at the six dead bodies, as the rest came running up. "You never told us you could do THIS."

"You never asked," Omega said simply. She sliced off one tentacle from the alien body at her feet, then wiped off her knives on the dead Persans' uniform tunics before re-sheathing them, apparently in a couple of warp pockets. "Now you know why I took the point." Then she grinned.

No one on the infiltration squad thought she looked amused. *Grim is more like it,* crossed the minds of several. The smile on her face was unnerving, to say the least, all the more so as it didn't begin to reach her eyes, and they were glad to be on her side.

After letting it bleed out on the floor and wiping the cut edge on a Scuttle uniform tunic, Omega tucked the section of tentacle into another warp pocket before looking up once more.

"All right," she said. "Let's get moving again before another goon squad comes after us. They know we're here; we have to get to Alexaan before they do, or he's dead."

She turned and started a swift jog — the others considered it a run — down the corridor to the desired junction.

* * *

"Holy shit," Zebra whispered. "What did she just do? Are they all dead?"

"Yeah," Echo said, proud. "She moved in too close and too fast for 'em to use their weapons effectively, then took 'em all out before they had time to think."

"Have you ever seen her do anything like that before, zun?" Fox wondered.

"Not exactly, no, but similar," Echo decided. "I think she's always had that ability to some extent, though it looks a lot more…honed, now. But yeah, I've seen her do things like that. Generally when she thought I wasn't watching. When she thought NOBODY was watching. Meg…well, she's tried not to do stuff like that where she can be seen. There was always too much negativity toward her modifications, and she didn't want to risk making things worse. But now that the worst of the naysayers have finally understood and become supportive, and given that those supporters are there, right now, backing her up? It looks like she's decided to risk it. Because we need it, here, and she has it to use."

"And nobody can see who isn't supportive," Fox added.

"Yeah."

"Look at her go! She looks like a ping-pong ball or something, running down the hall ducking and dodging beams an' shit," Zebra said, pointing at the images in the tank. "And the others are right in there with her!"

"Oh, I can't think THAT is good," Fox said, watching as well. "Be careful, tekhter!"

"What?" Echo exclaimed swiveling his head around; he had been talking to Fox, meeting his eyes, and had missed whatever brought on that remark. "What did she do?"

"She's baiting the booby traps," Fox noted, pointing. "Triggering them deliberately, before the others get there, so there isn't time for them to reset before the group has passed."

"Oh damn," Echo breathed, paling. "Baby, ease back."

* * *

Omega's goggle-glasses gave her a heads-up that there was a small but powerful booby trap ahead, so she put on a burst of speed to get well ahead of the rest of her team, as well as to build up sufficient momentum for what she had planned.

Just as she reached the threshold of the trap, she spun and leaped to the side at the same time she tapped a certain sequence on her cell phone. Omega ran up the wall, allowing her momentum and a certain special property that was built into the Suit components — notably the shoes — to carry her forward, much as Echo had once walked on the ceiling of a maglev train to take out an assassin.

Simultaneously, however, three fully-armed Scuttle guards appeared from a doorway. They quickly crouched and took aim at the runner-on-the-wall.

"MEG!" Romeo, Yankee, and Tare yelled simultaneously from farther down the hall, drawing blasters.

But Omega was already in action.

She drew both blasters while still running, dual-wielding in a gun fu sequence Echo had taught her long since, sweeping wide arcs and mowing down the three Scuttles, their upper bodies toppling to the floor as their lower bodies collapsed where they stood. Large puddles of blue-green blood and feculent goo spread across the floor.

As Omega angled down the wall toward the floor, she tossed something small into the air behind her. By the time it arced upward, then started down in its trajectory and hit the floor, the lead Praetorians — Romeo, India, Yankee, and Tare — were still ten feet away from the trap.

The tiny marble-like object popped like a firecracker as soon as it hit the floor.

The anti-personnel mine embedded in the floor blew upward.

The ceiling opened and vented the explosion up and away.

* * *

The Praetorians skidded to a halt, trying to see through the gas, smoke, and assorted debris, horrified at the notion that Omega might have been caught in it.

When it cleared and began to reset, she was already fifty feet down the hall.

"COME ON! Before it resets!" she yelled over her shoulder, and they charged ahead, sprinting to catch up.

* * *

The image in the tank flickered, then shifted slightly, as a notice came up on the side, near the bottom: DRONE D3 LOST.

Just then, an urgent-alert communiqué klaxon sounded on Fox's cell phone. He pulled it from his pocket and emergency-slap-activated it.

"Fox here. Zero?"

"Yes sir. Sensors report a sudden vent of hot gas and smoke from the roof of the target facility. There appears to have been an explosion."

"There has, but it seems to be nothing serious," Fox replied. "The Praetorians are, of necessity, setting off a few booby traps as they go. I think we just saw one of the traps vent itself, prior to resetting."

"Ah. Right, then, sir. You're watching in the remote tank?"

"I am, yes. As are Echo and Zebra, who are with me."

"Is progress good?"

"So far, so good. None of ours have been hurt yet, but quite a few of theirs have gone down."

"That IS good news."

"I'm surprised you're not watching the tank as well, meyn khaver."

"The data on it is apparently set at Directorial level, sir. We can't log in to see."

"Ah. Well, we might fix that. I expect Director Ulseleigh set that for the transmission, and I never thought to declassify it. Does the bridge crew want to see it?"

"That might be good, sir. We can be prepared for any actions we need to take, that way."

"Consider it done, Zero. Give me a moment, here…" Fox picked up his tablet and began working on it, looking for the classification on the various data packages as well as the incoming quantum-entangled telemetry from the drones, and resetting them to allow for the *Genesis* bridge crew to pull it up in their tank. "Aha. There we go. Try that, Zero."

There was a brief pause, then Fox heard several exclamations in the background of the phone's audio, followed by Zero saying, "Damnation! What the hell is going on, there?"

Uh-oh, Fox thought, trying not to smear his hand over his face. *They're going to see Omega at maximum…without her permission. I didn't think about that. Think fast, Franz, you idiot.*

"Oh, by the way," Fox responded smoothly, not quite lying through his teeth, but not telling the whole story, either. "Omega has been outfitted with quite a few bells and whistles, in her Suit, in her equipment, and more. Don't boggle because she's testing out some, ah, classified things for us. This was a situation that called for it."

"Ah," Zero replied. "That explains a lot, especially as regards the classification levels on the video data. Thank you, sir. We'll be ready if we're needed."

"Right. Fox out."

"Bridge out."

Fox deactivated the phone and returned it to his pocket. Echo stared at Fox. "Um," the younger man began.

"I know, I know," Fox sighed, holding up a hand in apology, "I nearly skrud aroyf, zun. I'm sorry; I was thinking in terms of prep for emergency response, and not giving away your wife's secret."

"No, I think you handled it fine, Fox," Echo said then. "I was gonna say, I didn't think about the bridge crew needing to know, to be able to watch. As it is, you gave Meg and me a good cover story if word of this gets out."

"Good," Fox said in relief. "That works, then."

* * *

Omega's goggle-glasses — its map hand-programmed by Omega with the most detailed information Director Ciarmhac Ulseleigh could provide — next depicted a bank of projectile weaponry built into the wall just past the left-hand turn at the end of the corridor. As the readout of its specific sensor suite popped up, she nodded to herself. *The baton won't cut it,* she considered. *It has to be organic. I'll do this the hard way, maybe, and just hope it works.*

Omega, well in the lead by this time, threw out a warning hand to those behind her, then leaped upward, grabbing the grid that supported the false ceiling, popping the adjacent tiles upward a bit to allow for her hands. A false ceiling on Earth likely would not have supported her weight, but on Kochav, they were intended to provide out-of-sight storage — though there was little indication the Scuttles had made use of this fact. *Though I'm betting that someplace in this big barn, they're bound to have booby traps in the ceiling crawl space,* she thought. *Maybe just not along the route we chose.*

She pulled her knees to her chest, then carefully 'walked' along the gridwork like a set of monkey bars, until she was near the spot that her glasses indicated was the center of the booby-trap device.

Then she lowered her legs to her body's full extension and swung once before pulling up swiftly into a tight tuck once more.

The projectile guns embedded in the right-hand wall began

to fire in a sustained burst, and Omega noted their origin points — two horizontal lines, roughly two and a half feet, and five feet, from the floor.

Omega threw her legs around the adjacent strut in the gridwork — heedless of ceiling tiles popped loose by the move — pulled a blaster with one hand, then let go with the other hand just long enough to dial down the beam to a pencil-thin diameter. She grabbed the grid again before her powerful abdominals could fail, aimed at the top line of guns, and fired, sweeping her weapon's beam back and forth until molten metal ran down the wall and that row of projectile guns stopped firing. She repeated the process on the lower row of projectile guns, then glanced upside-down at the rest of her unit, who had stopped where she had indicated.

"Somebody grab your phone and run the — UPDATED! — scanner app over this section of corridor," she ordered. "Make sure there's nothing else here before I let go an' come back down."

"Nope, that's got it, according to my scanner," Yankee averred scant seconds later, waving his phone around the corridor. "An' yeah, it's the update. I downloaded it as soon as you told us about it the other day."

"Good man. Thank you." Omega unwrapped her legs from the strut and lowered them, then released the grid with her hands and dropped lightly to the floor, landing easily on her feet.

"Let's go!" she ordered, and they moved out once more.

* * *

Likewise the movie in Omega's head continued to play.

Nreefluvan went into labor and delivered a healthy baby boy, as young Echo assisted in the birth.

She came home to the same quarters Echo and Omega currently shared, with the addition of a nursery off the master bedroom. Little Alexaan Daagnadan Bryant was a happy baby and grew rapidly.

A year later, Nreefluvan was pregnant again.

Omega shook her head in annoyance and ran onward.

* * *

"THAT was interesting," Zebra decided. "I knew, based on my readings, that Meg had some damn strong abs, but shit."

"What she said," Echo averred. "And yeah, she does, not to mention a helluva six-pack belly. You should see her in a bikini! But damn, that wasn't the way I'd have preferred she trigger the trap."

"No, but zun, we aren't there," Fox pointed out. "It may be that her various devices and scanners are showing her that, say, waving a collapsible baton in the target space would not trigger the sensors needed to activate the trap. And I know she has one, because I saw her stow it in a warp pocket."

"You mean, meat versus, say, metal? Or plastic, or the like?" Zebra asked.

"Exactly, bubeleh. Note she had someone run a more detailed scan using that phone app, before she would come down? And I know for a fact, she worked with the designer of that app recently, to help him upgrade it expressly for Alpha Line field use. Then ensured all of Alpha Line AND the Praetorians got the update! I think she has some tricks up her sleeve she didn't tell ANYone about." He shook his head, a wry grin on his face. "She's a sneaky one when she wishes to be, meyn beibi maydele."

"She can be, that," Echo agreed. "And I should know; I trained her!"

"But we're definitely on the clock now," Fox added. "They know there's an infiltration team, they know that team is skilled enough to get past several traps, and Omega and her people MUST get to the boy before they do…or he will almost certainly be killed."

"Damn," Zebra breathed.

* * *

(SIR!) Gree cried, bursting into Aggum's office. (Forgive my interruption, sir! We have invaders!)

(Oh?) Aggum responded, turning and pulling up an image

on his monitor. (Ah, I see. It is a human force. Then possibly our Kochavi adept was not as adept as she thought. She may even be dead.) He sighed. (That is a shame; we shall have to drop back and regroup as regards our plans for Division One. Perhaps we should try a different division…)

(What should we do, milord?)

(Nothing.)

(Nothing?)

(You heard me, Gree.) Aggum turned back to his plans.

(Why?)

(Do you think our security and our precautions insufficient?)

(Well, I did not…but they are inside the building!)

(And nowhere near us. There is a reason I chose this huge building, and placed our activity center where I did within it. They will be caught in a kill box sooner or later. I had it from my clutch-mate, Humn, that humans are not that intelligent. It was rather easy to take control of the Division One, and took a considerable effort to oust him. Even then, he survived the attempt, so they are weak into the bargain. Once I have gained some control in this galaxy, I plan to search out his whereabouts and extricate him from their imprisonment.)

(Do you not think, sir, that…)

(No, I do not.)

(Should we execute the youngling?)

(Why?) Aggum wondered. (They are not after him. They are after us. If his brooder is dead, then they have killed her. They almost certainly will not hesitate to kill the young male as well.) He gave the Persan equivalent of a shrug. (Leave him. Should they find him, they will take care of that loose end for us. And if they manage to trigger the trap on the door, then perhaps they will exit this life with him, and save me the trouble, twice over. You did tell me the informant was already dead, correct?)

(Yes, milord. He died of lack of nourishment several days ago. We have been venting the stench out of the structure.)

(Very good, then. And the youngling? Has he been fed and

watered?)

(He has, only until we heard back from his brooder if the plan had succeeded or not.)

(Very well. End his rations. We will allow the security system and the outlier guards to handle this matter,) Aggum waved at the monitor, which still displayed humans in black Suits making their way down a corridor, (and the matter of the youngling will take care of itself, soon or late.)

He switched off the monitor as his assistant Gree left the office.

* * *

Omega drove onward until they reached another 'machine gun nest,' this time composed of some sort of energy beams, according to the information provided by the Division Two Director. It wasn't far down their chosen path, but it was in a connecting corridor.

Hmph, she thought. *I needed more hands last time than I had, so…Let's try something a little different. If this one is laid out like the other one, this should work great.*

Before the others had quite caught up to her — they had been busy mowing down another squadron of some twenty or so Scuttles sent to intercept them from a side corridor, except the Scuttles had underestimated the speed at which the Praetorian infiltrators were moving, and failed to get into position soon enough — she had thrown herself onto her belly on the floor.

She quickly performed a military crawl until she was well into the target area, though below it.

"Meg!" Romeo hissed. "What th' hell you think you're doin', girl? Git outta there 'fore you fry your ass, an' Echo kills us! Whatchu doin'?!"

"This," Omega said, pulling the section of tentacle out of her warp pocket.

"It won't work," India said. "It's Persan. The sensors are cued on NOT-Persan."

"Which is why I'm down here," Omega pointed out. "It'll read me present, see the movement, and open fire. At least, that's my plan."

She held up the tentacle and waved it around; the tip flopped about, easily breaching any sensor beams that there might be.

Nothing happened.

"Mmph," India grunted, biting her tongue.

Omega waved the tentacle again, more vigorously this time, and suddenly the left wall opened up with THREE rows of some sort of energy beam. Omega dropped the tentacle and huddled against the floor, as flat as she could get; the bottom row was lower than she'd expected, and she was at risk of getting singed.

"TAKE 'EM OUT!" she yelled. "LIKE I DID THE PROJECTILE BANKS!"

The characteristic hum of multiple blasters in use sounded over her head; several small explosions ensued, and soon there was silence…and the smell of charred electronics.

"You're clear, per the scanner app," Tare called.

Omega leaped straight from the floor into a dead sprint, headed forward.

The others fell in behind.

* * *

We've got to MOVE, she kept thinking, even as she dual-wielded her blasters in rapid succession to take out another squadron of ten Scuttles sent to cut them off and take them down; over her shoulder, Alpha Two on her left and Four on her right, added to the barrage. *We're not going fast enough! They know we're here. The boy could be dead by now. Echo's son could be dead. No, no, no. I WILL NOT let that happen!*

So when they encountered the next trap — a laser grid from the schematics, intended to slice and dice — and her goggle-glasses showed it was already active, Omega became frustrated. *Enough is enough,* she thought. *Time to go off-book.*

"Glasses: Display overhead architectural view of current location to target location," she ordered. Instantly the goggle-glasses showed the desired view.

Thank You, God, for a one-floor structure, she thought in

gratitude. *Time to take a short-cut.*

"BLASTERS OUT!" she ordered. "Wide beam. We're going direct!"

"Vhat?" Kako wondered. "Ve are cuttink through?"

"It's taking too long, and they know we're here," Omega pointed out, adjusting her blaster. "The boy could be dead already. And I'm not having that."

"This ain't gonna be that fast either, pretty lady," Romeo noted. "We's movin' faster 'n you think; you're hyped up."

"She has a point, though, Romeo," Easy said. "There's too much shit between us an' the kid."

"Just do it," Golf declared. "This isn't a democracy, and we don't have time to argue. The boss-lady gave us an order."

"THANK you, Golf," Omega said, raising a chastising silver-blonde eyebrow at the others. "Glasses: Entire team. Project best opening to cut straight through to target."

Seconds later, Omega heard a chorus of, "Got it."

"Make sure you're not in anybody's way; arrange yourselves in ranks of three abreast. We'll take one minute of continuous fire in the first rank, then first rank moves to the rear, and second rank repeats. I want every rank switch to be accompanied by at least three steps forward! Keep following the best opening projections as we go. If any Scuttles get in the way, mow 'em down. Rear rank has responsibility for guarding our six. Everybody else, watch our sides. Swap out power packs as you need 'em, but step aside and move to the rear when you do, if you're in the firing rank. Person behind steps up."

"Yes, MA'AM!" came the chorus.

"And...FIRE."

They began to cut through the wall.

* * *

It took some doing, and after about ten minutes — two complete cycles through the team — everyone had to swap out power packs on their blasters. Those blasters were never intended to be what amounted to mining cutters, but they had brought along plenty of power packs, so that wasn't an issue.

What was an issue was how long it was taking.

He's gonna die, he's gonna die, ran the refrain in Omega's mind. *Echo's son is gonna die, and I can't bloody damn well stop it.* Frustrated, she spun and stepped away from the rank in which she stood—

—And triggered another booby trap.

The corridor seemed to erupt in front of her.

* * *

"OH SHIT!" a frantic Echo yelled, leaping to his feet, even as the tank image flickered again before stabilizing and posting the notice DRONE D1 LOST. "BABY! Meg! What were you THINKING?! Be okay, be okay, be okay! PLEASE be okay!"

"Hush, hush, zun," Fox said, moving to the younger man's side and taking his upper arm in a gentle grip. "Zebra, bubeleh, your technical analysis, please."

"Somebody let herself get frustrated and distracted, judging by that face she made," Zebra said, "and temporarily lost her situational awareness, as you lot put it. But she wasn't IN the blast; you can plainly see a gap between her and the actual blast in the drone display. Looks like it was another of those floor bomb things. She got hit by the shock wave, and I expect all of 'em are gonna have ringing ears, and she may need to sit on the floor and just be, for a few minutes. But India's there, and she's already running a medscanner over her..." she pulled out her own medscanner and looked at the display, "and I told her to set it up to relay to me, so we'd know the details if anybody got hurt. Meg's fine. A little shaken, but no serious damage. I think she's got a cut on her left cheek from a bit of plaster. That's it."

"Thank You, God," Echo breathed in intense relief.

"Amein," Fox averred. "Now come sit back down, zun, and let your own heart rate get back down to normal."

Echo did as he was told while Zebra gave him a quick scan, then she went and fetched a bottle of cool water from the wet bar refrigerator.

"Here," she said, handing it to Echo. "Sip on that, and let

things be, your own self, for a minute. Fox, if you can hide the tank for a couple min—"

"NO!" Echo exclaimed, throwing out a hand. "At least let me watch."

Zebra raised a skeptical eyebrow. "Are you gonna settle?"

"I will once I see Meg up an' moving."

"All right, zun," Fox agreed. "Drink on that water and lean back."

* * *

There was a general cry when Omega went down, and everyone instinctively ducked from the blast. But once again, most of the blast went upward, venting out the ceiling. They all turned, looking to help their lead, as India crouched over the downed Agent with her medscanner.

"Back at it, guys," Golf ordered. "Just 'cause Meg's down doesn't give us call to stop. We have a mission, and she'd be the first to say, get with it."

The cutting crew resumed, as Chi, Genova, Romeo, and India bent over a prone Omega.

"Umph," Omega grunted then. "Shit. Can y'all hear me?"

"Yes," India said, making sure to nod, in case Omega's ears rang too much to hear. "Can you hear us?"

"Uh…yeah, startin' to," Omega said after a few seconds. "Damn, did I pull a stupid. How bad am I hurt?"

"You have a scratch on your cheek, which I'm about to hit with some Rejuvic," India said, pulling her emergency field medikit from a warp pocket, "and maybe some bruising on the hand that broke the sensor beam and caught part of the blast wave, but nothing serious that I see. How do you feel?"

"Awake!" Omega said with a wry grin, as India swabbed a couple of places on her hand and her cheek. "That was one hell of an eye-opener. I got careless; sorry, y'all."

"You're worried an' frustrated we ain't goin' faster, pretty lady," Romeo noted. "It's okay. I think we all unnerstand it, 'specially those of us what got mates of our own."

* * *

Just then, there was a loud ruckus somewhere in the wall ahead of them; the rank of agents cutting through the facility had gotten well ahead of where Omega still sat.

"What the hell?" the Alpha Line assistant chief and Praetorian leader wondered, sitting up with Chi's help.

"Sounds like they're in a fight," Chi said, leaning over and trying to look down the tunnel the other agents had cut.

"I 'uz gonna say the same," Romeo agreed. "No, you sit right here," he shoved down on Omega's shoulder as she made to stand, "until India says you's ready to get up, girl. Th' guys 're all over this, an' Golf took the lead, while you 'uz down an' me an' India 'uz seein' to you. You been goin' flat-out since we started this. You c'n damn well sit an' catch your breath a sec."

"You have any water bottles in those pockets of yours, Meg?" India wondered.

"Um, yeah," Omega admitted.

"Good. Pull out a bottle of water and drink it. You sit tight until that's finished. THEN we can get back into this. Medical orders here, so don't argue with me, just DO it."

An obliging — and appreciative — Omega obeyed, while Romeo, Chi, and Genova kept watch, and India double-checked Omega's vitals readings. When the bottle was empty, she tossed it to one side and gave India a querying glance.

"Yeah, you can stand up," India decided. "I'd like to see you chug another of those, but we need to reach the child, too. Make sure you guzzle fluids and get a good meal in you when this is done, though."

"Right," Omega said, thinking, *I'll try. And hope I don't puke it back.*

Omega stood and steadied herself for a few moments, while India helped by holding onto her arm, then they headed for the opening where the rest of the team had, by this time, vanished.

* * *

They passed through the thick wall into the next corridor, where they found what looked to be around thirty Scuttle bodies all over the floor.

"It's hard t' tell how many f'r sure, though," Romeo said. "They's all in pieces-parts."

"And it reeks," Chi added. "Scuttle guts smell BAD."

"No shit," Genova agreed.

"That's what we're smelling, guys, shit," India pointed out.

"Ugh," Genova said, wrinkling her nose in disgust.

"Cut the banter and let's get a move on, y'all," Omega said. "We're getting close, and I'm the one tasked with getting little Alexaan out of here."

"According to the plan," India said. "But there's others can do that if necessary."

"We're supposed to see about recovering that Kochavi body and ascertaining its identity," Chi pointed out. "Me an' Genova, and Queen and Como."

"Let's go, then," Romeo said. "We do need t' get back inta th' ranks 'fore somethin' sneaks up on 'em…or on us."

They began to pick up the pace. In moments, they were moving at a run, behind Omega, in the lead.

* * *

By this point, they were past the external booby traps, and the progress was faster. Omega and the others rejoined the cutting queue, and within a couple of minutes they had reached the corridor where phone scanner apps confirmed the Division Two data — the boy was still there, and still alive.

"But my scanner app is showing we got a booby trap on the door," Golf told Omega.

"Okay, I expected this," Omega said, pulling out several specialized devices from a warp pocket in her Suit. "Did we verify that there's a dead Kochavi in the adjacent room down the hall?"

"We have," Chi said. "Most likely our missing professor."

"Yeah. Is that door also booby-trapped?"

"No ma'am," Como averred, looking up from his cell phone. "Scanner app shows there WAS one, but it has been deactivated. Most likely after he died."

"Good. Get out the body bag, put on your portable O2 masks — 'cause it's prob'ly not gonna smell good in there — don forensic gloves, and go load the poor guy inside the body bag," Omega ordered. "Beta Twenty-Eight, Beta Fifty-Two, that's your job. Go retrieve the fallen. We're on this."

The four agents trotted down the hallway as Omega turned to the booby-trapped door.

* * *

"Hmph," Omega grunted after a couple of minutes working with the lock on the door. "This one's pretty damn sophisticated."

"You gonna be able to get it, Meg, without blowing everybody sky-high?" Monkey wondered. "Or do we need to come at this from another direction? We DID just cut through the walls…"

"No, this is different," Omega noted, continuing to work. "This trap reaches into the walls. Or at least, into the electronics in those walls. Have Chi and Company retrieved the body yet?"

"Yeah, Omega, they left about thirty secs ago," Tare said.

"Do we need to send escorts with 'em, so they can carry the body while somebody else defends 'em?"

"No," Tare replied. "Chi had the body bag slung over his shoulders in a fireman's carry; the body didn't look to be too big. I signaled, asking if he needed help, and he shook his head. Indicated it was pretty light, and the others were gonna ride shotgun."

"They probably starved the poor guy to death," Yankee surmised. "I hope the kid is in better shape, or we could have a problem."

"Okay, y'all hush a minute, here," Omega ordered. "I gotta concentrate to figure something out."

The group fell silent, even as they watched the hall in both directions for Scuttles.

After a couple more minutes passed, Omega swore.

"Shit hellfire damnation," she grumbled, taking a leaf out of Echo's curse lexicon. "This is NOT gonna be fun, guys."

"What's wrong, Meg?" Romeo wondered. "Need me t' throw in my background? Will that help?"

"Thanks, but I don't think so, Romeo," Omega replied. "They got this thing rigged on a timer. I can't permanently deactivate it. Once I deactivate it, I got thirty seconds before it REactivates — and blows the room, and what looks like a significant chunk of the surrounding corridors, to Kingdom Come, along with all beings in that volume."

"Oh DAMN," Monkey expostulated, shocked.

"What do we do?" Quebec wondered.

"What kind of perimeter does the blast have?" Golf asked.

Omega looked up and down the hall.

"Okay," she decided. "If you're down the hall to our entrance tunnel, and about twenty feet inside it, you're probably safe." She gnawed her lip, considering. "Here's what we're gonna do, guys. Listen up, and listen close. 'Cause if things weren't complicated before, they damn sure are, now."

They all crouched around her except Dog, Quebec, Golf, and Easy, who were surveying the corridor; even they listened closely, however.

"Just tell us, Meg," India said. "We'll do whatever you need us to do."

"Good. Because you're not gonna like it," Omega said. "I'm the only one who stands a chance of outrunning this thing, so the rest of you are going to go back and get in the tunnel. Get out the kiddie-sized body armor Fox brought along for Alexaan, and have it ready. I'm gonna initiate this thing, run in, grab the kid and hope he doesn't struggle, and burn ass to get to y'all before this shit blows."

"You're right; I don't like it," Golf declared. "But I think maybe you have a point."

"Unfortunately, I think I agree with Golf," India said. "But Meg, just BE DAMN CAREFUL."

"I'm potentially rescuing Echo's son, India," Omega said, earnest. "I'm not gonna do anything that puts him in danger. And right now, I look like being his best shot at blowing this joint…excuse the pun."

"No," Yankee decreed. "There's gotta be a better way."

"You tell me what it is, 'cause I'm wide open to suggestions," Omega shot back. "I'm not thrilled about hangin' my ass out to dry either, y'all. An' I'm not tryin' to grandstand or show off. I just don't see any other way of doin' it that looks like it has a snowball's chance in hell of workin'."

They all thought for long moments, and several who had military backgrounds — including Romeo — took a look at the data she was getting from the booby trap. But nobody had any better ideas.

"Okay, y'all," Omega ordered, making her decision, "clear out. Get down the hall, around the corner, into the tunnel. Make sure you're at least twenty feet into the tunnel. Fifty would be better. Gimme a yell when you're in position and have the kiddie armor ready. Then I'm gonna do this."

The others turned reluctantly and headed back the way they had come.

* * *

"Oh, now this does not look good," Fox said, watching as everyone but Omega retreated to the tunnel they'd carved. "What the hell is Omega doing?"

"I gotta agree with you, Fox," Echo said, and Zebra leaned forward, anxious. "That looks like she's moving 'em outta danger."

"But she wouldn't put the boy she thinks is your son in danger, Echo," Zebra noted. "I think maybe she's…? I dunno…"

"Damnation, but I wish the tank software had more sound," Fox grumbled. "Somehow, I suspect this might be one of those things we need to stop, but I can't say for sure."

* * *

"Okay, we're in position an' ready. GO, Meg!" Romeo called.

Omega drew a deep breath, then hacked the electronic system and brought it down.

The door slid open and she launched herself from a kneeling position into a flat run, darting through the door and looking around for Alexaan.

"Oh hello!" the boy said in surprise, looking up from a little notebook in which he was drawing pictures. "You are not a Pers-thing. Who are you?"

"My name's Omega, your mama Nreefluvan sent me to rescue you, and we have to move fast," Omega replied, spitting out the words. "Come here, Alexaan."

The boy shoved the little notebook into a pocket and ran to the blonde human female, his arms extended. Omega grabbed him and swung him up to her shoulders.

"Wrap your legs around my waist, wrap your arms around my shoulders, and hang on tight," Omega warned. The boy obeyed without question, and once he had a firm grip, she spun and launched into a sprint.

They cleared the door scant seconds before it closed and latched once more, and Omega cornered hard, turning to the right and running down the corridor, which seemed to be lengthening moment by moment; she could have sworn the tunnel they'd carved through the walls was getting farther away, not closer.

Then her sensitive hearing caught Romeo's countdown.

"Eleven...ten...nine...eight...seven..."

Oh shit, she thought, and put on a burst of speed, pushing her body to its maximum limits.

* * *

When the three watchers in the secure suite aboard the *Genesis* saw the group huddled in the tunnel turn their backs and cover their faces and ears, they leaned forward, inching to the edge of their seats on the sofa.

"Oh shit," Echo breathed. "Move, baby. MOVE."

"She's hauling ass faster than I've ever seen a human run," Zebra murmured.

"But is she going to make it?" Fox wondered. "And she has the boy..."

* * *

Omega slid on the polished floor of the corridor as she reached the tunnel, her toes digging for traction. She made the turn, felt Alexaan tuck his face into the back of her neck as she entered the tunnel…and kept sprinting as hard as she could go.

"Move MOVE *MOVE*!" she cried as she came up hard on her teammates, still running at speed…

…As a titanic explosion shook the building and blew dust through the tunnel.

Chapter 12

"OH SHIT!" Echo exclaimed, then slumped on the sofa. The view in the tank shifted slightly as another of the drones was taken out by the blast; DRONE D5 LOST, read the message in the tank, and the resolution of the imagery degraded significantly — there were only two of the original five drones left.

"Are YOU gonna be all right?" Zebra wanted to know, as she turned to the head of Alpha Line.

"Yeah," Echo said, offering a sheepish grin. "I'm just used to being beside her, or generally with her, and I keep projecting myself into the mix."

"Ah," Fox said with a chuckle. "I've done that a time or two, myself, in the last hour or so, Echo. I'm just not as…" He paused, then shook his head. "I've already told you both that I learned to hide my reactions, my responses, in Majdanek," he said. "So I'm not going to be as demonstrative as you are, zun. Don't think I don't feel it, just because I don't show it. You'd be very wrong. I care a great deal about our meshuginah little family. And that young lady," he nodded at the tank, "is as near as I will have to a daughter — of the spirit, at least — for some time to come, I expect."

"No, I get it, 'Abba Fox,'" Echo said softly, laying a light hand on the older man's shoulder. "And you know I mean it, when I use that terminology."

"I do," Fox said, hazel eyes warming at the affectionate term.

"Good," Zebra said with a grin. "Nice male bonding moment, there. Now, what happened to our girl and our widdle kid?"

* * *

Instead of moving out of the way on Omega's orders, the Alpha Line Agents had linked arms and spread out across the width of the tunnel, bracing themselves in three tightly-spaced parallel ranks. Omega ran headlong into them, unable to ease back on her dead sprint in enough time to even slow down.

But the maneuver caused the linked wall of humans to serve as a kind of net or bumper guard, and Omega bounced backward…

…As Dog, Yankee, and Easy, centering the closest rank of 'human net,' spun and caught her outflung arms, keeping her upright and preventing her from landing on Alexaan.

"WHEEE!" Alexaan whooped, still clutching her waist and shoulders tightly with his arms and legs. "Can we do that again, Omega?"

"Oh," Omega panted heavily, even as Romeo swung the boy down from her back, "A-Alexaan, honey, I…I don't… think so."

* * *

"Sit your butt DOWN," India ordered Omega. "Right this second. You need to catch your breath, you need to chug some water, and I'd give a chunk of change if somebody — ANYBODY — had stowed some meal bars in all these damn warp pockets we got. We got tons of 'food' for the blasters, and none for our team lead, here."

"I'll be fine, India," Omega said, still panting. "We need to get the hell outta here."

"We need to get the boy into the body armor," Dog said, "and Yankee and Tare are doing that right now. We don't move until the child is armored up, so you have time to sit, rest, and hydrate."

"But I—"

"DO IT," India declared. "And that's an order. I'm pulling medical rank on you."

Omega threw up her hands and sat on an exposed section of a nearby I-beam, pulling another bottle of water from a warp pocket and sipping on it, as she fought to regulate her respiration into a more normal rhythm.

* * *

In only a few minutes, Alexaan was clad in small-person

body armor, including a full-head helmet with face mask, and Omega was shrugging into a special harness that would allow her to carry him more easily, without either of them wearing out arms or legs.

"Okay, y'all," Omega said, once Alexaan was comfortably settled on her back. "Assume guard position for retreat. Don't forget the trap resets."

"What is a trap reset?" Alexaan asked.

"Do you know what a trap is, a booby trap?" Omega wondered, as they began the retreat.

"Um, yes, kind of. Maman has talked to me about things like that because of having worked with my papan, and I like to watch Earth adventure movies."

"Do you remember the movie about the archaeologist? The one where he swaps out the gold idol for the bag of sand?" Omega queried.

"Oh yes! That is one of my favorites!"

"Do you remember how he would find a way through a trap, and it would sometimes reposition itself to catch the next person?"

"Ohhhhh…"

* * *

They were met at the exit by the rest of the Praetorians as well as the Alpha Line teams brought as backup. Oscar held up a hand, then dropped it hard, and after only a couple of seconds, the force field dropped…and stayed down. The rescue team walked over to where the Division Two personnel had come out of hiding and set up a triage center.

"I think my little buddy here is okay," Omega said, "but let's get this heavy armor off him, and have a look-see to make sure he's not hurt."

"I got 'im, Meg," Romeo said, lifting Alexaan out of the harness on her back. "Jus' hold still a sec. There." He sat the boy down on a gurney, and one of the Division Two medics ran a medscanner over him as Romeo commenced removing the body armor, and Omega shrugged out of the carry harness.

"Oh, this is very good," the medic said. "He is in surprisingly good shape, considering his captivity. The other captive did not fare so well; he had been starved and dehydrated, I fear."

"What does that mean?" Alexaan asked.

"The bad guys didn't give him any food or water," Omega explained.

"Oh no! Is he all right?"

"No, sweetie," Omega sighed, "he isn't. He didn't make it."

"What do you mean?"

"She means that he died, youngling," the medic explained, voice quiet. "They did not treat him as well as they did you. You do need a bit to eat and drink, and an extra meal for a few days will not hurt you. But you are otherwise in good health." He turned to Omega. "I gather you are taking him to his mother and father, aboard the Division One vessel?"

Omega's mouth went dry.

"Yes, we're taking him to his mother," India interjected smoothly. "The, ah, paternity question is still at issue."

"I see," the medic said with a nod. "He is cleared to go to his maman, then. Was anyone in your party seriously injured?"

"Surprisingly not," India said. "Oh, we had a couple close calls, but it all turned in our favor."

"You are the team medic?"

"I am," India said with a smile. "Agent India."

"Very good, then, Agent India; I am pleased to meet you. If your team lead will check in with our Director, you are all free to go."

"Right," Omega said. "Point me at Director Ulseleigh."

* * *

"…Ah. And so we are free to take control?" Ulseleigh asked, as Omega gave him a quick debrief.

"You are, sir, and glad of it," Omega determined.

"Very good. Thank you very kindly, Omega. Your team is most excellent; I intend to congratulate Fox heartily for your good work."

"Thank YOU, sir," Omega said. "Your help in this matter was appreciated more than we can say, and we made extensive use of it! Medical has cleared us; may we have your permission to take the boy to his mother?"

"By all means. Go, and keep me apprised of what happens there," Ulseleigh said. "It is a strange situation, according to what Fox has told me in private."

"It is, that," Omega agreed. "By your leave, sir."

"Go, Agent Omega."

* * *

Once Omega had carried the boy over to the *Praetorian One*, with Alpha Two guarding their rear, she took him through the hatch and set him down in one of the passenger seats.

"All right, little fella," Omega said with a smile, "let's get you belted in, then the rest of us will sit down and strap in, and we'll take you to your mama."

"Mama? You have said that several times; what is a mama?" Alexaan asked, as Omega went about fastening the five-point harness around the small body, then tightening it until it was secure. "Oh! You mean my maman?"

"Yup, that's exactly who I mean."

"Oh, it will be SO good to see Maman! I have missed her SO MUCH!" the little one cried. "Soon?"

"Very soon."

By this time, Omega was strapping in, and Alpha Two was already seated and belted.

"Canteen, cloak and lift off, please, ma'am," Omega ordered.

"Consider it done, Omega," Canteen replied with a smile.

Moments later, they were airborne, headed for orbit.

* * *

Ten minutes after that, the *Praetorian One* was settling in the hangar bay of the *Genesis*. Omega unstrapped and helped the little one unbuckle himself and slide out of the seat. A grinning Canteen opened the hatch.

"There ya go, Omega," she said. "Good job, and I hope

things work out well…for everybody."

"Thanks, Canteen," Omega murmured.

"You okay, pretty lady?" Romeo wondered.

"…Yeah, I'm fine, Romeo," she said then. "It is what it is. You know what I'm talking about."

"Yeah," Romeo said, his voice gentle. "I get it."

"I want you to see me when this is all done," India said softly. "Even if I wasn't the resident medic, I'm your friend and your adoptive sis. I wanna see about you."

Omega nodded, then turned to the little guy at her side.

"C'mon, Alexaan," she told him. "There's someone you need to meet."

"Is it safe now?" he wondered, somewhat plaintive.

"Yes, dear, it's safe now. You're safe on board the *Genesis*, the flagship of Division One Director Fox, and your maman is waiting with him, along with some friends. Come with me."

The boy pattered along right beside Omega, who slowed her pace to allow his shorter legs to keep up easier. Alpha Two guarded the rear.

* * *

They went up a couple of decks from the hangar deck. When they exited the elevator, Alexaan followed Omega down a corridor, around a corner, and through a door, where two human males, two human females, and a Chesharilzi male awaited, along with Nreefluvan Daagnadan, the child's mother. Omega headed straight for the younger of the two human males, kissing him before stepping back slightly.

"We made it back, Ace, Fox," she said, then indicated the child, still standing shyly near the door, flanked by India and Romeo. "Let me introduce you all to Alexaan Daagnadan. Alexaan, this is Director Fox, Assistant Director Echo, Dr. Zarnix Chif—"

"Echo?!" the boy exclaimed. "Did you say Agent ECHO??"

"That's me, youngling," Echo acknowledged.

"DADAAAAAN!" a delighted Alexaan cried out, running across the room to grab Echo in a fierce hug about his legs.

"Oh, Dadan! I knew you would come for me! I wanted to meet you for so long! Where have you been?"

Everyone in the room froze.

* * *

Echo looked down at the boy, the young face alight with happiness, and suddenly knew he couldn't say what he had been about to say to this little one. He crouched down to reach the boy's eye level.

"Hey, Alexaan," he said softly. "I'm sorry I haven't met you before now. I wasn't told about you, see. I didn't know your mommy made you."

"Ohhhhh," the little one said, nodding sagely in understanding. "Hokay. That is all right, then. But you know now."

"Yes."

"Good! Are we gonna be a famwy now? You, an' me, an' Maman?"

Echo's head shot up, and his gaze sought out Omega's face.

* * *

Omega watched as the boy met the man who, she considered, was most likely his father, and felt like her heart was ripping from her chest.

I waited for him, she thought, watching, *because my subconscious already knew him, loved him. But he didn't know about me. He didn't even know I existed. He was looking for the right one, and thought he'd found her in Nreefluvan. He was gonna marry her, or, well, 'make it permanent,' he said. I guess he couldn't have married her back then, 'cause we only just got the marriage amendment. But now they have a child. They have a FAMILY...if I'm out of the way. I thought I could find something in the rescue to take care of things where I was concerned, but that didn't work out — I had to get the boy out first, then I HAD him and...oh well. No idea what I was thinking with all that, anyway. It was stupid. So I guess now I'll just...just step back. I'll go to Fox and have him dissolve the life partnership and the defined partnership, and*

I'll probably have to talk hard to get Father Papa to dissolve the marriage. Or maybe see if the Ennead put a divorce clause in the marriage charter amendment. But then I'll...I guess I'll get with Fox and Pul and see if Pul still wants me to join his bodyguard corps. She swallowed hard. *Then at least I'll have something useful to do.*

Just then, the boy asked Echo if they—Echo, Alexaan, and Nreefluvan—were going to be a family.

And there it is, Omega thought, even as an invisible arrow fully an inch in diameter seemed to transfix her body, straight through her chest. *Even the child recognizes it.* She didn't quite manage to stifle a gasp of pain, instinctively putting her hand to her chest and grabbing a fistful of shirt as the intensity of the pain took away her breath.

She didn't expect her knees to buckle.

By the time she hit the floor — for the second time since Nreefluvan's arrival — everything had gone dark.

* * *

"Oh shit!" India and Zebra said in unison, as Omega fell to the floor in reaction to the boy's response. Dihl, who also waited there to assist and to find out if she had a grandchild, gave a cry of dismay. Echo, too, fairly yelled in alarm near to panic, gently freeing himself of the boy's clinging arms before running to the side of his wife and kneeling on the floor. The medical team clustered around, pulling instruments and scanners. Dihl promptly plopped onto the floor and eased Omega's head into her lap, delicately checking her throat for a pulse, even as Echo took Omega's hand in his own.

"Oh no!" Nreefluvan exclaimed, rushing to her son's side, even as the boy let out a wail of fear and confusion. "Hush, hush, Alexaan, hush. Omega is ill, my son."

"Maman! There you are! Oh, I am so glad to see you! But what is wrong with Omega, Maman?" the boy asked, worried. "She fall down go blat…"

"I do not know, boopyin," Nreefluvan murmured, holding the boy close; he wanted to run to Echo and Omega, even as the three physicians worked over the fallen Agent. "Stay here with me, boop-boop. Give them room to work. Those three there? They are physicians, and they are trying to find out what has happened. She may have been injured in rescuing you."

"No, no, no!" Alexaan exclaimed, worried and anxious. "She cannot be hurt! She must not! I liked her! She was good to me and took care of me!"

"She takes care of Echo, too," Nreefluvan murmured. "She and Echo are espoused."

"They…they are?"

"They are. They are partners in work and in life."

"But…but does that mean…we cannot be a family?"

"I do not know, son," the Kochavi woman said with a sigh. "I may have been wrong about Echo being your father. Or I might not. I think we will need to make sure he is before we do more."

"Oh," Alexaan said, seeming to collapse in on himself with disappointment. "He…he does not…want me?"

"I do not think it is that as much as it is…he was very surprised. I tried to reach him when you were very little — right after you were born — to tell him about you, but could not, and so it came as a shock to him when I told him recently. And he IS espoused to Omega, newly so, and they do not know how to handle it." Nreefluvan sighed. "This is probably beyond your understanding, boopyin."

"No, Maman," Alexaan said then. "I understand. He loves her, he did not know about me, and they are confused about what to do, because I am your child and not Omega's." He paused, watching the doctors work, then added, "Maybe, once they become un-confused, we can all be a family."

* * *

"What's wrong with her?" Echo wondered, as India, Zebra, and Zarnix scanned her, then began loosening her tie, collar, and belt, each taking one item and working until it was open or freed of Omega's body. "Is she okay?"

"Man, she let it all loose onna way t' get th' kid, let alone

315

on th' way out, with that last booby trap," Romeo said. "Never seen nothin' like it. I'm bettin' that's to do with this."

"She did that, all right," India agreed. "When she hit the floor, I was worried she was maybe having an infarct or something."

Echo paled.

"A heart attack?!" he whispered in horror.

"No, no. Yes, it was an initial concern, but I see no sign of it," Zarnix said, studying his medscanner.

"Me neither," Zebra agreed, "and she's got good color. I'm betting Romeo nailed it—she's upset over the whole concept of 'that's Echo's kid,' combined with blowing out all the stops, and I'm also betting, knowing her, she hasn't been eating that well as a result of all the emotional upset of late, never mind the reaction she had to the pheromones…"

"Ohhhh shit," India said, grasping where the other physician was going. "Lemme see." She quickly adjusted her medscanner and ran it over the prone form. "Yep, that's it, guys. I'm barely registering it. Her blood sugar is so low it's past all the sub-basements, and it's down below the foundation. She'd be, like, UNDER Headquarters."

"Damn," Echo muttered. "That's bad."

"It ain't good," Zebra agreed. "Zar, have we got any…?"

"Yes," Zarnix confirmed. "I brought along several complete emergency and triage kits; it occurred to me that we might need them, if the Persan foot soldiers put up much of a fight. We need to get her to our triage station right away, and I will put in a bag of glucose."

"I got her," Echo said, scooping up Omega's limp form, as Dihl rose to her feet. "Oh shit."

"What?" Zebra wondered.

"She's…it's hard to explain," Echo said, looking down at his wife in his arms, "but I can feel her body sort of, of jerking spasmodically…"

"She is having mild seizures, then," Zarnix declared. "That is another indication that Romeo's observation is the right one.

Are you having difficulties holding her?"

"No, not as long as it doesn't get worse. If it does, I might need some help."

"Then let us hurry, before it does get worse. For believe me, we do not want it to become worse."

"I have her. Let's go."

"Dadan, may we come?" a soft, high-pitched voice asked from behind. "Omega is a nice lady. I want her to be okay."

"Sure thing, Alexaan," Echo said, glancing over his shoulder at the boy as he followed the physicians out of the room and down the hall. "You and your mom come on. You can wait with me and Fox and Romeo while the medics tend to Meg."

"Is that what you call Omega?" the boy asked. "Meg?"

"Yeah. It's what we call a nickname on Earth. I have a couple for her, and she has some for me, too."

"Can I give her a nickname, too?"

"I suppose so. What did you want to call her?"

"Could I call her Amaman? Would she like that?"

"I think she might. Let's wait until she's awake again, and you can ask her."

"Hokay."

"What does 'Amaman' mean?" Romeo wondered, as he shadowed Echo to the right in case he needed to help carry Omega. Fox, likewise shadowing Echo to the left and also prepared to assist, raised a curious eyebrow.

"It's hard to translate into English," Echo said, glancing down at his wife in his arms, to see she was still unconscious and unresponsive. "It's sort of like stepmom, or maybe a very close aunt, but not quite either one. It has the connotation of a surrogate or alternate mother."

"Awww," Romeo said with a smile. "That's perfect f'r Meg."

"Yes, that fits our Mama Bear, all right," Fox decided.

"Yeah, it does," Echo agreed.

* * *

Once they got Omega onto a gurney, the trio of physicians commenced stripping off jacket, tie, and shoes, while Echo doffed her various holsters for them. Then, after shooing most of the rest of the party into the adjacent waiting room, India and Echo eased the shirt off Omega's torso, leaving her bra in place—it was one of the pretty nude-toned satin-and-lace bras that Echo liked—and Zarnix fetched a bag of saline and a bag of glucose, while Zebra began prepping Omega's arm for a standard noninvasive osmosive intravenous cannula.

"How well HAS she been eating, Echo?" Zebra wondered as she worked.

"Not that great, I don't think," Echo admitted. "You know how she was sick there for a bit, throwing up and stuff. This whole thing, first with Ree coming on to me so hard, and using the pheromones to muck with us, then with Ree claiming I accidentally fathered her son, all while y'all were tryin' to make it so Meg could even HAVE kids? Well, it just hasn't done her any favors at all, mentally OR emotionally."

"Has she been barfing up her toenails, as Romeo would say?" India wondered.

"Not that I know of, except for that one time. And with the nd't'lq, I don't think she could get that one by me without my knowing. But yeah, she's been, like, nauseated a good part of the time. Just not quite to the vomiting level."

"Well, we have that much," Zarnix decided, hanging the solution bags on the IV stand and giving the leads to Zebra. "But I suspect her appetite has been rather the worse for wear, even if she did keep it all down?"

"No doubting that," Echo confirmed, as Zebra seated the IV and adjusted the drip. "I've done the best I could to keep her eating, but to be honest, for at least a day or…three or four… there, when Ree had ramped up her pheromone game to the max, I…" He broke off and bit his lip. "I wasn't looking after my own wife like I should have. Dammit."

"We understand, Echo, and that's not your fault," India interjected, "so don't go blaming yourself."

"I knew I was off, I just didn't know why, or how to fight it," Echo confessed then. "And maybe now this is the result. How can I NOT blame myself?"

"Because you were being influenced from outside, and very strongly, at that," Zarnix said, running a medscanner over Omega again. "By a means that was calculated not to ALLOW you to figure out what was going on. Human olfactory responses are very nearly subliminal, in most respects. And pheromones are subtle, usually undetectable, at least consciously."

"Listen to the male," Zebra ordered. "Zar knows what he's talking about, Echo. It's part of that whole 'human nervous system study' he does. Never mind that...huh. Zar, are you seein' this?"

"Seeing what?" India wondered.

"Well, it looks to me like Meg may still be suffering from some of the aftermath of the pheromone storm she was caught in."

"I must agree with that," Zarnix affirmed, looking over Zebra's shoulder. "I am still seeing metabolites in her blood scans. Her system seems not to have cleared them as well as I would have expected."

"Oh, that explains it," India said, studying her scanner readings. "Yeah, wow. Guys, look at channel six-A."

Zarnix and Zebra adjusted their scanners, then hissed, perturbed by the readings.

"That ain't good," Zebra said. "We need to get that shit out of her, 'cause that's just complicating the whole metabolic situation. I woulda thought our last attempt would have worked for that, but evidently she doesn't metabolize 'em quite like the rest of us do. Damn you, Slug." She looked up at Echo. "So, see? Not your fault."

Echo drew a deep, frustrated breath. He wanted to be angry at Nreefluvan, but it was blatantly obvious to everyone there by this point that she had been in desperate fear for her son, and given she had had no knowledge of Omega before meeting her, had done what she felt was needful by doing her best to turn

Echo away from his own wife. It still irritated the ever-loving shit out of him—according to his way of thinking—but it was hard to condemn a desperate mother who was only trying to save her son from a ruthless warlord.

"All right," he finally sighed. "If you say so."

"I say so."

"Is Meg gonna be okay?"

"I am seeing signs that her body is metabolizing the glucose almost faster than we can run it into her," Zarnix said, still watching the scanner readings closely. "Dihl, go fetch another glucose bag, please; I think I want to hang an additional bag, here, to help her body catch up. We do not have to run it until the first runs out, but I want to maximize the flow rate, and that will exhaust this bag quickly."

"Whoa, Zar," Zebra said, eyebrows shooting up in surprise. "Are you sure? We don't want to set up a high blood glucose level, here. That way lies inflammation of all sorts, and potentially worse problems."

"Look, Zee," Zarnix said, holding out the medscanner for her to look at the readouts. "Look at the rate it is being metabolized. There is no way possible for Omega to develop too high a blood sugar level, at that rate. She will suck both bags in and we will have to hang a third, before we get her back to something even approximating normal levels."

"Damn," Zebra said, as her jaw slackened in shock at the readings.

"Wait, wait, wait," Echo said, startled. "Are you sure?"

"Very sure, Echo," Zarnix said, nodding. "The average human requires in the general vicinity of 100 grams of glucose per day, give or take, depending on the particular human— you know how that works. Body size, metabolic rate, activity level..."

"Yeah," Echo agreed. "But Meg isn't average..."

"No, she is not," Zarnix agreed. "On an ordinary day, I have estimated she requires some twenty-five to as much as thirty percent more glucose than human norms, give or take, and depending on her activity levels. I have seen her requirement go as high as nearly half again, if she has been very physical. But if she has truly 'pulled out all the stops' today — let alone given the worries of previous days, and the lack of proper nutrition — well, she may now require nearly double the average. And each of these bags is a standard glucose IV bag, containing about 25 grams of glucose in half a liter of fluid…"

"Oh shit," Echo said, shocked. "You're gonna have to knock down eight of those puppies into her before she's back to normal?!"

"Possibly," Zebra said, accepting the new glucose bag Dihl had fetched, and hanging it on the IV stand, before adjusting the drip rate on the IV. "Based on what I saw in the tank video, it wouldn't surprise me a bit at this point. Let's get a pump going here, too, so we can push it into her, then I'll daisy-chain the glucose bags, and let it run." Meanwhile, India was busy setting up vitals monitors so they didn't have to keep scanning the limp form with medscanners.

"Good idea," Zarnix agreed, and Dihl ducked into another room, returning with a pump, which she clamped onto the IV stand before she flipped on the power pack. "Given how her brain works, and what we have seen in the past, I suspect she is NOT going to return to consciousness until we have stabilized her blood sugar at something close to normal levels. And as you have just realized, Echo, that may take some time."

"And quite a few bags of glucose solution," Zebra added.

"We will need to monitor her levels, because I expect her body to slow its consumption as we gradually bring her levels closer to normal," Zarnix said. "We will slow the pump as that occurs, and likely eventually remove it altogether. But for now, we need to give it to her as fast as her body wants it."

"Echo, why don't you go outside into the waiting area with the others?" India wondered. "We need to get Meg into a medical jumpsuit, so we can have access as needed, anyway, and you look like you could stand sitting down…"

"Yeah, we don't need you on a gurney here, next to Meg,

just on account of you passed out from worry and busted your face open or something," Zebra agreed. "And she doesn't need you there, either."

"Listen to them, son," Dihl murmured, laying a light hand on his shoulder. "And trust us with your belovéd. We have this, son. I swear to you."

Echo sighed again, and turned for the door.

* * *

Echo emerged from the triage room, meeting four pairs of questioning eyes.

"She's still unconscious," he said, shaking his head. "Blood sugar was something close to nonexistent, to hear 'em tell it. They're running a bag of glucose into her now, and will probably need two or three more before she even comes close to regaining consciousness. She hasn't been eating right, and apparently has been burning through what she did eat like a wildfire in prairie grass. Especially after running that little obstacle course the Scuttles set up."

"Come sit down, zun," Fox murmured. "There is an excellent team working on her, and it will be all right. Yes, it can be serious, but I think everything is under control now, and we caught it in time thanks to Romeo's apt observation telling us what to look for. It could have been much worse."

"Yeah, coulda been 'er heart, like India 'uz afraid of," Romeo agreed.

"In a way, it still is," Echo sighed, sitting where Fox indicated, "it's just her emotional heart that's breaking, I suspect."

"What do you mean, Dadan?" Alexaan wondered.

"He means, boopyin, that I tried to come between them, when she loves him very deeply, and it has hurt her badly," a sad Nreefluvan told her son.

"But why did you do that?"

"Because the bad being that held you prisoner told me I must, else he would harm you."

"But why?"

"Let me try," Fox said softly. "Zun, my name is Fox, and I run Division One. You know about the Pan-Galactic Law Enforcement…?"

"Yes," Alexaan said with a nod. "Maman has taught me all about the galactic police, and how Echo is one of the 'portant agents an' everything. So you run Division One?"

"That's right. And now Echo is my assistant—he helps me run it. And one day, when I retire, he'll run it himself."

"Dadan? That's good!"

"Yes, and he's very good at it. But the bad being who held you prisoner is, according to information I got from a friend in the Andromeda Galaxy, the brother of another bad being who tried to take over our galaxy AND his own, and his brother — the one who kidnapped you — was trying to do the same."

"Ooo! He IS a bad being!"

"Yes, he is. So what he wanted to do was to have your mother in a position to control Echo," Fox explained, "by scaring her into thinking he would hurt you if she didn't follow his orders. Then she was going to have Echo take over from me," Fox chose to skip over the probable means of assassination, "and become the head of Division One, only obeying orders from the bad guy, as passed through your mother."

"He would have kept me prisoner…forever," Alexaan suddenly realized.

"Most likely, yes." Fox also chose to skip over the possibility — probability, in Fox's experienced opinion — that the boy would have been killed outright, while Aggum pretended to the mother that he was still alive.

"I am so sorry," Nreefluvan whispered. "I did not want to do it. Echo—I was glad to see Echo again, and had he still been unattached, I might well have wished to resume a relationship, if he were amenable. But I did not want to do any of the rest! It was only because he had Alexaan that I agreed to ANY of it! And then, when I saw the affinity between Echo and Omega, I…but I had no choice. Aggum made it plain that any failure meant Alexaan's death! I tried to…to 'fit into' the relationship, but they wanted none of that…and I understand that. Then I tried to make Omega want to go away, to leave Echo, but she would not. I…" The Kochavi woman's shoulders slumped. "Echo, once again I apologize, more deeply than you can imagine, but I have no real hope that you will ever—CAN ever—forgive me. And I do not blame you. I am not sure I can ever forgive myself! All I would ask is that you put up with me for the sake of this child, if he proves to be your son."

Echo drew a deep breath.

"Give me a chance to process everything, Ree," he said in a low, quiet voice. "And no, I don't hold anything against little Alexaan, here. But to put it frankly, you're going to have to earn my trust back, Ree. And that's a long way to go."

"I understand," Nreefluvan said, tears in her eyes, though they did not fall. "But you will give me a chance to do so?"

"I will," Echo said with a nod. "We'll have to see about Meg. I can't say how she'll feel about matters, after all this. And given she and I are married, if she doesn't want…"

"I…I understand," Nreefluvan said, voice catching. "What Omega deems as the thing to do, is what you will do, as well."

"Give Meg a chance," Echo said. "Let the medics bring her back to a semblance of normal, with time to heal and put her head back together, let alone on straight, and I'll discuss it with her."

"Speaking of," India's voice startled them all, and they looked up to see her standing there, now attired in a lab coat instead of her Suit coat. "We do have Meg stabilized now. She's not awake yet, and probably won't be for a bit, but there's enough glucose in her system now to ensure that she's out of any real serious danger, and Zarnix is convinced we reacted fast enough to prevent any lasting damage. It was just an abrupt drop in her blood sugar as a result of the truly amazing things she did earlier today, coupled with a bit of an emotional upset that sent her adrenaline surging after she'd calmed down from the mission. That adrenaline surge is what finally tanked her blood sugar below her body's ability to compensate, and down she went. But she's going to be fine now."

"Thank the good Lord," Echo breathed, slumping in his chair in utter relief.

"That," Fox agreed.

"Amen," Romeo averred.

"YAY!" Alexaan cried, shooting both fists straight up.

"Indeed, my little boop-boop," Nreefluvan murmured, also deeply relieved. "I must agree. I owe her so very much, for in the end, she personally rescued you, my dear son." She shook her head. "Despite all I did to her."

"That's jus' Meg," Romeo said. "She not gonna let a little one be hurt iffen she c'n help it. No matter what."

"Exactly," Fox affirmed. "So the news is good all around."

"Yup. I thought you'd all be happy to hear that," India said with a grin. "Now, Mr. Alexaan, Dr. Zarnix and I would like to check you out, to make sure you weren't hurt by the bad male from another galaxy. Our other medtech, Yorker, is already setting up the equipment in another exam room, while our chief medtech, Dihl, works with Zebra to see to Omega's needs. So. Would you and your mommy be so kind as to follow me?"

"Yes," Alexaan said, almost prim, but with chest swelling with pride at being addressed as 'Mr.' anything.

"India, you're going to run…?" Fox murmured in an aside.

"You betcha," India confirmed. "Like I said, Zebra said she'd look after Meg, and Dihl is with her, so that's all good. We have enough staff to handle everybody, this time."

"Come, Maman," an adorably-formal Alexaan declared, sliding out of his chair and turning to his mother. "Dr. India wants to see to us."

Alexaan and Nreefluvan followed India out of the waiting room, hand in hand.

* * *

As soon as the rest of the Praetorians, along with Alpha Line, cleared the building, Division Two moved in. Alpha Three ensured the force field stayed down despite several

325

efforts by the Scuttles to raise it, and several heavy armored vehicles — with turret guns — trundled up on antigrav 'wheels,' surrounding the building.

Director Ciarmhac Ulseleigh stepped up, wearing a headset.

"Load," he ordered, and clunks and clanks came from within the armored vehicles.

"Take aim," he ordered.

All the turret guns trained on various parts of the building.

"Fire," Ulseleigh commanded.

They all fired specialized rounds, designed to pierce the building. Loud concussions went up as the projectiles impacted and smashed through masonry walls, producing clouds of dust and chunks of rubble.

Gradually the silence returned, as the dust blew away in the breeze.

"Alpha Three," Ulseleigh said, "please bring up the force field, but maintain control of it. I do not wish it to go down until I give the word."

"Copy that, Director Ulseleigh," Kilo noted.

* * *

In Geretan Aggum's office, that being was preparing for his emergency escape.

(…And you say they actually RESCUED the youngling, rather than killed it?)

(Yes, milord. They were very careful to get him out safely and as swiftly as possible. Their feats were amazing, according to what I was told. They are as swift as an isegunt giving chase! Argat, our security chief, says she expects them to turn on us next.)

(Mmph. I fear I understand Humn's situation a bit better,) Aggum told Gree, more than a little rueful. (These humans are damnably unpredictable and belligerent. No matter. We will regroup and try again later. This WILL work.)

(Your essentials are packed and ready, milord,) Gree said, pointing to the small travel case near the door. (I would recommend we board your craft as soon as possible, if we want to manage our escape. They already have the boy out and gone.)

(What of the rest of them?)

(I do not know, sir. They have vacated the building, for certain. The head of security indicates she expects a major advance within the next half-hour.)

(Then let us make haste. Fetch the case and let us go at once.)

But before Gree could catch up the case, the room shook violently. The ceiling cracked, and masonry dust drifted down. Both males made use of their tentacle-legs to crouch low to the floor, spreading their multiple limbs wide to maintain balance.

Just then, a pointed-nose, cylindrical metallic object burst through the wall, and both males instinctively lunged away from it, even as one of the structural supports in the ceiling collapsed.

* * *

When the area around the building was clear of dust, and the force field dome had been erected once again, Ulseleigh spoke into the mic of his headset once more.

"Trigger payloads."

A soft hissing sound gradually increased in volume, and a few wisps of mist drifted out of various openings in the building, some of which had been caused by the rounds that were just shot into it.

* * *

Gree and Aggum were just about to make their escape, when the metal cylinder that had crashed through the wall of Aggum's office began to vent a white mist.

Within seconds, the two males began to gasp and wheeze. Gree staggered, spun about, and fell, dropping the case to the floor.

(Damnation,) Aggum panted, beginning to panic. (I must… must get away…)

He fell to the floor, and did not stir.

Moments later, the rest of the ceiling collapsed.

* * *

After about three minutes, timed off on his PGLEIA-issue wrist chronometer, Ulseleigh spoke again.

"Alpha Three, please drop the force field."

"Force field down, sir," Gustav replied seconds later.

"Thank you. Containment teams, don gas masks. Ensure you have plenty of force cuffs, and enter the building per plan; restrain every being you can find. Confinement, please bring up the police vans for the prisoners. Ensure maximum confinement on the cargo areas. Don gas masks, pick up stretchers, and enter the building behind the containment teams; please retrieve all restrained captives and place them in the cargo sections of the vans."

"Where do we take them from here, sir?" one of Ulseleigh's aides asked.

"We will be shipping them to Aleancë for war crimes trials," Ulseleigh noted. "Division One Director Fox indicated that President Entiyti was very interested in this lot…and not in a good way."

"Very good, sir."

* * *

It took 'Joe Bob' his entire shift, plus a couple of hours, to clean up the truly dreadful mess and properly decontaminate and sanitize the area, and then he had to carefully retreat to his quarters in the sub-basement to decontaminate himself. By the time he had finished all that, even with the oxygen mask, all he could smell was vomit and poop. He made no attempt to eat, because the situation was entirely too nauseating to deal with the concept of food. Consequently, he had not eaten since breaking the fast that morning.

Not to mention it was now well past his awake schedule and into his sleep period.

But at least I am finally clean. I need to call 'Gary', he thought. *He will be angry that I have no information, but there is no help for it. The cover story is important, and I cannot afford to lose it at this stage of things.*

He headed for the comm device, practically staggering with exhaustion.

However, much to his surprise, he got no response.

Then again, he considered, *I do not know what time it is there. I may have waited too late and in annoyance with me, he gave up and retired for the day. I think I should do the same, before I become incoherent with exhaustion. I will try again tomorrow.*

And he all but collapsed on the bed. He was asleep before his head hit the pillow.

Chapter 13

Over an hour after Echo had left it, Dihl came out of the triage room and went straight to…Fox.

"Omega is awake and asking for you, sir," she told him in a low voice. She shot an anxious glance at Echo.

"Oh good," Echo said in relief. "We can go see her now."

"No, son," Dihl said softly, holding up a staying hand. "She wants to see Fox right now. Just Fox."

"But…but why?" a hurt Echo asked, turning pale. "Damn, she's got a hard telepathic block up, too…"

"I do not know for certain, son," a worried Dihl replied, "but she told me to tell you to stay here and visit with your old girlfriend…and your son."

Echo went white.

"Shit," Romeo murmured, but said no more, after getting a good look at his former partner's face.

"Relax, zun," Fox said, laying a light hand on Echo's shoulder. "I'll take care of this. I have a sneaking suspicion what's up, here, and I can handle matters far better, at this stage. Trust me."

Echo nodded, swallowing hard.

Fox followed Dihl into the triage room, as Echo watched.

* * *

"…NO, Omega," Fox decreed not five minutes later, when she had put forward her request to dissolve all relationships with Echo and step aside. "I'm not going to do any of that. Not unless and until Echo and you BOTH come to me in agreement to do it. And even then, you're going to have to convince me you mean it. And, given the look on his face just a few minutes ago, I can tell you for a fact, and without hesitation, he does NOT want that."

"But Fox," a still-weak Omega protested. "I'm only trying to do…"

"I know, meyn tekhter, I know," Fox said, gentling his

voice. "You want to do right by the man you love more than life. But you're forgetting something important here, meyn kind. You're forgetting that he loves you, too. In fact, I would go so far as to say that he adores you, and that were anything to happen to you, he would not know what to do with himself. The rest of us would almost certainly have to work hard to keep him going, to keep him from what Romeo calls 'kamikazi'ing out.' You're also forgetting that he is convinced the boy is not his. And frankly, the evidence I've seen agrees with him."

"It does?" Omega wondered. "What do you mean? What evidence? What have you seen that I haven't?"

"The man and the boy. Face to face."

"Huh? I don't get it…"

"You were not in a position to see both their faces when Alexaan and Echo met, not at the proper angle," Fox pointed out. "I was. I saw them both, face to face, and could compare those faces. There is no resemblance there, Omega. Oh, undoubtedly Alexaan's father was dark-haired and brown-eyed. But there is no similarity of bone structure, of nose shape, eye shape, ear shape. Their profiles do not even remotely align. Echo has a firm, straight jaw and distinct chin, with that classic high cheekbone and straight brow of an Apache. Alexaan has a somewhat receding chin, average though slightly wide cheekbones, and a slightly rounded brow. None of which his mother has, either—Nreefluvan Daagnadan has a distinctly heart-shaped face. The bone structure could only have come from the father…who therefore cannot be Echo."

Omega struggled to sit up. Fox leaned down and assisted her, grabbing some extra pillows nearby and stuffing them behind her back to prop her up.

"You…you're sure?" she wondered.

"Very," Fox said, confident. "And right this moment, Zarnix and India are examining the boy and running a rapid-scan genetic profile on him. That will tell the tale on the paternity. And I will be extremely surprised if it comes back with Echo as the father. In fact, so convinced am I that I would lay every last thin dime I possess against Echo being the father."

"Um…okay."

"Now, here is what I want you to do, tekhter. I want you to rest, EAT, let your mind and heart be at ease until you know there is something to concern them. Eat some more. I want you to call for Echo and let him HELP you eat. I want you to let him know you love him with all your being, and I want you to ask him what HE wants to do, instead of just assuming it. Even if the boy IS Echo's—which, again, I doubt—there are any number of ways to work this which would be more pleasant than dissolving your marriage to the love of your life. Give the matter time to work itself out; don't jump the gun. And before you come to me with a request like this again, know that I will insist on BOTH of you coming to me, and being in accord about the necessity of it. And," he added, "don't you dare go behind my back to Pul about this. Family matters are one thing, and I will never mind you or Echo calling your 'uncle' for a chat, or even a bit of advice. But this isn't a family matter, not the way you're trying to work it; it's an organizational matter, and that, dear one, is MY purview. And I will not have you circumventing me. Is that understood?"

"Um, yes, sir," Omega said, mildly confused. "I wouldn't go around you, though, Fox. Not…I mean…"

Fox held up a hand, his face gentle.

"I know," he murmured. "And normally I would not have even added that warning. But child, your body chemistry is not at all right at the moment. You collapsed because you had dangerously low blood sugar. And I suspect that, between your body not having the nutrients and fuel it needed, and the lingering effects of the pheromone storm that Ms. Daagnadan produced that Zebra notified me about as still being resident in your system, it is no wonder you have been depressed over the situation, perhaps even unable to reason through it with your usual aplomb. Put bluntly, that magnificent brain of yours simply has not had sufficient fuel to operate at its accustomed levels."

"Oh," Omega said blankly. "I…hadn't even really thought about that…"

"I am certain you have not. Never mind the fact that the brain runs on blood glucose, yours requiring more than most. So I am certain your thought processes have been impaired, meyn kind. And you have been somewhat preoccupied with this whole matter, using up what brain power you had available," Fox pointed out, "and so now that matters look like being resolved one way or another, I want you to promise me something."

"What?"

"I want you to rest and get your body back to normal as much as you can. That, in turn, will allow your brain chemistry to stabilize, and you will realize just what — and who — you have around you…no matter what happens. Will you promise me, tekhter?"

Omega smiled shyly.

"Yes, Abba Fox, I promise," she murmured.

"Good, good," he replied in relief.

"And to that end," Zebra said, coming around the corner and through the door, "I've been working on how to flush the last of the metabolites of all those damn pheromones out of your system, girl. No, I wasn't eavesdropping, you two, I just heard the last little bit of the conversation as I came down the hall and through the door. Fox is dead right, Omega, sweetie. Zarnix and I both saw it on the scans; the pheromones you inhaled are still doing a number on you, gal. Not on anyone else, thank goodness. But Zar and I had a quick pow-wow on it, and we think maybe, since Slug engineered you and Mark Wright to mate, and part of that was pheromonal, you might be more sensitive to the shit than the rest of us. And it might stick around longer in you, for reasons like Wright an' shit."

"Well, crap," Omega grumbled. "Another damn repercussion. I thought we were done with those."

"Mostly, yes," Zebra noted with a smile. "Not that I blame you for being upset, but this is just sort of a 'didn't see that one coming' kinda thing. And one I think we now know how to handle." She hung another bag beside the saline and the glucose solutions, jacking it into the main IV line. "This ought to help you flush things out. That, and the crap-ton of water we're gonna make you drink. We've got you set up with a Foley already, because we've been pushing a lotta fluid into you while you were unconscious, and weren't sure when you'd wake up, so you don't even have to haul it across the room to the loo to pee."

Omega flushed. Then she sighed.

"All right," she capitulated. "Rest, eat, drink, pee, and talk to Echo. Not necessarily in that order."

"Right," Fox and Zebra said simultaneously. "And wait to see if things are what you fear, or not," Fox added.

"Okay. Um, Fox, would you mind going and…"

"Fetching Echo? I'd be happy to, tekhter."

* * *

"Yes, she wants to talk to you, zun, but you need to be really gentle," Fox told Echo in the waiting room, as Romeo listened. "It turns out that, not only was her blood sugar someplace under the East River, the metabolites of the pheromones are still in her system, and that, all put together, was doing a number on her emotions and moods. She sincerely thought all that she asked me was going to be the best thing for you."

"Aw, damn," Echo said, finally understanding. "She was trying to make me happy?"

"She was," Fox confirmed. "Never mind that SHE is what makes you happy, and we all know it. Unfortunately, with everything going on inside her, she had forgotten it. So perhaps a bit of reassurance is in order, there. Especially after the behavior that was…foisted upon you…by those same pheromones that Zebra and the others are trying to flush from her system as we speak."

"Right," Echo said. "I felt her telepathic block drop just a bit ago. Now?"

"Now would be an excellent time, zun."

Echo headed for the triage room door with determination.

* * *

"Hey, Ace," Omega murmured, when Echo slipped into the room where she currently sat alone. "How is Alexaan?"

"I dunno," Echo replied. "He and Ree went off with India to get him examined and…I suspect…scan his genetics."

"Oh." Omega looked down at the blanket. "Are, um…are you mad?"

"At who?"

"Anybody."

"I'm still kinda annoyed with Ree," Echo admitted. "More than a little, if I'm honest. But I gotta try to rein it in for the kid's sake, I guess. I dunno if he's old enough to understand or not…"

"What about…about me?"

"Why would I be mad at you, baby? You're not exactly well, according to what I was just told. And part of that is my fault for not noticing you weren't eating like you should have been. Never mind not being able to go with you to rescue Alexaan because I'm now the damn Assistant Director, and this whole mess targeted me, specifically." He shook his head. "I think I might should have ordered you not to go, given you had no partner along for backup."

"I had the whole Praetorians corps, Ace," Omega noted.

"Yeah—and then you opened up to max, with all your 'enhancements,' and they could barely keep up. That was deliberate, wasn't it?"

"I…yes and no. Part of me wondered if that would solve things for you, yeah." She shrugged. "Fox thinks that was the low blood sugar speaking, never mind the Kochavi pheromones still in my system. But seriously, you know me and kids, Ace. I couldn't risk failing to rescue him. I couldn't have lived with it. I had to do what I did, had to get him out, no matter what it took to do it."

"Yeah, I understand that," Echo decided. "Just do me a favor, okay?"

"What?"

"Don't do it again. Not without at least having a normal amount of food in you," Echo said, "and I think I'd prefer it if you carb-loaded beforehand."

"…Okay. That's fair. And it makes a lot of sense." She shrugged. "I just hadn't stopped to think about my appetite having been off."

"You do know that we could have lost you, right?"

"Huh?"

"You were starting to have minor seizures, baby," Echo told her. "Romeo and Fox hung close to me in case you went into full-blown seizures and I had trouble carrying you here. You, of all people, know the biology of the brain, I'm sure. Much lower blood sugar, and you might have d-died." He shook his head as his voice cracked. "And…and that's not something…I don't think I…" He broke off and bit his lip, glancing down and refusing to meet her sapphire gaze, as he wrestled with his emotions.

Omega's eyes widened, as she watched — and telepathically felt — her husband struggle with the notion of her death. Abruptly and instinctively she held out her arms, and Echo went into them, wrapping his arms tightly around her and gathering her close as she held him.

They sat like that, simply sharing their bond physically and mentally for a long time, until finally Dihl knocked on the side door with a tray of easily-digestible food for Omega.

To Dihl's delight, Echo promptly took over and fed his still-wobbly wife.

* * *

Even though it was a rapid scan test and the results were available almost by the time the scan finished, it would still take time to analyze the genetic scan data. And Alexaan's mental stress from the kidnapping and long days of imprisonment, isolated from his mother, began to manifest as the relief of rescue ebbed. So when he began to grow irritable and tired, the medical staff put him with his mother in a comfortable hospital room of their own, so the staff could watch for any medical problems that might have been brought on by the child's captivity.

That night, while in that room with his mother and down the hall from the one where Omega rested with a protective and solicitous Echo at her side, Alexaan had a nightmare. His high-pitched scream cut through the air of the sick bay like a knife.

"NO NO NO!" his shrill little voice could be heard all over the makeshift medlab, and all the staff came running. "MAMAN! HELP ME! MAKE HIM STOP! DADAN, WHERE ARE YOU?! OMEGA, AMAMAN, HELP ME!"

"Oh, dear Lord God," Omega breathed in horror, pushing up in the hospital bed, as she went from sleeping comfortably to startled awake. "Echo!"

"I'm right here, baby," Echo said, catching her hand and reaching for the light switch. "It's okay, I'm sure he's having a nightmare."

"Who is 'Amaman'? Is that his grandmother or something?"

"No, it's you," Echo explained. "He liked you, and 'amaman' is a Kochavi word that indicates…well, it's an additional mother, sorta. Sometimes Kochavi families are extended families, and often what we would call an aunt is a kind of surrogate mother, a mother figure when the actual mom isn't around. He told us he wanted to nickname you that."

"Aw," Omega murmured, even as several hiccups could be heard from down the hall. "Oh, they got him awake and calming down."

"Do you want me to carry you down there to see about him?" Echo wondered.

"You wouldn't mind?"

"Nah. Frankly, I had a few of those after the Cortians kidnapped me. I just didn't scream. So I know where the kid's coming from, in spades."

"Okay, let's go see about him."

He scooped her out of bed—Zebra had taken her off the

various monitors, as well as the IV and the catheter, earlier in the evening, once Omega's vitals fully stabilized and she proved steady enough to relieve her own bladder in the tiny head—and they wandered down the ship's corridor to see about the little fellow.

As soon as they entered the Daagnadan room, they were both enveloped in a group hug.

"We're headed for Earth in the morning," Zebra decreed.

No one complained.

* * *

'Joe Bob' tried to reach 'Gary' the next morning before beginning work, but again, he got no answer. This perturbed him, and he began to wonder if something had gone wrong.

If that is the case, he thought, *then I am what some call a 'kite' and am on my own. And that does not bode well. I wonder what has happened on Kochav. It seemed quite secure, so I cannot think that they were found out. Perhaps...some natural disaster?*

He shook his head.

I shall have to check the galactic news for any indication, I suppose, he decided. *Meanwhile, I have a cover identity to protect. It garners me nothing to be found out at this late date.*

He grabbed his janitorial cart and headed for the elevator.

* * *

Once the Agents got Alexaan and his mother back to Earth the next day, Alexaan was introduced to Ambassador Zz'r'p ob Tii'rkin of the planet Deltir, which was more commonly known to humans as Arcturus VII.

"Hello, youngling," the tall Deltiri said in a friendly fashion, crouching to place himself more nearly on a level with the little Kochavi male. "My name is Zz'r'p. Can you say that?"

"Zee-rup," Alexaan tried. Zz'r'p chuckled.

"Close enough," he declared. "May I call you Alexaan?"

"Can you call me 'Mr. Daagnadan'?"

"I can, but I want us to become friends, and that is a very formal kind of name," Zz'r'p tried.

"Hokay. Call me Alexaan. 'Cause you're what Amaman Omega calls 'cool.'"

"Oh? How do you know this?"

"She told me."

"Ah. I must thank her!" Zz'r'p laughed. "I call her my niece; did she tell you that?"

"No. But I do not understand. How can you be her unca if you are from one planet an' she is from another?"

"How can she be your amaman if you are from one planet and she is from another?"

"Ohhhh," Alexaan said, understanding. "I see now. Maman says it is called a kinda 'dopshun."

"Exactly, youngling," Zz'r'p said with a smile; his eyes tilted gently. "Do you know what a telepath is?"

"No. You are very blue, though. It is a very pretty color. I like it."

"Thank you. Yes, this is the skin tone of most of my people. There are a few that are purple, and some that are reddish, or even orange, but the majority are blue, like me. We have fun dressing to accentuate our color, and show off our ear-fins."

"Ooo," the boy said, grinning. "Like how Maman likes to match her eyes?"

"Something like, yes," Zz'r'p noted. "Now, you said you did not know what the word 'telepath meant…"

"No, I do not. Whatzit?"

"A telepath is someone who can 'hear' your thoughts, Alexaan," the Deltiri explained. "Almost all Deltiri, like me, are telepaths. We often use our skills in this to help people who have had bad things happen to them, and are having nightmares. Would you like me to do this?"

"Could you?" Alexaan asked, plaintive. "I do not like the nightmares at all…"

"Yes, I believe I can help, little one," Zz'r'p said. "With your permission, your mother's permission, and her presence while I work with you, I believe we can set those nightmares to rest, once and for all. It may take a few sessions of working on it, but we can do this."

"Good," Alexaan declared. "Do it please, Zee-rup."

* * *

'Joe Bob' was making the rounds of the Core when a large party came up the elevator from Grand Central Station and made straight for the Director's Office. He had to rein in his impulse to spin and stare; the party comprised Director Fox, Agent Echo, Agent Omega, several agents he did not recognize, Ambassador Zz'r'p ob Tii'rkin of Deltir, Nreefluvan Daagnadan...

...And Daagnadan's son.

'Joe Bob' cursed under his breath, as raw fury raced through his being.

Now I know what happened to Geretan, he realized. *THEY happened to him. Their rightful emperor! And he may well be dead by now! My oldest friend and mentor, you shall be avenged, if it means my life!*

'Joe Bob' left the Core quickly and headed down to Sub-basement Three...

...To acquire certain equipment he had carefully hidden in his quarters there.

Then he headed straight back to the Core, setting up near the base of the ramp to Fox's office, diligently mopping and cleaning.

* * *

In due time, eavesdropping on returning Agents discussing their most recent offworld mission told 'Joe Bob' all he needed to know — they had successfully assaulted his leader's base on Kochav, killing or taking prisoner all of the Persans they had found. Word came back that Geretan Aggum and his aide were found dead, crushed when the roof of their office, weakened by the somnolent mortar round, collapsed on their unconscious bodies.

'Joe Bob' grew calm. His anger still boiled beneath the surface, but he was harnessing it. When he released it at last, he intended it should be deadly.

Very deadly.

* * *

As Alpha One escorted Daagnadan and her son out of Fox's office, with Zz'r'p bringing up the rear, and Fox in the door to see them off, 'Joe Bob' eased into position. As they reached the main floor of the Core, he whipped out something that looked like a short broomstick, pointed it at little Alexaan...

...And opened fire.

* * *

Echo saw movement out of the corner of his eye, whipped his head around, and saw the janitor bringing a weapon to bear on the child. He leaped forward, reaching for his blaster, and took the round in the hip. It spun him around, and he went down.

Omega let out a howl of raw fury.

What happened next took fractions of a second.

* * *

It's okay, baby, I'm fine, Echo told her through the nd't'lq. *Well, my hip may be dislocated, but I'll live. I'll walk, too, once the medics get my hip back in place.*

Are you sure? Omega responded.

I'm fine. Then he let the anger show through. *He tried to kill Alexaan. A little kid. He's gotta be one of the embedded Scuttles, or working with 'em. Go get 'im.*

GONE!

* * *

'Joe Bob' suddenly found himself the center of attention, as numerous agents spread across the Core turned toward the group when Omega screamed as Echo fell.

This will not do, he thought. *I do not have the same abilities like this that I do in my normal form. I will be at a distinct disadvantage, battling these humans when I am shaped like them. I think it is at last time to drop this damned-by-the-gods cover story.*

He slapped the side of his thigh, then ripped off his uniform coverall.

341

Instantly he morphed — before he could even fully free his now-naked body of the shredded coverall — and his natural form was revealed, looking like a multi-level octopus, with two full rows of tentacles below a short, liver-colored torso and a bulbous head. The lower row of tentacles served as legs, and the upper row as arms. His eyes were orange, with odd, W-shaped irises. He spread his 'legs' for stability before reaching out with one of his long arm tentacles and grabbing the child, pulling him in close.

* * *

"It's an Uzshei!" Fox cried from his vantage on the Director's Balcony.

"ALEXAAN! It has Alexaan!" Nreefluvan screamed. "Someone save my son! It has Alexaan!"

"Not for long," Omega snarled.

She spun and sprinted past Zz'r'p, who was ducking out of the way, back up the ramp.

Halfway up, she turned and vaulted over the railing, feet-first, aimed at the Uzshei's torso. She landed as hard as she could, knocking the wind out of the creature, but in no wise killing it, as she had the Ka'agand on Kochav; their internal structures were very different. Killing an Uzshei was much harder than killing a Ka'agand.

'Joe Bob,' whose real name was Arnmuggih Gerthbum of the Andromeda Galaxy, tried to pull the boy closer to his body, only to find out that Omega had analyzed her target landing point very carefully — her body was in the way.

But that is of little consequence, Gerthbum decided. *Human males are no match in strength for an Uzshei, and human females are even weaker. I will simply grab her with a couple of my other tentacles, pull her loose from my body, break her neck, and throw her aside. Then I will do the same to the boy, pull the rest of my weapons from the cart, and take as many of these bastards with me as I can.*

As Gerthbum wrapped tentacles around Omega's body, however, he felt her legs tighten around what passed for his

342

torso, between his arm tentacles and his leg tentacles...and squeeze. He gasped, surprised at how powerful the pressure was that this human female exerted. *But I will simply slide out,* he thought. *Uzshei have so few bones that...*

* * *

Omega felt the Uzshei trying to escape her grip and tightened her legs even more around the creature's body, even as it tried to gain a hold on her in turn.

"Oh, no you don't!" she exclaimed. "You hurt my husband and tried to kill my stepson! Bastard!"

She drew back her fist and punched it squarely between its eyes, which somewhere in the back of her mind, she vaguely thought resembled cuttlefish eyes. It blinked hard, and staggered badly, dropping Alexaan.

* * *

Echo, whose hip was injured from the projectile impact, managed to reach out and grab the boy by one foot and pull him away from the fight. As soon as the boy was clear, he leaped up, hugged Echo, and ran to his maman, who was sobbing in fear.

With that, a contingent of Praetorians and Alpha Line members, who happened to be passing through the Core when all perdition had broken out, ranked themselves between the fight and everyone else, with weapons drawn. Several also ran up and joined Fox, who was leaning over the balcony railing with his own blaster drawn, looking for a good shot at the Uzshei that would not hit Omega.

* * *

Dizzy after the punch to his face, Gerthbum staggered badly and nearly passed out. He hung onto consciousness with an effort, however, and realized that he could not get free of the human female's entwining legs.

How can she possibly have a grip equal to my own? he thought in shock, as Omega continued to pummel him with incredibly powerful fist blows. *Humans are inferior in every way to the Uzshei! She has BONES in those limbs! They are not nearly so flexible! But I can neither slide out, nor pull her away from me! This is a HUMAN FEMALE! She should not be able to do this, even though she is angry! How strong IS she?! I must reconsider my plan, if she is typical! I have been misled!*

Just then, Gerthbum managed to get a grip on her ankle with one tentacle, even as another managed to wrap around her face. Prying hard with both limbs, he loosened her grip on his torso long enough to yank her away from his body.

Gerthbum flung the female Agent at the others, and turned to run on multiple limbs.

After all, he considered, *if I survive this, I can certainly try again at another time. My old friend Geretan WILL be avenged if it is my last act in this life.*

* * *

Yankee and Tare both reacted when they saw Omega flying away from the Uzshei. They stepped forward, arms out, and caught her before she could hit the floor, then eased her to the floor on her feet.

"You okay, Meg?" Yankee asked.

"Madder than hell, but fine," Omega declared. "Hang on, and try to sorta screen what I'm about to do from casual bystanders, okay?"

"You got it, Meg," Tare agreed instantly, understanding immediately what she had planned.

Omega took off after the fleeing Uzshei at a sprint — HER sprint.

* * *

Gerthbum ran at his maximum speed for the Grand Central Station main concourse, intent on finding a small niche he could force his way into, in order to hide until he could spirit himself aboard an outbound craft.

Rather than using the elevator or the escalator, he simply used his suckers to go over the rail and down the wall near the escalator. Once on the concourse floor, he glanced around.

The day before, while he was cleaning up all the vomit and fecal matter, he had seen a maintenance crawlway whose hatch was askew; it would be perfect for a hiding place.

There, he thought, as he spotted it.

He began to run again.

* * *

Omega headed straight for the station overlook beside the escalators, running as fast as she could...at least, without the impetus of a bomb behind her. As she reached the rail, very near where Gerthbum had crawled over, she reached out.

* * *

Echo looked around from handing off Alexaan to his mother, just in time to see Omega heading for the overlook at breakneck speed.

"MEG!" he shouted. "STOP! What the hell are you doing?!"

She vaulted over the rail and vanished from his sight.

"MEG!" he yelled, then turned to the Firewall Team. "Get me up and over to that railing, NOW," he ordered.

Monkey, Kako, Tare, and Yankee all bent to help lift him to his feet.

* * *

As she vaulted the railing, Omega scanned the floor below for the fleeing Uzshei. Spotting him, she pushed a little harder with her arms and aimed her body once again for his.

And I better get it right, or I'm gonna land awful damn hard, she told herself.

* * *

Gerthbum had almost reached the maintenance crawlspace when he was suddenly and powerfully impacted from behind and above. The force of the impact bore him to the floor, and he felt something inside his body rupture. He let out a low-pitched scream of pain, then lashed out with all his tentacles, arcing behind his head, desperately slapping whatever had hit him so hard and caused him injury.

Whatever it was rolled off quickly, out of his reach, and he clambered back to what passed for feet, scrambling for the crawlspace.

Though I no longer know if it will do me much good, he

thought, trying to ignore the severe pain. *I am badly injured inside. I may not survive to reach a ship, let alone get off this bedamned planet. I am beginning to think the gods have cursed it.*

* * *

Omega targeted her quarry well; she hit him hard, with the full force of her body's weight dropped from that height. As she hit, she heard a hollow popping sound, like a drum being hit, and she wondered if she had injured the Uzshei.

Just then, however, it fought back, slapping hard at her with all fourteen limbs, and she briefly took a beating before she doubled up to protect her abdomen and rolled off its back.

The Uzshei promptly scrambled onto whatever limbs it could get under it and started heading for an open maintenance crawlway.

Shit. If he gets in there, with those suckers on his legs and arms, we'll never get him out, she realized. *We'd have to rip out part of the wall...by which time, he'll have crawled someplace else.*

She grabbed for the nearest limb she could reach.

* * *

He was unable to actually walk, but the four members of the Firewall Team got Echo to the railing, mostly by carrying him. Once he was there, he leaned against the rail and surveyed the scene below.

Omega had survived the drop; she currently had the Uzshei by one tentacle, hauling back on it for all she was worth, as the being tried hard to crawl away. A purple fluid trickled from one trailing orifice, and Echo realized it was seriously injured, likely when Omega had landed on it.

But she's losing ground in the tug-of-war, he realized, *because he's got suction cups on his feet and hands, and she doesn't. And if he drags her into that crawlspace with him, he's got the advantage, injured or no.*

The entire analysis took fractions of a second.

"MEG!" he yelled then. "ALPHA-RED-THIRTY-EIGHT

BRAVO!"

"GOT IT!" she yelled back, then wrapped her legs around the tentacle she held, released it with her hands, and flung her body backward as hard as she could...

...As Echo drew his primary blaster and took aim.

* * *

The soft ululation of a blaster firing filled the air, and Omega felt the tentacle she held fall limp. She held on for a few seconds longer, but the Uzshei did not move.

"You can let go now, baby," Echo's voice called. "I nailed it in the head, with a little help from some friends in getting here. Never mind they were prepared to help me turn it into a colander."

Omega released the tentacle, crawled away a few feet, and stood.

There was something that looked rather like purple blood streaking the floor, where it trickled out of some orifice or other. *That's probably what I heard pop,* she decided. *I must have ruptured an internal organ when I landed on it. It was probably dying anyhow.*

But the clean hole in its head, where Echo's blaster shot had hit, had taken care of matters, and ensured a swift exit from this world for the Uzshei.

She turned and gave her husband a thumbs-up.

* * *

Echo stood, leaning hard against the overlook rail, until his wife and partner gave him the all-clear thumbs-up signal. He returned it, then sighed in pain.

"Okay, guys," he told Yankee, Tare, Kako, and Monkey. "Can y'all help me get to the medlab, so I can get this hip popped back into place? Damn, this thing hurts."

"All over it, boss-man," Monkey said with a grin.

* * *

Omega stood guard, keeping the travelers away from the dead body, until Fox could get Security to the Grand Central Station main concourse with the appropriate materials for containing and carrying away the body. It didn't take long. A coroner in Forensics would handle the autopsy.

Then she rode the escalator back up to the Core, where she met Fox.

"Good job, tekhter," he told her. "Impressive. I don't know many humans who could take on a trained Uzshei and live to tell of it, let alone best it."

"I dunno about besting it," she said, flushing. "I'd say Echo did that. That floor down there is entirely too slick for good traction. And with those suckers on what passed for its hands and feet, it was pulling me along for the ride."

"Mm. We may need to look at some texturizing, then," Fox mulled, "to allow our people that kind of traction. And perhaps update the shoe app to allow for variable traction, as well."

"I think those are both good ideas. Where IS Echo?" Omega asked, looking around. "Where's everybody, for that matter?"

"I had the Core cleared of bystanders, Zz'r'p has escorted Ms. Daagnadan and her son to their quarters in the Kochav Embassy with a couple of Alpha Line Agents for protection, there's a few of the Praetorians hidden here and there keeping a watchful eye out, and several of the Alpha Line teams carried Echo down to the medlab. That bullet he took...well, it's a damn good thing he was wearing his body armor or matters would be a lot worse, but the way it hit, it did dislocate his hip. Nothing's broken, and nothing's torn; it just popped the condyle out of its socket. So he's got some sprains in there from that, too, but nothing worse. I've already heard from Zebra, and she's about to put it back in place, then run a Regenic IV on him, to help tighten up all the tendons and cut down on the bruising. She said we'd probably hear him howl all the way up here when she popped it back in, though, because it was way the hell out, according to her."

"After the Cortians got done with him, I doubt we'll hear a peep outta him," Omega pointed out. "Still, if everybody's safe and accounted for, I'll head on down there to keep him company, with your permission, Fox."

"By all means, my dear girl, go," Fox said. "You have a few bruises — not to mention a black eye that's already developed — that could stand treating, as well. That Uzshei beat on you rather badly, there, it looks like. No worries. Everything is fine here. The Boys already have Security doing a comprehensive sweep for any other embedded Scuttles, as your people call them. I don't know that they'll find any; I know that the man we hired for that position was legitimately human as of his last physical, which he had last quarter, according to Zarnix. So I suspect this was a spy sent along after Ms. Daagnadan, to make sure she either did what she was supposed to do, or got offed before she could rat them out."

"I guess he failed, then," Omega decided.

"I expect so. But that bodes ill for our real janitor." Fox sighed. "Given the special incinerator is next to his quarters, I suspect I know what happened to him, too."

"Ow," Omega murmured, wincing. "I bet I know what happened to our cold case Sluuite serial killer, too." She pointed down the escalator.

"Oh, damnation. I hadn't even thought of that. And in every case, 'Joe Bob' cleaned over the murder scene before anyone got there…which argues that he did it, then cleaned up after himself. So you may well be right." He shuddered for a moment, then added, "I hate to think what HE did with the Sluuite bodies. But I expect they never made it to the incinerator." Fox huffed, then said, "Well, that's on me to sort out, at this point. You head on down to the medlab and see to Echo."

"Okay. Hey, do you wanna come along? Or do you feel safer staying here?"

"With the dual-embodied head of the Praetorians and the assistant chief of Alpha Line at my side? I couldn't be safer," Fox said with a smile. "Let's go, meyn tekhter. You have a husband to see to. And even if he doesn't scream, I expect he might like to have his wife holding his hand when MY wife pops his femur back into position."

They headed for the medlab.

* * *

The next morning, Omega's bruises were healed, and though the leg and hip were stiff and sore, Echo was mobile again.

Fox had already had reports from Zz'r'p that little Alexaan had had some severe nightmares in the night, but Zz'r'p had been prepared, and the Deltiri had responded at once, helping Alexaan to see that the nightmares were nothing more than expressions of his fears, and calming him back to sleep.

* * *

In the end, it turned out that Alexaan was only badly frightened by everything that had happened. The thought that Aggum might have harmed him — and the realization that the 'janitor' almost did — had also turned loose his imagination on what might have happened, and his subconscious had a field day with it during his sleep periods.

A team of Deltiri, working together under their ambassador, eased the child's fears, and ensured him that he was in safe hands at last, and everything would settle out soon.

"But we also got some other information," Whiskey reported to Fox and Alpha One in Fox's office. "Little Alexaan IS half-human…"

Omega swayed, and Echo grabbed her shoulders to steady her, even as he bit his lip.

"…But that human genetic contribution did NOT come from Echo," Whiskey finished. "Definitive. Echo is not the father. End of story."

Omega all but slumped into her partner's arms; Echo leaned hard on her, as well. Fox glanced at them in concern, ascertaining that they would be all right; when Echo nodded, he turned back to Whiskey.

"Whose are they, then?"

"We're not sure," Whiskey said. "Zarnix is running a search through our database now, but hadn't hit a match as of the time I came up to your office to report, sir." He shrugged.

"It would help if we had a direction to go with it, but right now, we're just running a general search through the database of all male agents who were in Headquarters at that time. It's…quite a list."

"I expect so," Fox agreed. "Keep me posted, please."

"Will do, sir."

"That means that Ree cheated on me, I guess," Echo said with a sigh. "Not only did she dump me for being an immature kid, she was seeing somebody on the side."

"Maybe not, Ace," Omega said. "I mean, I know the whole mess hurts you; I can feel it through the nd't'lq. And you've told me about getting dumped, and how much that hurt, especially how she did it."

"Eh. I really was little more than a kid; Ree's a couple decades older than me, when you get down to it. But the Kochavi lifespan and their phases of life are a little different than humans, so we kinda made it work…at least for a while. When we started sorta going 'out of phase,' things changed, and that's more or less when she broke up with me."

"Yeah, but still," Omega pressed. "I guess the thing I'd like to know is: did she leave Earth immediately, or did she hang around Headquarters for a while? Or one of the other Offices?"

Echo stared at her, suddenly grasping where she was going with the query.

"I have no idea," he said.

* * *

"OH! No, I did not leave at once," Daagnadan said, when they got her into Fox's office to query her; Whiskey headed back to the medlab to help corral a rambunctious and curious youngster. "I had to do a few things before I could leave. As I did not intend to return, I had to tender my resignation to the embassy where I had been functioning as secretary to the ambassador, and I needed to pack my personal belongings and see them shipped back to Kochav. So I was here a few more days — close on a lunation, if I recall correctly; the ambassador requested I stay until after a treaty was signed, so I might help

351

him with the administrative work — after Echo and I…after I broke off the relationship." She threw Echo an apologetic look. "I…am sorry for the pain I caused you, Echo. I was still only realizing how young you truly were, and I had no idea…"

"It's okay, Ree," Echo said quietly. "I found the right one in the end." He put an arm around Omega.

"Yes, it seems you did," Daagnadan said with a slight, wistful smile. "I envy you that. At least you left me with a son."

Echo and Omega glanced at each other in consternation.

"Well, that's just it," a slightly hesitant Fox gently interjected then. "Our genetic tests indicate that the boy IS half-human, but that half didn't come from Echo. At all."

"What? But I…oh my," Daagnadan said, badly startled. "But…" She thought hard. "I cannot recall…it has been so long…and I have been so frightened for Alexaan, I…"

"Hush now. That is why I am here," Qq'k'l ob Sii'stek said. "I have helped you this far; I can assist in a bit more."

"Oh yes!" Daagnadan said in relief. "The kind, gentle Deltiri. My dear friend Qq'k'l. It would help so very much if you did! Thank you most deeply, Qq'k'l, even if you cannot determine what happened; you have helped me so much, in so many ways, already…"

"It was ever my honor," Qq'k'l said with a nod. "Do I have your permission to try to retrieve the memories of your time on Earth between the point where you and Echo ended your relationship, and the point where you left for your homeworld?"

"Yes, please," Daagnadan agreed at once. "I am so confused now. I want to find out what happened!"

"Very well. Relax as much as you can, and I will see what I can find."

Daagnadan closed her eyes and leaned back in her chair, then shuddered slightly as the Deltiri telepath entered her mind. The two were quiet for long minutes while the others watched. Finally Qq'k'l stirred, and Daagnadan opened her eyes.

"Oh," she murmured, seeming surprised. "I…had forgotten all about that. How did I forget that?! How COULD I forget that?"

"Forget what?" Omega wondered.

"There was another agent," the Kochavi woman said. "I had completely forgotten. After Echo and I ended our relationship, he approached me. It seems that he had had…I think X-ray used to call it, 'a crush'…on me for much of the time Echo and I were seeing each other. Now that I was free, he wanted to try to convince me to stay…with HIM."

"I take it, he didn't?" Fox wondered.

"He came very, very close," she admitted with a slight, wry smile. "And he tried hard. But after ending matters with Echo, I was…wary…of beginning another relationship, especially so soon. I did what X-ray used to call, 'knee-jerk.' And so I did not stay, despite a growing wish to do so. In retrospect, and looking at the memories our Deltiri friend here just helped me retrieve, I think he may have truly loved me." She sighed. "How I wish I had known then what I know now. It might have…worked." She shrugged. "At any rate, I spent some few nights with him, in his quarters. I suppose…I suppose he is the father of young Alexaan. I should, perhaps, seek him out?"

"Certainly," Fox said quietly, sitting down at his desk and activating the virtual keyboard. "I'll be glad to help. What is his code name?"

"He is called Quail."

A few quick commands to the keyboard, and Fox studied the information that came up on his virtual desktop screen.

"Uh-oh," he murmured after several moments. He hit a couple more keystrokes, then put the desktop screen in split-screen mode to display the two windows side by side, looking back and forth. "Oh damnation."

"What's wrong, Fox?" Omega wondered.

"Agent Quail is dead," Fox told them sadly. "He died in a particularly violent firefight with a dangerous perp…about a month after Ms. Daagnadan, here, left Earth."

"Shit," Echo murmured, suddenly understanding. "He checked out deliberately, because he was too heartbroken to keep going."

"Damn," Omega breathed.

"Oh no," Daagnadan whispered; it was almost a groan. "No, no, no. Poor Quail. Poor Quail! I did not mean…" She turned to Echo, as a tear slid down her cheek. "I did it all wrong, did I not? I hurt you, I hurt him…I left my son with no father…"

"You did the best you could with the experience and knowledge you had at the time, Ree," Echo tried to comfort. "You can't do more than you know to do."

"But that does mean that the boy is the son of one of our agents," Fox said, "and therefore we have a responsibility to him—and to his mother."

"Oh?" Daagnadan sat up in surprise, even as a tear of regret slid down her cheek.

"Yes. And given what almost went down, and given I'm going to run a flag up through channels to make sure that the entire PGLEIA knows that there are still embedded Andromedans in our midst, that's probably a good thing, in the end, because it revealed their presence," Fox said. "So. I propose you and your son stay on Earth, Ms. Daagnadan, as part of the Agency—or, rather, I want to offer you a job in the Agency, where you and your son can stay safe, where you'll be accepted, and where your son can obtain dual-planet education. Then, when he is of age, he'll be offered a PGLEIA position, and have the option of choosing Earth and Division One, or Kochav and Division Two."

* * *

Fox, Qq'k'l interjected silently, *be careful, my friend. Omega is becoming very perturbed, and Echo is anything but entirely comfortable, in addition. They do not want her around while they try to start a family of their own. Especially Omega. She feels Daagnadan is entirely too dangerous to their relationship. Especially with her skills at pheromone manipulation. At least potentially. She trusts Echo, but Daagnadan has proven she can undermine even Echo's iron will. And Echo knows it, and is concerned, as well.*

Understood, and I've already considered it, Fox replied. *Tell them to hang in there, and hear me out; I'm going to try to do right by everyone.*

Very well.

* * *

"What did you have in mind, Director Fox?" Daagnadan wondered.

"I had in mind to put you into our intel system," Fox said. "Given your abilities with pheromones, I'd like to see what you can do when it comes to obtaining information. I think you might make an excellent intelligence operative."

"I…I do not think I want to be what X-ray used to call 'a spy,'" Daagnadan admitted. "I have had enough of that kind of dealing with this drekul."

"You don't have to be a spy, as such," Fox explained. "There are other ways of functioning as an intelligence operative. Interrogation is one of those."

"I would be happy to work with her on interrogation techniques, Fox," Qq'k'l offered. "We might get some interesting results if a Kochavi of her abilities and a trained Deltiri telepathic interrogator teamed up on an interrogation."

"Even better," Fox declared. "Meanwhile, Ms. Daagnadan, your son Alexaan can enter into our educational program—we do have agents with children, and not all of those have mates that are human, after all, plus we have ambassadors, envoys, émigrés, and others whose children must be educated—and then, as I mentioned before, once he reaches his majority, he's welcome to join up if he wants, or go back to Kochav, or move into another position in the Coalition. I am bosom friends with both Coalition President Pulgey Entiyti and his second, Lady Teela Krimnet, and while they may no longer be in those positions by the time Alexaan grows up, I expect with their help I could manage to find young Alexaan entrée to any organization he develops an interest in."

"This all sounds…very good," Daagnadan admitted, "except…"

"Except what?" Fox wondered.

Daagnadan threw an uncertain glance at Echo and Omega.

"I think…perhaps…Headquarters is not where we should be," Daagnadan confessed. "Not only is it a little more dangerous here, given how many people come through and, ah, recent events, it is…" She sighed. "I do not know that any of the three of us," she gestured at Alpha One, "would be comfortable with Alexaan and me here. And while for me, there are memories that are good, I think they would make me lonely, and sooner rather than later. And I know they would make Echo uncomfortable, and I suspect Omega even more so. And I do not wish to do that to them…or me."

"If you truly do feel like that now, I think I can deal, Ree," Omega said then, using Echo's nickname for the Kochavi woman—and meaning it, for the first time. "Do what you think is best for you and your son."

"And Echo?" Daagnadan wondered. "What of him?"

"If Meg's okay with it, I'll manage, too," Echo said. "I agree with her; do what's best for you and Alexaan."

"Do you wish me to rename him?"

"What?"

"My son. Should I rename him?"

"Only if you and he want to," Echo said. "I'm honored that you named him after me. And my family sometimes named kids after old friends, plus my real name isn't much known around here, so it isn't a problem that way."

"I have a suggestion that may mitigate a great deal of angst, as well as provide for additional care for the youngling. Ms. Daagnadan, are you familiar with the Earth concept of 'godparents,' by any chance?" Fox wondered.

"Actually, yes, I am," Daagnadan said. "I remember some stories X-ray used to tell, you see." She shrugged. "He and I may not have always gotten along, but he was an honest, knowledgeable male and I learned much from him."

"Ah. Well, then may I suggest that, in the unlikely event something were to happen to you before the child has grown up," Fox said, "I suspect you might have Alexaan's godparents, standing right here?"

Alpha One glanced at Fox, startled. Then they stared at each other.

* * *

What the hell? Wow. THAT was an unexpected bomb from Fox! How do you feel about that, baby? Echo asked through their telepathic bond.

I...dunno, Ace, Omega replied, taken off guard. *I just... don't know. I guess I'd be okay with it. The little guy was funny, and cute, and had a wicked cool curiosity. He was smart as a whip, too. I swear, he was asking me questions — 'why' this, and 'how does it work' that — the whole time I was carrying him out of the facility! But he still had enough sense to be quiet and just hang on, when I was trying to get us away from the booby trap on his room. I sorta related to him, if I'm honest with you. In the end, the fact that he's NOT yours is kinda a relief, too, and it sort of frees me to...I dunno how to explain it. It frees me to...accept him? Accept a relationship between us and him? Am I making any sense?*

Yeah, you are. And I understand what you're saying — I get it. It allows you to put some perspective in place. And that perspective, in turn, lets you see him as just another little boy, without all the emotional baggage that came along with 'Echo's son by another woman.' And that's something you can accept.

Yeah. I think you nailed it on the head. So...yeah, I think I could. I think I could probably help raise him if something happened to Ree. As long as you're there to help.

Yup. Right alongside our own?

Assuming we get that chance, sure. I don't see why not.

* * *

Alpha One came up for air and smiled at Fox, then at Daagnadan, who caught her breath in shocked surprise.

"You...you would do that? Both of you? After everything?" she whispered.

"Sure, Ree," Echo said, his voice calm, almost, but not quite, gentle. "I'm not a kid any more. I'm not THAT kid any more, the one you knew, way back when. I'm a man with a wife he loves, looking at starting a family of his own with that wife, so I'm in a damn good place in my life. Besides, you were being blackmailed over this whole big mess: 'Do what I say or I kill your son.' Yes, the entire thing upsets me, but I can't blame you for that. And the guy to blame is dead, according to Director Ulseleigh."

"Flip the genders, and that's pretty much me, too, on all of it," Omega averred. "Alexaan already wants to call me Amaman. And I'm okay with that. Maybe, if there's the equivalent for the father…"

"There is," Echo said. "Adadan."

"Okay, then. Amaman and Adadan. It works. If your son ever needs godparents, we'd be happy and honored to fill the job. If YOU want us to."

"Yes," Nreefluvan said with a watery smile. "Yes, please!"

"All right. I'll see that all the legal matters are taken care of, to make Alpha One the godparents for little Alexaan," Fox said. "Meanwhile, Ms. Daagnadan, let's sit down and look at which Office you might enjoy working in…"

* * *

"Director Fox, could you tell me, please, what ever became of my good friend and university professor, Diipik Baaxegis?" Nreefluvan wondered then.

"Ah," Fox said, then sighed.

"Oh, that does not sound good," Nreefluvan said, apprehensive.

"It isn't, I'm afraid," Fox said, stifling another sigh. "He didn't survive. I'm still waiting for the final autopsy result, which is being done by Division Two personnel, but the preliminary examination indicates that, once the Scuttles had the information they needed from him — namely, information about you and your son — he was locked away and abandoned. He eventually died of dehydration and starvation."

"Oh no," Nreefluvan groaned. "That is not the news I wanted to hear at all. What will happen to the…the body?"

"Once the autopsy is complete — we want to determine if he was tortured or not, to add to the war crimes charges that will be levied, but the high probability is that he was, in order to force the information out of him, and our medical people saw probable evidence of same — then his body will be returned to his family, who had reported him missing," Fox said. "I don't know what plans they have for the funeral or memorial service."

The room was silent, as Nreefluvan finally broke down and wept in grief and regret.

Chapter 14

Within the week, a very heavyhearted Nreefluvan Daagnadan and a happy, excited, energetic Alexaan Daagnadan-Quailan — he had taken the news that Echo was not his father with some considerable disappointment, but having Alpha One as his Adadan and Amaman, it seemed, more than made up for it — were en route to the Los Angeles Office. There, Nreefluvan would not only learn to use her pheromone abilities in interrogation skills alongside Qq'k'l ob Sii'stek—who was at least temporarily transferring with her; Fox had a sneaking suspicion there was more that had transpired between the pair in recent days than met the eye, and Qq'k'l might well stay with Nreefluvan, in many respects—she would also be assisting with some of the more clandestine aspects of that Office's Hollywood business.

"Because I know exactly how I can use her," Juliet, the head of that Office, told Fox with a wicked grin. "And I think she'll like it out here. It's a lot like certain parts of her homeworld. I'll see her son gets off to a good start, too. We have a really good interstellar school at the L.A. Office, because of all the offworld actors here. He'll fit right in."

"This sounds like a very good plan, Juliet," Fox said, as Daagnadan and her son smiled.

* * *

"…And yes, we did confirm there were several crushed but otherwise intact locator beacons in various parts of the Uzshei's digestive tract," the coroner from Forensics verified, as he met with Fox, Crutch, and Alpha One in Fox's office.

"How many?" Crutch asked.

"We counted a total of five," the coroner noted. "Strictly speaking, one of those was somewhat fragmentary, and we didn't find a complete device for it, but there was enough there to count it."

"That would do it," Echo determined. "And that explains

what happened to our missing Sluuites. The bastard ATE 'em."

"Which was what I suspected," Fox sighed. "In my experience, some Uzshei, at least, are disgusting beings."

"Well, it explains why none of us could find any bodies," Crutch pointed out.

"No shit," Omega said, pulling a disgusted face. "Any sign of heating on the locators?"

"No," the coroner replied. "If he ate the Sluuites — and I must agree that's what happened, judging by the fecal remains; there were tiny bones in there — when he ate them, he ate them raw, and likely freshly murdered."

"Ugh," Omega grunted.

"What she said," Crutch agreed.

"I'll third that," Echo added.

"I'll fourth it," Fox averred.

"I'll fifth it," the coroner added, screwing up her face, "and you can add my assistants and most of the rest of Forensics, which comprises everyone that's heard about it so far."

There was silence for long moments.

"Well, at least we can close THOSE cold cases," Omega decided.

"We can close one more, tekhter," Fox said quietly, as the coroner left the office, in company with Crutch.

"Oh?" Omega wondered.

"Yes. It seems that some of your abilities with pheromones derive from Kochavi genetics," Fox explained. "I set Zebra on it, and she and Zarnix confirmed it for me. I used Ms. Daagnadan's contacts on Kochav to verify that about two decades ago, one of their lesser adepts went missing and was never found."

"Oh," Omega murmured, face falling. "So Slug knew about the adepts, too."

"Well, if he didn't when he started, he probably did when he was through," Fox pointed out. "He was a telepath, after all. It's entirely possible, though, that he simply grabbed someone with the abilities he wanted, and was unaware that there was even such an organization of adepts until discovering it in his victim's mind."

"Damn," Echo said. "That…makes a lot of sense."

"I guess," Omega sighed, "we need to send out another condolence letter?"

"I'm already on it, tekhter," Fox said softly. "I'm using the same one we sent out the first time, complete with your comments. I'm just modifying it for the time that has passed, is the only change. Is that all right with you?"

"Yes, that sounds good." Omega shrugged, then offered a wry grin that didn't reach her eyes. "Well, as good as something like that can be, anyway, I guess."

"And another door of the past is closed," Echo decided. "Now to see if our people can ever forgive me in the present."

"I think you'll find it's better than you think, zun," Fox said. "I've sort of been greasing the skids for you."

"Thanks, Fox," Omega said, seeing Echo's jaw and throat tighten. "C'mon, honey. Let's just go do this."

Echo nodded, and they headed for the Alpha Line Room.

* * *

"Okay, guys, thanks for meeting us," Echo said, hiding his anxiety with an effort as Omega stood by his side at the front of the Alpha Line Room, fifteen minutes later. Before them sat the combined Alpha Line/Praetorian contingent; given the overlap between the two groups, it had seemed a logical meeting place, though Fox was working with Omega and the Facilities department to develop a smaller meeting room for the Praetorians next door. "We kinda thought, under the circumstances of your last mission, maybe you might like to hear the end of the matter."

"That sounds good, boss-man," Easy noted. "First off, are you two okay?"

"We're fine, Easy," Omega said with a slight smile. "In every sense of the word."

"Good," came the murmur from several voices.

"So," Echo said, "first of all, Aggum is definitely dead;

the room he was in was compromised when the somnolent munition crashed through the wall. After the knockout gas was released, he and his assistant passed out, and then the roof fell in on them. It wasn't intended, and his family is being notified of the fact…through the Persan Premier Hsrs Syrsh. The rest of the Scuttles that survived are in custody and going to trial on Aleancë like the first batch did. Once the Ennead is finished with 'em, the Persis Federation gets a shot at 'em. I strongly suspect, one way or another, none of 'em is any longer for this world than the first batch was. Oh, I suppose a few of 'em are going to end up on the maximum-security prison on Armik; if they're lucky, they'll get to look down at Aleancë and see what a real government looks like."

"Although this Aggum seemed to be under the impression that his brother was alive someplace and being held as a political prisoner, and apparently passed that belief on to his followers," Omega added. "I think Pulgey Entiyti is likely to disabuse them of the notion fairly fast, though."

A burst of applause and cheering went around the room.

"Now, as to the boy, Alexaan Daagnadan, you should know that he is in fact half-human," Echo said, and a soft gasp went up, "but that half didn't come from me."

"But I thought she 'uz your ol' girlfriend, Echo, an' when y'all broke up, she left Earth," Romeo said.

"She was, but she didn't leave right away," Echo said. "She had matters of two weeks' notice and the ambassador wanting her to stay on a couple more weeks to help finalize a treaty, and some other shit like that to deal with, and meanwhile she hooked up with another agent. How many of you were around to remember Agent Quail?"

A smattering of hands went up among the longer-term agents.

"Aw shit," Queen remarked. "Don't tell me…he was in love with her, he got her pregnant, but neither of 'em knew until after she'd left…"

"And he never knew at all," Echo said, nodding in

confirmation. "And, we think, he kamikazi'ed out when she left him."

"Shit," and "Dammit," came from several places in the room.

"Is she at least remorseful?" India demanded to know.

"Very much so," Omega averred. "In fact, she wanted to find Quail and let him know he had a son, and maybe see what could be done to repair relationships. She did like him, I think, and maybe cared about him — possibly even loved him; we're pretty sure he loved her — but she had been afraid at the time that it was just a rebound relationship after breaking up with Echo."

"And I've come to realize that the reason her breakup with me was so awkward and painful was because she didn't really want to," Echo explained, "she felt she had to, because of the age difference, given the different species."

"Ooo," several hummed, thoughtful.

"So Ms. Daagnadan has been offered a position working with Division One, here on Earth," Echo added, "so that we could put Alexaan into our educational process."

"Not at Headquarters, I hope," Chi grumbled.

"No, at another field Office," Omega said with a smile. "At her request, let me add. And because she was targeted, that location isn't being disclosed; we're treating it as sort of a witness protection program. Everything's fine there. In fact, at Fox's suggestion, Echo and I have been made Alexaan's godparents."

"Whoa! That's great! Congrats!" the cry went up. A smiling Echo held up his hands for silence.

"But is that wise?" Yankee wondered, when the room quieted.

"I think things are gonna level out now," Omega said. "Echo and I had a long heart-to-heart with Ree — with her Deltiri interrogator present, in Fox's office; evidently Deltiri aren't susceptible to most Opdip-standard pheromones — and she had been panicked and frightened for Alexaan. And was definitely being blackmailed. Despite her best efforts, though, she never really was able to break our relationship, Echo an' me. She grasped that the bond between the two of us is really damn strong, but not WHY. Let alone HOW."

"And we still haven't enlightened her as to details," Echo said. Then he shrugged. "And don't plan to."

"Well, that's really nobody's business anyway," India observed. "Some of us were at the wedding, and we saw a few things, and inferred a few others, but we're not asking, and you're not telling. And shouldn't."

"Which is egg-zackly how it oughta be," Romeo declared.

"Right, damn straight, it's all cool," came the chorus around the room.

"Anyway," Omega tag-teamed, "the matter is over and done. Alexaan and Nreefluvan are disappearing into the Agency, Aggum round two and his — well, his forces, anyway, have been apprehended and are likely to be convicted and executed — if not by the Pan-Galactic Coalition, then by the Persis Federation — and from the feedback I've gotten from Fox and Echo, the Praetorians more than lived up to expectations, especially when backed by a good portion of the rest of Alpha Line."

"Commendations are being arranged all around," Echo said. "Congratulations, everybody, and thank you VERY much." He paused, then added, "And thanks for overlooking my recent, chemically-induced behavior, too." He shook his head. "I want to apologize to each and every one of you. I've already apologized to Meg and Fox. Several times each."

"Nah. Wasn't you, man," Romeo said, as the others nodded vigorously. "Wasn't anything like th' man we've come t' know an' respect, after all the shit we been through together. So we knew somethin' weird was up."

"Alla that, dude," Tare agreed.

"Yup," Yankee asserted. "You were being controlled by Daagnadan just as much as Omega was controlled by Slug, back in the day. And Daagnadan herself was being blackmailed to control HER. I say the people to blame are already heading to Aleancë for punishment."

"Or dead," Kako amended.

"Bingo," Monkey declared.

"I guess my concern would just be, how do we defend against another pheromone storm from an adept like that?" Golf asked.

"That's being worked on," Omega declared. "We have samples of the pheromones that were being used against Echo and me, that he and I collected. I took them to Zebra, and we brought in Item, over in the Sciences department — she's a research chemist, in addition to heading the department — and Item pinged me this morning that she'd had a breakthrough on how to neutralize them. Thing is, she said, we still have to know it's happening. Because pheromones are a normal, natural thing for so many species, a subtle but important form of communication, we don't want to just eliminate them willy-nilly."

"Oh, I get it," Adam said. "Because it's important in friendships and romance and stuff. You gotta know if the other person likes you or not."

"Exactly," Echo confirmed. "So one thing we're going to do is to put some high-speed air samplers around Headquarters, to start — then follow up at the other Offices — with some testing equipment attached, so we'll KNOW if there's a pheromone adept in the area. Then we can look at implementing the neutralization protocol that Item is ginning up."

"Well, that's a definite step in the right direction," Golf decided. "Keep us posted on the research on it, Omega, if you don't mind."

"Sure thing, Golf. I'd have done that anyway, for what it's worth. And will probably put my hand in on the research as it goes on, to boot. So. Does this mean y'all are good with us, with Echo an' me?" Omega wondered.

"All hands in favor?" India said.

Every hand in the room went up.

"All opposed?" Romeo asked.

No hands went up.

"Yup. Y'all 're good," Romeo said with a grin. "Anything else, boss-man an' -lady?"

"Nope," Echo said, his relief obvious. "And, well, thanks again, y'all."

"'Nuff 'a that, now," Romeo decreed. "What's next?"

"We got nuthin'," Omega noted. "Things quieted back down again. We're good."

"For a change," India interjected.

"Amen," both members of Alpha One pronounced benediction.

"I haff an idea," Kako piped up then, a big smile on his face. "Monkey, Yankee, Tare, and I haff requested Facilities temporarily join our four qvarters, and ve haff stocked up on beer and ordered many pizzas. Fox and Zebra haff already been notified, as vell, and some of zose pizzas are kosher for him. So ve vould like to issue an inwitation. Vill you all come to our joint qvarters to celebrate? Ve must properly inaugurate zhe Praetorians!"

A cheer went up, and the lot of them filed out of the Alpha Line Room, headed for the elevator to the agents' quarters.

* * *

When Alpha One arrived in the medlab after receiving the summons two days later, Zebra and Zarnix were both waiting.

"Come on in here," Zebra said, leading the way into the small consulting conference room. "We wanted to talk to you two in private."

"What's up?" Echo wondered, as Zarnix closed the door and they all sat down around a small table.

"Well, it's about having kids," Zebra said. "While you two were off Earth, before she was scheduled to meet up with us on the *Genesis* for the trip to Kochav, your mom had a bit of a brainstorm recently, Echo."

"Oh? What about?"

"We believe we may have been a bit too high-tech in

our thinking about your reproductive conundrum," Zarnix explained. "The answer, at least in the near-term, may be much simpler. But first, we wanted to ask you both a few things…"

"What?" Omega wondered.

"How determined are the two of you to, uh, make a baby the natural way?" Zebra tiptoed delicately around the personal subject.

Taken off guard, Echo and Omega stared at each other for a few moments, then shrugged in unison.

"I gotta say, we enjoy the practice," Echo said with a mischievous grin, watching Omega flush with a sheepish grin of her own. "But I don't think that we gotta have every bit 'natural,' as you put it, if it gets us healthy kids that won't be trying to kill me at some point in the future."

"That," Omega said, her own gaze twinkling. "Alla that. Especially with an nd't'lq to work with. Or maybe I should say 'through.'"

It was her turn to grin broadly as she watched Echo flush.

* * *

Zarnix and Zebra both bit their lips to keep from laughing outright, as the couple before them teased each other unmercifully, revealing some very private matters to their doctors in the process.

"So you are both all right with the concept of using a variant on *in vitro* fertilization?" Zarnix queried, when he could be sure of making the statement without interjecting a bark of laughter.

"If that's what it takes, sure," Echo said.

"Rather do it the old-fashioned way, but if it gets us healthy kids, yeah," Omega agreed. "I'd still carry the baby, right?"

"Exactly," Zebra soothed. "So far we've not seen any indicators that you'd be prevented from doing that, but even if you were, there are now cutting-edge galactic techniques to gestate the baby outside the womb. That much, at least, is NOT an issue! So we think we've come up with a good solution in the interim…"

"Let's hear it," Echo said.

"It is fairly simple, and has the advantage of allowing us to work on other facets of the puzzle in the meanwhile," Zarnix said. "Based on what we know of you both, especially in the light of recent events, neither of you is ready to leave the field quite yet, anyway, which you really should do if you become parents."

"Right," Alpha One said in unison. "But I'm already taking on more of the Assistant Director duties," Echo added, "and when Fox and Zee decide to resign from PGLEIA and go to work for Pulgey, then I'll step into the Director's office and Meg will step into the Alpha Line department lead role, and we'll both largely leave field work at that point."

"And that's when we've been talking about starting a family," Omega added. "We just needed to have all the ducks in a row over the genetics, first."

"Exactly, exactly," Zarnix said, nodding vigorously. "Very good. Which means that, until that happens, we can be working on exactly what Omega's genetic complement should be in her eggs, as well as watching the cutting-edge research in the field in case something pertinent comes along to our problem. And who knows? In the meanwhile, we might actually come up with a technique that enables you to do it, ahem, 'naturally.'"

"And I plan on helping with all this, even after Fox resigns," Zebra said. "I think a nice break for him, before he goes back into harness with Pul, will be good for him. So it'll work. At the point where you're ready to start a family, see, we'll biopsy Meg's ovaries, grab a couple immature eggs, and modify the genetics so that they have what we'll have already determined is the correct normal-human-for-her genetic components..."

"Then we mature the eggs, perform an *in vitro* fertilization from Echo's sperm," Zarnix tagged, "allow the fetus to develop to the proper degree while we prep Omega for a pregnancy with the appropriate hormonal signals, then implant the fetus in her uterus. The development and birth progresses nominally from there."

"Ooo! And then we have babies," Omega said with a smile,

unable to suppress a happy wriggle. Echo grinned and put an arm around her.

"I might almost think you liked kids, baby," he said then.

"You know I originally thought you did NOT like 'em, right?"

"You did?"

"Yeah. Remember how things went at the toy store, my first Christmas with the Agency? I mean, it ended decent, I guess, and you looked like you really got into it after a few minutes, but I swear I thought you didn't like 'em, there for a bit. Never mind what happened when the kids swarmed us."

"Eh," Echo grunted. "In this job, I just was never around 'em all that much to be used to it. At least until you showed on the scene. Now…I'm good. I didn't want to even risk kids with any of my previous girlfriends, but with you, baby? Yeah. I want kids."

"And we believe we can now ensure you have those," Zarnix said with a smile.

"Does that make you feel better, baby?" Echo wondered. "Now that you know Alexaan wasn't my son, and YOU can give me children?"

"More than any of you know," Omega said simply. "What about the egg genetics?"

"That's begun long since," Zebra said. "Trust us: The 'Omega Team' is on the job and on top of things."

"Who-all is that?" Echo wondered. "This 'Omega Team' you referenced."

"Me, Zebra, India, Dihl, occasionally Doron, when we can catch him," Zarnix said. "From time to time we consult with specialists around the galaxy, but Omega, let me assure you that we are extremely careful to keep private matters private."

"Thanks," Omega said, nodding in gratitude. "So…what?"

"We move on," Zebra said. "We're making good progress on the genetics now, and I think it's safe to say, based on what I know of Fox's plans, by the time you two are ready to start the process, we will be, too."

"And by then, we may even have a process to proceed more 'naturally,' without needing *in vitro*," Zarnix said, "as I mentioned, but if not, we do still have the *in vitro* process."

"And I expect the procedure — whatever we settle on — will become more sophisticated with later kids, assuming you want more than one," Zebra added.

"Sounds great," Echo said with a grin. "Meg, how do you feel?"

"Wonderful," Omega decided. "For the first time in a really long time, I feel like a full, complete human being."

"Specifically, a female human being," Zebra said with a smile.

"A woman," Echo corrected. "My wife, and the future mother of my children."

"Couple that with 'Alpha Line leads,' and I think that says all that needs saying," Omega declared.

"Amen," Echo averred.

"I have a future," Omega decided.

"WE have a future, baby," Echo corrected. "Together. Alpha One is gonna BE a family, in addition to having one."

"And that's the best news I've heard in a long, long time," Zebra said. "'Cause that makes Fox and me grandparents!"

All four beings smiled in happiness.

Author Notes

And we're back! Once more we delve into the Division One universe! I'm very excited about how this series is progressing!

Unfortunately, as I said in the notes for Mega Moth, I have had to back off on the rapid production in this series, though not in production overall; this past year, I wrote and released an entire trilogy in Richard Weyand's excellent Empire series, and they've been well received. I'll be writing at least one more trilogy in that series, possibly two, in the next couple of years.

The next book in the series might be a little different; I'm looking at a collaboration with a budding author. Anthony Thompson had the idea for The Bounty Game, and so he and I are going to try to co-author that story. That'll help me out with you Division One fans in that you won't have to wait a whole year before the next book, since he can be writing on that while I'm writing on the Empire trilogy, and then I can swap up and keep my brain fresh! Much thanks to him for the assistance!

Also thanks to Mom & Dad, Colene & Steve Gannaway, for their continuous support. Mom is still doing therapy after her strokes, and Dad is trying to keep everything together. Prayers are probably in order, please. 2020 has been exceptionally hard on us as a family, between the shutdowns and the pandemic and the numerous tropical storms, which cause Mom's joints to ache really badly. I love my family to pieces, but I'm in another state from the rest of 'em, which makes it kind of hard, some days.

Thanks to my beta readers Jim Woosley, Randy Jones, and Anthony Thompson for much assistance and brainstorming on this one; your suggestions and recommendations only made the story deeper and richer, I think.

And I'm sure many of you can recognize the ongoing characters that have been Tuckerized in this series; I thank you for allowing me to fictionalize some of you!

On that note, here's to leaving 2020 behind us, and I hope that 2021 is much better for ALL of us!

~Stephanie Osborn
December 2020
Huntsville, Alabama

About the Author

Stephanie Osborn is a former payload flight controller, a veteran of over twenty years of working in the civilian space program, as well as various military space defense programs. She has worked on numerous Space Shuttle flights and the International Space Station, and counts the training of astronauts on her resumé. Of those astronauts she trained, one was Kalpana Chawla, a member of the crew lost in the Columbia disaster.

She holds graduate and undergraduate degrees in four sciences: Astronomy, Physics, Chemistry, and Mathematics, and she is "fluent" in several more, including Geology and Anatomy. She obtained her various degrees from Austin Peay State University in Clarksville, TN and Vanderbilt University in Nashville, TN.

Stephanie is currently retired from space work. She now happily "passes it forward," teaching math and science via numerous media including radio, podcasting, and public speaking, as well as working with SIGMA, the science fiction think tank, while writing science fiction mysteries based on her knowledge, experience, and travels.

For more, or to subscribe to Stephanie's newsletter, go to her website,

For more, go to http://www.stephanie-osborn.com/.

Don't miss any of these highly entertaining SF/F books by Stephanie Osborn!

The *Division One* series by Stephanie Osborn:
Alpha and Omega
A Small Medium At Large
A Very UnCONventional Christmas
Tour de Force
Trojan Horse
Texas Rangers
Definition and Alignment
Phantoms
Head Games
Break, Break, Houston
Tourist Trap
Mega Moth
Byegones

Coming soon:
The Bounty Game
Everywhere Signs
Shake, Rattle and Roll
Die Glocke
Diplomatic Catfight
Forming Terra
Minimum Age
With more on the way!

* * *

The Burnout series by Stephanie Osborn (from Twilight Times Books and Chromosphere Press):
The Fetish
Burnout: The mystery of Space Shuttle STS-281

Coming soon:
Escape Velocity
* * *

*Sherlock Holmes: Gentleman Aegis series by Stephanie Osborn
(from Pro Se Productions):
Sherlock Holmes and the Mummy's Curse*

Coming soon:
*Sherlock Holmes in the Wild Hunt
Sherlock Holmes and the Tournament of Shadows*
* * *

*The Displaced Detective series by Stephanie Osborn (being rereleased by Enigma House Press, an imprint of Hydra Publications):
The Case of the Displaced Detective: The Arrival
The Case of the Displaced Detective: At Speed
The Case of the Cosmological Killer: The Rendlesham Incident
The Case of the Cosmological Killer: Endings and Beginnings
A Case of Spontaneous Combustion
Fear in the French Quarter*